Around the Day
in
Eighty Worlds

by

Julio Cortázar

Translated by

Thomas Christensen

NORTH POINT PRESS
San Francisco

*This translation is for Carol,
Claire, and Ellen*

Contents

Translator's Note: *Para Llegar a Julio Cortázar, Enormísimo Cronopio*

"Cada vez que me ha tocado revisar la traducción de uno de mis relatos (o intentar la de otros autores, como alguna vez con Poe) he sentido hasta qué punto la eficacia y el sentido del cuento dependían de esos valores que dan su carácter especí-fico al poema y también al jazz: la tensión, el ritmo, la pulsa-ción interna, lo imprevisto dentro de parámentros pre-vistos, esa libertad fatal *que no admite alteración sin una pérdida irrestañable."*

Julio Cortázar, "Del cuento breve y sus alrededores"
("On the Short Story and Its Environs")

In an essay in this book, "On the Short Story and Its Environs," Julio Cortázar insists on the importance of writing from within the story itself, of moving from the inside outward. Reading what Pablo Neruda called his "fabrications, myths, contradictions, and mortal games," we reverse this process: by the end of the story we too are inside (like the ants in "A Country Called Alechinsky"), caught within another of his remarkable worlds.

Cortázar continually worked against the accepted grain, seeking from that friction the spark that (in Ezra Pound's phrase) would make the book into a ball of light in our hands. In *Hopscotch*, for example, he offered the reader a choice of readings: either straight through the first two of the three parts (ignoring the third "with a clean conscience"), or, following an alternate set of instructions, jumping back and forth among the chapters of all three parts. (In the latter reading, one begins with chapter 73 and concludes in a perpetual dance between chapters 58 and 131. A machine to facilitate reading this magisterial work is described in the present volume.)

Later, in two "collage books," *La vuelta al día en ochenta mundos* (*Around the Day in Eighty Worlds*), 1967, and *Ultimo round* (*Last Round*), 1969, Cortázar (whom the critic Evelyn Picon Garfield has termed a "collage-personality") obtained an analogous effect through more traditional means: loosely modeled on the old-fashioned almanac, these were books for browsing, releasing us to construct our own book by skipping back and forth without a Virgil to guide us through their layered worlds; the juxtaposition of texts and images also reflects the author's abiding interest in surrealism. From these volumes, in 1980, he selected sixty-two texts for a single, shapelier French edition, divided into two parts corresponding to the Spanish volumes: you are holding an English version of that book, translated from the Spanish but following the French arrangement of texts (although Cortázar deleted many of the Spanish pieces, he left the order intact, except for moving "Siestas" to the final position). The number *sixty-two* is significant: In *62: A Model Kit*, following a strategy described here in "The Broken Doll," Cortázar expanded on theories of his fictional novelist Morelli (to whom he alludes in "Morelliana Forever")—theories presented in section sixty-two of *Hopscotch*.

A few years before the first versions of this book appeared, Cortázar published *Historias de cronopios y famas* (*Cronopios and Famas*, Paul Blackburn, trans., 1969), setting out his whimsical personal mythology of creative Cronopios, overbearing Famas, and striving Esperanzas; these intriguing creatures recur here—"Louis Super-Cronopio," originally published in *Buenos Aires Literaria* in 1952, had, in fact, marked their first appearance in print. To translate Cortázar is to grow Cronopian. (It is possible to change one's stripes in this way: the first thing a Cronopio son does, Cortázar wrote in *Cronopios and Famas*, is to be grossly insulting to his father, "in whom he sees obscurely the accumulation of misfortunes that will one day be his own." So Cronopios turn to Famas for help in fecundating their wives. But when they educate these children, "within a few weeks [they] have removed any resemblance to the famas"—this is encouraging and will give hope to all Esperanzas.) As the translator writes (perhaps, as in "Nights in Europe's Ministries," of the writer translating), he feels the dim green Cronopian glow gradually brighten within him. Perhaps this is why Cortázar has been so

well served by his English translators, Elaine Kerrigan, Paul
Blackburn, Suzanne Jill Levine, and Gregory Rabassa, and I am
honored to take my modest place among this select company.

Julio Cortázar died in February, 1984. In a photo taken the year
before, when he was sixty-eight, he appears as youthful as ever:
Carlos Fuentes mistook him for his son when they first met. As he
writes in "On Feeling Not All There," he carried a child within
him, and in this sense his life was cut off in his youth. But somewhere still, I imagine, he is weaving webs of words for worthier
Cronopios than we.

De distancias llevadas a cabo, de resentimientos infieles,
de hereditarias mezcladas con sombra,
de asistencias desgarradoramente dulces
y días de transparente veta y estatua floral,
¿qué subsiste en mi término escaso, en mi débil producto?
Pablo Neruda, "Diurno doliente"

Ah crevez-moi les yeux de l'âme
S'ils s'habituaient aux nuées.
Aragon, "Le Roman inachevé"

I

This Is the Way
It Begins

I am indebted for the title of this book to my namesake, and for the liberty of altering it without offense to the planetary saga of Phileas Fogg, Esq., I am indebted to Lester Young. One night when Lester filled the melody of "Three Little Words" with smoke and rain, I understood better than ever the way the great jazzmen would stay faithful to a theme by playing against it, transforming it, and rendering it iridescent. Who could forget Charlie Parker's imperious entrance in "Lady, Be Good"? That night Lester took up the profile, almost the absence, of its theme, evoking it as matter might evoke antimatter, and I thought of Mallarmé and of Kid Azteca, a boxer I knew in Buenos Aires in the forties who one night, by means of imperceptible feints, turned his opponent's chaos into a perfect absence, forming an encyclopedia of holes into which his opponent's pathetic thrusts disappeared. And with jazz I open myself to openness, I am released from my crustacean identity to attain the quality of a sponge, a porous simultaneity, a participation that on the night when Lester played was a pulsation of stars, palindromes, and anagrams inexplicably recalling my namesake, and suddenly there appeared before me Passepartout and the beautiful Aouda: it was around the day in eighty worlds because the analogy was moving through me like Lester's melodic theme, bearing me to the reverse of the weaving where the same threads and colors form a different pattern.

What follows has as much as possible (it's hard to break away from fifty years of crustaceous everyday life) the quality of the sponge's respiration, where the fish of memories come and go along with thunderous alliances of

times and states and matters that Seriousness, that Lady too often heeded, could never reconcile. I like to think of this book and some of its foreseeable effects on that person much as Man Ray was thinking of his tack-studded flatiron and other extraordinary objects when he said: "The aesthetic pretensions and plastic virtuosity usually expected from works of art could never be attributed to them. As a result, visitors to my show were confused—they didn't dare to have fun, because a gallery is considered a sanctuary where one doesn't joke about art."*

They didn't dare to have fun. Man Ray, how you would have enjoyed hearing what I overheard a few months ago in Geneva, where a gallery in the Old Town put on a tribute to Dada. There was the very tack-studded flatiron, and, as the aforementioned Lady contemplated it with a stony face, a woman with chestnut hair turned to one whose hair was blonder, and they exchanged these exemplary remarks:

"Actually, it's not so different from one of my irons."

"How so?"

"Well, with this one you prick yourself and with mine you burn yourself."

Or, to return to Lester, what about the time a music critic just as serious as our Lady asked him what grave aesthetic considerations led him to give up drums for tenor sax, and Lester answered: "Drums are a dead end. It's no use checking out the pretty women in the crowd, because by the time you get packed up, they've already all been taken."

You may have noticed the quotes raining down, and that's nothing compared to what will follow (that is, almost everything). In the eighty worlds of my trip around the day there are harbors, hotels, and beds for Cronopios, and besides, in quoting others we cite ourselves, it's been said and done more than a few times, only pedants quote to be correct, whereas Cronopios

*Man Ray, *Autoportrait* [Self-Portrait], Laffont, 1964, p. 319.

quote because they are terrible egotists and they want to gather their friends together, like me with Man Ray and Lester and those who follow—Robert Lebel, for example, who described this book perfectly when he said: "Everything you see in this room, or in fact in this building, was left here by the previous tenants. So you won't find much that pertains to me, yet I prefer these random appurtenances. Their diversity keeps me from being limited to a single mode of reflection; and in this laboratory, whose resources I have systematically inventoried (with the opposite of the conventional valuation, of course), my imagination is less inclined to measure its steps."* Which is something I know it would have taken me more words to say.

The person who speaks through Lebel is none other than Marcel Duchamp. To his ways of creating a richer reality—for example, by making art from dust or creating new units of measure by the method (no more arbitrary than any other) of dropping a piece of rope onto a surface smeared with glue and recording its shape and length—I add here another method that I cannot articulate very well but that will perhaps *be articulated*, will emerge from all this. I am alluding to a feeling of substantiality, to the "life force" missing from so many of our books, to what prevents writing and breathing (in the Indian sense of breath as ebb and flow of universal being) from having two different rhythms. Something like what Antonin Artaud was getting at when he said: "My concern is with the minimal thinking life in the brute state— not yet arrived at speech but containing a movement toward it— without which the soul cannot live and life is as if it did not exist."†

And there is more: eighty worlds and within each one eighty more, and within each of these . . . stupidities, coffee, information of the sort that constitutes the obscure glory of miscellanies like *The Admirable Secrets of Albert the Elder,* including: "If a man bites another man while he is eating lentils, the wound will never heal," as well as this marvelous formula:

HOW TO MAKE A GIRL DANCE IN A SHIFT

Take wild marjoram, pure marjoram, wild thyme, verbena, myrtle leaves, three walnut leaves and three little fennel spurs; pick them all on St. John's Eve, in the month of June,

*Robert Lebel, *La Double Vue, l'inventeur du temps gratuit,* Soleil noir, 1964, pp. 121–122.
†Antonin Artaud, *L'Ombilic des limbes, Œuvres complètes,* vol. 1, Gallimard, 1956.

before the sun comes up; dry them in the shade, reduce them to powder and pass it through a silk sieve; and when you want to play this pretty jest, blow the powder into the air, in the place where the girl is, so that she will breathe it, or else have her smoke it like tobacco; the effect will appear instantly. A famous author adds that this effect will appear more infallibly if the merry experiment is conducted in a spot illuminated by lamps employing the grease from hares and young he-goats.*

A formula I will be sure to try in the Haute Provence glens so full of the perfumes that all these herbs exhale, not to mention young girls. And it seems to me there are poems, poems that suffer neglect they may deserve, but you never know, and also an air, a tune that I want to be like that of the great Audiberti's *Dimanche m'attend*, and *The Unquiet Grave*, and so many pages of *Le Paysan de Paris*, and always in the background Jean the Fowler, who snatched me from my foolish Buenos Aires adolescence to tell me what Jules Verne had been repeating so often without my understanding at all: there is a world, there are eighty worlds a day. There are Dargelos and Hatteras, there is Gordon Pym and there is Oppiano Licario (little known, I realize, but we will speak of Lezama Lima again, and someday perhaps of Felisberto† and Maurice Fourré) and especially there is the gesture of sharing a cigarette, or a walk through the more furtive sections of Paris, or through other worlds; but that will do, you get the idea what awaits you, so let's recall the words of the great Macedonio‡: "I hate to finish my writings, so I stop before the end."

Les Secrets admirables du grand et du petit Albert, Garnier Frères.
†Felisberto Hernández, Uruguayan writer, 1902–1965. (translator's note)
‡Macedonio Fernández, Argentine essayist and poet, 1874–1952. (translator's note)

Summer
in the Hills

Yesterday afternoon I finished making the Bishop of Evreux's cage, I played with the cat Theodor W. Adorno, and I discovered in the sky above Cazeneuve a lone cloud that reminded me of the René Magritte painting *The Battle of Argonne*. Cazeneuve is a small town in the foothills of the Luberon range, and when the mistral blows that burnishes the air and its images I like to look out from my house in Saignon and imagine its residents all crossing the fingers of their left hands or putting on purple wool hats, especially last night when this extraordinary Magritte cloud caused me to interrupt not only the incarceration of the bishop but also the pleasure of wrestling in the grass with Theodor, an activity we enjoy more than almost anything. In the philosophic sky of Haute Provence, still sunlit and with a waxing moon at nine in the evening, the Magritte cloud was suspended exactly over Cazeneuve, and I sensed again that pallid nature imitates ardent art and that this cloud was plagiarizing the vital, always ominous suspension in Magritte, as well as the occult powers of a text that I wrote many years ago and never published, except in French, which read:

THE SIMPLEST WAY TO DESTROY A CITY
Hidden in the grass, wait for a large cumulus cloud to drift over the hated city. Then shoot a petrifying arrow; the cloud will turn to stone and the consequences go without saying.

My wife, who knows that I'm working on a book of which the only things certain are the desire and the title, reads over my shoulder and asks:

"So it will be a book of memoirs? Arteriosclerosis has already begun, then? And where are you going to put the bishop's cage?"

I answered that at my age my arteries had surely begun their insidious vitrification but that the memoirs were far from the narcissism of intellectual andropause, residing rather in the Magritte cloud, the cat Theodor W. Adorno, and a phenomenon no one has described better than Felisberto Hernández in *Lands of Memory*, where he discovered that his consciousness continually vacillated between infinity and sneezing. As for the cage, I had not yet installed the bishop who is also a mandrake, so I had to consider where to put his flickering fire. Our house is rather large, but I have always had a tendency to combat a void, while my wife struggles in the opposite direction, which has given our marriage one of its exalting aspects. If it were up to me, I would hang the bishop's cage in the middle of the living room, where the episcopal mandrake could participate in our lyrical summer: he would see us drink maté at five and coffee at the hour of Magritte's cloud, to say nothing of our tortuous war against horseflies and spiders. My dear Maria Zambrano, who passionately defends all the various manifestations of Arachne, must forgive me if I mention that this afternoon I applied a shoe and seventy-five pounds against a black spider that kept climbing up my pantsleg, an operation that resulted in drastically curtailing his activity. The remains of the spider then became part of the food intended for the Bishop of Evreux, who would be mounted in a corner of the cage where a candle stub would show off bits of rope, Gauloise butts, dried flowers, snails, and a heap of other ingredients that would have won the approval of the painter Alberto Gironella, even though the cage and the bishop would have seemed to him the work of an amateur. Anyway, it would be impossible to hang the cage in the living room; it would remain suspended like the Cazeneuve cloud in a disturbing manner over my work table. I have already incarcerated the bishop—with a pair of wrenches I've fastened a clasp around his neck, only allowing him a tenuous support for his right foot. The chain that holds up his cage creaks whenever I open the door of my room, and I see the bishop facing forward, then in a three-quarters view, sometimes in profile; the chain tends to bring the cage to rest in a certain position. At dinnertime, when I light the candle, the bishop's shadow will be projected onto the whitewashed walls, and his mandrake shape will stand out in the shadows.

Since there are very few books in Saignon, beyond the eighty or a hundred that we read over the summer, and the ones we buy at the Dumont bookstore when we go down to Apt on market days, I have few references about the bishop, and I don't know if he was free or bound within his cell. As bishop I prefer him chained by the neck, but as mandrake this treatment troubles me. My dilemma is greater than Louis XI's, for he had only to face the episcopal problem, whereas I have the bishop, the mandrake, and a third thing, a mandrake-shaped root about half a foot long with a large, confused sex, a head crowned with two horns or antennae, and arms that could reach out hypocritically to a condemned man on the rack or to a servant who hadn't learned to stay out of the hayloft. I elect the bonds and a diabolical alimentation: for the mandrake there will be an occasional saucer of milk; and someone has told me that if you stroke a mandrake with a feather it will be pleased and will grant your wishes.

The irony of my wife's question had been hanging over me rather like the cloud over Cazeneuve. And why not a book of memoirs? If I feel like it, why not? What a continent of hypocrites South America is, always afraid that we will appear vain or pedantic. If Robert Graves and Simone de Beauvoir write about themselves, they are greeted with immense respect and deference; but if Carlos Fuentes and I publish our memoirs, everyone will say that we think too much of ourselves. One of the proofs that our countries are still undeveloped is the lack of *naturalness* in our writers; another is the absence of humor, because humor only arises from the natural. In other countries it is the combination of naturalness and humor that gives the writer his personality; Graves and de Beauvoir write their memoirs the very day it occurs to them, without either them or their readers thinking it the least bit unusual. But we are timid products of self-censorship and the constant vigilance of friends and critics, so we limit ourselves to writing vicarious memoirs, peeping like Fregoli out of our novels. And while it is only natural for all novelists to do this to some extent, we remain inside our books, we take up legal residence in our novels, and when we go out into the street we are dull gentlemen in dark blue suits. Let's ask ourselves: why shouldn't I write my memoirs now that I have entered my crepuscular years, I have

finished the bishop's cage, and I have been responsible for quite a few books, which would seem to give me a certain right to the first person singular?

This question was settled by Theodor W. Adorno's jumping perversely on my knees with the resulting scratches, because when I play with him I forget about memoirs, and I would rather explain that his name was not given to him ironically but because of the infinite joy that we bring to my wife and because of certain Argentine correspondences that occur to me. But before explaining that I should mention that I am happier talking about Theodor and other cats or people than I am talking about myself. Or even about the mandrake, if the truth be known, of which I have said very little.

Albert-Marie Schmidt informs us that the Adam of the Cabalists was not just expelled from Paradise, but the Holy Spirit, that domineering little bird, also kept Eve from him.* In a dream the image of the woman he loved appeared vividly to Adam, and desire overtook him, and the sperm of the first man fell upon the ground and gave birth to a plant that took human form. In the Middle Ages (and in German cinema), the belief was spread that the mandrake is the fruit of the gallows, of the last sinister spasm of the hanged man. It took a Cronopio with very long antennae to bridge the gap between two such dissimilar versions. Jesus: wasn't he the new Adam? Wasn't he hanged from a tree as it says in the Acts of the Apostles? Christian decency spirited away—literally—the root of the belief, which was degraded to the level of a Grimm's fairy tale, the one about the adolescent virgin who was unjustly hanged and at whose feet the mandrake was born; but this adolescent was Christ, whose involuntary fruit is found throughout folklore, for want of a worthier descendence.

More on Cats and Philosophers

What exceptional good fortune to be a South American and specifically an Argentine and not feel obligated to write seriously, to

---

*La Mandragore, Flammarion, chap. 3.

be grave, to sit in front of the typewriter with shined shoes and a sepulchral notion of the gravity-of-the-moment. Among the lines I most precociously loved as a child was one spoken by a classmate: "What a laugh, everyone cried." Nothing is more comical than seriousness understood as a virtue that has to precede all important literature (another infinitely comical notion to hear proposed), the seriousness of the person who writes like someone obliged to attend a wake or to give alms to a priest. On this topic of wakes I should tell you something that I heard once from Dr. Alejandro Ganedo, but instead I return to the cat, since now is the time to explain why he is called Theodor. In a novel I cooked up on a low burner there was a section I took out (I took so much out of that novel that, as Macedonio might say, one more and it would be the end), and in that section three none too serious or important Argentines were discussing the Sunday supplements in Buenos Aires papers and related topics, along these lines:

I've mentioned a black cat and now is the time to explain that he is named Theodor in indirect tribute to the German thinker, and that the name was given to him by Juan, Calac, and Polanco after extensive reading in literary materials sent by faithful aunts from the Río de la Plata, in which many sociologists had embellished their works with references to Adorno, whose flamboyant name seemed to lend credibility to what they wanted to say. At that time, almost all such articles seemed to be sprinkled with references to Adorno, or to Wittgenstein, so that Polanco insisted the cat should be named Tractatus, but that motion was poorly received by Calac, Juan, and the cat himself, who, however, did not seem to mind at all being named Theodor.

According to Polanco, who was the oldest, for analogous reasons twenty years before the cat would have had to have been called Rainer Maria, a little later, Albert or William (seek and you will find), and still later, St.-Jean Perse (a great name for a cat when you think about it) or Dylan. Waving old journal clippings before the dazed eyes of Juan and Calac, he was able to demonstrate conclusively that the sociologists who produced these columns must have been one and the same and that the only things that had changed over the years were the citations; that is, the most important thing was to keep your references fashionable and to avoid, for fear of being discredited, all mention of the authors used for this purpose in the preceding decade. Pareto: a bad word; Durkheim: vulgar. As soon as the clippings would arrive, the three Tartars would hurry through them to see what the sociologists were up to that week, ignoring the names at the ends of the articles, because the only thing that interested them was calculating the number of references to Adorno or Wittgenstein—without which the articles would have been inconceivable—per column inch. "Just wait," said Polanco, "before too long it's going to be Lévi-Strauss's turn, if it hasn't already started, and then you'll see, my friends." Juan added in passing that the most prestigious jeans in the United States were made by a certain Levi Strauss, but Calac and Polanco pointed out that he was getting off the subject, and the three then began to study the recent activities of the Fat One.

The Fat One was almost the exclusive property of Calac, who knew dozens of the celebrated poet's sonnets by heart and recited them interchanging quartets and tercets without anyone knowing the difference; so even though the Fat One of Sunday the eighth had two names, while she of the twenty-ninth had only

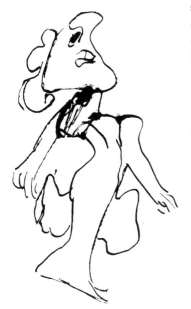

one, the fact remained that there was really but a single Fat One, who lived in various homes under different names, with different husbands, but who always wrote, in a style that never failed to be wrenching, the same sonnet, or nearly so. "It's pure science fiction," said Calac. "In these journals we have witnessed a mutation: there's a multiple protoplasm that has not yet learned that it's possible to live paying only one rent. Investigators are going to have to arrange a meeting between The Sociologist and The Fat Woman to see whether a genetic spark will ignite that will produce a terrible step forward." Of course, Theodor did not pay too much attention to all this, as he nudged his saucer of milk toward Calac's bed, the agora where they studied these weighty problems of South American destiny.

Julios in Action

Throughout the nineteenth century, refuge in metaphysics was the best antidote for *timor mortis*, the miseries of the *hic et nunc*, and the sense of the absurd by which we define ourselves and the world. Then came Jules Laforgue who, like a cosmonaut, preceded another Jules and showed us a simpler solution: what is the use of ethereal metaphysics when we have a palpable physics within our reach? In an epoch when all sentiment acted like a boomerang, Laforgue flung his like a javelin into the sun, against the despairing cosmic mystery. That he was right, time has proved: in the twentieth century nothing can better cure the an-

---

Encore à cet astre

Espèce de soleil! tu songes: —voyez-les
Ces pantins morphinés, buveurs de lait d'ânesse
Et de café; sans trève, en vain, je leur caresse
L'échine de mes feux; ils vont étiolés!—

—Eh! c'est toi qui n'as plus que des rayons gelés!
Nous, mais nous crevons de santé, de jeunesse!
C'est vrai, la terre n'est qu'une vaste kermesse,
Nos hourrahs de gaieté courbent au loin les blés.

Toi seul claques des dents, car tes taches accrues
Te mangent, ô soleil, ainsi que des verrues
Un vaste citron d'or, et bientôt, blond moqueur.
Après tant de couchants dans la pourpre et la gloire,

Tu seras en risée aux étoiles sans cœur,
Astre jaune et grêlé, flamboyante écumoire!

It is said in passing (but a very special passage) that in 1911 Marcel Duchamp did a drawing for this poem that became the basis for his *Nude Descending a Staircase*: a typical pataphysical progression.

thropocentrism that is the author of all our ills than to cast ourselves into the physics of the infinitely large (or the infinitely
small). By reading any text of popular science we quickly regain
the sense of the absurd, but this time it is a sentiment that can be
held in our hands, born of tangible, demonstrable, almost con-
soling things. We no longer believe because it is absurd: it is absurd because we must believe.

My readings of the Science pages of *Le Monde* (appearing
Thursdays) have a further benefit: rather than turning me away
from the absurd, they encourage me to accept it as the natural
mode by which we are shown an inconceivable reality. This is not
the same as accepting reality though believing it absurd; it is discovering in the absurd a challenge raised by physics without
being able to know how or where the mad race through the double

tunnel of tele- and microscopes will end (but is that tunnel really double?).

What I mean is that a clear sense of the absurd *situates* us better or more lucidly than the post-Kantian assurance that phenomena are mediators of an inaccessible reality that will somehow assure them at least a year of stability. From childhood, Cronopios have an eminently constructive notion of the absurd, so it startles them to see that Famas can take in stride reports like this: "The new elementary particle 'N asterisk 3245' has a relatively longer lifespan than other known particles, even though it does not exceed a millionth of a millionth of a millionth of a millionth of a second" (*Le Monde*, Thursday, July 7, 1966).

"Say, Coco," says the Fama after reading that, "bring me my suede shoes. I have an important meeting at the Society of Authors. We're going to discuss the floral games of Curuzu Cuatia and I'm already twenty minutes late."

Certain Cronopios have been quite excited to learn that the universe itself may be asymmetrical, a fact that runs counter to one of the most illustrious of received ideas. A researcher named Paolo Franzini and his wife Juliet Lee Franzini (have you noticed how a writing Julio, working with an illustrating Julio, has already considered two more Julios and now a Juliet, in reference to an article that appeared on 7 *July*?) know a great deal about the neutral meson *eta*, which only recently emerged from anonymity and which has the curious quality of being its own antiparticle. The moment it decomposes, it produces three pi-mesons, one of which, poor thing, is neuter, while the other two are positive and negative, which is a great relief to everyone. And then we discover (this is what the Franzinis have shown) that the conduct of the two charged pi-mesons is not symmetrical; the harmonious proposition that antimatter is the mirror image of matter is deflated like a balloon. What does this mean to us? The Franzinis are not concerned: it's fine that the two pi-mesons should be warring brothers because that helps us to recognize and identify them. Even physics has its Talleyrands.

Cronopios will feel a dizzying rush in their ears when they read the conclusion of this report: "Thus, thanks to this asymmetry, we will be able to identify celestial bodies composed of antimatter, if such bodies exist, as some have claimed based on the rays they emit." This, always on Thursday, always in *Le Monde*, always with a Julio somewhere in view.

As for the Famas, Jules Laforgue, on one of his interplanetary voyages, wrote:

La plupart vit et meurt sans soupçonner l'histoire
Du globe, sa misère en l'éternelle gloire.
Sa future agonie au soleil moribund.

Vertige d'univers, cieux à jamais en fête!
Rien, ils n'auront rien su. Combien même s'en vont
Sans avoir seulement visité leur planète.

PS. When I wrote, above, "a perfectly typical pataphysical progression," about the Laforgue–Duchamp connection, in which I am forever somehow entwined, I did not imagine that I would once more take passage into the realm of transparent vastness. This very afternoon (11/12/66), having completed this text, I went to see an exhibition of Dada. The first painting that I saw on entering was *Nude Descending a Staircase*, especially sent to Paris from its museum in Philadelphia.

On Feeling
Not All There

Jamais réel et toujours vrai
(on a drawing by Antonin Artaud)

I will always be a child in many ways, but one of those children who from the beginning carries within him an adult, so when the little monster becomes an adult he carries in turn a child inside and, *nel mezzo del camino*, yields to the seldom peaceful coexistence of at least two outlooks onto the world.

This can be taken metaphorically, but it aptly describes a temperament that has not renounced the child's vision as the price of becoming an adult, and this juxtaposition, which creates the poet and perhaps the criminal, as well as the Cronopio and the humorist (a question of different dosages, of end or penultimate stresses, of choices: now I play, now I kill), shows itself in the feeling of not being completely a part of those structures, those webs, that make up our lives, wherein we are at once both spider and fly.

Much of what I have written falls into the category of *eccentricity*, because I have never admitted a clear distinction between living and writing; if in my life I have managed to disguise an only partial participation in my circumstances, I still cannot deny that eccentricity in what I write, since I write precisely because I am only half there or not there at all. I write by default and dislocation, and since I write out of an interstice I always invite others to discover one of their own and to see for themselves the garden where the trees bear fruits that turn out to be precious stones. The monster remains in charge.

This kind of ludic constant explains, if it doesn't justify, much of what I have written or lived. They accuse my novels—that game on the edge of the balcony, that match next to the bottle of gasoline, that loaded revolver on the end table—of being an intellectual search for the novel itself, which would mean a kind of continuous commentary on the action and often the action of commenting. I am tired of arguing *a posteriori* that throughout the course of this magical dialectic a man-child is struggling to keep winning the game of his life: *yes, no, this is it*. Because isn't a game, if you look at it right, a process that begins with disequilibrium and ends with equilibrium, with an established orientation—goal, checkmate, free stone? Isn't it the fulfillment of a ceremony that marches toward its ultimate crowning?

People today are anxious to believe that their philosophical and historical information will take them beyond ingenuous realism. In university conferences and cafe conversations they will admit that reality is not what it appears to be, and they are always quick to agree that the senses deceive and that the mind fabricates a tolerable but incomplete vision of the world. Whenever they think metaphysically they feel "sadder but wiser," but this admission is momentary and exceptional, whereas the continuity of life places them firmly in the realm of appearance and draws up all sorts of definitions, functions, and values around them. This type of person is a realistic naïf rather than a naive realist. You have only to observe his behavior before the extraordinary: he either reduces it to an aesthetic or poetic phenomenon ("it was really surreal, let me tell you") or rejects at once any attempt to discern in it a dream, a failed act, a verbal or causal association beyond the normal, a disquieting coincidence, any of the momentary disruptions of the continuous. If you ask him, he will say that he does not believe in everyday reality, that he only accepts it pragmatically. But you can bet he believes in it, it's all he believes in. His sense of life is like his mechanism of sight. At times he has an ephemeral sense that his eyelids occasionally interrupt the vision that his consciousness has decided is permanent and continuous, but almost immediately the blinking again becomes unconscious, the book or the apple is fixed in obstinate appearance. There is a sort of gentleman's agreement between circumstances and the circumstanced: you don't meddle with my habits and I won't prod you with my stick. But it so happens that the man-child is not a gentleman but a Cronopio who does not understand very well the system of vanishing lines that either creates a satisfactory perspective on circumstances or, like a badly done collage, produces a scale inconsistent with those circumstances, an ant too big for a palace or a number four that contains three or five units. I know this from experience: sometimes I am larger than the horse I ride and sometimes I fall into one of my shoes, which always is alarming, to say nothing of the difficulty of climbing out, the ladders constructed knot by knot from the laces, and the terrible discovery, there on the brink, that the shoe had been put up in the wardrobe and that I am worse off than Edmund Dantes in the Castle of If because there is no one in my closet to come to my aid.

And I am pleased, I am terribly happy in my hell, and I write. I write and I live threatened by that laterality, that *parallel truth*, by always being a little to the left or behind the spot where I should be for everything to resolve itself satisfactorily into another day without conflicts. Ever since I was young I have accepted with clenched teeth this condition that separated me from my friends and at the same time made me guide them toward the strange, the different, made me be the one to stick his fingers into the fan. I did not lack happiness; it's just that I sometimes longed for someone who like me had not adjusted perfectly with his age, and such a person was hard to find; but I soon discovered cats, in which I could imagine a condition like mine, and books, where I found it quite often. In those years I could have addressed to myself those perhaps apocryphal lines of Poe:

> From childhood's hour I have not been
> As others were; I have not seen
> As others saw; I could not bring
> My passions from a common spring—

But while the Virginian regarded this as a stigmata (luciferian and thus monstrous), which isolated and condemned him—

> And all I loved, I loved alone

—I was not cut off from those whose rounded worlds I touched only tangentially. Subtle hypocrisy, an aptitude for all sorts of mimicry, a tenderness that crossed over the limits and concealed them from me—the surprises and the afflictions of that early time were full of sweet irony. I remember when I was eleven I lent a friend a copy of *The Secret of Wilhelm Stroritz*, where Jules Verne as usual told me of natural and intimate commerce with a reality that was not so different from the everyday one. My friend returned the book: "I didn't finish, it's too fantastic." I will never forget my scandalized surprise at that moment. Fantastic, an invisible man? So we can approach each other only through football, *café au lait*, and first sexual confidences?

As an adolescent I thought, like others, that my continuous alienation announced the coming of a poet, and I wrote the sort of poems one will, which are always easier to write than prose at the age that repeats in the individual the stages of literature. Over the years I discovered that if all poets are dispossessed, all the dispossessed are not poets, in the generic sense of the term. Here I enter a polemical terrain, so go ahead and pass the hat. If we use the word *poet* in the functional sense of one who writes poems, the reason he writes them (we will not discuss quality) springs from his personal estrangement, which gives birth to a challenge-and-response mechanism; so that when the poet feels his laterality, his extrinsic situation in an apparently intrinsic reality, he reacts poetically (I might almost say professionally, especially once he has matured technically); put another way, he writes poems that are like little petrifications of that estrangement, what he sees or senses in place of, by the side of, on the bottom of, or opposite of, applying this *of* to what others think they see correctly, without distortion or self-doubt. I doubt there is a single great poem that has not been born of such estrangement, or that does not translate it, and moreover that does not activate and strengthen it through a sense of the poem as an interstitial zone through which what the poet sees meets the accepted reality. In a similar way, the philosopher deliberately estranges and dislocates himself in order to discover the fissures in appearance, and his search too arises from a challenge and response; in both cases, although the results differ, there is a formal response, a technical attitude to a defined object.

But we have already seen that not all the estranged are poets or professional philosophers. They almost always begin by being one or wanting to be one, but the day arrives when they realize that they cannot or do not feel obligated to produce the almost mandatory response of the poem or philosophy in the face of the challenge of estrangement. Their attitude becomes defensive, egoistic if you like, since it is an effort to maintain their lucidity through it all, to resist the sly deformation that the codified quotidian imposes on consciousness with the active participation of reasoning intelligence, the information media, hedonism, arteriosclerosis, and matrimony, *inter alia.* Humorists, certain anarchists, more than a few criminals, and many story writers and novelists inhabit this ill-defined region where the condition of estrangement does not necessarily produce a response on the poetic level. These nonprofessional poets have adjusted to their condition more naturally, if with less brilliance, and we might even say that their sense of estrangement is ludic compared to the lyric or tragic response of the poet. While poets engage in constant combat, the merely estranged integrate themselves in eccentricity to the point that the exceptional, which raises the challenge for the poet or philosopher, becomes a natural condition, desired and used by the estranged one to adjust his conduct to that insidious acceptance. I think of Jarry, of a slow commerce based on humor, irony, familiarity, which ends by tipping the scale in favor of the exceptional, by annihilating the scandalous difference between the exceptional and the ordinary, by approaching day-to-day life—without any direct response since there is no longer a challenge—on a level that for want of a better word we can continue to call reality, even though that must remain a *flatus vocis,* a token word, or it will be less than nothing.

Returning to Eugénie Grandet

Maybe now something of what I am trying to do in my writing can be better understood, correcting a misunderstanding that has unduly augmented the earnings of the houses of Waterman and Pelikan. Those who reproach me for writing novels in which what has just been affirmed is almost continually placed in doubt or what we have every reason to doubt is stubbornly affirmed insist that my most acceptable work consists of some stories that appear univocally created, without glances back or little Hamlettian strolls within the very structure of the story. To me it seems that this taxonomic distinction between two types of writing is based less on the objectives and techniques of the author than on the convenience of the reader. What is the use of reiterating the well-known fact that the more a book is like an opium pipe the more the Chinaman reader is satisfied with it and tends to discuss the quality of the drug rather than its lethargic effects? The partisans of those stories pass over in silence the fact that each story is also the record of an estrangement, when it is not a provocation aimed at recreating it in the reader. It has been said that in my stories the fantastic takes off from the "real" or is inserted into it and that this abrupt and usually unexpected disruption of a reasonable and satisfying perspective with an invasion by the extraordinary is what makes them effective as literary works. But what does it mean that the stories are narrated without a break in the continuity of an action that seduces the reader, if what finally captures him is not the unity of the narrative process but the break in its univocal appearance? Accomplished technique can seduce the reader without giving him the opportunity to exercise his critical sense as he is reading, but it is not in their narrative skill that these stories distinguish themselves from other efforts; well or badly written, most of them are of the same fabric as my novels, openings onto estrangement, instances of a dislocation in which the ordinary ceases to be tranquilizing because nothing is ordinary when submitted to a silent and sustained scrutiny. Ask Macedonio, Francis Ponge, Michaux.

One might say that it is one thing to show an estrangement as it appears or as it can be conveniently paraphrased in literature and quite another to debate it on a dialectical level, as often happens in my novels. The reader has every right to prefer one or the other vehicle, to choose participation or reflection. Nonetheless, he shouldn't criticize the novel in the name of the story (or vice versa, if anyone is so inclined) because the central attitude remains the same and the only thing different is the perspective from which the author multiplies his interstitial possibilities. *Hopscotch* is in a sense the philosophy of my stories, an investigation of what for many years determined their materials and impulses. I reflect little or not at all when I write my stories; as with my poems, I have the impression that they write themselves, and I don't think I am bragging if I say that many of them participate in the suspension of contingency and belief that Coleridge regarded as the distinctive sign of the highest poetical operation. The novels have, on the other hand, been more systematic enterprises in which poetical estrangement intervenes only intermittently to move forward action slowed by reflection. But has it been sufficiently recognized that those reflections are less concerned with logic than with prophesy, less dialectical than verbal or imaginative association? What I am calling reflection here may deserve a better name or at least another connotation; Hamlet too reflected on his action or inaction, as did Musil's Ülrich and Malcolm Lowry's consul. Yet it is almost inevitable that the breaks in the trance, in which the author demands an active participation from the reader, should be received by the clients of the opium vendor with considerable consternation.

To conclude: I too like those chapters of *Hopscotch* that the critics are nearly unanimous in singling out: the concert of Berthe Trepat, the death of Rocamadour. And yet I do not believe that in them lies the real justification of the book. I cannot help but see that those who praise these chapters are inevitably praising a link that is most within the novelistic tradition, within a familiar and orthodox terrain. I prefer those few critics who have seen in *Hopscotch* the imperfect and desperate denunciation of the establishment of letters, at once the mirror and the screen of the larger establishment that is making Adam, cybernetically and minutely, into what his name signifies when it is spelled backwards in Spanish: *Adán, nada,* nothing.

Theme for
Saint George

Every so often Lopez found himself obliged to go to work, because he had discovered that money has a disagreeable tendency to keep diminishing, and all of a sudden a big beautiful hundred-franc bill emerges from the wallet as fifty francs and then, before you know it, it's only a ten, and next a horrible thing happens, the wallet weighs more and emits a pleasant tintinnabulation, but these agreeable phenomena are caused by only a few one-franc coins, and there you go. So our poor hero exhales cavernous sighs and signs a one-month agreement with one of the many firms where he has already done temporary work many times before, and Monday, 7/5/66, at exactly 9:00 A.M. he enters once again into Section 18, Floor 4, Stairway 2, and woop! he's up against the monster.

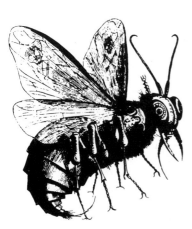

Of course, it's difficult to accept the reality of this cordial monster, since at first he isn't there; how could there be a monster there when the boss and all his fellow workers greet him with open arms and each shares some news and offers him cigarettes? The presence of the monster manifests itself otherwise, it imposes itself diagonally or backwards through what happens this and succeeding days, and he has to admit its existence even though nobody sees it because this monster is a monster of nonexistence, it is there like a living nothingness, a kind of vacuum that envelops and possesses and, say, listen to what happened to me last night, Lopez, and then my wife . . . And that is how he suddenly recognizes the monster, because, get this, kid, they've promised us a raise in February, and we'll see, maybe the minister . . .

If he had to define its form he would cover it with a talc of words to reveal its size and shape, and maybe such things as Suarez's pipe, the cough that comes at regular intervals from Mrs. Schmidt's office, the lemon perfume of Miss Roberts, Toquina's jokes (did you hear the one about the Japanese?), Dr. Uriarte's habit of underlining his sentences in pencil, which gives his prose the quality of soup struck with a metronome. And also the light that filters through the trees and clouds to form a pattern of plumage as it passes through the polarizing glass of the windows, the wagon that brings the coffee and croissants at ten-forty, the dust that billows up from the carpet of files. None of this actually is the monster, or it is, but only as an insignificant manifestation of its presence, like its footprints, droppings, or a faint sound that it makes. Nonetheless, the monster lives in the pipe or the cough or the pencil underlinings, these things make up its blood and its character, especially its character, because Lopez finally realizes that it is different from other monsters he knows; everything depends on how the monster materializes, what coughs or windows or cigarettes circulate in its veins. If he ever imagined that it was always the same monster, something ubiquitous and inevitable, he had only to work for another company to discover that there was more than one, although, in a sense, they were all the same monster, because the monster revealed itself only to him, not to his fellow office workers, who seemed unaware of its presence. Lopez finally realized that the monster of Azincourt Place, the one of Villa Calvin, and the one of Vindobono Street differed in obscure qualities and intentions and tobaccos. He knew, for example, that the one of Azincourt Place was a garrulous hail-fellow-well-met, a friendly monster, if you like, a child monster, always ready to fool around and joke and forget, a monster they don't make them like anymore, whereas the monster of Vindobono Street was lean and dry, uncomfortable with itself, a resentful and unhappy monster that thrived on gadgets and vulgarities. And now Lopez has again entered one of the firms that employs him, and, seated at a desk covered with papers, he has sensed forming little by little before his eyes, as he smokes and listens to the anecdotes of his colleagues, the slow, inexorable, indescribable crystallization of the monster who was waiting for his return to come truly to life, to awake and rise up with all its scales and pipes and coughs. For a while he continues to think it absurd that the monster has been waiting for him to come to life again, that it has been waiting for him, the only one who hates and fears it, that it has been waiting specifically for him and not for one of his coworkers, who either do not know of its existence or, if they suspect, are not bothered by it; but maybe that is why it ceases to exist when only they, and not Lopez, are there. It all seems so ridiculous that he wants to go away and not work, but that would be futile because his absence would not kill the monster, who would continue to live in the smoke from the pipe, in the sound of the ten-forty coffee wagon, in the one about the Japanese. The monster is patient and agreeable, it never says a word when Lopez departs, leaving it blind; it just waits there in the shadows with an enormous pacific and somnolent availability. The morning when Lopez takes his place at his desk and is surrounded by his coworkers greeting him and shaking his hand the monster is pleased to wake again, it is pleased, with a horrible, innocent pleasure, that its eyes again are Lopez's eyes that see it and hate it.

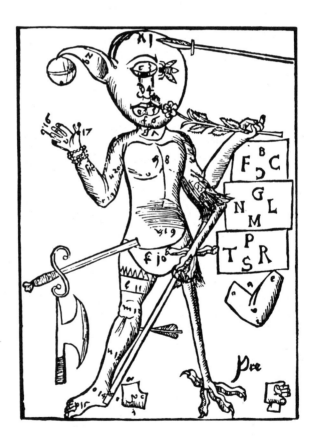

On the Sense
of the Fantastic

This morning Theodor W. Adorno did something very catlike: in the middle of a passionate discourse, half jeremiad, half caress against my pantsleg, he froze, all his muscles tense, and stared steadily at a point in space where I could see nothing, in front of the wall where the Bishop of Evreux's cage, which had never interested Theodor at all, was hanging. An English lady would have said that the cat had seen a morning ghost, the most authentic and verifiable kind, and that his change from rigidity to a slight movement of his head from left to right, ending in the direction of the door, clearly showed that the ghost had just left, probably disturbed by that implacable detection.

It might seem strange, but the sense of the fantastic is not as natural to me as to some others who have never written fantastic stories. As a child, I was more aware of the marvelous than the fantastic (for the different meanings of these often misused terms one might profitably consult Roger Callois*), and except for a few fairy stories, I believed, like the rest of my family, that external reality appeared every morning with the same punctuality and unalterable rubric as *La Prensa*.

That a train must be pulled by a locomotive was a fact that frequent trips from Banfield to Buenos Aires had proved to my satisfaction, and the first time I saw an electric train pull into a station apparently without a locomotive I began to cry so furiously that, according to my aunt Henrietta, it took more than three scoops of ice cream to quiet me down. (One obtains a more complete notion of my abominable realism during this period when I confess that I often found coins in the street—coins that I stole at home and casually dropped while my aunt studied a store window, in order to pick them up afterwards and claim the right

*Preface to *Anthologie du fantastique*, Club Français du Livre, 1958.

to buy candy. My aunt, on the other hand, must have been quite accustomed to the fantastic, for she never found this too frequent occurrence strange, but actually shared my excitement, as well as an occasional caramel.)

I have already mentioned my astonishment when a classmate found the story of Wilhelm Stroritz fantastic, a story I had read with a total suspension of disbelief. I realize now that I had accomplished an inverted and rather difficult operation: to place the fantastic within the real, to *realize* it. The prestige of all books simplified this task: how could one *doubt* Jules Verne? Following the example of Naser-e-Khosrow, an eleventh-century Persian, I felt that a book "has only one spine, but a hundred faces," and that I had to transfer those faces from their coffer into my personal circumstances, my little room under the roof, my fearful dreams, my treetop reveries at siesta time. I think that in my youth I never saw or felt the fantastic directly: words, sentences, stories, libraries distilled it into external life through an act of will, of choice. I was scandalized that my friend rejected the case of Wilhelm Stroritz: someone had written about an invisible man, wasn't that irrefutable proof of the plausibility of his existence? In the end, when I wrote my first fantastic story, I did nothing but intervene personally in an operation that until then had been mere substitution. Another Jules replaced the first with a tangible loss for both.

This World That Is Ours

In his *Illuminations*, Rimbaud depicted a young man submitting to the "temptations of Saint Anthony," prey to "tics of puerile pride, abandon, and fright." From that subjection to contingency, one emerges with a desire to change the world. "You will set yourself to work," Rimbaud says, and he tells himself, "All the harmonic and architectural possibilities will vibrate around your central axis. True alchemy lies in this formula: 'Your memory and your senses are but the nourishment of your creative impulse.' As for the world, when you leave it what will it become? Of its present appearance, at least, nothing will remain."*

If the world is not limited to external appearances, it is because the creative spirit of which the poet speaks has metamorphosed the pragmatic functions of memory and the senses: all "combinatory arts," the apprehension of subsurface relations, the sense that all reverses deform, multiply, and annul their obverses are natural for those who *live for the unexpected*. Extreme familiarity with the fantastic leads still further: in a certain sense we have already received what has yet to arrive, the door allows a visitor to pass who will come tomorrow or who came yesterday. The order is always open; one never reaches a conclusion because nothing ever starts or finishes in a system in which we possess only the immediate coordinates. At times I have feared that the functioning of the fantastic is even more rigid than physical causality; I didn't understand that I was witnessing particular applications of a system that gave the impression of inevitability, of a Calvinism of the supernatural, by dint of its exceptional *force*. Then, little by little, I realized that these overwhelming instances of the fantastic reverberated through realities that cannot be understood pragmatically: the practical aids you, the study of so-called chance enlarges the billiards game, multiplies the possibilities of the chessboard to that personal limit beyond which only powers other than your own can gain access. There is no closed fantastic, what we come to know of it is always partial and that is why we think it fantastic. One comes to realize that, as always, words merely plug the gaps.

A story by W. F. Harvey provides an example of restrained and seemingly inevitable fantastic.† The narrator begins to sketch on a hot August day; he realizes that he has mechanically rendered a trial scene: the judge has just pronounced a death sentence and the condemned, a fat, balding man, looks at him with an expression that shows more dismay than horror. The narrator puts the

*Rimbaud, *Jeunesse* [Youth], IV.
†W. F. Harvey, "August Heat," in *The Beast with Five Fingers*, Dent, 1962.

drawing in his pocket and goes for a walk, ending up very tired at the door to a marble cutter's workshop. Without knowing quite why, he addresses the cutter, who is in the process of carving a tombstone: it was he whose portrait the man had drawn two hours before, without knowing him. The cutter greets him cordially and shows him a slab he is just finishing on which the narrator finds his own name, the date of his birth, and that of his death— that very day. Amazed and incredulous, he learns that the slab is intended for an exhibition and the marble cutter has inscribed on it a name and dates that were, for him, imaginary.

As it goes on getting hotter and hotter they enter the house. The narrator shows his drawing and the two men realize that the double coincidence goes beyond all explanation and its absurdity renders it horrible. The marble cutter proposes that the narrator remain there until midnight to avoid all possibility of an accident. They take refuge in an isolated room and the marble cutter occupies himself sharpening a chisel while the narrator writes down what has just happened to him. It is eleven o'clock in the evening, one more hour and all danger will have passed. The heat grows more and more intense; as the last lines of the story put it, "This heat is stifling. It is enough to send a man mad."

The admirably symmetrical plan of the story and the inevitability of its conclusion should not cause us to lose sight of the fact that the two victims knew no more than a single twist of the net that ensnared and destroyed them. It is not so much the specific events related in the story that make it fantastic, as it is their resonance, the thrilling beating of a heart not our own, an order that can at any moment place us in one of its own mosaics, breaking us out of our routine to set in our hands a pencil or a chisel. When the fantastic visits me (sometimes I am the visitor, and my stories are born of twenty years of that reciprocal education), I often recall that admirable sentence of Victor Hugo's: "Everybody knows what the velic point of a boat is: the point of convergence, the mysterious point of intersection for the boat-maker himself, where all the slight forces along the sails accumulate." I am convinced that Theodor saw a velic point in the air this morning. It isn't hard to find them or even to conjure them up, but one condition is essential: to entertain a very special notion of the heterogeneities permitted in the convergence, not to fear the chance (which really isn't) encounter of an umbrella and a sewing machine. The fantastic breaks the crust of appearance and thus recalls the velic point; something grabs us by the shoulders to throw us outside ourselves. I have always known that the big surprises await us where we have learned to be surprised by nothing, that is, where we are not shocked by ruptures in the order. The only ones who really believe in ghosts are the ghosts themselves, as the famous dialogue in the picture gallery proves.* If we accepted what is natural in the fantastic, poor Theodor would not be the only one to freeze, looking at something that as yet we cannot see.

*It is so famous that it is almost an insult to cite its author, George Loring Frost (*Memorabilia*, 1923), and the book that won it fame, *The Anthology of Fantastic Literature* (Borges, Silvina Ocampo, Bioy Casares).

I Could Dance
This Chair,
Said Isadora

*In Wölfi we observe neither a particular and isolated inspi-
ration nor a very distinct cognitive conception or imagination; moreover, his thought, like his method of working, has
neither beginning nor end. Hardly pausing, he begins a new
page as soon as one is finished, and without stopping he goes
on writing and drawing. If he is asked at the beginning what
he plans to draw on the page, he will sometimes answer without hesitation, as if he had planned everything out, that it
will represent an enormous hotel, a high mountain, a great
goddess, etc; but often he will be unable to tell you, just before commencing, what he is going to draw; he does not yet
know, it has to take shape: and often he will irritably refuse
to answer this sort of question, saying leave him alone, he
has more interesting things to do than chat.*
Morgenthaler, "An Alienated Artist," (translated from the
French, "Un Aliéné Artiste," in *L'Art Brut 2* , pp. 42–43)

A broken leg and the work of Adolf Wölfi call forth these reflections on an attitude that Lévy-Bruhl would have called prelogical,
until the negative connotations of that term were pointed out by
other anthropologists. I am referring to the intuition of archaic,
magical origin that there are phenomena, even physical objects,
that are what they are and the way they are because, in some sense
they also are or could be other phenomena and other things; that
the reciprocal action of a conjunction of elements that the intelligence perceives as heterogeneous can release analogous interactions in other conjunctions apparently separate from the first—
as is understood in sympathetic magic and by at least four fat and
cranky women who still stick pins into wax figures; and that there

exists a profound identity between one conjunction and the other, outrageous as that may seem.

This all smacks of the tom-tom and mumbo jumbo, and also sounds a little technical, but not when you suspend routine and open yourself to that permeability in which Antonin Artaud saw the poetic act *par excellence*, "the recognition of the dynamic and internal destiny of thought." You need only follow the advice of Fred Astaire, *let yourself go*, by thinking, for example, of Wölfi, many of whose creations were perfect manifestations of this attitude. I discovered Wölfi through Jean Dubuffet, who published a report by a Swiss doctor who was working with him in an asylum, a text that fails to sound intelligent even when translated into French, but is full of goodwill and anecdotes, which are what interests us, for we can apply the intelligence ourselves. Refer to the report for his full *curriculum vitae*; in the meantime we might merely recall how the giant Wölfi, hirsute and tremendously virile mountaineer, all shorts and deltoids, a maladjusted primate even in his mountain village, ended up in a cell for the disturbed after violating several minors, and there followed similar offenses, imprisonment, new scandals in the hay, prison again, and more ravishments, until some wise men at the penitentiary recognized the irresponsibility of the supposed monster and put him in an asylum. There Wölfi made life miserable for all God's children until one day it occurred to a psychiatrist to offer this chimpanzee a banana in the form of colored pencils and sheets of paper. The chimp commenced to draw and write, and even rolled one of the sheets of paper

into a musical instrument, and for twenty years, hardly stopping to eat, sleep, and torment his doctors, Wölfi wrote, drew, and executed a perfectly delirious oeuvre that it would pay many of those artists who for some reason remain at large to consult.

I base these remarks on one of his pictorial works entitled (I have to refer to the French version) *La ville de biscuit à bière St. Adolf* (The Beer Biscuit City St. Adolph). This is a drawing in colored pencil (they never gave him oils or tempera, too expensive to waste on madmen), which according to Wölfi represents a city—that much is certain *inter alia*—but this city is of biscuit (if the translator is referring to the earthenware called biscuit, then the city is porcelain, a "biscuit" for beer, or a beer mug, but the translator may intend the other sense of *bière*, meaning coffin, so it is either a biscuit, or an earthenware beer mug, or a casket . . .). Let's pick the likeliest possibility: city of St. Adolph beer biscuits, and here we must explain that Wölfi believed in a certain Sankt Adolph, among others. The picture, therefore, contains in its title the perfectly univocal apparent plurivision of Wölfi, who sees it as city (of biscuit [beer biscuit {St. Adolph's city}]). It seems clear to me that Saint Adolph is not the name of the city but, as for the biscuit and the beer, the city *is* Saint Adolph, and vice versa.

As if that weren't enough, when Dr. Morgenthaler became interested in the meaning of Wölfi's work, and Wölfi deigned to answer his questions (which was unusual), to the question "What does it represent?" the giant responded, "This"—and taking his roll of paper he blew a melody that for him was not just the explanation of the picture but the picture itself, or the picture was the melody, as is suggested by the pentagrams full of musical compositions that many of his drawings include, as well as by his many works containing texts in which his vision of reality reappears verbally. It is odd and disturbing that Wölfi could disprove (and at the same time confirm by his forced confinement) the pessimistic sentence of Lichtenberg: "If I were to write of such things, the world would think me mad, so I hold silent. It is as impossible to speak of this as to play on the violin, as if they were notes, the ink stains upon my table."

If the psychiatric study insists on that dizzying musical explanation of the painting, it says nothing of the converse possibility, that Wölfi *painted his music.* As a stubborn inhabitant of interstitial zones, I find nothing more natural than that a city, a biscuit, beer, Saint Adolph, and a melody should be five in one and one in five; there is an antecedent in the Trinity, and there is *Je est un autre.* But this would all be much more static if these quintuple univocals did not accomplish in their internal destiny and dynamics (transferring to their sphere the activity attributed by Artaud to thought) an action equivalent to that of the elements of the atom, so that, to use the title of Wölfi's work metaphorically, the eventual action of the biscuit in the city could bring about a metamorphosis in Saint Adolph, so that the slightest gesture of Saint Adolph could completely alter the nature of the beer. If we now extrapolate this example to less gastronomic and hagiographic conjunctions, we get what happened to me with my broken leg in the Cochin hospital, which consisted in knowing (and not in sensing or imagining: the certainty was of a sort that would do Aristotelean logic proud) that in my infected leg, which I regarded from the observation point of fever and delirium, miniature skirmishes were taking place: it was a field of battle, with all its geography, its strategy, its reverses and counterattacks, and I was a detached and at the same time involved observer, for each stab of pain was a regiment launching an assault, hand-to-hand combat, and each wave of fever was a headlong charge or a host of flags unfurling in the wind.*

It is impossible to have dived to this depth without returning to the surface with the conviction that the battles of history were tea with toast in a rectory in the county of Kent, or that the effort I have been making for the past hour to write these pages may equal an anthill in Adelaide, Australia, or the last three rounds of the first fight last Thursday in Dawson Square in Glasgow. I give primary examples, reduced to an action that proceeds from X to Z by means of a coexistence between Z and X. But what is the significance of that, next to a day of your life, *un amour de Swann*, the conception of the cathedral of Gaudi in Barcelona? If people are astonished when they comprehend the significance of a light-year, the volume of a dwarf star, the content of a galaxy, what will they say about three brushstrokes of Masaccio that are perhaps the burning of Persepolis that is perhaps the fourth murder of Peter Kürten who is perhaps the road to Damascus which is perhaps the Lafayette Galeries which are perhaps the black cat of Hans Magnus Enzensberger who is perhaps an Avignon prostitute named Jeanne Blanc (1477–1514)? And saying this is saying less than nothing, because it's not a matter of interexistence in itself, but of its dynamic (its "internal and dynamic destiny"), which naturally takes place beyond the scope of all measurement or detection based on our Greenwiches or Geigers. Metaphors that point in this vague, insistent direction: the clack of a triple carom, the play of the bishop that changes the complexion of the entire board; many times I have felt that a thunderous soccer

---

*Many years later I discovered another quote from Lichtenberg: "For the soldiers, wars are diseases."

combination play (especially one by River Plate, a team I followed faithfully in my Buenos Aires days) could provoke an association of ideas in a physicist in Rome, unless this very association is what gives him birth, or, even more staggering, that the physicist and the soccer were elements in another process that could culminate in a cherry bough in Nicaragua, and from these three, in turn . . .

One Julio
Speaks of Another

This book is proceeding like one of those mysterious dishes in some Paris restaurants where the main ingredient has been ready for maybe two centuries, a hotchpotch stew to which meats, vegetables, and spices are continually added in a never-ending process that preserves in its depths the accumulated flavor of infinite cooking. Here is a Julio who stares at us from a daguerreotype, a little scornfully I fear, a Julio who writes and revises page after page, and a Julio who takes and organizes all the pages, armed with patience that does not prevent him from addressing a rotund "shit" to his nearest namesake or to the scotch tape that's gotten wrapped around his finger with that vehement need of scotch tape to demonstrate its efficacy.

The eldest Julio stays silent, the other two work, talk, and every so often grill a steak and smoke Gitanes. They know each other so well, they are so used to being Julios, to raising their heads at the same time when someone calls their name, that one of them is suddenly startled to realize that the book is advancing and there has been no mention of the other, the one who collects the pages, who at first regards them exclusively as measurable, pasteable, and diagrammable objects, only beginning to read them later when he is alone, and who now and again quotes a sentence or drops an allusion between cigarettes a few days later to let Julio-scribe know that he too enjoys it from the inside. Then Julio-scribe knows that it is time to say something about Julio Silva, and the best thing might be to tell how he came to Paris from Buenos Aires in fifty-five and a few months later visited me and

spent a night talking about French poetry, referring frequently to a certain Sara, who was always saying the most subtle if a bit sibylline things. I didn't know him well enough then to pursue the identity of this mysterious muse who guided him through Surrealism and we had nearly finished talking when at last I realized that he meant Tzara, pronouncing his name the way this Cronopio, who does not need proper pronunciation to teach us his own rich language, always will.

We became close friends, thanks largely to Sara, and Julio began to show his paintings in Paris and to disturb us with drawings in which perpetually metamorphosing fauna somewhat comically threatens to take over our living room, which is really something to see. In those years incredible things would happen, like the time Julio traded a painting for a tiny car that looked like a jar of yogurt, which you entered through a Plexiglas roof shaped like a time capsule. Firmly convinced that he had mastered its operation, he went to get his flashy acquisition, while his wife waited at the door to be taken for an inaugural spin. He entered the yogurt with some difficulty right in the middle of the Latin Quarter, but when he got it going he felt the trees along the sidewalk were retreating instead of advancing, a small detail that didn't bother him too much until a glance at the dashboard confirmed that he was in reverse, a way of getting about that has its disadvantages in Paris at five in the afternoon and culminated in an unfortunate encounter between the yogurt and one of those unbelievable stands where a shivering little old lady sells lottery tickets. While he was figuring out what had happened, his noxious exhaust pipe had penetrated the stand, causing the wizened vendor to emit those alarums with which Parisians now and again rend the courtly silence of their high civilization. My friend tried to get out of the car to assist the semi-asphyxiated victim, but since he didn't know how to open the Plexiglas he found himself as imprisoned as Gagarin in his capsule, to say nothing of the incensed crowd that surrounded the distressing scene of the accident and began to talk about lynching the foreigners, as any self-respecting mob evidently must.

This sort of thing often happened to Julio, but what my esteem for him was based on more than anything was the way he took possession little by little of an excellent flat in a house located on the rue de Beaune, no less, where the musketeers lived (you can still see the iron supports from which Porthos and Athos would hang their swords before entering their houses, and you imagine Constance Bonacieux on the corner of the rue de Lille, timidly watching the windows behind which D'Artagnan dreamt of duels and diamonds). In the beginning Julio had a kitchen and an alcove; over the years he gained access to another, larger, room, with a forgotten door that leads up three steps to what is now his studio, all acquired with mole-like obstinacy and the subtlety of a Talleyrand in calming the owners and the neighbors, who were understandably alarmed at this expanding phenomenon never studied by Max Planck. Today he can boast of a house with doors opening on two streets, which adds to the atmosphere in which you can imagine Cardinal Richelieu attempting to disband the musketeers, when there were all sorts of Scaramouches, and ambushes, and swaggards' oaths, as the musketeers always say in the Spanish translations that disgraced our youth.

Today this Cronopio receives his friends with a collection of technological marvels, including an enlarger, a photocopier that emits disturbing rumblings and may start up at any moment, not to mention a collection of African masks that make you think you're what you are, a poor white man. And the wine, whose systematic selection I will not explain, since it is good that people have their secrets, and his wife, who endures with endless goodwill the Cronopios who roam the atelier, and the children, no doubt inspired by a magical painting, *El pintor y su familia* (*The Painter and His Family*) by Juan Bautista Mazo, son-in-law of Diego Velásquez.

This is the Julio who has given form and rhythm to our flight around the day. I think that if the other Julio had known him he would have placed him by the side of Michel Ardan in the lunar projectile, to multiply the joyful chances of improvisation, fantasy, and game. Today we see another kind of astronaut in space, and that's too bad. Might I close this portrait with an example of the aesthetic theories of Julio (which should preferably not be read by ladies)? One day when we were talking about different approaches to drawing, the great Cronopio lost patience and told me, once and for all, "Look, in drawing you have to have your balls in your hands." At which point I think it will be decorous to conclude.

About Going from Athens to Cape Sounion

. . . and the recollection of that absence of tree, that nothingness, is more vivid to me than any memory of the tree itself.

E. F. Bozeman, *The White Road*

Memory plays a dark game, of which psychological studies can furnish many examples—I am referring to the arrhythmia of man and memory, which either will not come to him or else pretends to be an impeccable mirror, but when tested turns out to have lied scandalously. When Diaghilev restaged the Ballets Russes, some critics complained that the colors of *Petrushka* had lost their original brilliance; yet they were the same sets, perfectly preserved. Bakst had to brighten the colors to make them match apotheotic memory. Movie-goers, how does your memory compare with the films of Pabst, Dreyer, Lupu Pick?

A strange echo, which stores its replicas according to some other acoustic than consciousness or expectation, memory sometimes places some Persian satraps in its museum of Roman busts, or, more subtly, onto the face of Commodus or Gordianus it places a smile that comes from a Nadar daguerreotype or a Carolingian ivory, if not from an aunt who served us tea cakes and madeira in Tandil. The archive of supposed photocopies actually offers up strange creatures; the green paradise of childhood loves that Baudelaire recalled is for many a future in reverse, an obverse of hope in the face of the gray purgatory of adult loves, and in this silent inversion that allows the belief that life has had its moments, since at least there was that distant Eden and innocent happiness, memory resembles the schizophrenic spiders in labo-

ratories where they study hallucinogens, who spin aberrant webs
with holes, interlacings, patches. Memory weaves and traps us at
the same time according to a scheme in which we do not participate: we should never speak of *our* memory, for it is anything but
ours; it works on its own terms, it assists us while deceiving us or
perhaps deceives us to assist us. Be that as it may, one gets from
Athens to Cape Sounion in a crowded bus, as my friend Carlos
Courau, an indefatigable Cronopio if there ever was one, explained to me in Paris, along with other Greek itineraries, yielding to the pleasure of all travelers of reliving their travels by talking about them (which is why Penelope forever waits) and of
enjoying a vicarious trip, the one that will be made by the friend
to whom the traveler describes how to get from Athens to Cape
Sounion. Three journeys in one, the real but now elapsed one,
the one that is imaginary but present in the words spoken, and the
one that will take place in the future, following the footsteps of
the past and based on the counsels of the present; which is to
say that the bus left an Athens plaza at ten in the morning but you
had to get there earlier because it quickly filled up with locals
and tourists. And that night, in that itinerary of excursions and
monuments, the spider made a curious choice, because finally,
how demonic, the stories Carlos told me about arriving at Delphi, or his sea journey to the Cyclades, or the beach at Mykonos
at twilight, any of the hundred stories including Olympus and
Mistra, the view of the canal of Corinth and the hospitality of the
shepherds, these were all more interesting and exciting than his
modest advice about arriving early at the bus to avoid being left
without a seat among baskets of chickens and "marines" with
Paleolithic jawbones. The spider heard all this and, out of this
succession of images, perfumes, and plinths, it forever fixed the
imaginary image of my going to the plaza that you had to get to
early and waiting for the bus under the trees.

A month later I went to Greece, and the day came when I
sought out the plaza, which naturally was not at all like the one in
my imagination. At that moment I did not compare them, external reality invaded my consciousness like the jab of an elbow, the
place occupied by a tree left no room for other things, the bus was
crowded as Carlos had said, but it did not resemble the one I had
seen so clearly while he had been speaking; luckily, there were
seats available, I saw Cape Sounion, I found the signature of By-
ron on the temple of Poseidon, on a secluded beach I listened to

the muffled sound of a fisherman repeatedly pounding an octopus against the rocks.

Then, on returning to Paris, this happened: when I told my story and spoke of my trip to Cape Sounion, what I saw when telling about my departure was Carlos's plaza and Carlos's bus. At first I was amused, then I was surprised; when I was alone I made an effort to recall the real scene of that banal departure. I remembered fragments, a pair of farmers on the seat next to me, but the bus remained the other, Carlos's bus, and when I reconstructed my getting to the plaza and waiting there (Carlos had mentioned the heat and the pistachio vendors) the only thing I saw without a struggle, the only thing really true was that other plaza that had appeared in my house in Paris while I listened to Carlos; and the bus in that plaza waited in a square beneath trees that shielded it from the blazing sun, and not on a corner like the one I know from that morning when I took the bus to Cape Sounion.

Ten years have passed and the images of a quick month in Greece have faded and been reduced more and more to a few moments selected by my heart and the spider. There was the Delphi night when I sensed the noumenon and didn't know death, that is, birth; there were the early hours at Mycenae, the stairs of Phaistos, and the details that the spider retained for a design that escapes us, the design of a mediocre fragment of mosaic in the Roman Gate at Delos, the smell of ice cream in a Plaka lane. And there is also the journey from Athens to Cape Sounion, and it is still Carlos's plaza and Carlos's bus, invented one night in Paris when he told me to arrive early to get a seat; they are his plaza and his bus, and the ones I sought and knew in Athens no longer exist for me, they have been dislodged, disproved by these phantasms that are stronger than the world they invent only to destroy in the end, in the false citadel of memory.

Clifford

That difficult custom of being dead. Like Bird, like Bud, *he didn't stand the ghost of a chance*, but before dying he spoke his most obscure name, he had long held the thread of a secret discourse, damp with the modesty that quivers on the Greek stelae where a thoughtful young man gazes at the white night of the marble. Clifford's music in these moments captures something that usually escapes in jazz, that nearly always escapes from what we write or paint or love. Suddenly, near the middle of the piece we sense that the unerringly groping trumpet, searching for the only way to sail beyond the limit, is less a soliloquy than a contact. It is the description of an ephemeral and difficult affirmation, of a precarious relinquishment: before and after, normality. When I want to know what the shaman feels in the highest tree on the path, face to face with a night apart from time, I listen once more to the testament of Clifford Brown, a wing-beat that rends the continuum, that invents an island of the absolute within disorder. And afterwards, once again the custom wherein he and so many others are dead.

Remember Clifford (Clifford Brown, 1930–1956)
Mercury disk MCL 268
"The Ghost of a Chance" (Young-Crosby)
penultimate track on the second side

Nights in
Europe's Ministries

It's worth being a free-lance translator because
one by one you see the ministries of Europe at
night, and it's strange, and there are statues and
hallways where anything can happen, and often
does. When I say ministry you should understand me to mean not only ministry but also palace of justice or legislative assembly, all sorts of
enormous marble edifices with lots of carpet and
lugubrious watchmen who speak Finnish, English, Danish, or Parsi, according to the year and
place. That's how I got to know a ministry in Lisbon, then Dean's Yard in London, a ministry in
Helsinki, a sinister annex in Washington, D.C.,
the Palace of the Senate in Berne, and there I stop
from modesty, but I will add that it was always
night, I mean, even if I visited them in the daytime when I was called for conferences, the true,
furtive meetings took place at night, and I can
boast that not many have known so many nights
in Europe's ministries as I, nights when the ministries rearranged their syllables to be revealed as
mysteries, the way you remove a mask, and they
became again what they really were, mouths of
shadows, hell-mouths, rendezvous with a mirror
in which the ties and lies of midday are not reflected.

Things always went like this: the work sessions
stretched late into the afternoon and you found
yourself in an unknown country where they
spoke languages that drew mysterious polyhe-
drons and all sorts of objects in your ears, which

is to say that for the most part it did no good to understand a few words that probably meant something else and usually directed you down a hallway that did not lead to the street but to the archives in the basement, or before a guard who was too polite not to be disturbing. In Copenhagen, for example, the ministry where I worked had an elevator the likes of which I have never seen anywhere else, an *open* elevator that operated continuously like an escalator, but in place of the security provided by those mechanisms, where if you miscalculate your entrance you only fall back a little awkwardly onto the next step, the Copenhagen elevator presented a vast black chasm from which the revolving elevator cage slowly emerged, so you had to time your entrance perfectly and let it take you up or down, moving slowly past hallways leading to unknown, shadowy regions or, worse yet, as once happened to me through a suicidal mania I can never sufficiently repent, reaching the point where the elevator, passing the final floor, revolved in total darkness within an absolute enclosure, where you felt on the verge of an abominable revelation, because, besides the complete darkness, there was a long moment when, creaking and swaying, the cage navigated the zone between ascent and descent, the mysterious point of balance. Of course, I got used to that elevator and even, after a while, found it amusing to enter one of its cages and smoke a cigarette as it slowly circled, presenting myself eight or nine times to doormen on various floors who stared dumbfounded at this passenger who was certainly not Danish, who wouldn't stop descending and act sensibly; but at night there were no doormen, in fact there was no one except an occasional night watchman waiting for the four or five translators to finish working, and precisely then I would begin to walk through the ministry, and in that way I came to know them all, and after fifteen years they have found homes in my nightmares, which have also collected galleries and elevators and stairways with black statues hung with banners, and rooms full of apparatus, and strange encounters.

Maybe the imagination can comprehend the privilege of those moments in the ministries, the almost incredible fact that a foreigner could roam at midnight through regions that a citizen of the country could seldom penetrate. The cloakroom of Dean's Yard in London, for example, its racks of jackets, almost all with vests and sometimes a portfolio or a raincoat or a hat left there by who knows what idiosyncrasy of the honorable Cyril Romney or Dr. Humphrey Barnes, Ph.D. What incredible freak of irrationality permitted a sardonic Argentine to wander at this hour among the clothes racks, opening the portfolios or studying the lining of the hats? But what was most hallucinatory was to go to the ministry in the middle of the night (there were always last-minute documents that needed translating), passing freely through a side door, a true Phantom-of-the-Opera door where the watchman let me in without checking my pass card, leaving me free and almost alone, sometimes completely alone, in the ministry full of archives and files and endless carpets.

To cross the deserted plaza, approach the ministry, and look for the side door, often watched sus-
piciously by native nightworkmen who could
never enter what was in a sense their building,
their ministry, in this way: this scandalous rupture of a coherent Finnish reality put me in
an appropriate frame of mind for what I would
find inside, for my slow and furtive wanderings
through corridors and stairways and empty
spaces. My occasional colleagues preferred to
limit themselves to the familiar territory of the
office where we were working, the shots of
whisky and slivovitz prior to the final round of
urgent documents; but at that hour something
called me and though I was a little afraid, with
cigarette in mouth I walked the passageways,
leaving behind the lighted room where we
worked, and began to explore the ministry. I have
already mentioned black statues and now I recall
the gigantic, grotesque sculptures in the gallery
of the Senate in Berne, in darkness barely light-
ened by a few blue bulbs: forms bristling with
spears, bears, and banners that beckoned me
ironically as I entered the first enormous gallery:
there each step resounded distinctly, marking
out the ever-increasing darkness, the distance
that separated me from the known world. I have
never liked closed doors, corridors where a double line of oak molding prolongs a sordid play of
repetition. Each door placed before me the exasperating possibility of bringing to life an empty
room, of knowing what a room is when it's empty
(I'm not speaking of imagining or postulating an

empty room, superficial tasks that others might find reassuring);
the hallway of the ministry, of any of these midnight ministries,
where the rooms were not only empty but also unknown (Would
there be long tables with green cloths, files, desks, or antecham-
bers with paintings and documents? What color would the carpets be? What shape would the ashtrays be? Would there be a dead
secretary in the closet? *Would there be a woman shuffling papers*
in the outer office of the president of the Supreme Court?), the
slow walk down the exact middle of the hallway, not too close to
the closed doors, that walk might lead me at any moment to a
lighted area where familiar faces were speaking Spanish. In Helsinki one night I chanced down a hallway that made an unex-

pected departure from the regularity of the Palace; a door opened onto a vast room where
moonlight illuminated a scene from a Delvaux
painting; I climbed a balcony and discovered a
secret garden, the garden of the minister or of a
judge, a small garden enclosed by high walls. I
descended an iron staircase from the balcony and
everything was on a miniature scale, as if the minister were a dwarf. I felt again the incongruity of
my being in this garden inside this palace inside
this city inside this country thousands of miles
from the place I had lived all my life, and I
thought of the white unicorn imprisoned in a
small enclosure imprisoned in the blue tapestry
imprisoned in the Cloisters prison in New York.
Passing back through the large room, I noticed a
card file and I opened it: all the file cards were
white. I had a blue felt pen with which I drew
five or six labyrinths, adding them to the other
cards; it amused me to think that a dumbfounded
Finn would find my drawings some day and that
a memorandum would circulate, functionaries
would ask questions, secretaries would be con-
sternated.

As I am falling asleep I often recall the ministries of Europe that I knew by night; my memory
mixes them up until there remains but a single
interminable palace in shadow—outside it might
be London or Lisbon or New Delhi, but inside
there is only one ministry and in some corner of

this ministry is what called out to me in the night and made me walk faint-hearted down stairways and hallways; once again I will light a cigarette to console me as I lose myself in rooms and elevators, searching vaguely for something I do not know and do not wish to encounter.

Of Another Bachelor Machine

Fabriquées à partir du langage, les machines sont cette fabrication en acte; elles sont leur propre naissance répétée en elles-mêmes; entre leur tubes, leurs roues dentées, leurs systèmes de métal, l'écheveau de leur fils, elles emboîtent le procédé dans lequel elles sont emboîtés.

Michel Foucault, *Raymond Roussel*

N'est-ce pas des Indes que Raymond Roussel envoya un radiateur électrique à une amie qui lui demandait un souvenir rare de là-bas?

Roger Vitrac, *Raymond Roussel*

I don't have the means at hand to check it, but in Michel Sanouillet's book on Marcel Duchamp he maintains that the *marchand du sel* was in Buenos Aires in 1918.* As mysterious as it seems, this trip must have responded to the laws of the arbitrary whose keys have been sought by a small band of literary irregulars, and for my part I am convinced that its inevitability is proved on the opening page of *Impressions of Africa*: "15 March 19 . . . , with the intention of making a long journey through the curious regions of South America, I embarked at Marseille on the *Lyncée*, a fast passenger liner of heavy tonnage destined for the latitude of Buenos Aires." Among the passengers who filled Raymond Roussel's incomparable book with the poetry of the exceptional should have been Duchamp, who must have been traveling incognito since there is no mention of him; yet he would surely have played chess with Roussel and talked with the ballerina Olga Tcherwonenkoff, whose cousin, who had lived in the Republic of Argentina since childhood, had recently died, leaving her a small fortune amassed through coffee plantations (sic). Nor is there any

*M. Sanouillet, *Marchand du sel*, Le Terrain Vague, Paris, 1958.

doubt that he would have been bound by friendship to such men as Balbet, pistol and fencing champion, La Ballandière-Maisonnial, inventor of a mechanical fencing foil, and Luxo, a pyrotechnist who was going to Buenos Aires to attend the wedding of the young Baron Ballesteros, where he would fashion a fireworks display that would spread the image of the young bride across the sky, a notion that according to Roussel exposed the extravagance of the multimillionaire Argentine, but which, he adds, did not lack originality. I think it less likely that he would have conversed with the members of the opera company or the Italian tragedienne Adinolfa, but he certainly spoke at length with the sculptor Fuxier, creator of smoke pictures and liquid bas-reliefs; in short, it is not hard to deduce that the better part of the *Lyncée*'s passengers would have interested Duchamp and would have benefited in turn from contact with a person who in a way contained nearly all of them.

Serious critics, of course, know that none of this is possible: in the first place, the *Lyncée* is an imaginary ship; secondly, Duchamp and Roussel never met. (Duchamp relates that he saw Roussel only once, in the Café La Régence, the one in the poem by César Vallejo, and that the author of *Locus Solus* was playing chess with a friend. "I am afraid I neglected to introduce myself," adds Duchamp.*) But others do not allow these physical difficulties to obscure the truth of a more worthy reality. Not only did Duchamp and Roussel make the journey to that city but they also met an echo from the future there, linked to them in ways that serious critics would likewise fail to credit. Juan Esteban Fassio prepared the ground by inventing in the heart of Buenos Aires a machine for reading the *New Impressions of Africa* during the same period when I, without knowing him, wrote Persio's first monologues in *The Winners*, using a system of phonetic analogies inspired by Roussel; years later, Fassio attempted to fashion a new machine for reading *Hopscotch*, unaware that my most obsessive work during those years in Paris was with the obscure texts of Duchamp and the works of Roussel. A double im-

*Jean Schuster, "Marcel Duchamp, vite," *Bizarre*, no. 34–35, 1964.

pulse gradually converged upon the austral vertex where Roussel and Duchamp would meet once again in Buenos Aires, when an inventor and a writer—who perhaps years earlier had also watched each other across a cafe in the heart of the city, neglecting to introduce themselves—would meet through a machine conceived by the first to facilitate the reading of the second. If the *Lyncée* navigated the coasts of Africa, still some of its passengers reached our American shores, and the proof is in what follows, a sort of joke designed to lead astray those who search for treasure with solemn faces.

Cronopios, Red Wine, and Little Drawers

It was through Paco and Sara Porrúa, two sides of the mysterious polygon that makes up my life, along with other sides named Fredi Guthmann, Jean Thiercelin, Claude Tarnaud, and Sergio de Castro (there could be others I don't know, parts of the pattern who will show themselves one day or never), that I met Juan Esteban Fassio on a trip to Argentina in 1962. Everything began as it should, which is to say in the cafe of the Plaza Eleven station, since anyone who has a profound appreciation of what a railway station cafe is will understand that encounters and departures take place there that lead to a marginal territory, transitory, on the border. That afternoon there was a dark, thick, and material will, a negative tar, separating Sara, Paco, my wife, and me, who were to meet at a certain hour and failed to meet, telephoned, searched for each other among tables and railway platforms, and finally met after two hours of incessant complications, with the feeling of following in one another's paths as if in a nightmare where everything is dust and delay. The plan was to go from there to Fassio's place, and if at the time I didn't anticipate the resistance of the material world to that intention, later it seemed to me almost inevitable, since all established order forms a line of resistance against the threat of rupture and places its meager forces at the service of *continuity*. That everything should continue as usual is the bourgeois standard of a reality that is indeed bourgeois precisely because it is standard; Buenos Aires and especially the Cafe Eleven secretly conspired to prevent a meeting from which no good could come for the Republic. Just the same, we arrived at Mission Street (there are names that . . .) and by eight o'clock were drinking the first glass of red wine with the Provider and Disseminator of American Mesembrisia, the Antarctic Administrator and Grand Competent CEO, and also the Regent of the Chair of Practical Rousselian Studies. I had in my hands the machine for reading *New Impressions of Africa* and also the *Valise* of Marcel Duchamp; Fassio, who spoke little, served sandwiches that were, on the other hand, of ordinary dimensions, and a good deal of red wine; he concluded by taking out a Kodak that dated from the pterodactyl period and photographing us beneath an umbrella and in other poses worthy of the occasion. Not long afterward, I returned to France, and two years later I received the following documents, secretly forwarded by Paco Porrúa, who had worked with Sara in the experimental stages of the mechanical reader of *Hopscotch*. It is worth reproducing here, first of all, the heading of that transcendental communication:

> ## INSTITUTO DE ALTOS ESTUDIOS PATAFISICOS DE BUENOS AIRES
>
> CATEDRA DE TRABAJOS
> PRACTICOS ROUSSELIANOS
> Comisión de Rayuela
> Subcomisiones Electrónica y. de
> Relaciones Patabrownianas

> [Institute of High Pataphysical Studies of Buenos Aires: Chair of Practical Rousselian Studies: Hopscotch Committee: Electronic and Patabrownian Relations Subcommittee]

There followed numerous diagrams, plans, and drawings, and a sheet explaining the functioning of the machine in general terms, as well as photos of the scientists of the Electronic and Patabrownian Relations Subcommittee hard at work. Personally, I never understood the functioning of the machine very well, because its creator did not deign to send me complete explanations, and since I have not returned to Argentina I still cannot comprehend some details of this delicate mechanism. I have even succumbed to this perhaps premature and immodest publication in the hope that some clever reader will decipher the secrets of the HOPSCOTCH-O-MATIC, as the machine is called in one of the drawings (fig. 1), which, frankly, suggests the deplorable intention of introducing it in the marketplace, particularly considering the trade name that appears at the bottom:

FIG. I

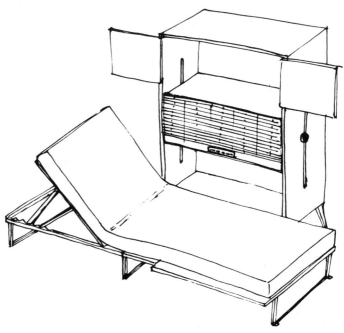

FIG. 2

It will be noted that the true machine is the one that appears on the left; the piece of furniture that resembles a triclinium is in fact an authentic triclinium, because Fassio saw immediately that *Hopscotch* is a book for reading in bed on nights when one cannot get to sleep in any other way, which can be most annoying. Figures 2 and 3 admirably illustrate this pleasant ambience, especially figure 3, where neither the maté nor the bottle of gin is lacking (I could swear that there is also an electric toaster, which seems to me an excessive refinement):

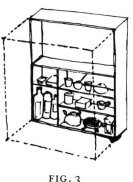

FIG. 3

I have never understood why some of the drawings were numbered while others were left to go anywhere, a disposition I have respectfully retained. This should give a general idea of the machine:

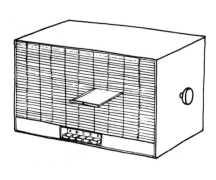

It doesn't take Wernher von Braun to figure out what is kept in the drawers, but the inventor has taken the trouble to add the following instructions:

A) Begin the process with chapter 73 (pull out drawer 73); when this is closed, no. 1 will open, and so on in order. If you want to interrupt your reading, say in the middle of chapter 16, press this button before closing the drawer.

B) When you are ready to resume your reading, merely press this button and drawer 16 will reappear, continuing the sequence.

C) All the springs are released by simply pulling this little knob, so that any drawer can be opened. This shuts off the electrical system.

D) Button used in reading the "First Book," that is, from chapter 1 to chapter 56 in order. On closing drawer 1, no. 2 opens, and so on, successively.

E) Button for interrupting the process at any time once the final circuit is reached: 58–131–58–131–58, etc.

F) In the model with a bed, this button opens the lower portion, releasing the made-up bed.

Figs. 1, 2, and 4 allow one to appreciate the model with bed, as well as the manner in which it emerges and opens up when button F is pushed.

Mindful of the probable aesthetic demands of our product's consumer, Fassio has designed special models of the machine in the Louis XV and Louis XVI styles.

A supplemental reference alludes to a button G, which the reader will press in extreme cases, the function of which is to send the whole apparatus flying.

Unable to send me the machine for logistical, legal, and strategic reasons that the College of Pataphysics is neither able nor willing to study, Fassio included with the drawings a graph of the reading of *Hopscotch* (either in bed or sitting up).

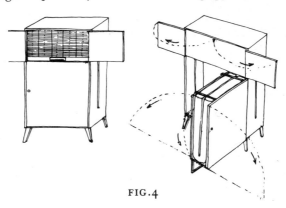

FIG.4

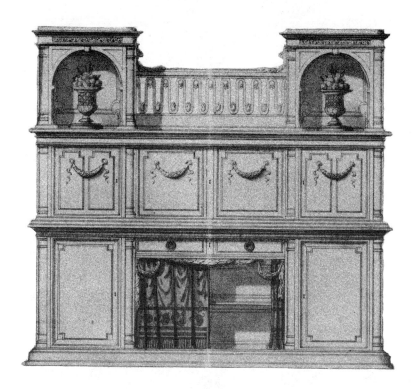

The general interpretation is not difficult: the principal points are indicated clearly: the starting point (73), the midpoint (55), and the two chapters of the final cycle (58 and 131). From this a design emerges that seems to be a meaningless scribble, but specialists may some day be able to explain to me why the lines tend to converge on chapters 54 and 64. Structural analysts will have a field day with these apparently disorderly projections, and I wish them lots of luck.

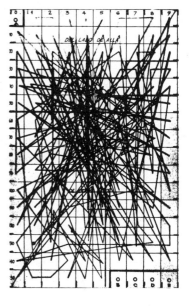

Only a Real Idiot

This is something I've known for years, it's something I'm used to, but I never thought I would write about it, since idiocy isn't a pleasant topic, particularly if it's the idiot who is talking. Maybe the word *idiot* is too strong, but I want to spell it out right from the start and have my friends say I'm exaggerating, rather than use some other word like *fool*, *clown*, or *simpleton* and have those same friends think that I've stopped short of the truth. Actually, being an idiot isn't so terrible, but it does set you apart from others, and while that is sometimes good, at other times you feel a certain longing, a desire to recross the road and join your family and friends, to be reunited there on the sidewalk by a common intelligence and understanding, to mingle with them a little and feel that you are all about the same and that everything is fine. But the unfortunate thing is that when you're an idiot nothing is fine. There is, for example, a performance of Czech mimes or Thai dancers at the theater where I go with my wife and a friend, and I know that once the show starts I am going to find it all marvelous. I am entertained, deeply moved; the dialogues or the dancers' motions seem like supernatural visions to me. I applaud wildly, and sometimes the tears well up in my eyes or I laugh until I have to pee; in any event, I am glad to be alive and to have had this opportunity to go to the theater or to the movies or to an exhibition, anywhere extraordinary people make or show things never before imagined, where they invent a place of revelation or communication, something that washes away the moments when nothing is happening, nothing but what always happens.

So I am overwhelmed, I am so delighted that at the intermission I rise up enthusiastically and continue to applaud at length, and I tell my wife that the mimes are a marvel and that the scene where the fisherman casts out his line and hauls in a phosphorescent fish half the height of the stage is absolutely fantastic. My wife, too, has enjoyed herself and has applauded, but I see at once (there is something wounding in this moment, an oozing, jagged cut) that her pleasure and applause are not the same as mine;

furthermore, we nearly always have a friend along who has also enjoyed and applauded, but never like me, and now I realize that he is saying, intelligently and sensitively, that the show was nice and the actors weren't bad, but there was not, after all, much original about the concept, not only that but the colors of the costumes were mediocre, and the staging rather banal, and so on, and so on. When my wife or my friend speaks this way—politely, with no ill will— I understand that I am an idiot; but the unfortunate thing is that I forget it every time something marvelous occurs, so that this sudden descent into idiocy is like being a cork that has spent years stoppering a bottle in the cellar and all of a sudden, a tug—pop!—and it's nothing but a bit of cork again. I would like to come to the defense of the Czech mimes or the Thai ballerinas, because I really did admire them, and the intelligent and sensitive words of my friends or my wife are like torture to me, even though I understand perfectly how right they are and that the show was not as good as it had seemed to me (although really it did not seem either bad or good to me, I was simply transported, idiot that I am, and that was all I needed to visit the place I love where I can so seldom go). It never occurs to me to discuss the show with my wife or my friends, because I know that they are right and that really they have done well not to be carried away with enthusiasm, since the pleasures of the intelligence and sensibility must arise from a considered judgement and, above all, a comparative spirit based, as Epictetus says, on using what we already know to judge what we have just encountered, for this and nothing else is the essence of culture and of Sophronism. I do not attempt to converse with them, and I move a few steps away to keep from overhearing their series of comparisons and judgements, as I try to retain the last images of the phosphorescent fish; but my recollections have already, inevitably, been altered by the intelligent criticisms I have just heard, and the only thing I can do is to admit the mediocrity of what I have just seen, which only filled me with enthusiasm because any form or color that is a little out of the ordinary is enough to transport me from ordinary life; then the memory of what I have enjoyed this evening troubles me, and it becomes my accomplice, it becomes the work of other idiots who have danced badly, fished poorly, in costumes and choreographies that were mediocre, and in the end I find it a sinister consolation that we are so numerous, we idiots who met in that room to dance, fish, and applaud. But the really unfortunate thing is that two days later I open the paper and read a review

of the show, and it repeats, sometimes in the same words, what my friends had said so intelligently and relevantly. Then I am convinced that not being an idiot is one of the most important things for making your life run smoothly, yet, little by little, I forget, the most unfortunate thing of all is that I end up having forgotten; for example, I have just seen a duck on the lake in the Bois de Boulogne, and it possessed such marvelous beauty that I had to stop and sit down by the side of the lake for I don't know how long, admiring its grace, the insolent joy in its eyes, that delicate double line carved by its breast in the surface of the water, which gradually widened until it disappeared in the distance. My enthusiasm was not just aroused by the duck but came from something that was given material form in it, that might also appear in a dead leaf balanced on the edge of the bank, or in an orange crane, enormous and delicate, framed against the blue evening sky, or in the smell of a train car as you enter with a ticket for a trip of several hours when everything will rush by, stations, a ham sandwich, the buttons for turning on and off the lights (one white and the other violet), the automatic ventilation system: all of this seems to me so beautiful, so nearly impossible, that to have it there within my reach fills me with a kind of inner sauce, so deliciously green that I never want to come to the end of it. But many people have told me that this enthusiasm is a sign of my immaturity (they wanted to say idiocy but they chose their words with care), that it is not possible to be so enthusiastic about a spider web shining in the sun, because if I get so carried away by a spider web covered with dew, what will I do in the evening when we are going to see *King Lear*? This surprises me a little, because in truth this enthusiasm is not something that you use up when you're an idiot: you only use it up when you're intelligent and have a sense of the values and history of things, so if I run along one side or the other of the Bois de Boulogne to get a better look at the duck, it will not prevent me from shouting with enthusiasm tonight if I like the way Fischer-Dieskau sings. Now that I think about it, it seems to me that's what idiocy is: the ability to be enthusiastic all the time about anything you like, so that a drawing on the wall does not have to be diminished by the memory of the frescoes of Giotto in Padua. Idiocy must be a kind of presence, a continuous beginning over: now I like this little yellow pebble, now I like *Last Year at Marienbad*, now I like you, my dear, now I like that incredible smoking locomotive in the Gare de Lyons, now I like that dirty and torn poster. Now I love, I love so much, now I am me, I become again the idiot who has perfected his idiocy and does not realize he is an idiot, who enjoys his enjoyment, until the first intelligent sentence returns him to an awareness of his idiocy and makes him nervously grope with clumsy hands for a cigarette, as he looks down at the ground, understanding and sometimes accepting, because idiots have to live too, at least until the next duck or the next poster, and so on, forever.

Louis, Super-Cronopio

Louis Armstrong concert
Paris, 9 November 1952

It seems that the imperious bird known as God breathed into the side of the first man to animate him and give him soul. If Louis instead of the little bird had been there for that breath, man would have turned out much better. Chronology, history, and other concatenations are a total disaster. A world that began with Picasso instead of ending with him would be a world exclusively for Cronopios, and the Cronopios would dance Tregua and dance Catalan on every corner, and perched on a lamppost Louis would blow for hours, making huge chunks of raspberry syrup stars fall from the sky to be eaten by children and dogs.

These are the things you think of while taking your seat at the Champs Elysées Theater when Louis is about to appear, since he arrived in Paris this afternoon like an angel, in other words on Air France, and you imagine the tremendous confusion in the cabin of the plane, with innumerable Famas clutching briefcases full of documents and balance sheets, and Louis among them dying of laughter, waving his finger at passengers the Famas would rather not see because they have just finished vomiting, poor things. And Louis eating a hot dog that the girl on the plane had brought to make him happy and because if she hadn't Louis would have chased her all over the plane until he got it. While all this was going on, the airplane landed in Paris and the journalists flocked around, and as a result I already have a *France-Soir* photo of Louis surrounded by white faces, and without prejudice I can say that in this photo his face is the only human one among so many faces of reporters.

Now you see how things are in this theater. Here, where the great Cronopio Nijinsky once discovered secret swings and stairs in the air that lead to happiness, Louis will appear any moment and the end of the world will begin. Of course, Louis does not have the slightest idea that he will plant his yellow shoes in the spot Nijinsky's dancer slippers once were set, but one virtue of Cronopios is the way they don't dwell on what happened in the past or whether the gentleman in the box is the Prince of Wales. Nor would Nijinsky have attached any importance to the fact that Louis would play the trumpet in his theater. These things are left to the Famas, and also the Esperanzas, who occupy themselves in recording the chronicles and fixing the dates and putting it all in moroccan leather and cloth bindings. Tonight the theater is copiously furnished with Cronopios who, not satisfied with lining the hall and climbing up to the lights, have invaded the stage and seated themselves there, have curled up in all the free spaces and the spaces that are not free, to the great indignation of the ushers who only the day before at a flute and harp recital had a public so well educated that it was a pleasure, not to mention that these Cronopios do not tip well and seat themselves whenever possible without consulting an usher. Most of the ushers are Esperanzas, who are clearly depressed by the Cronopios' behavior, and sigh heavily, flicking their penlights on and off, which in Esperanzas is a sign of great melancholy. Another thing the Cronopios immediately do is whistle and shout, calling for Louis who splits his sides with laughter making them wait just a moment longer, so the Champs Elysées Theater swells like a mushroom as the Cronopios yell for Louis, and paper airplanes rain down from all sides, landing in the eyes and down the necks of the Famas and Esperanzas, who twist around indignantly, and also of the Cronopios, who rise up furious, grab the airplanes, and hurl them off with terrible force, and so things go from bad to worse in the Champs Elysées Theater.

Now a man comes out to say a few words into the microphone, but since the public is waiting for Louis and this gentleman is going to stand in the way, the Cronopios are outraged and they protest vociferously, completely drowning out the speech of the

gentleman who can be seen opening and closing his mouth, looking remarkably like a fish in a tank.

Since Louis is a Super-Cronopio, he regrets missing the speech and suddenly appears through a side entrance, and the first thing that appears is his great white handkerchief floating in the air, and behind it a stream of gold also floating in the air, which is Louis's trumpet, and behind that, emerging from the darkness of the entrance, is another darkness full of light, and this is Louis himself, advancing onto the stage, and everyone falls silent, and what occurs next is the total and definitive collapse of the bookshelves and all their hardware.

Behind Louis come the guys in the band, and there is Trummy Young, who plays the trombone as if he were holding a nude woman of honey, and Arvel Shaw, who plays the bass as if he were holding a nude woman of smoke, and Cozy Cole, who sits over the drums like the Marquis de Sade over the buttocks of eight bound and naked women, and then come two other musicians whose names I don't wish to recall and who I think are there through an impresario's error or because Louis ran into them on the Pont Neuf and saw their hungry faces, and besides, one of them was named Napoleon, which would be an irresistible inducement for a Cronopio as Super as Louis.

And now the apocalypse is loosed, Louis merely raises his golden sword and the first phrase of "When It's Sleepy Time Down South" falls upon the audience like a leopard's caress. From Louis's trumpet the music unfurls like the enribboned speeches of primitive saints, his hot yellow writing is drawn in the air, and after this first sign "Muskrat Ramble" is unleashed, and in our chairs we hang on tightly to everything there is to hang on to, including our neighbors, so that the hall appears to contain a horde of crazed octopuses, and in the middle is Louis with his eyes white behind his trumpet, with his handkerchief waving in a continuous farewell to something unknown, as if Louis always has to say good-bye to the music that he makes and unmakes in a moment, as if he knows the terrible price of his marvelous freedom. Of course, after every number, when Louis laughs the laugh of his final phrase and the gold ribbon is cut as if by a shining shears, the Cronopios on the stage jump several yards in every direction, while the Cronopios in the hall writhe enthusiastically in their seats, and the Famas attending the concert by mistake or because they have to or because it costs a lot regard each other with polite reserve, but of course they haven't understood a thing, their heads ache horribly, and in general they wish they were at home listening to good music selected and explained by good announcers, or any place else so long as it was miles from the Champs Elysées Theater.

One thing you shouldn't miss is that not only does an avalanche of applause fall on Louis the moment he finishes his chorus, but he is obviously just as delighted with himself, he laughs through his great teeth, waves his handkerchief, and comes and goes about the stage, exchanging words of approval with his musicians, quite pleased by the proceedings. Then he takes advantage of Trummy Young hoisting his trombone and blowing a phenomenal succession of staccato and gliding masses of sound to dry his face carefully with his handkerchief, and not just his face but also his throat, and even the insides of his eyes to judge from the way he rubs them. And now we realize that Louis brings his sidemen with him because he enjoys them and they make him feel at home on the stage. Meanwhile, he uses the platform where Cozy Cole sits like Zeus dispensing supernatural quantities of rays and stars to hold a dozen white handkerchiefs that he picks up one after another as the preceding one turns to soup. But this sweat naturally comes from somewhere and in a few minutes Louis feels he is getting dehydrated, so while Arvel Shaw is locked in terrible amorous combat with his dark lady, Louis pulls from Zeus's platform an extraordinary, mysterious red vessel, tall and narrow, which appears to be either a dicebox or the container of the Holy Grail, and when he takes a drink it provokes the wildest speculations from the Cronopios in the audience: some maintain that Louis is drinking milk, while others flush with indignation at this theory, declaring that such a vessel could only contain the blood of a bull or wine from Crete, which amounts to the same thing. Meanwhile, Louis has hidden the vessel, he has a fresh handkerchief in his hand, and now he feels the urge to sing, so he sings, but when Louis sings the established order of things is suspended and from his mouth that had been writing pennants of gold now rises the lowing of a lovesick deer, the cry of an antelope toward the stars, the buzz of honeybees in sleepy plantations. Lost in the immense cavern of his song, I close my eyes, and with the voice of the Louis of today all his voices from other days come to me, his voice from old records lost forever, his voice singing "When Your Lover Has Gone," singing "Confessin'," singing "Thankful," singing "Dusky Stevedore." And although I'm lost in the perfect uproar of the crowd, which is swinging like a pendulum from

Louis's voice, for a moment I return to myself and think of 1930 when I met Louis through a first record, and of 1935 when I bought my first Louis, the "Mahogany Hall Stomp" from Polydor. And I open my ears and he is there, after twenty-two years of South American love he is there singing, laughing with his whole unreformed child's face, Cronopio Louis, Louis Super-Cronopio, Louis joy of those who are worthy of him.

Now Louis has learned that his friend Hughes Panassié is in the house, and this naturally makes him very happy, so he runs to the microphone and dedicates his music to him, and he and Trummy Young begin a counterpoint of trombone and trumpet that makes you tear your shirt to pieces and fling them—one by one or all together—into the air. Trummy Young attacks like a bison, with falls and rebounds that make you prick up your ears, but now Louis fills in the holes and you begin to hear nothing but his trumpet, to understand once again that when Louis blows, everybody falls in and lends an ear. Afterwards comes the reconciliation, Trummy and Louis grow together like two poplars, and the air is split from top to bottom by a final slash that leaves us all sweetly dumb. The concert has ended, already Louis is changing his shirt and thinking of the hamburger they're going to make him in the hotel and the bath he's going to take, but the hall remains full of Cronopios lost in their dreams, multitudes of Cronopios who slowly, unconcernedly, start for the exit, each one still with his dream, and at the center of each dream a little Louis is blowing and singing.

Around the Piano
with
Thelonious Monk

Concert of the Thelonious Monk Quartet
Geneva, March, 1966

During the daytime in Geneva there is the United Nations office but at night you have to live, and suddenly you notice a poster everywhere with news of Thelonious Monk and Charles Rouse: no wonder the rush to Victoria Hall for fifth row center, the propitiatory drinks in the bar at the corner, the itch of joy, nine o'-clock which is interminably seven-thirty, eight, eight-fifteen, the third whisky, Claude Tarnaud who proposes a fondue, his wife and mine who look at each other with consternation but then eat the major portion, especially the end, which is always the best part of the fondue, the white wine that taps its little feet inside the glass, the world you leave behind you, and Thelonious like a comet that five minutes from now will carry off a piece of the earth, just as in *Hector Servadec*, a piece of Geneva anyway, with the statue of Calvin and the Vacheron and Constantin clocks.

Now they lower the lights, we look at each other with that faint tremor of farewell that possesses us whenever a concert is about to begin (we have crossed the river, another time has been established, the obol has been paid), and the bass player raises his instrument and tests it, the brush shivers briefly over the kettle-drum, and from backstage, taking a completely unnecessary detour on the way, a bear with a cap that is half fez, half skullcap walks up to the piano, putting one foot in front of the other with such caution that you think of abandoned mines or those flower beds of Sassanid despots where each crushed flower meant the slow death of a gardener. When Thelonious sits down at the piano the whole hall sits down with him and produces a collective sigh as great as his relief because the diagonal progress of Thelonious across the stage contained something of the risk of piloting a Phoenician sailing ship with probable grounding in sandbars, and when the ship loaded with dark honey and its bearded captain reach the port the masonic wharf of Victoria Hall receives it with a sound like air escaping from the sails as the ship's bow touches the pier. Then it's "Pannonica," or "Blue Monk," three shadows like masts surround the bear exploring the beehive of the keyboard, his good rough paws coming and going among disorderly bees and hexagons of sound; barely a minute has passed and already we are in a night outside of time, the primitive and delicate night of Thelonious Monk.

Yet this is unexplained: A rose is a rose is a rose. We are becalmed, someone intercedes, perhaps somewhere we will be redeemed. And then, when Charles Rouse steps toward the microphone and his sax imperiously shows us why it is there, Thelonious lets his hands fall, listens a moment, tries a soft chord with his left hand, and the bear rises, swaying like a hammock, and, having had his fill of honey or in search of a mossy bank suited to his drowsiness, he leaves the bench and leans against the end of the piano, where, as he marks the beat with a foot and his cap, his fingers go gliding over the piano, first at the end of the keyboard where there should be a beer and an ashtray but instead there is only *Steinway & Sons*, and then imperceptibly his fingers set off on a safari across the piano, while the bear sways to the beat, because Rouse and the bass player and the drummer are entangled in the mystery of their trinity, and Thelonious makes a dizzying journey, barely moving, progressing inch by inch toward the end of the piano, but he won't reach it, you know he won't reach it because to get there he would need more time than Phileas Fogg, more sail-sleds, more hemlock-honey rapids, elephants, and high-speed trains to leap the abyss where the bridge is down, so

Thelonious travels in his own way, resting on one leg and then the other without moving from the spot, teetering on the point of his *Pequod* grounded in a theater, every so often moving his fingers to gain an inch, or ten tenths, otherwise remaining still, as if on guard, measuring the heights with a sextant of smoke and refusing to go forward and reach the end of the piano, until his hand abandons the shore, the bear gradually spins around, anything could happen in that moment when he is without his prop, when he glides like a halcyon bird on the rhythm through which Charles Rouse is casting out the last, long, intense, wonderful swashes of violet and red, we feel the emptiness of Thelonious away from the shore of the piano, the interminable diastole of one enormous heart where all of our blood is beating, and just at that moment his other hand falls from the piano, the bear teeters amiably and returns through the clouds to the keyboard, looks at it as if for the first time, passes his indecisive fingers through the air, lets them fall, and we are saved, it is Thelonious the Captain, we have our bearing again, and Rouse's gesture of moving back as he takes apart his sax contains something of the delivery of powers, of the legate who renders to the Doge the keys of Highest Serenity.

With Justifiable Pride

In memoriam K.

None of us recalls the text of the law that obliges us to collect the dead leaves, but we are convinced that it would not occur to anyone to leave them uncollected; it's one of those things that goes way back, to the first lessons of childhood, and now there is no great difference between the elementary acts of lacing your shoes or opening your umbrella and what we do in collecting the dead leaves on the second of November at nine in the morning.

Nor would it occur to anyone to question the appropriateness of that date, it's part of the customs of the country and needs no justification. The day before is reserved for visiting the cemetery, where we simply tend the family tombs, sweeping away the dead leaves that hide them and make it hard to read the names, although on this day the leaves have no official importance, so to speak, at most they are a nuisance that we have to get out of the way before changing the water in the flower vases and cleaning the snail tracks off the tombstones. Occasionally someone has insinuated that the campaign against the dead leaves could be moved up two or three days so that on the first of November the cemetery would already be clean and families could gather around the tombs without the troublesome sweeping that always provokes disagreeable scenes and distracts us from our duties on this day of remembrance. But we have never accepted these suggestions, just as we have never believed that the expeditions to the northern forests can be halted, no matter what they cost us. These are traditions that have their reasons for existing, and we have often heard our grandparents respond sharply to these anarchic voices that the accumulation of dead leaves on the tombs is a vivid illustration to us all of the problems the leaves present each autumn and thus motivates us to participate more enthusiastically in the work to be done the next day.

Each of us has a specific task to be done in this campaign. The next day, when we return to the cemetery, we see that the municipality has already installed a white kiosk in the middle of the plaza, and as we arrive we line up and wait our turn. Since the line is interminable, most of us don't get home until late, but we have the satisfaction of having received our card from the hands of a city employee. Thereafter our participation is recorded each day in the little boxes on the card, which a special machine perforates as we carry the sacks of leaves or the cages of mongooses, according to the task we have been assigned. The children enjoy themselves the most because they are given very large cards that they love to show their mothers, cards that assign them to various light tasks, especially observing the behavior of the mongooses. We adults have the hardest job, since in addition to directing the mongooses we have to fill the bags with the leaves that the mongooses collect, and then carry them on our shoulders to the municipal trucks. To the elders are assigned the compressed air pistols used to cover the leaves with powdered snake essence. But it is the work of the adults that carries the greatest responsibility, because the mongooses often get distracted and don't do what we want; when that happens our cards soon reflect the inadequacy of our work and the likelihood increases of our being sent to the northern forests. As you might expect, we do everything possible to avoid that, but if it happens we realize that it's just a custom that is every bit as natural as the present campaign; still, it's just human nature to apply ourselves as much as possible to the task of making the mongooses work in order to get as many points as possible on our cards, and therefore we are strict with the mongooses, the elders, and the children, all essential to the success of the campaign.

We have sometimes wondered where the idea

came from to powder the leaves with snake essence, but after some fruitless speculation we have eventually concluded that the origin of customs, especially when they are useful and successful, is lost in the mists of time. One fine day the city must have realized that its population was inadequate for the collection of each year's leaf fall and that only the intelligent utilization of the mongooses, which abound in the country, could overcome this deficiency. Some functionary from the towns bordering the forests must

have noticed that the mongooses, completely indifferent to dead leaves, would become ravenous for them if they smelled of snake. It must have taken a long time to reach this conclusion, to study the reaction of the mongooses to the dead leaves, to powder the leaves so the mongooses would go after them with a vengeance. We have grown up in an era when this was already established and codified, the mongoose raisers have the necessary personnel for training them, and the expeditions to the forests bring back an adequate supply of snakes each summer. So these things seem so natural to us that it is only rarely and with great effort that we can ask the questions our parents answered so sharply when we were children, thereby teaching us how to answer the questions our own children would someday ask us. It is curious that this desire to question only occurs, and then very rarely, before or after the campaign. On the second of November, when we have received our cards and reported for our assigned tasks, the justification for all these activities seems so obvious that only a madman could doubt the utility of the campaign and the manner in which it is completed. Nevertheless, our authorities must have foreseen that possibility because the text of the law printed on the back of the cards details the penalties to be administered in such cases, but no one remembers it ever having been necessary to apply them.

We have always admired the way the city distributes our work so that the life of the state and the country is unaffected by the campaign. Adults dedicate five hours a day to the collection of dead leaves, before or after our regular work in government or trade. Children continue to attend gymnastics classes and civic and military training, and the elders take advantage of the daylight hours to leave their rest homes and assume their respective places. After two or three days the campaign has accomplished its first objective and the streets and plazas of the central district are free of dead leaves. Then those of us in charge of the mongooses have to redouble our precautions, for as the campaign progresses the mongooses show less zeal for their work and it's our grave responsibility to inform the municipal inspector from our district of this fact, so he can order replacement supplies of powder. The inspector only gives this order after making sure that we have done everything possible to get the mongooses to collect the leaves, and if he concludes that we have requested new supplies frivolously we run the risk of being mobilized immediately and sent to the forests. But when we say *risk* we obviously exaggerate, since the expeditions to the forests form part of the customs of the state just as much as the campaign itself and nobody would think of protesting something that is just a duty like any other.

It has sometimes been whispered that it is a mistake to assign the powder guns to the elders. Since this is an ancient custom it cannot be a mistake, but it does sometimes happen that they get distracted and squander a good part of the snake essence in a small section of street or plaza, forgetting that they should be distributing it in the widest area possible. Then the mongooses savagely attack a heap of dead leaves, collect them in a few minutes, and bring them to where we are waiting with our sacks; but afterwards, when we confidently assume that things are going to proceed with the same dispatch, we see them pause, sniff among themselves as if confused, and give up their task with obvious signs of fatigue and even disgust. In such cases the leader uses his whistle and for a few moments the mongooses gather a few leaves, but it doesn't take long for us to realize that the powder has been used up and the mongooses naturally resist a task that has lost all interest for them. If we could count on an adequate supply of snake essence, we wouldn't have these tension-filled situations in which the elders, the adults, and the city inspector are all called to task and suffer greatly; but from time immemorial it has been the case that the supply of snake essence has barely covered the needs of the campaign, and that the expeditions to the forest have in some cases not accomplished their objective, requiring the city to call upon its scanty reserves for the new campaign. This situation intensifies our fear that a greater number of recruits will be called up during the next mobilization, although *fear* is obviously too strong a word, since the increase in the number of recruits is just as much a part of the customs of the state as is the campaign proper, and no one would think of protesting something that constitutes a duty like any other. We seldom speak among ourselves of the expeditions to the forests, and those who

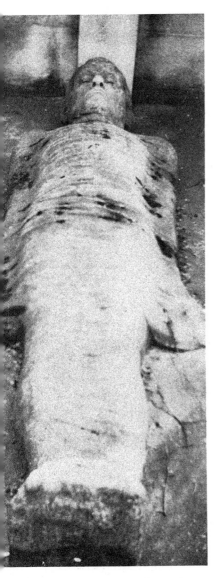

return from them are required to remain silent by a law we hardly notice. We are convinced that the authorities wish to spare us all concern about the expeditions to the forests of the north, but, sadly, no one can overlook the losses. We try not to draw conclusions, but the deaths of so many friends and acquaintances in each expedition leads us to believe that the searchers for snakes in the forests must constantly face fierce resistance from the inhabitants of the border country, sometimes with heavy losses and rumors of viciousness and cruelty. Although we don't say so openly, we are all indignant that a nation that does not collect its dead leaves should oppose our gathering snakes from the forests. We have never doubted for a moment that our authorities are prepared to guarantee that our expeditions enter their territory with no other intention and that the resistance they encounter can only be attributed to a stupid and senseless foreign pride.

The generosity of our authorities is boundless, even in matters that could disturb the public peace of mind. Therefore we will never know—nor do we wish to know, it goes without saying—what becomes of our glorious wounded. As if to save us from unnecessary suffering, they only publish a list of the expeditioners who are unhurt and another naming those who have died, their coffins arriving in the same military train that carries the expeditioners and the snakes. Two days later, authorities and citizens alike gather at the cemetery for the burial of the casualties. Rejecting the vulgar expedient of mass burial, our authorities want each expeditioner to have his own tomb, easily identifiable by its gravestone and any inscriptions the family wishes to have carved there; but since the number of the fallen has gotten larger each year lately, the city has appropriated the adjoining lands for the enlargement of the cemetery. So you can imagine the size of the crowd that gathers there on the morning of November first to honor the fallen. Unfortunately, autumn is already well along by this time and dead leaves cover the paths and tombs, so it is very difficult to orient ourselves; often we become completely confused and spend many hours wandering around and asking directions before locating the tombs we are looking for. We almost all carry rakes, and often we remove the leaves from a tomb thinking that it is the one we have been looking for, only to discover that we were mistaken. But we eventually locate the tombs, and by the middle of the afternoon we can sit down and rest. In a way we are glad to have had so much trouble locating the graves because this seems to justify the campaign that will begin the next day, as if our dead themselves were urging us to collect the dead leaves, even though we don't have the mongooses yet: they will be brought the following day, when the authorities distribute this year's ration of snake essence, carried back by the expeditioners along with the coffins of the dead, and then will the elders powder the dead leaves, which the mongooses will gather.

To Reach
Lezama Lima

Después que en las arenas, sedosas pausas intermedias,
entre lo irreal sumergido y el denso, inrrechazable apare-
cido, se hizo el acuerdo métrico, y el ombligo terrenal superó
el vicioso horizonte que confundía al hombre con la repro-
ducción de las arboles.

José Lezama Lima, *Para llegar a la Montego Bay*

"Est-ce que ce monsieur est fou?" me dit-elle.
Je fis un signe affirmatif.
"Et il vous emmène avec lui?"
Même affirmation.
"Ou çela?" dit-elle.
J'indique du doigt le centre de la terre.

Jules Verne, *Voyage au centre de la terre*

These pages on José Lezama Lima's novel *Paradiso* (Ediciones
Union, 1966) are not intended as a study of Lezama's novelistic
technique, which would require a rigorous analysis of all his work
as a poet and an essayist, informed by the most significant developments in the field of anthropology (Bachelard, Eliade, Gilbert
Durand . . .); rather, they represent the sympathetic approach
that Cronopios employ to establish commerce with each other.
Why Lezama Lima? Because, as he says describing one of his
characters:

"What I like about him," Cemí answered, "is his way of putting himself at the umbilical center of issues. It gives me the
impression that during every moment of his growth he was
endowed with grace. He has what the Chinese call *li*, that is,
behavior of a cosmic orientation, configuration, the perfect
form that comes before a fact, perhaps what our classical
tradition might call beauty within a style. Like a strategist
who always offers a flank well guarded against attack, he

can't be surprised. As he advances, he seems to keep an eye on the rear echelon. He knows what he lacks and looks for it avidly. He has a maturity that doesn't become enslaved as he grows and a wisdom that doesn't reject the immediate happening but at the same time doesn't render it a worshipful idolatry. His wisdom has excellent luck. He's a student who always knows what question he's going to be asked; but fate, of course, acts in a continuum where the answer leaps forth like a spark. He begins by studying the hundred questions in such a way that he can't miss, and the question that the bird of fortune brings in its beak is precisely the fruit he likes, which is the best one and the one the most worth the trouble of polishing and inspection." (279–80)*

So are we both crazy? Where can I emerge, desperate for air, from this deep swim through the hundreds of pages of *Paradiso*? And why does Jules Verne pop up all of a sudden in a discussion of a book where nothing seems to evoke him? And yet, yes, certainly it evokes him, doesn't Lezama speak of parallel existences, hasn't he somewhere said that it is "as if, without realizing it, by switching on the lights in his room a man initiated a waterfall in Ontario"—a Vernian metaphor if ever there was one. Don't we place ourselves in that tangential causality when we remember that the moment Saint George stuck his lance into the dragon the first to fall dead was his horse, just as lightning will sometimes pass down the trunk of an oak and run inoffensively through thirteen seminarians absorbed in eating Gruyère and hunting for four-leaf clovers, before carbonizing a canary stridulating in a cage fifty yards away? So, yes, Jules Verne, so to reach Montego

*Quotations from *Paradiso* for which page references are given are translated by Gregory Rabassa and refer to the edition published by Farrar, Straus and Giroux, Inc., 1974.

Bay you surely must pass through the center of the earth. It is not only certain but it is literal, and here is the proof: very rare reader of *Paradiso* (I imagine, in my vanity, a very exclusive club of those who, like you, have read *The Man Without Qualities*, *The Death of Virgil*, and *Paradiso*; in this alone—I am referring to the club—I resemble Phileas Fogg), do you realize that the explicit reference to Verne diabolically appears in an episode of eroticism like the one some researchers are cautiously beginning to attribute to the father of the *Nautilus*? In this episode the priapic oarsman Leregas will receive a visit from the unsuspected athlete Baena Albornoz. Baena descends to the underworld of a Havana gymnasium where, like a consenting Adonis, he is penetrated by the boar's tusk that makes him bite the bed in an ecstasy of delight. During Leregas's tense wait for the humiliating visit of the Hercules who, after many diurnal labors, spins the feminine thread of his true condition in the night, "the memory of the crater of Iasshole went down to the basement, the shadows of Scataris also reached there. The ringed shadow of Scataris over the crater of Sneffels . . ." (243). Fiendishly, the innocent island orography resonates through a lasciviously erotic situation, and Arne Saknussemm, marvel of our youth (*Descends dans la cratère du Yocul de Sneffels que l'ombre du Scartars vient caresser avant les calendes de Juillet, voyageur audacieux, et tu parviendras au centre de la Terre . . .*) proposes through sounds and images a lubricious revelation. Iasshole ("Yoculo"), ringed shadow ("il a perdu ses trente deux plis," a character of Jean Genet's would say, referring to another Baena Albornoz), Sneffels, who makes you think of "to sniff," Scataris, who in this context evokes the scrotum, and the images of descent into the crater, of caresses, of shadowy regions . . . O Phileas Fogg, O Professor Lidenbrock, what are we doing to your father?

I will let the recluse of Nantes and his speleologists lie in peace, but first I want to consider another passage so significant that Lezama could have placed it, like a blazing light, at the head of all that follows:

> Enfin, mon oncle me tirant par le collet, j'arrivai près de la boule. "Regarde, me dit-il, et regarde bien! il faut prendre des *leçons* d'abîme."
>
> Jules Verne, *Voyage au centre de la terre*

In ten days, stopping only to breathe and feed my cat, Theodor W. Adorno, I read *Paradiso*, completing (completing?) a journey begun several years before with the reading of some of its chapters in the review *Origenes*, along with other objects of Tlon or Ugbar. I am not a critic; some day, far in the future most likely, this prodigious oeuvre will find its Maurice Blanchot, because it will take someone like that to forge the way. I intend only to point out the shameful ignorance of this work and to strike a blow in advance against the misunderstandings that will arise when Latin America finally hears the voice of the author of *Paradiso*. The ignorance does not surprise me; twelve years ago I did not know of Lezama Lima either, until Ricardo Vigon, in Paris, told me about *Oppiano Licario*, which had just been published in *Origenes*, and which now closes (if anything can) *Paradiso*. I doubt that in these dozen years the work of Lezama has reached anywhere near the audience that has greeted the work of Jorge Luis Borges or Octavio Paz, after an equal time, even though

Lezama's work is undeniably on their level. Difficulties of matter and manner are the first causes of that ignorance: reading Lezama is one of the most arduous and at times frustrating tasks that one can undertake. The perseverence demanded by writers who work the limits, such as Raymond Roussel, Hermann Broch, or the Cuban master, is rare even among "specialists": thus the vacant chairs in our club. Borges and Paz (I chose them to set our sights on our countries' crowning achievements) have the advantage over Lezama of being writers of midday light, I would almost call them Apollonian in the sense that they possess perfectly composed styles and coherent organization of thought. Their difficulties and even obscurities (Apollo also knew how to be nocturnal, to descend into the abyss to kill the serpent Python) respond to a dialectic evoked by *Le Cimetière marin*:

. . . Mais rendre la lumière
Suppose d'ombre une morne moitié.

Endpoints of a tradition of Mediterranean origin, Borges and Paz produce their best effects without first posing the three riddles that turn the reader of Lezama into an eternal Oedipus. And if I say that this is an advantage they have over Lezama, I refer to those readers who have an almost moral abhorrence for the trials of Oedipus, who seek the greatest yield with the least effort. In Argentina, at least, there is a tendency to shy away from hermeticism, and Lezama is not only hermetic in the literal sense that the best of his work supposes an apprehension of essences through the mythical and the esoteric in all their historic, psychic, and literary forms, combined in an absolutely vertiginous manner within a poetic system where a Louis XV chair will often serve to seat the god Anubis; but he is also hermetic in the formal sense, as much by an innocence that leads him to believe that the most irregular of his metaphoric systems will be understood perfectly as by his original baroque style (one that is baroque *in origin,* as opposed to a baroque lucidly *mis en page,* as Alejo Carpentier's). You can see how difficult it is to join this club when so many obstacles stand in your way, except that the pleasures begin with these very difficulties, which make me, for one, read Lezama in the spirit of someone trying to decode the cipher *messunkaSebrA.icefdok. segnittamurtn,* etc., which finally is resolved into *Descends dans le cratère du Yocul de Sneffels. . .* : one might say that haste and the sense of guilt caused by bibliographic proliferation have led the modern reader to reject, at times with condescension, all *trovar clus.* Add false asceticism and the solemn blinders of wrongheaded specialization, against which a spirit represented by structuralism is now arising. In a work of masterful unitive intuition Goethe melded philosophy and poetry, previously separate in his century; until Thomas Mann (I am speaking now of the novel) it seemed that authors and readers would retain that synthesis, but already in Robert Musil (to stay in the German literary tradition) this sort of achievement no longer met the acclaim it deserved. Today the reader tends to adopt the specialist's attitude as he reads, often unconsciously rejecting works that offer mixed waters, novels that enter the realm of poetry, or metaphysics applied to an elbow on the bar counter or a bedpillow used for amorous activities. He is fairly tolerant of the extraliterary cargo any novel carries, as long as the genre observes its basic assumptions (which, I might add in passing, nobody understands very well, but that is another question). *Paradiso,* a novel that is also a hermetic tract, a poetics and the poetry that results from it, will have trouble reaching its readers: Where does the novel begin and the poetry end? What is the meaning of this anthropology embedded in an augury that is at the same time a tropical folklore that is also a family chronicle?

One hears much these days of "diagonal" (interdisciplinary) sciences, but the *diagonal reader* is slow to appear, and *Paradiso*, that transverse slice of essences and presences, will encounter the resistance that greets anything opposed to the direct file of received ideas. Yet the slice has been made; as in the Chinese story of the perfect executioner, the decapitated one will remain standing, not realizing that the first sneeze will send his head rolling across the ground.

If the difficulties of his expression are the first reason why Lezama is not well known, our political and historical circumstances are the second. Since 1960, fear, hypocrisy, and guilty consciences have combined to separate Cuba, its intellectuals, and its artists, from the rest of Latin America. Known writers such as Guillen, Carpentier, and Wilfredo Lam have surmounted this barrier by means of international reputations acquired before the revolution, so they cannot be ignored. Lezama, at that time still inexcusably near the bottom of the hierarchy of values drawn up by Peruvian, Mexican, or Argentine scholars, has remained on the other side of the barrier, so that those who have heard of him and want to read *Tratados en la Habana*, *Analecta del reloj*, *La fijeza*, *La expression americana*, or *Paradiso* cannot find copies. Like many other Cuban poets and artists, he has been forced to live and work in an isolation of which we can say only that it is sickening and shameful. Of course we must close the door to totalitarian communism. *Paradiso*? Nothing that could justify that label could emerge from its inferno. Rest assured, the OAS is watching over you.

There is also, perhaps, a third, and more hidden, reason for the oppressive silence that surrounds Lezama's work: I am going to speak of it without mincing words precisely because the few Cuban critics familiar with his work have chosen not to mention it, but I know its negative effect in the hands of many Pharisees of Latin American letters. I am referring to the numerous formal errors in Lezama Lima's prose, which, in contrast to the subtlety and profundity of its content, produce a scandalized impatience that the superficially refined reader can rarely get beyond. Lezama's publisher does a very poor job on the typographic level and *Paradiso* is no exception, so when the novel's internal perplexities are compounded by the carelessness that produces orthographic and grammatical extravagances, the eyes of the stuffed shirt within us have to roll. Several years ago when I began to show or read passages of Lezama to people who didn't know his work, the astonishment caused by his vision of reality and the audacious images that communicate it was nearly always tainted by an ironic smile of superiority. I soon realized that a defense mechanism entered into play and that, threatened with the absolute, people quickly exaggerated the importance of his formal faults as an almost unconscious pretext for remaining on this side of Lezama, rather than following him as he boldly plunges into deep waters. The

undeniable fact that Lezama seems to have decided never to write correctly any English, French, or Russian name, and that his quotations from foreign languages are replete with orthographic fantasies, induces the typical Rio Plata intellectual to see him as a no less typical autodidact of an underdeveloped country, which is quite accurate, and to find in this a justification for not appreciating his true significance, which is most unfortunate. Of course, among particular Argentines, formal correctness in writing as well as in dress is a guarantee of seriousness, and anyone who announces that the earth is round in the proper "style" deserves more respect than a Cronopio with a spud in his mouth but plenty to say behind it. I speak of Argentina because I know it a little, but when I was in Cuba there too I met young intellectuals who smiled condescendingly in recalling the peculiar way Lezama pronounced the name of some foreign poet; the difference came out when we began to discuss the poet in question: while these young people never got beyond good phonetics, in five minutes Lezama had them staring at their hands, at a loss for words. One of the indices of underdevelopment is our fastidiousness toward anything that peels away the cultural crust, appearances, the lock on the door of culture. We know that Dylan is pronounced *Dilan*, not *Dailan*, the way we said it ourselves for the first time (and they looked at us ironically or corrected us or made us feel we had done something wrong); we know exactly how to pronounce Caen or Laon and Sean O'Casey and Gloucester. And that's fine, like keeping your underarms clean and using deodorant. What is really important comes later, or not at all. For many of those who dismiss Lezama with a smile, it will arrive neither sooner nor later, and yet their armpits, I assure you, are perfect.

The remarkable ingenuity of Lezama's narrative has the same effect on many readers as its surface flaws do. Yet it is because of my love for that ingenuity that I am speaking about him here—not bound by any scholastic canon, it possesses an extraordinary efficacy: while many search, Perceval meets; while many talk, Mishkin comprehends. The baroque that arises from many sources in Latin America has produced writers as different and yet as alike as Vallejo, Neruda, Asturias, and Carpentier (I am speaking of substance rather than genre), but in Lezama's case it is distinguished by a quality that I can only call, for want of a better word, ingenuity. An American ingenuity, insular in both a literal and a broader sense, an American innocence. An ingenious American innocence, opening its eyes eleatically, orphically, at the very beginning of Creation. Lezama Adam before the fall, Lezama Noah identical to the one in the Flemish paintings who sagely directs the file of animals: two butterflies, two horses, two leopards, two ants, two dolphins. . . . A primitive, as everyone knows, an accomplished *sorbonnard*, but American the way the dissected albatross of the prophet of Ecclesiastes did not become a "sadder but wiser man," even though his science was metempsychosis: his knowledge is original, jubilant, it is born of the water of Tales and the fire of Empedocles. Between the thought of Lezama and that of a European writer (or his Rio Platan homologues, much less American in respect to the matter under discussion), we find the difference between innocence and guilt. All European writers are "slaves of their baptism," if I may paraphrase Rimbaud; like it or not, their writing carries baggage from an immense and almost

frightening tradition; they accept that tradition or they fight against it, it inhabits them, it is their familiar and their succubus. Why write, if everything has, in a way, already been said? Gide observed sardonically that since nobody listened, everything has to be said again, yet a suspicion of guilt and superfluity leads the European intellectual to the most extreme refinement of his trade and tools, the only way to avoid paths too much traveled. Thus the enthusiasm that greets novelties, the uproar when a writer has succeeded in giving substance to a new slice of the invisible; merely recall symbolism, surrealism, the "nouveau roman": finally something truly new that neither Ronsard, nor Stendhal, nor Proust imagined. For a moment we can put aside our guilt; even the epigones begin to believe they are doing something new. Afterwards, slowly, they start to feel European again and each writer still has his albatross around his neck.

While this is going on, Lezama wakes up on his island with a preadamite happiness, without a fig leaf, innocent of any direct tradition. He assumes them all, from the Etruscan interpreting entrails to Leopold Bloom blowing his nose in a dirty handkerchief, but without historic compromise, without being a French or an Austrian writer; he is a Cuban with only a handful of his own culture behind him and the rest is knowledge, pure and free, not a career responsibility. He can write whatever he pleases without saying now Rabelais . . . now Martial . . . He is not a chained slave, he is not required to write more, or better, or differently, he doesn't have to justify himself as a writer. His incredible gifts, like his deficiencies, spring out of this innocent freedom, this free innocence. At times, reading *Paradiso*, one has the feeling that Lezama has come from another planet; how is it possible to ignore or defy the taboos of knowledge to this extent, the *don't-write-like-this*es that are our embarrassing professional mandates? When the innocent American makes his appearance, the good savage who accumulates trinkets without suspecting that they are worthless or out of fashion, then two things can happen to Lezama. One, the one that counts: the erup-

tion, with the primordial force of the stealer of
fire, of a brilliance stripped of the inferiority
complexes that weigh so heavily on Latin Americans. The other, which makes the impeccably
cultured reader smile ironically, is the Douanier
Rousseau route, the route of Mishkin simplicity,
the person who puts a period at the end of an
extraordinary passage in *Paradiso* and writes
with the utmost tranquility: "What happened to
young Ricardo Fronesis, while the story of his
ancestors was being told?"

I am writing these pages because I *know* that
sentences like the one I have just quoted count
more with the pedants than the prodigious in-
ventiveness with which *Paradiso* creates its
world. And if I quote the sentence about young Fronesis it is
because, like many other gaucheries, it annoys me too, but only
the way I would be annoyed by a fly on a Picasso or a scratch from
my cat Theodor while I am listening to the music of Xenakis.
Anyone who finds himself incapable of grasping the complexities
of a work hides his withdrawal behind the most superficial pretexts because he has not gotten past the surface. Thus, I knew a
gentleman who refused to listen to classical records because, he
said, the sound of the needle on the plastic prevented him from
enjoying the work in its absolute perfection; mo-
tivated by this lofty standard, he spent days listening to tangos and boleros that would curl your
hair. Whenever I quote a passage from Lezama
and am met by an ironic smile or a change of subject, I think of that man; those who are incapable
of penetrating *Paradiso* always react that way:
for them everything is the scritch of the needle, a
fly, a scratch. In *Hopscotch* I defined and at-
tacked the Lady Reader who is incapable of wag-
ing true amorous battle against the book, a battle
like that of Job with the angel. For those who
question the legitimacy of my attack, one exam-

ple will suffice: at first the respected critics of Buenos Aires could
not understand the two possible ways of reading my book; after
that they went on to the *pollice verso* with the pathetic assurance
that they had read the book "in the two ways demanded by the

author," when what the poor author had offered was an option: I never had the vanity to believe that in our time people were going to read a book twice. What then would you expect from the Lady Reader faced with *Paradiso*, which, as one of Lewis Carroll's characters said, would try the patience of an oyster? But there is no patience where we have lost humility and hope, where a conditioned, prefabricated culture, adulated by those writers we can call functional, with its rebellions and heterodoxies carefully controlled by the marquises of Queensbury of the profession, rejects all works that go truly against the grain. Willing to confront any literary difficulty on the intellectual or psychological plane as long as the Western rules of the game are observed, ready to play the most arduous Proustian or Joycean chess game as long as it employs known pieces and divinable strategies, she retreats indignant and ironic when she is invited into an extrageneric territory, to react to language and action that are part of a narrative that is born not of books but of long *readings of the abyss*; and I have now finished my explanation of my epigraph and it is time to pass to another subject.

Is *Paradiso* a novel? Yes, inasmuch as it is tied loosely together by the life of José Cemí—from which the multiple episodes and connected and unconnected stories arise and to which they return. But right from the beginning this "argument" has curious characteristics. I don't know if Lezama realizes that the beginning of his book recalls the delights of *Tristram Shandy*, for while José Cemí is indeed alive at the beginning of the book, whereas Tristram, who tells his own story, is not born until the middle of the book, still the protagonist around whom *Paradiso* revolves remains in the background while the book proceeds leisurely to describe the lives of his grandparents, parents, aunts, and uncles. More importantly, *Paradiso* lacks what I would call the unifying reverse-field, the fabric that makes a novel, however fragmentary its episodes. This is not a defect, for the book does not at all depend on its being or not being what we expect from a novel; my own reading of *Paradiso*, as of all of Lezama, begins by expecting the unexpected, by not demanding a novel, and then I can concentrate on its content without useless tension, without that petulant protest that arises from opening a cabinet to get out the jam and discovering instead three fantastic vests. Lezama has to be read with a suspension prior to the *fatum*, just as one gets into a plane without asking the color of the pilot's eyes or his religious beliefs. What irritates the critical intelligence in the Bureau of Weights and Measures seems perfectly natural to any critical intelligence thrust into the cave of Ali Baba.

Paradiso may not be a novel, because of its lack of a plot capable of providing narrative coherence to the dizzying multiplicity of its contents, as much as anything. Toward the end, for example, Lezama interjects a chapter-long story that seems to have nothing to do with the rest of the novel, although its atmosphere and impact are the same. And the two final chapters are dominated by Oppiano Licario, who had hardly appeared previously, while José Cemí has all but disappeared, along with Fronesis and Foción; consequently, these chapters have something of the nature of appendixes, of *surplus*. But more than its unconventional structure it is its lack of a viable (that is, "life-like") spatio-temporal and psychological reference that is not novelistic. All of the characters are seen more in essence than in presence; they are archetypes more than types. The first result of this (which has raised some eyebrows) is that, while the novel tells its story of several Cuban families at the end of the past century and the beginning of this one, with profuse historical detailing of geography, furniture, gastronomy, and fashion, the characters themselves seem to move in a perfect continuum outside historicity, talking to each other in a private, unchanging language that does not pertain to either the reader or the story and has no reference to psychological or cultural verisimilitude.

And yet, nothing is less inconceivable than this language when one is freed from the persistent notion of the realism of the novel, which is primary even in the novel's fantastic or poetic forms. Nothing is more *natural* than a language that emerges from native roots and origins, that always lies between oracle and incantation, that is the shadow of myths, the murmur of the collective unconscious; nothing is more human, finally, than such a poetic language, disdainful of prosaic and pragmatic information, a verbal radiaesthesia that divines the deepest waters and makes them gush forth. No one who understands he is reading an epic is put off by the language of the *Iliad* or the Norse sagas; the speeches of the Greek chorus are barely noticed in the amplitude of the tragedy (and this applies to a Paul Claudel or a Christopher Fry as well). Why then not accept the fact that the characters of *Paradiso* always speak *desde la imagen*, that they are presented through a poetic system that Lezama has often described, whose key is the power of the image as the supreme expression of the human spirit in search of the reality of the invisible world?

Thus, when two Cuban boys form a friendship at school, they speak like this:

> "From the first day of class," Fibo told José Eugenio, "I could see that you were the son of a Spaniard. You never did anything bad; you never looked surprised; you never seemed to notice other people doing bad things. Still, after we settled into our desks, a person's eyes would light on you. You've got a bottom like a root. When you're standing up you look as if you're growing, but inwardly, toward a dream. Nobody ever notices that kind of growth."
>
> "When I went into that classroom," José Eugenio replied, "I was so disturbed that it clouded over, it seemed to be raining. I was touching mist, I was pinching the ink of a squid. So your jabbing point made me realize where I was, it straightened me out, it touched me and I wasn't a tree any more." (87)

And a dialogue like this occurs during a family meal:

> The chill of November, cut by gusts of north wind which rustled the tops of the Prado poplars, justified the arrival of the glistening turkey, its harsh extremities softened by butter, its breast capable of attracting the appetite of the whole family and sheltering it as in an ark of the covenant.
>
> "The Mexican turkey buzzard is much tenderer," the older Santurce child said.
>
> "Not turkey buzzard, just turkey," Cemí corrected. "Once for my asthma they recommended a soup made from the young of that disgusting bird, if I can avoid using its ugly name, but I said I'd rather die than drink that oil. That kind of soup must taste like the sow's milk that the ancients thought caused leprosy."
>
> "We really don't know what that disease comes from," Dr. Santurce said. As a doctor, he did not feel it improper to talk about illnesses at dinnertime.
>
> "Let's talk about the Peking nightingale instead," Doña Augusta said, annoyed at the turn of the conversation. Cemí's reference to sow's milk had been comical because it was so unexpected, but Santurce's development of the theme

at that moment was as frightening as the possibilities of a tidal wave that the evening papers had begun to brood over.

"The red stains on the tablecloth must have favored the Vulturidae theme, but remember too, Mother, that the Peking nightingale sang for a dying emperor," Alberto said as he started to parcel out the winy, almondy turkey.

"I know, Alberto, that every meal must pass through its gloomy whirlwind, because a happy family gathering couldn't get by without death trying to open the windows, but the aroma of that turkey can be a spell to drive away Hera the horrible." (182–83)

Doña Augusta invokes Hera, any servant recalls Hermes, Nero, or Yi King. Lezama makes absolutely no effort to make his characters' speech appropriate to their conditions, to have them vary their speech in different situations or when speaking to different people; yet this is the magic of the novel, for as one's reading advances the characters differentiate and define themselves, Ricardo Fronesis reveals his most secret depths, Foción is set against him like an antistrophe, the way *yin* calls forth *yang*, José Cemí and Alberta Olalla, Oppiano Licario and Doña Augusta, José Eugenio and Rialta, each of these is a person, just as Andromache and Philoctetes and Creon are in the realm of tragedy. Lezama accomplishes the non-Goethean feat of creating the individual out of the universal, almost disdainfully rejecting the novelist's usual strategies of typification for character and exaggeration for portraiture. Because characters aren't important to Lezama, the important thing is the total mystery of human experience, "the existence of a universal marrow which controls series and exceptions" (p. 328). Thus the author's favored characters live, act, think, and talk in conformity to a total poetics that appears in the following passages, several more doors through which we can enter the verbal universe of *Paradiso*:

But neither the historical nor futurity nor tradition awaken man's exercise or conduct, and he's been the one who has seen it most clearly and deeply. But the desire, the desire that becomes choral, the desire that, when it penetrates, succeeds, by the surface of the shared dream, in elaborating the true warp of the historical, that escaped him. *Difficult it is to fight against desire; what it wants it buys with the soul:* Heraclitus' aphorism encompasses the totality of man's conduct. The only thing attained by the suprahistoric is desire, which doesn't end in dialogue but reflects on the universal spirit, prior to the actual appearance of the earth.

We may discuss Nietzsche's will to transvaluate all values, but the values that must be found and established are very different now than the ones he considered. A gathering of scholars who approach new assignments in the future, for example: the history of fire, of the drop of water, of the breath, of the emanation of Greek *aporrhoea*. A history of fire, beginning with a presentation of its fight with the Neptunic or aqueous elements, the dissemination of fire, fire in the tree, colors of the flame, the blaze and the wind, the burning bush of Moses, the sun and the white rooster, the sun and the red rooster among the Germani, in short, the transformations of fire into energy, all those themes which are the first that occur to me and which today's man needs to enter new regions of depth.　　　　　　(305)

On Foción's homosexual love for Fronesis:

The error that Foción's senses brought as he neared Fronesis consisted in that the image was the form which for him acquired the insatiable. But just as he intuited that he would never be able to sate himself with Fronesis's body (for a long time he had been convinced that, without even proposing it to him, Fronesis was playing with him, gaining a perspective where in the end he was always grotesquely knocked off his horse), he had made a transposition in which his verbum of sexual energy no longer solicited the other body, that is, no longer sought its incarnation, going from the fact to the body, but, on the contrary, starting out from his body he attained the aeration, the subtilizing, the absolute pneuma of the other body. He volatilized the figure of Fronesis, but there was his insatiability, reconstructing the fragments to attain even the possibility of his image, where his senses again felt shaken by an unsupported fervor, one could say a falcon in pursuit of a pneuma, the very spirit of flight. (326)

The worldview of Fronesis, Cemí, and Foción:

When the rest of the students appeared disdainful and mocking and the majority of professors were unable to overcome their aphasias and lethargyrations, Fronesis, Cemí, and Foción scandalized people by bringing the new gods, the word without breaking, in its pure yolk yellow, and the combinatorials and the proportions that could trace new games and new ironies. They knew that conformity in expression and in ideas took on in the contemporary world innumerable variants and disguises, because it exacted from the intellectual a servitude, the mechanism of a causative absolute, so that he would abandon his truly heroic position of being, as in the grand epochs, creator of values, of forms, the salutatorian of creative vitalism and the accuser of what is enshrouded in blocks of ice, which still dares to float in the river of the temporal.   (329)

José Cemí conversing with his grandmother:

"Grandmother, every day I am more aware of how Mama is coming to look like you. Both of you have what I would call the same interpreted rhythm of nature. Lately, people have a trapped look, as if they had no way out. But you two seem guided, as if you were giving effect to the words that made their way into your ears. All you have to do is listen, follow a sound . . . You are free from interruptions, when you talk you don't seem to look for words but rather to follow a point that will make everything clear. It's as if you were acting in obedience, as if you'd sworn to keep the quantity of light in the world from diminishing. We know that both of you have made a sacrifice, that you've renounced vast regions, life itself, I would say, if something had not appeared within you, a life so miraculous that the rest of us don't even know what we exist for, or how to live out our days, because it seems that we are mere fragments of the upper sphere that the mystics talk of, and have not yet found the island where stags and senses leap."

"But, my dear grandson Cemí, you observe all this in your mother and myself precisely because your gift is to grasp that rhythm of growth for nature. An infrequent lingering, that lingering of nature, before which you place an observant lingering which is itself nature. Thank God that the linger-

ing in bringing observation to a fabulous dimension is ac-
companied by a hyperbolic memory. Among many gestures,
many words, many sounds, after you've observed them between sleep and waking, you know the one that will accompany your memory over the centuries. The visit of our
impressions possesses an intangible swiftness, but your gift
of observation lies in wait, as if in a theater through which
must pass again and again those impressions that later become as light as larvae, that allow themselves to be caressed
or show their disdain; afterwards memory gives them a substance like primal mud, like a stone that collects the image of
the fish's shadow. You talk about the rhythm of growth in
nature, but one must have much humility to observe it, follow it, revere it. In that, too, it's apparent you belong to our
family, most people interrupt, prefer the void, make excla-
mations, stupid demands, or deliver phantom arias, but you
pay attention to the rhythm that makes a complement, the
complement of the unknown, but which, as you say, has
been dictated to us as the principal mark of our lives. We've
been dictated to, that is, we were necessary for the complement of a higher voice to touch the shore, feel itself on solid
ground. The rhythmic interpretation of the higher voice,
almost without the intervention of the will, that is, a will
already wrapped in a superior destiny, gave us the enjoyment
of an impulse which was simultaneously a clarification . . ."

(370–71)

Although Lezama's synthesis is not easy to convey, this passage
may give an idea of the occult rhythms that animate his narrative:

The exercise of poetry, the verbal search for unknown fi-
nality, developed in him a strange perspicacity for words
which acquire an animistic relief when grouped in space,
seated like sibyls at an assembly of spirits. When his vision
gave him a word in whatever relation it might have to reality,
that word seemed to pass into his hands, and although the
word remained invisible, freed of the vision from whence it
had come, it went along, gathering a wheel on which gyrated
incessantly its invisible modulation and its palpable modelization; then between intangible modelization and almost
visible modulation, he seemed finally to be able to touch
its forms, if he closed his eyes a little. Thus he went on
acquiring the ambivalence between gnostic space, which ex-

presses, which knows, which has a difference of density that contracts to bring forth, and quantity, which in the unity of time revives the look, the sacred character of what in one instant passes from undulant vision into fixed look. Gnostic space, tree, man, city, spatial groupages in which man is the median point between nature and the supernatural.

(355–56)

Meditating on that, José Cemí approaches an antiquarian's window, where a group of statuettes and other objects seem to suffer from a lack of harmony, from the reciprocal relation of their forces, which vainly seek coincidence, articulations, fraternal rhythms. Cemí understands that every time he chooses and buys an object, his choice is due to "his glance having distinguished and isolated it from the rest of the objects, moving it forward like a chess piece that penetrates a world that instantaneously reconstitutes all its facets," an intuitive process that the reader of *Paradiso* perceives in every episode, every decisive crossroads within the story. Cemí knows that "the piece advanced represented a point that synthesized an infinite current of relations": there could not be a better description of the process that, like Valéry's *Achille immobile à grand pas*, at once sets in tumultuous movement and immobilizes the innumerable animate creatures and inanimate objects that inhabit every page of the book.

Trusting the infallible choice of his inner vision, Cemí chooses two statuettes, a bacchante "gently swaying to the rhythms of the dance," and a Cupid without a bow who, thus disarmed, resembles an angel, "a youth in a Persian miniature" with something as well "of the Greek or Inca athlete following the prodigious Veracocho." He places these objects on his dresser and what happens then associates the initial meditation on words-become-objects with what will happen to these objects that become words in their subtle chain of *similitudes amies* (to quote Valéry again):

Days before, in his own study, he had studied a cup of solid silver which he had brought from Puebla, beside a Chinese buck worked out of a single piece of wood. At his side, by itself on another table, a fan disquieted the buck (more than is natural for such animals) as he drew near the silver cup, his fear ancestral, cosmological, of the hour of watering, after running through the grazing lands. The buck, frightened because he saw a sudden storm wind rise, no longer stood beside the cup in his usual pleasant pose, his

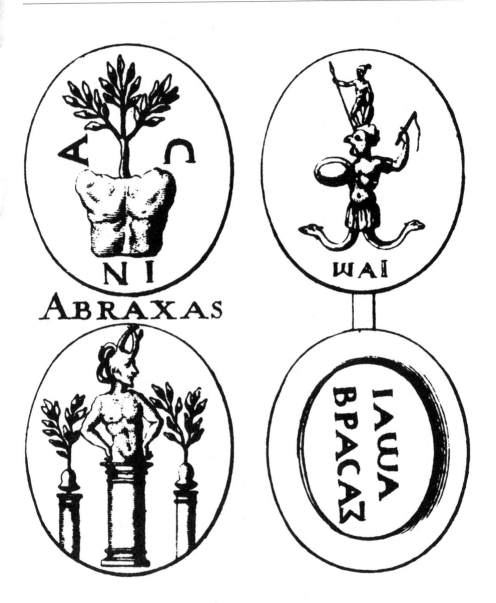

ABRAXAS

skin trembled, as when he felt the gust passing over the grass, the serpent's fumes on the protective cloak of the dew.

To give the wooden buck peace, not only had the cup to be moved away, but the fan had to be turned off. Cemí lifted the Pueblan cup to the upper reaches of the little cabinet, setting it between the angel and the bacchante. He realized that the chaotic tastelessness of the show window on Obispo calmed itself in the polished mahogany that topped the cabinet, when he set the cup between the two bronze statuettes. The angel appeared to run and jump without dizzying himself along the circle of the cup's lip, and the bacchante, exhausted from striking her cymbals and making gaudy leaps, collapsed at the foot of the cup, from where the angel resolved to retrieve her for the games of the round light at the cup's lip.   (357)

The final step is metaphysical; it is the axis around which the system that makes *Paradiso* possible crystallizes, a system that uses the image to make visible the world of essences we can usually visit only momentarily. But then Cemí notices that the serene pleasure these groupings bring him, "where a field of force succeeds in establishing itself in the center of the composition," provokes in others "a cross and even confused reaction, as if of supreme mistrust." The imaginary cities he has seen rise up in the conciliation and harmony of the rhythms provoke angry gestures in those who remain outside an architecture at once intuited and set into operation by the spirit. In a passage that has the "dark clarity" of Corneille's famous line, Lezama crowns his vision:

That brought him to meditate on the manner in which those spatial rearrangements were produced in him, that ordering of the invisible, that feeling for stalactites. He was able to establish that those groupings had temporal roots, had nothing to do with spatial groupings, which are always a still life; for the viewer, the flow of time converted those spatial cities into figures, through which time, as it passed back and forth like the labor of the tides on the coral reefs, produced a kind of eternal change of the figures, which by being situated in the distance were a permanent embryo. The essence of time, which is the ungraspable, by its own movement that expresses all distance, achieves the reconstruction of those Tibetan cities which enjoy all mirages, the quartz doe of the contemplative way, but into which we are not able to penetrate, for a time in which all animals begin to speak has not been bestowed on man, everything external producing an irradiation which reduces him to a diamond essence lacking walls. The man knows that he cannot penetrate into those cities, but in him there is a disquieting fascination with those images, which are the only reality that comes toward us, that bites us, a leech that bites without a mouth, that by a completive method sustains the image, like most of Egyptian painting, and wounds us precisely with what it lacks.   (358)

In our mooring at Lezama I have assumed that the reader does not know *Paradiso*, which, like so many other Cuban books and indeed all of Cuba, is still waiting for the rest of Latin America to decide to confront its true destiny. That is why I hasten to clear up the misunderstanding that would result from assuming that the whole book is in the tone of the passages I have quoted. These passages offer some keys to the novel, but it actually operates on many levels, from everyday domestic descriptions to extreme erotic, magical, and imaginary situations. It is impossible to convey the multiplicity of connected or free episodes, the sequential and cross-referential scenes, the inexhaustible fantasy of a man who uses the image as a fabulous falconry in which the falconer, the falcon, and the capture triangulate a primary series of reactions that multiply into a vast crystal containing an entire world, a "Tibetan city" of absolute enchantment. I offer an example that I hope will provide a sense of the lifeblood that runs through *Paradiso*, the human presence that hypostatizes all that is Cuban and American, the arduous proposition of recording height and length, above and below, myth and folklore, and at the same time letting us in on games and table talk, longing for absent loves, empty opera halls, and the Havana waterfront at daybreak after an endless walk. So:

José Cemí remembered the Aladdin-like days when Grandmother would get up in the morning and say, "Today I feel like making a pudding, not the kind they eat these days, which is like restaurant food, but something closer to a custard or a thick pudding." Then the whole house was at the old lady's disposal. Even the Colonel obeyed her, imposing a religious submission, as with a queen once regnant who years later, when her son the king was obliged to visit armories in Liverpool or Amsterdam, reassumed her old prerogatives and heard once more the whispered flattery of her retired servants. She asked what boat had brought the cinnamon, then held it aloft by the root for a long time and ran the tips of her fingers over the surface, the way one tests the antiquity of a parchment, not by the date of the work hidden in it but by the width, by the boldness of the boar's tooth that engraved the surface. She lingered even more over the vanilla, not pouring it directly from the bottle, but with drops soaking her handkerchief, and afterwards, in irreversible cycles of time that only she could measure, she went on sniffing until the message from that dizzying essence faded away, and only then would she pronounce it worthy of participation in a dessert mixed by her; or else she poured the bottle's contents into the grass in the garden, declaring it harsh and unusable, obeying, I think, some secret principle to destroy whatever was deficient and unfulfilled, so that those who settle for little would not come across the rejected matter and preserve it. She reestablished herself with loving domination, a trait whose ultimate refinement was its obvious balance, and said to the Colonel, "Get the irons ready to singe the meringue, because soon we'll paint a mustache on Mont Blanc," voiced with an almost invisible laugh, intimating that the creation of a dessert elevated the house toward the supreme essence. "Now don't beat eggs in milk. Mix the two after you beat them separately; each should grow in itself, and then you put together what they've blossomed into." The sum total of these delicacies would be put on the fire as Doña Augusta, watching it boil, saw it form into the yellow ceramic-like pieces, served on plates with a dark red surface, a red that came out of night. Then Grandmother passed from her nervous commands to an impassive indifference. There was no need for praise, hyperbole, encouraging love pats, importunate reiteration of its sweetness. Nothing seemed to matter to her any more and she took up talking to her daughter again. Now she seemed to be asleep, while her

daughter was telling her something. Or she was mending
socks, while the other was talking. They would change
rooms, one as if she were looking for something she remembered at that moment, leading the other by the hand, talking, laughing, whispering.   (12–13)

Thus we learn of the death of Andresito and of Eloisa, and of
the marriages of José Eugenio, with the delicious episode of the

boots of his sweetheart Rialta, mother of José
Cemí and the most enchanting feminine figure
in the book; the disappearance of José Eugenio
brings the life of his son to the forefront, and
from him and with him we get to know Deme-
trious and Blanquita and are present at the marvelous game of chess when Uncle Alberto reads
mysterious messages hidden inside the jade
pieces, creating a magical atmosphere, until José
Cemí secretly discovers that the little pieces of
paper were actually blank and that the magic was
even heavier for being imaginary and poetic. The phallic rituals
of Leregas and Farraluque have something of an aping parody
anticipating the extraordinary debate on homosexuality that reveals the character of Fronesis and Foción at the same time that it
defines a mythic and poetic anthropology. The chapters that lead
to the end of the work are the most novelistic in regard to narrative
and character: the drama of Foción before Fronesis, the bitterly
humorous story of Fronesis's father and Sergei Diaghilev, culmi-
nating in the hallucinatory episode of Foción's madness. This is a
poor summation of a novel that will not tolerate summarizing,
that demands a *literal* reading, but in the meantime it would be
selfish to resist the urge to cite twists, discoveries, and jests like
these:

The olive green of his uniform contrasted with the yolk-like
yellow of the melon; when he shifted it to relieve its fatiguing
weight, the melon took on the vital appearance of a dog.

                                                             (14)

Andresito, Doña Augusta's eldest son, before shaking the
sweat several times from the bow of his violin, would begin
to fold the pages of his score, and with that silence of a stout
commodore before the first notes . . .   (40)

The President crossed the ballroom like a nicety on the lid of a cigar box. (105)

On waking, he sensed the undefined collection of silences that surround a tiger, a silence lying in wait, unfolding under the tiger's auditory captation. (229)

It caused the sensation of being a transmuter of hours, it bore the secret of the metamorphoses of time, the hours inhabited by a dormouse or a terrapin, it transformed them into the hours of a falcon or a cat with electrified whiskers. (327)

They'll consider him a victim of high culture, like those victims in detective stories who prefer to enter their houses through the window. (429)

The house, the candles in their holders, seemed to stress its metals, as if preparing the fireflies of memory for the future. (119)

Once Uncle Alberto, arguing with his mother, Doña Augusta, broke a Sèvres tureen with pastoral scenes, the goats left with just one jawbone, a pair of short pants left without a leg in the morning rehearsal of courtly dances. Doña Augusta continued her contralto imprecations, refusing to sell her last shares of Western Union; then the French cut-crystal ashtray, jumping like a quartz mine under the puffing and mad running of gnomes, deposited its fragments in the woven wicker basket. (77–78)

Its owner was Colonel-of-Independence Castillo Dimás, who spent three months on the plantation during the harvesting and grinding season, three months on some keys he owned near Cabañas, a completely Eden-like locale, where he slept like a gull, ate like a shark, and bored himself like a marmot in the Para-Nirvana. (213)

Then he caught up with a former mistress, Hortense Schneider, an Isoldic and light-fingered Prussian beauty, then in her diminishing forties, with circles under her eyes and lips as communicative as the pines of the Rhine. Growing old in such a Wagnerian way, in her immoderate concept of grandeur, she had switched continents, and now in China she went on playing her Isoldic role, restricting herself to being the emperor's mistress. (441)

Paradiso is like the sea, and the preceding quotes suffer the sad fate of any medusa detached from its green belly. Surprised at first, now I understand the gesture my hand makes to reach out and turn the pages of this huge volume one more time; this is not a book to read in the way that one reads books, it is an object with obverse and reverse, weight and density, smell and taste, a center of vibration you will never succeed in knowing intimately unless you approach it with a certain amount of tact, seeking the entrance through osmosis and sympathetic magic. How admirable that Cuba has given us two great writers who defend the baroque as the code and emblem of Latin America, and that their work possesses such a richness that Alejo Carpentier and José Lezama Lima could be the two poles of the vision and manifestation of the baroque, Carpentier the impeccable novelist of European technique and lucidity, the author of literary works without a trace of innocence, maker of books refined to the tastes of that Western specialist, the reader of novels; and Lezama Lima, intercessor in the dark operations of the spirit that precedes the intellect, of those zones that provide pleasure we don't understand, of the touch that hears, the lips that see, the skin that perceives the flutes at the Pannic hour and the terror of crossing streets under the full moon. In its highest moments, *Paradiso* is a ceremony, something that surpasses all readings with literary ends and modes in mind; it has that zealous presence typical of the primordial vision of the Eleatics, amalgam of what would later be called poem and philosophy, naked confrontation between man's face and a sky full of columns of stars. A work like this isn't *read*; it is consulted, you move through it line by line, essence by essence, with an intellectual and sensory involvement as tense and deeply felt as that contained in these lines and essences, which seem to reach out to us and expose us. Pity the poor soul who tries to travel through *Paradiso* the way you go through "the book of the month," that television show on the pages of ordinary novels. Since my first encounter with the poetry of Lezama I have known that this *Paradiso* would be the crowning of an imperial work. And therefore, as to reach Montego Bay,

> después que en las arenas, sedosas pausas intermedias,
> entre lo irreal suergido y el denso, irrechazable aparecido,
> se hizo el acuario métrico, y el ombligo terrenal
> supero el vicioso horizonte que confundia al hombre con la reproducción de los arboles,

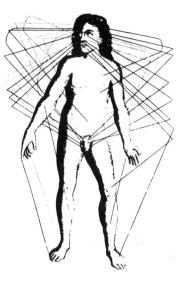

we must remember the myth of the Idumeans, who reproduced vegetatively, without "obligo terrenal," without time, "acuario métrico," so, in the same way, every dark and risky page of *Paradiso*, every uprooting or estranging image, requires a humble but profound love of the first morning discovered in the garden of Eden, a deciphering of herbs, seclusions, and comportments, a ritual cadence that in the middle of the trance and enchantment opens the doors of a great mystery that is resolved in the brilliance of this masterwork. Thanks to *Paradiso*—as in their day one thanked *Locus Solus* or *The Death of Virgil*—I return to the written word in the spirit of a child who slowly passes a finger over the maps in the atlas, over the contours of the images, who savors the inebriating pleasures of the incomprehensible, of words that are incantations, rhythms, and rites of passage: "Before the calends of July . . . Fifteen men on the coffin of the dead . . . They departed for the conquest of the Tower of Gold . . . Open, Sesame . . . The monsoons and the trade winds . . . Don't forget that we owe Esculapio a cock . . ." These days we weigh the dead albatross, we have become wise, but the fundamental attitude remains the same, because it is that of all poets who seek or transmit a participation in the essential. *Paradiso* can be read in the manner of Orphic hymns, or bestiaries, or *Il Milione* by the Venetian, or Paracelsus, or Sir John Mandeville, and in the oracle's cadenced consultation, where a certainty palpitates that transcends enigmas,

the absurdity and incredulity of intellectual technique, the reader passes into the verb and through the verb to a transcendent encounter, he is before the entrails the soothsayer reads, before the mantic tablets, the signs of the I Ching and the *libris fulguralis*. To read *Paradiso* this way is to look at the fire in the fireplace and enter into its whirlwind of creation and annihilation, its classical moment in which it is the sacrificial fire, its romantic hour full of sparks and unexpected explosions, its baroque of blue and green smoke that multiplies ephemeral statues and cornucopias, its Aura Mazda instant, its Brunhilda instant, the cosmic sign of Empedocles, the spiral turns of Isadora Duncan, the analytic sign of Bachelard, and, underneath, always, the old women of the hyperborean coasts who read in the flames the fate of those on the high seas who confront the Kraken and the unchained leviathan. Man has reached the moon, but twenty centuries ago a poet knew the enchantments that would make the moon come down to earth. Ultimately, what is the difference?

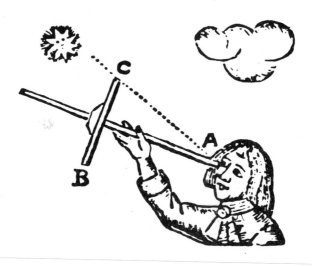

The Fire
Where Burns a

He was the first to accuse me of
Without proof and perhaps with regret and yet there were those
    who
Everyone knows that in a town hidden among
Time holds still and only every
People obsessed with trifles, with slow
They may have hearts but when they speak it is
What can they accuse me of, if only we had
Surely not just spite, after that
(Maybe the full moon, the night when he took me to
In love a bite is not so strange, especially when one has
I moaned it is true and in a moment I could
Afterwards we didn't talk about it, he seemed proud of
They always seem proud when we moan, but then
How would hatred change the memory that follows the
Why did we desire each other more in those nights than if
Beneath the moon in the sands mixed together and smelling of
(I would have bitten him, yes, but in love to bite is not so
He never spoke to me but only attended to
I perfumed my breasts with the herbs that my mother
And he, the pleasure of tobacco in his beard, and so much
He never cried when we went down to the river but sometimes
A black and white handkerchief that he gently gave me while
We called each other by sweet animal names and trees that
There was no end to that interminable beginning of each
(I would have bitten him while within me he
At a certain point our voices always mixed if
It could have lasted like the hard green sky over my
Why if embracing we held the world against
Until the night, its memory like a stake in my mouth, I felt
Oh, the moon on his face, that loving death on a skin that before

Why did he stagger, why did his body act as if
Are you sick? Cover yourself, let me
I felt him tremble as if from fear or dampness and when he looked
  at me
Again my hands covered him, seeking that beating, that warm
  drum and
Until dawn I was his faithful shadow and I hoped that again
But another moon came and we were together and I understood
  that now
And he trembled with fury and tore off my blouse like
I helped him, I was his dog, I licked the whip waiting
I faked the cry and the sob as if his flesh really
(I no longer bit but moaned and begged to give him
Now he could believe, he got up with his smile from before, when
When he left he stumbled and I saw him turn, grimacing and
Alone in my house I waited with my arms around my knees until
The first to accuse me was
(I did bite him, in love a bite isn't
Now I know that the morning when I
He will lack the nerve to take the torch to the
Another will do it for him while in his house he
The half-open window facing the plaza where
Until it is over I will watch that window while
I will bite him to the end, in love to bite is not so

III

Suspect Relations

They say miracles are past; and we have our philosophical persons, to make modern and familiar, things supernatural and causeless. Hence it is that we make trifles of terrors, ensconcing ourselves into seeming knowledge, when we should submit ourselves to an unknown fear.

Shakespeare, *All's Well That Ends Well*

Encounter with Evil

These are trying times. A writer needs to *reify* his imagination in his life's most lunar intersections; when he cannot—when to do so would be horrible—he has to be satisfied with putting one word after another and, with the three trapped tigers of paper and pencil, conjuring up De Quincey on the number 92 bus that connects the Porte de Camperret with the Gare Montparnasse, on a winter night in the sixties. There's no one like De Quincey for an encounter that certain of my nightmares are still refining, De Quincey who could blaze a trail through the most terrifying London nights to follow the footsteps left in the fog by Williams and show us his inexplicably pale face, his astonishing yellow-orange hair.* De Quincey sensed that Williams's unnatural pallor was a *key* to his senseless murders; perhaps this time too he could have identified the distinguishing mark that we, crowded within a Paris bus, could not recognize. You leave work in the midst of a cold wave, you step into the bus, watching the empty faces in the silence that is the unwritten law of Paris. I don't know where the man in the overcoat and the black hat came from, all of a sudden he just seemed to appear among us, like the rest of us he must have given his ticket to the conductor and taken his place among us, staring down at the ground and occasionally glancing up at other overcoats, other gloves, newspapers, and women's bags. By the time we reached the Pont d'Alma, before the first stop in the Avenue Bosquet, some of us had noticed him and had drawn back

*Thomas De Quincey, "On Murder Considered as One of the Fine Arts," in *Selected Writings*, Random House, 1937.

instinctively, seeking a protective distance among other passengers who were still unaware of him. Many people got off at the École Militaire stop; we were entering the last leg of the run and the bus was hot with a foul air, with slack bodies under innumerable vests and mufflers. Then I became aware of the fear that had gradually spread through the bus, where no one had thought that they would be afraid. I don't know how to describe such a thing: it was an aura, a radiation of evil, an abominable presence. The man in the black overcoat, with the lapel turned up, hiding his mouth and nose, and the brim of his hat pulled down over his eyes, knew or desired this; never did he look at anyone, but what was worse, the menace that emanated from his lack of comunication became so intolerable that we passengers were united and yet defenseless, waiting for something. I remember that the conductor, a gray-haired man with a calm manner, looked at the man and then almost immediately at the three or four passengers who were still standing. It was as if we had formed an alliance, and the man in the overcoat knew that we had joined together, and he remained still, holding onto the vertical bar with one hand, his eyes fixed on his shoes; it got worse and worse and endured forever. No women remained and we men didn't move, but I know that each of us waited for the moment of getting off like a flight, a return to the life outside.

To say that it was Evil is to say nothing; we know its smiling faces and its many pleasant games. What is intolerable (and this the conductor knew in his simplicity, we all knew from our different perspectives) was the lack of any outward sign; madness must be something like this, where a pencil could suddenly be death or leprosy and yet remain just a pencil in a contradiction that annuls any defense, and reason is more than anything else a defense. The man remained still, his face almost hidden, looking down at his shoes; it emerged from him like a patch of nothingness, a stench of shadow, a potency. I am sure that if he had raised his head suddenly to look at one of us, the response would have been a scream or a blind run to the exit. In that suspension of time, forces came into play that had nothing to do with us; the fear was like a living being and the confused question occurred of what would happen if someone *from outside* should innocently

LANDRU

board and push aside that heavy mass affixed to the vertical bar. In that subconscious alliance, that terrible communication by means of the stomach's mouth and the hair of the neck, any rupture would be even more intolerable than the unbearably slow passage of the 92 bus through the night. When no one got on or off at the Avenue de Lowendal stop, I realized that it was up to me to approach the man and ring the bell, and just then I saw, we all saw, his hand climb up the support bar, seeking the bell button. I know I kept as far back as possible, hoping that others would also be getting off at the rue Oudinot stop, but nobody moved; he had rung the bell to get off and the 92 was moving down the street approaching the stop, braking lightly at the end to avoid skidding on the layer of snow and ice. When the automatic doors opened and the man, with an abrupt yet interminable motion, turned his back to us to get off, the conductor waited with his hand on the lever that closed the door, until three of us decided at the same moment to descend. The avenue's silent darkness blinded us and we had to move carefully to keep from falling on the slush. The three of us who had got off together waited for the bus to set off before crossing the street, without speaking (what could we have said to each other, what legitimate relation bound us together?), as if ashamed by the complicity that lingered among us. The man had reached the sidewalk after passing the trees that ran along the road and was standing on the corner of the avenue and rue Oudinot, without looking at us. Behind him was the wall of the Institute for the Blind; perhaps he would enter there or go into one of the secluded homes in this district of convents and enclosed gardens. My two companions began to cross the avenue, slipping on the wet snow, and I stayed close behind them, knowing that I would have to enter the rue Oudinot alone, as always at this hour, and that the man might begin to follow me. The other two were already setting off down the avenue in the direction of the rue de Sèvres, where lights were shining in the distance; we walked together, preserving our alliance. I slipped and had to grasp the trunk of a plane tree; when I ventured a furtive glance behind me the corner was deserted. For several months I continued to take the 92 bus, always at the same hour; I frequently had the same conductor with the peaceful demeanor and shared some companions from that night. The Evil never boarded again, and we, who didn't really know each other, never spoke of that night; anyway, it's not the sort of thing you do in Paris.

On the subject of Williams, De Quincey's insistence on the abnormal features of his face, his striking pallor contrasted to his yellow-orange hair, clearly points to something more than the desire to frighten the reader. De Quincey must have realized, as did Dostoyevski later, at the end of *The Idiot*, that certain types of crime are governed by different values, in a system where judgement and conscience are consumed by a nameless horror that possesses both the criminal and the victim. It is not simply the fear that stimulates and facilitates a series of murders, as in the cases of Jack the Ripper or the Vampire of Düsseldorf; even in a murder that is not presaged by the notoriety of an unknown criminal there may be circumstances that I am tempted to call ceremonial, a double dance linking the victimizer and the victim, a complicity.

PETER KÜRTEN

Victimology has existed as a discipline for many years; one might call it the antimatter of criminology. Baudelaire, who understood these things, was perhaps the first to sense the profound alliance between the villain and the victim. What would I have done that night on the bus if the man in the overcoat had followed me down the deserted rue Oudinot? I don't know, of course, but I can rule out some things I wouldn't have done, such as running away: I think the absurdity of the situation would have restrained me. I would probably have provoked some act on the part of my follower, speaking to him, asking him for a light; but this would have been the conduct of the victim, the first step in the ceremony.

JULIO BONINI

Dr. Karl Berb's study of Peter Kürten (whom everyone always imagines having Peter Lorre's face; but in fact, while I'm not sure exactly what he looked like, he seems to have resembled Max Jacob, who would have found the resemblance quite amusing) reveals in some victims a behavior that only great novelists have been able to predict. If the crimes of literature are not very convincing, still, Rogozhin's story about the murder of Natasha and the description of Meursault on the African beach are forever inscribed on the memory that *recognizes*; there is about them an aura of fatality and consent that came alive for me

DR. PETIOT

JOHN CHRISTIE

MYRA HINDLEY

IAN BRADY

that night on the bus. The physical resistance of the victim often obscures a more profound acquiescence, but now I know, as Natasha and many of the victims of Kürten or the Ripper knew, that the absurd negative of flight can be a form of acceptance, even if there is a desperate struggle afterwards to avoid strangulation or the knife. The case of Maria Butlies is a perfect example of this surrender of the most vital defenses. Düsseldorf was in the grip of total panic, an unknown "vampire" had murdered, violated, and removed the blood from numerous women and children, and everyone was living in constant fear of a new crime, when Maria Butlies let herself be picked up by a well-dressed man who took her to a park where he made love to her and, at the critical moment, attempted to strangle her. In Charles Franklin's study of Kürten he notes that several women had suffered the same treatment, which for some reason stopped short of completion, but that it did not prevent them from meeting Kürten on other occasions, *of course* without suspecting that this was the vampire.* Maria Butlies survived the attempt at strangulation, which she must have taken for a stimulating caprice, and then agreed to go to Kürten's house, where he could have killed her, as he had already done with Rudolf Scheer. But the unconscious consent went still further; Maria, impressed by Kürten's conduct, wrote to a woman friend describing the adventure in the park and the fear she had felt. The friend realized at once that Kürten was the vampire and sent the letter to the police. Maria was not an idiot; she lived in Düsseldorf and was able to write letters recalling her amorous experiences. How can we explain this block, this astonishing amnesia regarding the menace the vampire represented for the young women of the

*See Charles Franklin, *A Mirror of Murders*, Transworld Publishers, 1964. Enthusiasts can find picturesque variants of this episode in *Encyclopedia of Murders*, Pan Books, 1964.

city? The special relation that is sometimes established between the murderer and the murdered can be of an almost hypnotic order, creating an inhibiting atmosphere like the one we experienced that night on the number 92 bus; there was a subtle suspension of defenses, a mental anesthesia that some criminals—Kürten, the Ripper, Landru, Christie, and the almost unbelievable Bela Kriss—have the power to administer to their victims in the same gesture with which they offer them their arm or buy them a flower.*

Jack the Ripper Blues

I've no time to tell you how
I came to be a killer.
But you should know, as time will show,
That I'm a society pillar.
(from a poem sent by Jack to a
London journal, 1888)

GOYO CARDENAS

The letters and poems attributed to Jack at the time of his murders are still discussed in his homeland, that happy country in which the years are of no consequence where the pleasure of seeking the solution to a puzzle is concerned. If we think of how water and salt invent each other, it will come as no surprise that Great Britain has produced some of history's most memorable mysteries and also some of the most arduous efforts to resolve them. Who was Shakespeare? Who was Jack the Ripper?

We Argentines can be proud: Jack died in Buenos Aires. For their part, the Russians will not conceal their satisfaction if, in place of the previous sentence, we substitute this one: Jack died in Saint Petersburg. Last but not least, the English will smile cheerfully: Jack died in their country, for he was none other than Queen Victoria's own doctor. As you can see, this is rather like the

---

*De Quincey was aware of this dialectic, and it seems apropos to quote him: "In particular, one gentle-mannered girl, whom Williams had undoubtedly designed to murder, gave in evidence that once, when sitting alone with her, he had said: 'Now, Miss R., supposing that I should appear about midnight at your bedside armed with a carving knife, what would you say?' To which the confiding girl had replied: 'Oh, Mr. Williams, if it was anybody else, I should be frightened. But, as soon as I heard your voice, I should be tranquil.'" (De Quincey, "On Murder," pp. 1034–1035.)

EL SAPO

three authentic heads of St. John the Baptist that decorate an equal number of Italian churches. I will eliminate at once the theory promulgated by the Russians and championed by William Le Queux, according to which the Ripper was a certain Pedachenko, a distinguished psychopath sent to London by the Okhrana to annoy and discredit the English police. In fact, while I have often trembled before the Russians' suspicious mastery of foreign languages, the first step no doubt toward the mastery of all the rest, I can't see any Pedachenko being able to write, between one murder and another, this little poem about which you can say what you like, but it certainly isn't cockney:

> I'm not a butcher,
> I'm not a Yid,
> Nor yet a foreign skipper.
> But I'm your own light-hearted friend.
> Yours truly, Jack the Ripper.

I regret that Charles Franklin, who seconds my disdainful elimination of the Slavic theory, is equally skeptical about the fat queen's doctor and most of all that he does not understand the grandeur of the Argentine theory. First, to eliminate in this offhand way the fat one's doctor shows little sense of the dangerous corners, as Priestley calls them, those "if"s that could alter, perhaps beautifully, the course of history, beginning with Cleopatra's nose. It is enough to imagine Jack accomplishing on so vast and royal a field of operation what he had to content himself with doing so modestly on Mary Kelly, which, out of respect for impressionable persons, I summarize in the upside-down note below.* This imaginative exercise (you have already read the note,

* "What Jack had done to Mary Kelly horrified the most hardened policemen of that(?) time. Her mutilated body lay nude and dripping blood on the bed. He had slit her throat from ear to ear, and the cut reached to the spinal column. He had cut her ears and nose and had opened and gutted her stomach. He had removed her breasts and had placed them with her heart and kidneys on a table by the bed. Her intestines were draped around a painting. In a macabre touch of diabolical symmetry, her clothes had been carefully folded and placed at the foot of the bed."
(Franklin, *A Mirror*, p. 116. The question mark is mine.)

because you don't think of yourself as an impressionable person) will appear in a favorable light if you think of the famous photograph of Queen Victoria on horseback or that other one where she is seen holding the bridle of the unfortunate animal, which has miraculously survived the excursion. Faced with such documents one can easily understand how Jack would shiver, but here we are wasting time because I have never believed in this theory; not in vain am I Argentine, and the hypothesis of Leonard Matters is the one that appeals to my most patriotic sentiments.* Therefore, although I will always believe that the Ripper was a surgeon (because I have never doubted his qualifications, and all the available documents prove that his mutilations were performed with a profound knowledge of anatomy and use of the surgical knife), I persist in supporting those who, after rejecting vague Slavic anarchists and royal doctors, bow respectfully before Doctor Stanley, who died in Buenos Aires at the turn of the century after confessing his bloody saga to a family split between astonishment and fainting.

QUEEN
VICTORIA

If I am convinced that Doctor Stanley was the Ripper, I remain uninformed of the reasons for his exile in Argentina, other than imagining him a sort of symmetrical counterpart of Juan Manuel de las Rosas.† On this level of mirrors and repetitions outside of historical time, there is another element that supports the theory. Franklin believes that Stanley wanted to avenge his son, whom Mary Kelly had afflicted with a virulent strain of syphilis years before he began his methodical fractioning. Perhaps to keep in practice or because he mixed up the girls who could look so much alike in those bonnets under those gas lamps, Jack only arrived at Mary Kelly after long practice, and with her he closed the series, proving that his ven-

---

*Quoted by Franklin, Colin Wilson, etc.
†A brutal Argentine despot who was deposed in the middle of the nineteenth century and spent his last three decades as a gentleman farmer in Southampton, England. (translator's note)

geance had been completed and that he could now enter into Argentine history, as has been true of so many English matters. And now, in his study of the case, Franklin observes with his customary facility that this theory is full of holes, beginning with the fact that Mary Kelly did not suffer from syphilis. I will not be the one to accuse that girl of a sickness that she may not have had, but experience teaches me, as it must have taught Franklin, that any more or less famous allusion to syphilis is carefully obscured when Buenos Aires enters the picture; of Pedro de Mendoza, founder of that industrious city, the history books say primly that "he was very ill" when he reached the Rio de la Plata, when the truth is that his Roman debaucheries had placed him in the same condition as the son of Stanley. So I think this leaves Franklin's Anglophilic argument fairly well demolished.

Ah, how I would like to know about Jack's life in Buenos Aires, if he ever left what is called (in a curious inversion of terms) "the English colony" to take a turn through the southern district or to descend to the river, where the odors and some faces might recall Whitechapel and Spitalfields. Maybe some rogue made fun of his accent at a coffee shop counter; maybe he cured the liver of one of my grand-uncles. Why do I feel sympathy for Jack? A while ago a lady accused me sotto voce of bad taste, maybe because the little *upside-down* note turned her *inside-out*. Look, dear Lady, in the first place I did all I could to keep you from reading it, and besides, what really bothered you was talking so freely about Queen Victoria, so I will explain to you why I feel more sympathy for Jack and Mary Kelly than for the glorious monarch. In my florid conception of a better world, Jack came to earth to disembowel the queen. When I say *Jack*, when I say *queen*, maybe you already understand me; and if it's still not clear, learn that a certain Henry Mayhew, cited by Franklin in his study of the Ripper, reported that in the time of the glorious monarch living conditions in London were so monstrous that the number of prostitutes was more than *eighty thousand*. Unemployment, misery, social despotism offered these women only gin, venereal disease, and the knife; for every Moll Flanders, how many ended up like Nancy in *Oliver Twist*? Of course, the statisticians and the fat-cheeked sovereign knew nothing of this. Nothing better sums up the Victorian paradise than the sentence of one of the East End girls, when she was told not to work the streets to avoid the Ripper: "Bah, let him come. So much the better, for one like me."

Therefore, dear Lady, as horrible as were the crimes of the

Ripper, they were like acts of mercy compared to the genocidal hypocrisy that has far from disappeared in many parts of the world; and consequently, in my imagined world, Jack was meant to gut Queen Victoria, and the poem that I placed at the beginning is accurate and Jack is a pillar of society. In his film on Peter Kürten, the Frenchman Robert Hossein lucidly poses the problem: the city of Düsseldorf, which trembles before the repeated murders of the vampire, impassively tolerates the Nazis' canings of the Jews, the first destruction of libraries, the parades of Hitler youths. Voilà, Madame.

To Put an End to Suspect Relations

Some years ago I imagined Jack in a more personal context, searching for the face that would hide the mask, and I said this:

JACK THE RIPPER

Because I haven't known intimacy, because my hands
show me only their commerce with pennies and rings,
and since my day is a lavatory where hairs float,
and my inaccessible night is another belly
from which my mother rejects me before we bathe in beer,

I need this triangular mirror,
something that plunges me in mystery
so later, hidden in the fog
and respectability
I see her red cloud
and taste her bleeding.

Season
of the Hand

Someone in my family recently found in Buenos Aires some of my papers that had entered that shadowy region of houses where old mattresses, issues of Para Ti, *broken toy soldiers, incomplete tea sets, and empty but still usable tins or maybe full ones but you don't know of what, which are consequently dangerous, go on collecting in a corner favored by lint, spiders, and the vague hopes of children at naptime; and wrote to me with the disconcerting courtesy of someone who has found something that falls outside the usual domestic categories, that without actually being trash at least occupies a spot that could better serve for a bar of yellow soap or that sweet tomato paste they make in Argentina that brings back memories of impossible sauces and loves. I was curious about these tracks left by my hand in other times (having thought I had burnt, along with my bridges, all my papers one day in November of 1951); I thus rediscovered the journal of a trip I made in Chile in 1942 and a sort of short story that I had completely forgotten, which was rather stupid and in fact concerned a hand. Pretentious, ingenuous, and full of decadent aestheticism recalling Vernon Lee, it drew me into the defenseless past. I offer it without revision, recalling the words of Corot quoted by Jean Cocteau in* Opium *that describe my feelings perfectly: "This morning I had the extraordinary pleasure of seeing again a little painting of mine. There was nothing at all in it, but it was charming, as if painted by a bird."*

I let it in one afternoon by opening the window facing the garden a crack, and the hand descended lightly on the edge of my work table, which it grasped easily in its palm, its fingers spread slightly apart as if ill at ease until it found the spot it wanted on the piano, on the frame of a portrait, or sometimes on the wine-colored rug.

I liked that hand because it was not at all demanding and it made me think of birds and dry leaves. What did it know of me? It would appear at my window without fail in the afternoon: sometimes hurriedly—its little shadow suddenly cast over my papers—apparently urging me to open it; other times leisurely, ascending the stairs of ivy where its passage left a deep path. Our pigeons knew it well; often in the morning I heard a sustained and frantic cooing and I knew that the hand was walking among the nests, palm cupped to hold the white breasts of the youngest birds, the rough feathers of the robust males. It loved the pigeons and pitchers of clear, fresh water; how many times I found it on the edge of a glass vase, with one finger plunged gently into the water that soothed it and made it dance. I never touched it; I knew that it would cruelly free itself from that mysterious grasp. And for several days the hand went among my things, opening books and notebooks, drawing its index finger—with which it seemed to read—across my favorite poems and seeming to slowly approve them, line by line.

Time passed. External events, which at that time saddened and marked me, began to lose their force, to soften their whip that now struck me aglance. I neglected my math, moss grew on my best suit, I almost never left my room, waiting each day for the hand to reappear, hopefully listening for the first—the farthest and most hidden—rustling of the ivy.

I gave it names: I liked to call it Dg, because that is a name that makes you think. I tempted its probable vanity by leaving rings and bracelets on the mantle and secretly observing its behavior. Once I thought that it was going to adorn itself with the jewels, but it just studied them, going round them without touching them, like a cautious spider; and although the day came when it slipped on an amethyst ring, it was only for a second, and it dropped it as if it had been burned. When it had gone I quickly hid all the jewels and thereafter it seemed more content.

Thus the seasons passed, some uneventful, others with weeks full of violent lights, but those strident cries did not penetrate into our refuge. Every afternoon the hand would return, often drenched by the autumn rains, and I would watch it lie on its back on the rug, drying itself carefully one finger after another, sometimes with little shudders of satisfaction. On cool evenings its shadow had a purple tint. Then I would light a brazier by my feet and it would huddle up and barely budge, except to peevishly get a record album or a ball of yarn that it liked to twist and tie. I soon realized that it was incapable of remaining still for long. One day it discovered a bowl of clay and fell upon it; for hours and hours it modeled the clay while, with my back to it, I pretended not to be interested in what it was doing. It molded a hand, of course. I let it dry and put it on my desk to show that its work pleased me. That was a mistake: Dg turned out to be disturbed by the contemplation of that rigid and somewhat convulsed portrait. When I hid it, the hand discreetly pretended not to have noticed.

My interest soon turned analytical. Tired of being confounded, I wanted to *know*: invariable and regrettable end to all adventures. Many questions arose about my guest: Did it feed, feel, understand, love? I left traps, I made experiments. I had noticed that the hand, while able to read, never wrote. One afternoon I opened the window and set a pen and some white paper on the table, and when Dg entered I went away so as not to disturb it. Through the keyhole I watched it make its usual rounds; then, uneasily, it went to the desk and took the pen. I heard the scratching of the quill and after a nervous interval I entered the studio. On a slant, with elongated letters, Dg had written: *This resolution annuls all the preceding until the next order.* I never succeeded in getting it to write again.

After this period of analysis I began to truly love Dg. I loved its way of looking at flowers in their ceramic vases, its slow circle all around a rose, reaching out to touch the petals with the tips of its fingers, and its way of cupping its palm to surround the flower without touching it, its way perhaps of smelling the fragrance. One afternoon when I was cutting the pages of a book, I noticed that Dg seemed secretly to want to imitate me. I went out to look for more books, thinking that it might like to have its own library. I found some curious works that seemed to have been written by hands, just as others seemed to have been made by lips or heads, and I bought a small page-cutter as well. When I placed these objects on the rug—its favorite spot—Dg regarded them with its usual caution, and only decided to touch them several days later. I cut the pages of more books to give it confidence, and one night (have I mentioned that it only left at dawn, disappearing with the darkness?) it began to open the books and to examine their pages. It soon achieved an extraordinary dexterity; the page-cutter entered the white or opalescent flesh with a dazzling grace. Its task completed, Dg placed the page-cutter on the mantel beside its other favorite objects—yarn, drawings, burnt matches, a wristwatch, little piles of ashes—and then it descended, lay face down on the rug, and began to read. It read with great speed, marking the words with a finger; when it encountered an illustration it stretched out over the page and seemed to be sleeping. I observed that my selection of books had been appropriate; it returned again and again to certain pages (*Étude de mains* by Gautier, *Le Gant de crin* by Reverdy) and it placed strands of yarn to mark their places. Before going, while I was sleeping, it shut its volumes in a little dresser that I had provided for that purpose; and there was never anything out of place when I awoke.

In this thoughtless manner—in the simplicity of the mystery—we lived together for a time in mutual respect and consideration. Having left curiosity behind, having abolished surprise, what absolute perfection we enjoyed! Our life then was purposeless satisfaction, a pure, spontaneous song. Dg would enter through the window and initiate an experience that was entirely mine, apart from the constraints of parents and obligations, repaid by my desire to please what in some way liberated me. And thus we lived, for longer than I can say, until in my weakness I succumbed to the intervention of reality. One night I dreamed: Dg was in love with my hand—the left one, probably, since Dg was a right hand—and it took advantage of my sleep to kidnap its loved one by amputating it with the page-cutter. I woke up terrified, comprehending for the first time the madness of leaving a weapon within reach of such a mystery. Still awash in the turbid waters of that vision, I looked for Dg; it was curled up on the rug and really did seem to be watching the movements of my left hand. I got up and went to put the page-cutter out of its reach, but then I repented and put it back, hoping that Dg would forgive or forget. Dg seemed disillusioned and linked its fingers in an undefinable smile of sadness.

I know it will never return. My shameful conduct had infected its innocence with resentment and disdain. I know it will never return! Why do you reproach me, pigeons, clamoring up above for the hand that will return no more to caress you? Why do you incline so, Flanders rose, that it will no more encircle your delicate dimensions? Emulate me, who have returned to my figures, put on my good suit, and shown the world the appearance of a proper citizen.

The Most
Profound Caress

No one at his house said anything to him about it, but he couldn't believe they hadn't noticed. It would have been possible for them not to have noticed at first, and he felt sure that the hallucination, or whatever it was, would go away, but now that he had to go around buried up to his elbows it seemed incredible that his parents and sisters didn't see what was happening and do something about it. It's true that so far he had not had the slightest difficulty moving around, and while that was the strangest thing, what disturbed him the most was that his parents and sisters didn't realize that he was buried to his elbows.

How dull that things evolved, as usual, from less to more. One day, crossing the patio, he felt that his feet were pushing something soft, like cotton. Looking closely, he discovered that his shoelaces seemed to be barely above the ground. At first he was so dumbfounded that he was speechless, unable to say anything to the others, afraid that he would sink away altogether and wondering if the patio had melted from being washed, for his mother washed it every morning and even sometimes in the afternoon. But in a moment he grew bold enough to lift a foot and take a step, carefully: all went well, except that he again sank up to his shoelaces. He took several more steps, then shrugged and went to the corner to buy *La Razón* because he wanted to read a film review.

Since he was not one to make a fuss, he gradually got used to walking around this way, but several days later his shoelaces disappeared, and one Sunday he could no longer see the cuffs of his pants. After that his only way of changing his shoes and socks was to sit on a chair, raise his leg, and set it against the edge of the bed. So he managed to wash and dress himself, but as soon as he stood up he would sink back down to his ankles, and he went about that way everywhere, even on the stairs to his office or the railway platform. Even now he did not dare ask his family about it, and

still less a stranger on the street, whether they didn't notice anything odd about him; nobody likes to be looked at askance and taken for a fool. It seemed clear that he was the only one who realized that he was sinking little by little, but what was intolerable (and therefore the most difficult thing to mention to others) was his suspicion that there might be witnesses to that slow immersion. The first time that he analyzed the situation calmly, in the shelter of his bed, he was struck by his incredible estrangement from his mother, his fiancée, and his sisters. How could his fiancée, for example, when she felt his hand on her elbow, fail to notice that he was several inches shorter? He now had to stand on tiptoes to kiss her when they parted in the street, and he felt that in so doing he sank a bit deeper still, slid more easily down; that is why he decided to kiss her as little as possible and limited himself to little terms of endearment she seemed to find disconcerting. He decided that his fiancée must be pretty dumb to put up with such treatment. As for his sisters who had never loved him, they had a unique opportunity to humiliate him since he no longer rose above their shoulders, and yet they continued to treat him with that cordial irony that they had always considered so clever. He never much wondered at the blindness of his parents because they had always been like that with their children, but the rest of his family, his colleagues, and all of Buenos Aires saw him and

acted like it was nothing. He thought, logically, that it was all illogical, and the rigorous consequence of this was a brass plaque on Serrano Street and a doctor who examined his tongue and legs, xylophoned him with his little rubber mallet, and chatted about the hair on his back. On the examining table all was normal, but when he got up it was the same story; he mentioned this to the doctor more than once. With a condescending air the man of science leaned down to feel his ankles below the ground; the floor must have become transparent and intangible for him because not only did he explore his tendons and toes but he also tickled the bottoms of his feet. Then he asked him to be seated again and listened to his heart and lungs; he was a very expensive doctor and he had to use up a good half hour before delivering a prescription of sedatives and the classic advice of a temporary change of scene. He also changed a ten-thousand-peso bill with a six.

After that there was nothing he could do but endure his torment stoically, go to work every day and rise desperately on his toes to meet the lips of his promised one and reach his hat on the office rack. Two weeks later he sank to his knees and one morning when he got out of bed he again felt the sensation of moving through cotton, but this time it was with his hands, and he saw that the floor had risen to midthigh. Nonetheless, he still could not detect any sign of surprise in his parents or his sisters, even though he had been watching them for a long time trying to catch them in some flagrantly hypocritical expression. Once he felt that one of his sisters bent over a little to render the cold kiss on the cheek that they exchanged on waking and he thought that they had discovered the truth and were attempting not to betray anything. But no, he still had to go on stretching up a little more each morning, until the ground reached his knees, whereupon he said something about the stupidity of these buccal customs that were just primitive vestiges, and limited himself to a smile and a greeting. With his fiancée he resorted to more drastic measures: he

arranged to take her to a hotel and there, having won in twenty minutes a battle against two thousand years of virtue, he caressed her without stopping until it was time to get dressed; this strategy succeeded perfectly and his love did not seem to notice that he kept himself at a distance betweentimes. He stopped wearing a hat so he wouldn't have to hang it up at the office; he managed to find a solution to every problem, modifying them in measure as he sank, but when the earth reached his elbows he felt that he had exhausted all his resources and would have to ask someone for help.

He then stayed in bed for a week, faking the flu; he managed to get his mother to give him her undivided attention and his sisters to position the television at the foot of his bed. The bathroom was just a few steps away but to be safe he only got up when no one was near. After these days when the bed, like a lifeboat, kept him afloat, it seemed less likely than ever that his father, if he entered unexpectedly, could fail to notice that he only rose above the floor from chest up and that to get his toothbrush glass he had to climb on the bidet or the toilet seat. That is why he stayed in bed when he knew someone was going to visit and why he telephoned his reassurances to his fiancée. He sometimes imagined, childish fantasy, a system of communicating beds that would allow him to pass from his own to the one where his fiancée awaited him, then to another at his office, another at the movie house, the cafe, a whole system of beds bridging Buenos Aires. He would never entirely sink into the ground so long as he could hold onto a bed and fake bronchitis.

That night he had a nightmare and woke up crying, his mouth full of earth; it wasn't earth but saliva, a bad taste, and fright. In the darkness he thought that if he stayed in bed he would be able to believe that it was only a nightmare, but immediately he began to fear that he had actually got up in the middle of the night to go to the bathroom and had sunk up to his neck, so that the bed would no longer protect him against what was coming. He managed to convince himself that he must have been dreaming, yes, certainly, he had dreamt that he had got up during the night; nonetheless, he would wait until he was alone to go to the bathroom, climbing onto a chair, stepping from it onto a stool, then moving the chair over again, and so on to the bathroom and back to bed; he told himself that once he had forgotten his nightmare he would be able to get up and that it would be almost pleasant to sink only up to his waist.

The next day he had to find out, he couldn't stay away from

work forever. Sure enough, the dream had been an exaggeration, the earth didn't enter his mouth, there was just that cottony contact that he had noticed at the beginning; the only important change was that his eyes were looking out almost at ground level: he discovered a spittoon quite close to him, his red slippers, and a little cockroach that looked at him with an attention that his sisters and his fiancée had never given him. To brush his teeth, to shave, were arduous operations; to have to pull himself up by his arms onto the bidet, then the sink, exhausted him. His family breakfasted together, but since his chair had rungs he could climb up and get on his seat very quickly. His sisters were reading *Clarin* with the concentration appropriate to such a patriotic morning paper, but his mother looked at him for a moment and pronounced him a bit pale from all his days in bed and lack of fresh air. At which his father said to her that he was the same as ever and that she would ruin the boy by spoiling him. Everyone was in a good mood because the new government had announced salary increases and pension adjustments. "Buy yourself some new clothes," his mother advised him. "You will surely be able to buy on credit now that salaries are going up." His sisters had already decided to replace the refrigerator and the television; he noticed that there were two kinds of jam on the table. He occupied himself with these little bits of news and trivial observations, so when everyone got up to go to work he thought he was back in his prenightmare state, having grown accustomed to sinking only to his waist; suddenly he saw his father's shoes quite close in front of him: they grazed his head and went out to the patio. He hid under the table to avoid the sandals of one of his sisters who was taking up the tablecloth, and tried to calm himself. "You dropped something?" his mother asked. "My cigarettes," he replied, staying as far as possible from the sandals and slippers that continued to circle the table. In the yard there were ants, geranium leaves, and a piece of glass that nearly cut his cheek; he quickly reentered the house and climbed into bed just as the telephone rang. It was his fiancée, who asked if he was still feeling better and if they could get together that afternoon. He was so upset that he couldn't collect his wits in time and before he knew what he was doing he had set up a meeting for six at the usual street corner, after which they would go to a movie or the hotel depending on how they felt. He stuck his head under the pillow and slept; he couldn't even hear himself crying in his sleep.

At a quarter to six he dressed himself, seated on the corner of his bed and, taking advantage of a moment when there was no one around, crossed the patio, keeping his distance from the sleeping cat. When he got to the street he began to worry that all the shoes that were passing at eye level would step on him and crush him, since to their owners he did not seem to be where he was. The first hundred yards he made a series of zigzags, especially to avoid the women's shoes, the most dangerous because of their spike heels and pointed toes. Then he realized that he could proceed without all these precautions, and he got to the street corner before his fiancée did. He had a stiff neck from looking up to try to make out something besides the shoes of the passersby, and finally the crimp became so painful that he stopped looking up. Fortunately, he knew all his fiancée's shoes quite well from having so often helped her take them off, so when he saw her green shoes approaching all he had to do was smile and listen attentively in order to respond to her greeting as naturally as possible. But this evening his fiancée said nothing, which was quite unlike her; the green shoes remained fixed not far from his eyes and he got the impression, without knowing exactly how, that his fiancée was waiting; in any case, the left shoe was turned in a little, while the other supported her weight; in a moment there was a change, the right shoe turned out and the left was set more heavily on the ground. "It's been quite hot all day!" he said, to open the conversation. His fiancée said nothing and perhaps that is why, waiting for a reply as banal as his comment, he suddenly noticed the silence: the roar of the street, the clack of shoes on the pavement, and then, suddenly, nothing. He waited a little longer and the green shoes advanced slightly and then waited again; the heels were worn, his poor fiancée did not make a lot of money. He waited and, wishing he could do something to express his affection, he stroked the more worn of the heels, the one on the left shoe, with two fingers. His fiancée did not move, as if she continued absurdly to wait for his arrival. It must have been the silence that gave him the impression of time being drawn out, interminably, and his eyes being stuck full of things that made images appear to be far away. With an almost unbearable pain, he raised his head once more to look at the face of his fiancée, but all he saw was her heels, this time at such a distance that he no longer noticed their imperfections. He raised an arm, then the other, trying to caress those heels that spoke so poignantly of his poor fiancée's life; he managed to touch them with his left hand, but already his right hand could not reach them, and then neither could. So of course she went on waiting.

Melancholy
of Luggage

Summer is drawing to a close; this afternoon around five it rained and an admirable double rainbow linked the distant image of Cazeneuve with the romanesque church of Saignon—there was, for a moment, a passage, there was a bridge, and to the astonishment of Theodor I uttered invocations to Valhalla and I saw Wotan and Freya, I understood that for us too, minor southern gods, the twilight was commencing. The proof of this is that in a week I will be lugubriously translating reports for Interpol in Berne, where they have had the mad idea of holding their annual conference, an occasion for discussing opium trafficking, counterfeiting techniques, and the incidence of long hair and guitars in the dreams of Dr. Perez and his colleagues.

The topic of counterfeiters (who are not themselves absolutely fake, it is the term that is badly coined, for many counterfeiters are great and authentic Cronopios) could occupy countless pages, so I will restrain myself to a few paragraphs: I will say only that my strange (to say the least) visits to Interpol have introduced me to almost alchemical labors, vocations that bordered on martyrdom or poetry, beginning with a gentleman who falsified bills of the maximum denomination (because anything less wouldn't have been worth the trouble) by a procedure that consisted of cutting vertical slices of half a millimeter from two hundred legitimate bills so that their reduction in size would be so slight as to pass unnoticed, later to make from the two hundred bills the two hundred and first that represented his profit.

After martyrdom, poetry: an old Mexican cobbler made a "golden eagle" every four or five months, serenely went to exchange it, and returned to his shoes until the next time. The police initially jailed him but, for reasons of local philosophy of which I am ignorant, they considered such a modest sin pardonable; later some students who had lost all hope of paying their room and board and beer came to the cobbler to ask him to make them an eagle. Full of good will toward youth, the old man worked for them twice with no reward except his pleasure. Vespasian could have been right, but in this case the money smelled of flowers.

The days are growing shorter, Theodor senses that soon we will be leaving, is full of tricks, and bounds in all directions, with special preference for a cherry tree where he sharpens his claws and attempts to resemble an Aduanero painting, with regrettable results. My wife has surpassed herself in the preparation of a ratatouille that has fortified us for the moment when we must think of luggage and wheels. We have received a telegram from Carlos Fuentes and Emir Rodriguez Monegal, informing us of an imminent auto trip from Ramatuelle; we await them with a lamb roast and a reasonably clean house; we get another telegram informing us the black death is raging, stop. For good measure, this message bears the signature of Charlie Parker. My mood darkens and this evening, after the rainbow, I play some bop and then another Jimmy Heath record, on which a pianist answering to the bucolic name of Cedar Walton lets loose with all the petulant beauty with which the theme of "My Ideal" inspires him, which is more than a little.

Take It or Leave It

Now that I have returned, I would like to speak of jazz *takes* because this morning in my courtyard in Paris you could see a good deal of rain coming down, which made me nostalgic and wet, and instead of listening, for example, to Xenakis who is a Cronopio for dry, Apollonian, and, in a word, Cretan days, I sought the only thing, besides rum, coffee, and a bad Robt. Burns cigar (if it's Robt. Burns it's not the cigarillo), that would help: old Bessie Smith records and also some by Lester Young and Bird. But for quite a while now I have been completely inhibited in talking about jazz, because a Uruguayan critic who knows a lot has stated in the weekly *Marcha* that the discographic dates given in *Hopscotch* are full of errors, and he has demonstrated this in a column signed with initials, really a solomonian column in the way this fellow judges me. This pentelic stone hit me on the head last month as I was innocently attempting to pick up a little Uruguayan culture in one of Albergo Ateneo's beds in its questionable setting near the Piazza della Fenice in Venice. This foolishness of reading Montevidean periodicals in Venice results from Esther Calvino's receiving them in Rome, coming afterward to the canals to attend several festivals and eat in the Malamocco restaurant and, under the pretext of raising my level of culture, depositing in my arms five or six pounds of printed paper. Thus was I in bed absorbing the spirit of the Rio Plata with commendable dedication until the moment came when it was demonstrated that I knew nothing of the groups to which Zutty Singleton and Baby Dodds belonged, as well as other abominations of the same sort. It spoiled my evening to think that neither Ronald nor Oliveira nor Babs nor Wong knew much about what they were listening to, poor angels. So.

The instructor who taught me to drive told me that if I ever cracked up, the only thing that could keep me together would be to get in another car as soon as possible and keep on driving as if nothing had happened. So let fall the cords that bind Saint Sebastian, let the solitary column stand, and let's talk of takes, which, as everyone knows, even me a little, are the successive recordings of a single theme during the course of a recording session. The definitive record will include the best take from among them all, and the others will be archived and sometimes destroyed; when a great jazzman dies the record companies begin to print the archival takes of a Bud Powell or an Eric Dolphy. Then it is a great marvel to listen to four or five takes of a theme that you only had one version of (not always the best one, but that introduces another problem); but it is even better to let go and *listen* (to be an *écouteur* in the same sense you can be a *voyeur*) to the central laboratory of jazz, and so come to understand a few things better.

It goes like this: in the middle of the recording (we have already forgotten that it is an exhumed take, what is called an homage and what I call more dollars for the head of the company) Bird tears loose brutally with a long sax riff, there is a sort of coitus interruptus like an earthquake, an inconceivable fracture, you hear a grumble from Bird, *Hold it!*, and sometimes Max Roach continues for a couple more measures, or the piano of Duke Jordan completes a phrase, and then there follows a mechanical silence because the engineer has stopped the recording, with a curse, probably. Strange power of the record, which can open for us the workshop of the artist, let us attend his successes and failures. How many takes are there in the world? This edited one can't be the best; in its turn the atom bomb could someday be the equivalent of Bird's *Hold it!*, the great silence. But will there be other usable takes, afterwards?

The difference between *practice* and *take*. Practice leads little by little to perfection, what it produces doesn't matter, it is present only as a function of the future. In the take creation contains its own criticism, so it often interrupts itself to begin again; the inadequacy or failure of a take has the value of practice for the one that follows, but the next one is not an improved version of the preceding one, rather, if it really is good, it is always another thing entirely.

The best literature is always a take; there is an implicit risk in its execution, a margin of danger that is the pleasure of the flight, of the love, carrying with it a tangible loss but also a total engagement that, on another level, lends the theater its unparalleled imperfection faced with the perfection of film.

I don't want to write anything but takes.

Journey to a Land of Cronopios

The Embassy of the Cronopios

In many lands Cronopios live surrounded by vast numbers of Famas and Esperanzas, but for some time there has existed a place where the Cronopios have taken the colored chalks they always carry and written an enormous THAT'S IT on the walls of the Famas and added in smaller, cramped letters YOU DECIDE on the walls of the Esperanzas, and these inscriptions have caused such a commotion that there can be no doubt that every Cronopio will do all he can to visit this country as soon as possible.

Once he has decided to visit this country as soon as possible, the Cronopio presents himself at its embassy, where several employees are directed to expedite the explorer Cronopio's journey, and the following dialogue ensues:

"Buenos salenas, Cronopio Cronopio."

"Buenos salenas, you will leave by plane on Thursday. Please fill out these five forms and attach five photos."

The traveling Cronopio expresses his thanks and returns home, where he feverishly completes the five forms, which he finds terribly complicated, but, fortunately, he discovers when he has completed the first one that he need only copy over the same errors onto the others. Then the Cronopio goes to a photo machine and is photographed in this manner: the first five photographs he is very serious, on the sixth he sticks out his tongue. This final one he keeps for himself, and he is very satisfied with it.

On Thursday the Cronopio gets his bags ready early, which is to say he throws two toothbrushes and a kaleidoscope into them and then sits back to watch his wife fill them with the necessary things; but as she is as much Cronopio as he, she forgets the most essential things, so that they have to sit together on the luggage to get it shut, and at that moment the telephone rings and the embassy informs them that there has been a mistake and that he was supposed to take last Sunday's plane, which precipitates a dialogue full of pointed remarks between the Cronopio and the embassy, and they hear the snap of the luggage opening, and fuzzy teddy bears and dried starfish escape, and the end of it all is that the plane will leave next Sunday, and please bring five full-face photos.

Thoroughly perturbed by *the turn events have taken*, the Cronopio rushes to the embassy, and the moment they open the door he cries at the top of his lungs that he has already submitted the five photos, along with the five forms. The employees play down the matter; they tell him not to worry, that the photos are not actually all that important, but the problem is the visa for Czechoslovakia, information that violently upsets the journeying Cronopio. As everyone knows, Cronopios are likely to get upset over the slightest thing, so enormous tears roll down his cheeks, as he sighs:

"Cruel embassy! Futile journey, useless preparations, please return my photos."

But that's not what happens, and eighteen days later the Cronopio and his wife depart from Orly and stop over in Prague, after a flight during which the most sensational thing, as usual, is the plastic tray full of stuff to eat and drink, and not the least of it the little tube of mustard, which the Cronopio keeps as a souvenir in his vest pocket.

Prague is blanketed by a modest temperature of fifteen below zero, so the Cronopio and his wife don't move from their stopover hotel, where incomprehensible people circulate in the carpeted hallways. In the afternoon they rouse themselves and take a tram to the Carolus Bridge, and everything is so covered with snow, and there are so many children and ducks playing on the ice, that the Cronopio and his wife take each other by the hand and dance the Tregua and dance the Catalan, and speak as follows:

"Prague, legendary city, pride of Central Europe!"

Afterwards, they return to their hotel and anxiously wait for someone to come get them to continue their journey, which, miraculously, happens not the following month but the very next day.

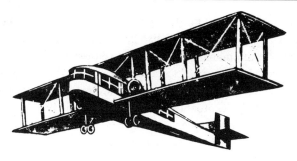

The Airplane of the Cronopios

The first thing that you noticed on entering the Cronopios' airplane was that since they had very few planes they were obliged to utilize space to the maximum, so that the airplane more nearly resembled a streetcar, yet this did not diminish the good cheer aboard because except for a few Esperanzas almost all the passengers were Cronopios returning home, and the rest were foreign Cronopios, who at first contemplated the enthusiasm of those returning with stupefaction but finally came to share their fellow Cronopios' enthusiasm, and within the airplane a din of conversation reigned that could only be compared to the rumble of the ancient motors.

It happened that the plane was to depart at nine-thirty, but the passengers had hardly got seated and begun to tremble, as is the custom on such occasions, when a ravishing stewardess appeared and delivered the following address:

"The cap'n says to tell you everybody off and come back in two hours."

It's a known fact that Cronopios don't let this sort of thing bother them, and they immediately imagined that the airline would serve them many glasses of different colored juices in the airport bar, not to mention the opportunity to buy postcards and send them to other Cronopios, and this not only transpired but the airline also served them a delicious dinner at eleven-thirty, so the Cronopios fulfilled a lifelong dream, which was to eat with one hand while writing postcards with the other. Then they returned to the plane, which had an air of wanting to take off, and right away the stewardess brought them green and blue blankets, and even tucked them in with her beautiful hands, and turned out the lights in case they wanted to sleep, which they only did much later, to the great annoyance of the Esperanzas and some of the foreign Cronopios, who were accustomed to sleeping as soon as the lights were turned off, no matter where they were.

The traveling Cronopio had long since tried all the buttons and levers within his reach, which had filled him with delight, but his attempts to summon the stewardess to request another juice and be better tucked in proved vain, for it was soon clear that she had fallen asleep across the three seats that astute stewardesses always reserve for such eventualities. The Cronopio had just decided to resign himself to sleeping as he was when all the lights came on and a steward began passing out trays, at which the Cronopio and his wife rubbed their hands and said:

"Nothing like a good breakfast after a good night's sleep, especially if it comes with toast."

Such understandable delusions were cruelly destroyed by the steward, who began to distribute drinks with mysterious and poetic names, such as "Aged on the Rocks," which makes you think of a stamp depicting an old Japanese fisherman, or "Mojito," which also calls to mind something Japanese. In any case, the Cronopio thought it extraordinary that they had interrupted his sleep with the sole object of immediately inducing an alcoholic delirium, but he soon realized that matters were even worse, because the stewardess appeared with plates containing, among other things, a tortilla, almond ice cream, and a plantain of astonishing dimensions. Since they had been served a complete dinner in the airport only five hours before, the Cronopio felt that this meal was quite unnecessary, but the steward explained that nobody could have foreseen that dinner would have been so late, and if he didn't like the food he didn't have to eat it, a possibility that the Cronopio completely ruled out, so, after having downed the

tortilla and the ice cream with great perseverance, he saved the plantain in his left interior vest pocket, while his wife put hers in her purse. This sort of thing did have the virtue of seeming to shorten trips taken in the airplane of the Cronopios and, after another stopover in Gander, where nothing worth mentioning happened, because the day something happens in a place like Gander will be the day a groundhog wins a chess tournament, the airplane of the Cronopios entered into bluer skies over an even bluer sea, and everything was so blue everywhere that all the Cronopios swelled with enthusiasm, and soon palm trees appeared, at which a Cronopio exclaimed that now it made no difference if the plane crashed, a patriotic pronouncement that was received with a certain reserve by the foreign Cronopios, and especially by the Esperanzas, and with that they arrived at the land of the Cronopios.

So it is, surely, that the Cronopio will visit this country, and one day, when he returns, he will write down his memories of the trip on little papers of different colors and distribute them on the street corner by his house for everyone to read. He will give the Famas little blue sheets, because he knows that reading his account will make them turn green, and everyone knows how much Cronopios like this combination of colors. As for the Esperanzas, who will redden considerably on receiving this gift, he will give them little white pages, with which they will cover their cheeks, and from his street corner the Cronopio will watch the many different colors traveling off in all directions, carrying away his memories of his trip.

Gran Reverbero "Inexplosivo Cubano"

Morelliana Forever

*Ici se sont fermés des yeux à travers lesquels l'univers se
contemplait avec amour et dans toute sa richesse.*

Epitaph of Johann Jacob Wagner

Like the Eleatics, like Saint Augustine, Novalis sensed that only
through the interior world can one truly reach out to the external world and come to understand that the two
worlds will be one when the alchemy of this journey produces a new, perfectly realized man.

Novalis died without attaining the blue flower;
Nerval and Rimbaud in their turn descended to
Les Mères and condemned us to the terrible liberty of thinking ourselves gods risen from the
muck. Thanks to them, thanks to what now and
again rends the veil of the quotidian, we know
that only from the very bottom of the well can you
see the stars at midday. *Well* and *sky* might not
convey much, but you have to pay attention, to
trace the abscissas and coordinates; Jung offered
his nomenclature, each poet creates his own, anthropology has charted nocturnal and diurnal regions of the psyche and imagination. As for me,
I know well that when external circumstances
(music, love, any small surprise) take me outside
my waking mind for a moment, what takes shape
and flourishes carries with it complete certainty, a sense of exultant truth. I suppose that this is what the Romantics called inspi-
ration, and that mania is the same.

None of this can be articulated, yet there are those who insist
on doing just that: the poet always, the painter, and sometimes
the fool. This reconciliation with a world we can no longer attain,
trapped as we are in a deceitful Western dualism (which the East
annuls with systems and expressions of which we can only make
out deformed, distant echoes), can be glimpsed in indistinct

texts, in exceptional lives foreign from our own, and, very rarely, at the edges of our own searching. If it cannot be spoken we will have to invent the word, because our insistence will surround it and through its holes we will pull the threads that tie it down; like a pause in Webern's music, the plastic harmony within a Picasso painting, a jest of Marcel Duchamp's, the moment when Charlie Parker begins to soar in "Out of Nowhere," these lines of Attar:

Having drunk of the sea we were surprised
that our lips, like the sands, were still dry,
and we went again to the sea to immerse ourselves, not seeing
that our lips are the sands and we ourselves the sea.

There, and in many other traces of the encounter, are the proofs of that reconciliation, there Novalis's hand picks the blue flowers. I am not talking about formal studies, about methodical asceticism, I am talking about the tacit intentionality that gives direction to the poet's stirrings, that turns him into his own wings, the oars of his boat, the weathervane of his wind, and that reaffirms the world at the price of descent into the hells of night and the soul. I detest the reader who has bought his book, the spectator who has bought a ticket, and from his soft spot on his pillow *takes advantage* of it for hedonistic enjoyment or in admiration of genius. What does Van Gogh care for your admiration? What he wanted was your complicity, the effort to see as he saw, with eyes scorched by a Heraclitean fire. When Saint-Exupéry sensed that to love is not to gaze into each other's eyes but to gaze together in the same direction, he went beyond the love of a couple, because all true love goes beyond the couple; and I spit in the face of anyone who comes to tell me he loves Michelangelo or e.e.cummings without showing that at least once, in one extreme moment, he knew that love, he was the other, he looked in the same direction with him rather than merely at him, and he learned to see with him into the infinite opening that waits and beckons.

The Chameleon's Station

Il eut jusqu'au bout le génie de s'échapper mais il s'échappa en souffrant.

René Char, "L'Âge cassant"

Regarding the Synchronicity, Urchronicity, or Anachronicity of the Eighty Worlds

I told you, dear Lady, do not expect too much coherence from this trip around the day. Some of my eighty worlds are small, old planets where I once arrived long ago, somewhat like Saint-Exupéry's Little Prince, so despised by the guardians of Literature but so moving to those who remain faithful to *City Lights*, to Jelly Roll Morton, to *Oliver Twist*. For a long time during the forties I inhabited one of those worlds that seem vulgar and hackneyed to young people and that it is considered bad taste to allude to *hic et nunc*: I am referring to the poetic universe of John Keats. I even wrote six hundred pages that were then and perhaps still are the only complete study on the poet in Spanish. Timid and unknown, I let a friend push me up to the door of the British Consulate of Buenos Aires, where a gentleman bearing a remarkable resemblance to a lobster perused with an air of consternation a chapter in which Keats and I walked through the Flores District, speaking of many things, and then handed the manuscript back to me with a cadaverous smile. That was unfortunate, for it was a handsome book, bold and unkempt, full of interpolations and leaps and grand wing-beats and dives, the sort of book that poets and Cronopios love. It comes to mind because this morning in Paris a committed writer—you know the kind I mean—attempted to convince me of the necessity of an ideology without contradictions. And as I tried to look like I was listening, I became lost in a fog in which cognac was not absent, and Keats's image appeared to me from the far-off world of the waterfront at Lavalle and Reconquista, when we met on the terrritory of a still-white page and went off to live in the night. Maybe now you will understand what follows, the theory of chameleons and sparrows, which I present to vex those good consciences trapped in their monocratic truths.

Enter a Chameleon

> *A man who had not seen Mr. K. for a long time greeted him with these words: "You haven't changed at all." "Oh!" cried Mr. K., turning very pale.*
>
> Bertolt Brecht, *Histories of Mr. Keuner*

The day has arrived when reporters, critics, and those who write dissertations about the artist expect, extrapolate, or even invent for him a full ideological and aesthetic panoply. It so happens that the artist *also* has ideas, but it is rare that he has them systematically, that he has been coleopterized to the point of eliminating all contradictions the way philosophical or political coleoptera have, in exchange for casting aside or ignoring everything born beyond their elytriferous wings, their rigid, measured, and precise little feet. Nietzsche, who was an unparalleled Cronopio, said that only idiots fail to contradict  themselves three times a day. He was not talking about those false contradictions that are exposed as deliberate hypocrisies when you scratch their surface (the gentleman who gives to panhandlers in the street but exploits fifty workers in his umbrella factory) but about a willingness to join the rhythm of the four hearts of the cosmic octopus that throb side by side, each with its own function, moving the blood that sustains the universe, about the great chameleon that all readers will encounter and love or hate in this book and any book where the poet rejects the coleoptera. Today there are eighty worlds, a figure chosen to make you understand and to please my namesake, but there could be five and then this afternoon a hundred and twenty, nobody can tell how many worlds there are in the day of a Cronopio or a poet, only bureaucrats of the spirit decide that their day is composed of a fixed number of elements, of chitinous little feet that agitate furiously in order to progress along what is called the upright path of the soul.

To begin to understand each other a little, all that I've said has to be taken several ways, has to go beyond the beetle with his blue and red file cards: we can say that a Cronopio contradicts himself, he thinks and feels differently in world fourteen than in world nine or twenty-eight; but we must understand the grave and marvelous fact, which the coleoptera seldom admit ("Ah, if only Shelley had remained true to his beliefs" . . . "Pushkin kissing the hand of the czar, an inexplicable ceremony" . . . "Aragon, that Surrealist who obeyed the Party" . . .), that the Cronopio or the poet knows that his contradictions do not run counter to nature but are, so to speak, preternatural, and that they will be resolved if the antagonistic rhythms of the great octopus's hearts move the same blood at some deep level. I insist, dear Lady, that it is not a matter of surface contradictions, since in that respect the artist is no better than a councilman or a gynecologist or comrade Brezhnev, and it could well happen that Shelley was guilty of, etc., and that Pushkin, etc. I am talking about sponges, osmotic powers, barometric sensibility, a dial that captures the spectrum of waves and orders them or ranks them in a way that has nothing to do with the rules of the International Communications Union. I am talking about the responsibility of the poet, who is irresponsible by definition, an anarchist enamored of a solar order and never of the new order or whatever slogan makes five or six hundred million men march in step in a parody of order, I am talking about something that profoundly disgusts the commissars, the Young Turks and the Red Guard, I am talking about a condition that no one has described better than John Keats in a letter that years ago I called "the chameleon letter," which deserves to be more famous than the "lettre du voyant." It was anticipated in a sentence written the year before, as if in passing. Keats was writing to his friend Bayley, who never wanted any happiness beyond the pure present, and he added, apparently carelessly: "If a Sparrow come before my window, I take part in its existence and pick about the Gravel . . ." In October of 1818 the swallow had turned into a chameleon in a letter to Richard Woodhouse: "As to the poetical character itself . . . it has no self—it is everything and nothing—It has no character—it enjoys light and shade, it lives in gusto, be it foul or fair, high or low, rich or poor, mean or elevated—It has as much delight in conceiving an Iago as an Imogen. What shocks the virtuous philosopher delights the cameleon Poet. . . . A Poet is the most unpoetical of any thing in existence; because he has no Identity—he is continually informing—and filling some other Body. . . . [T]he Poet has . . . no identity—he is certainly the most unpoetical of all God's Creatures."

When you look at his life—you have only to read his correspondence—Keats was as capable as anyone of taking sides and, like Sartre, supporting what he thought good or just or necessary, but this sensibility of the sponge, this insistence on a lack of identity that would later occur to Robert Musil's Ülrich, points to a special chameleonism that rigid coleoptera will never understand. If to know something is to participate in it in some way, to apprehend it, then poetic understanding is profoundly disinterested in the conceptual, chitinous aspects of the thing; rather, it proceeds by eruption, by assault and affective ingression into the thing, what Keats called taking part in the existence of the sparrow, what the Germans later termed *Einfühlung*, which sounds very nice in treatises. All these things are known, but we live in a time in Latin America when, even apart from a true Reign of Terror, there are little nocturnal fears that trouble the writer's dreams, the nightmares of escapism, of not compromising, of revisionism, of literary libertinism, of gratuity, of hedonism, of art for art's sake, of the ivory tower: the list is long with synonyms and stupidity. The commissars are all quick to see in the poet a deviant or a cokehead or a wastrel—and the most terrible thing is that there was once a commissar named Plato. For me, as for those who will follow, there will be commissars who will condemn this book for its effervescent playfulness. Why defend myself? Once again I will walk with Keats, but first we will write with chalk on the wall of the commissariat these things that someday will be understood even there. Yes, dear Lady, of course there is no loss of identity in the act of

rational knowledge; on the contrary, the subject tries to reduce its object to categorizable and petrifiable terms, in search of a logical simplification at its own level (which the commissar will translate into ideological, moral, etc., simplifications that will not trouble the proselytes). The logical conduct of a person tends always to defend the subject, to hide behind a carapace when faced with the osmotic eruption of reality, to be the antagonist *par excellence* of the world, because the person who is obsessed with knowledge is always a little hostile, for fear of *getting mixed up*. The poet, on the other hand, you see, refuses to defend himself. He refuses to conserve his identity in the act of knowing because the unmistakable sign, the clover-shaped mark under the fairy-tale teat, is precisely what very early on gives him the constant sense of an other, the ability to escape from himself into the entities that absorb him, binding him in the spell of the object of his song, the physical or moral material whose lyrical combustion provokes the poem. Thirsty for being, the poet ceaselessly reaches out to reality, seeking with the indefatigable harpoon of the poem a reality that is always better hidden, more *re(g)al*. The poem's power is as an instrument of possession but at the same time, ineffably, it expresses the desire for possession, like a net that fishes by itself, a hook that is also the desire of the fish. To be a poet is to desire and, at the same time, to obtain, in the exact shape of the desire. This determines the different forms of poets and their poetics: the one who submits to the aesthetic delight of the word and proceeds according to its impulse of possession; the one who invades reality like a thief of essences and finds in and through himself the lyric instrument that enables him to fashion a response to the *other* that can return the other to himself, that can make the other his, and therefore ours; poems like the *Dueño Elegies* or *Piedra de sol* forever abolish the false Kantian division between our spiritual skin and the great cosmic body, the true homeland. Understand, dear Lady, that human experience alone cannot make a poet, but it can enlarge him if it runs parallel to the poetic condition and if the poet understands the special perspective from which he must articulate it. Here we meet the errant Romanticism of Espronceda or Lamartine, the belief that the poetic condition must be subsumed within personal experience (experience of the sentiment and the passions, experience of moral and social imperatives) when in fact such experience, enriched and purified by a poetic intuition of the world, must generate the word and carry it beyond the merely personal to produce the poem, a truly human work. Why in Keats, a man with clear-cut moral and intellectual beliefs, do we find an apparent contradiction between his personal "humanity" and the never anecdotal, never "engaged" tone of his work? To what does his relentless replacement of himself with various poetic objects, his refusal to appear personally in his poems, respond?

Dear Lady (and this we will write with capital letters on the door of the commissariat), here lies the essence of the problem. Only the weak use their literary aptitude as compensation to make them seem strong and solid and on the right side. Their works are often autobiographical and panegyric (poems to heroes or to the political hero of the hour, which amounts to the same thing), while at other times they are racist, through weakness or a shameful sense of inferiority. Why give examples that anyone can think of, the poems that so many celebrated people would like to remove from their oeuvres? Keats's personal security in his inner strength, his confidence in his intrinsic spiritual humanity ("It takes more than manliness to make a man," said D. H. Lawrence, who knew about these things) liberate him from the confessional narcissism of Musset as well as from the ode to the liberator or tyrant. Faced with the commissars who demand tangible compromises, the poet knows that he can lose himself in reality without forfeit, can let himself hold, can be the one who fearlessly holds—with the supreme liberty of one who has the key to return, who knows that he will always be there to wait for himself, solid, his feet on the ground—the hive, waiting for the return of the exploring bees.

Personal Coda

Therefore, dear Lady, I tell you that many will not understand this chameleon's stroll over the variegated carpet, and that my preferred colors and directions can just be made out if you look a little closer—everyone knows I live a little off to the left, on the red. But I will not say any more about that, or rather, yes, I promise or deny nothing. I think I am doing something more important than that, and that many will understand. Even some commissars, because nobody is hopelessly lost, and many poets keep writing with chalk on the walls of the commissariats of the north and the south, of the east and the west of the horrible, beautiful earth.

II

The Witnesses

When I told Polanco that there was a fly in my room that flew on its back there followed one of those silences that resemble holes in the vast cheese of the air. Polanco, being a friend, finally asked politely if I was sure. I'm not sensitive, so I explained in some detail that I had discovered the fly on page 231 of *Oliver Twist*; I mean, I was in my room with the doors and windows shut reading *Oliver Twist* when, raising my eyes just as evil Sykes was about to kill poor Nancy, I saw three flies flying near the ceiling, two conventionally and one upside down. What Polanco said to me then is completely crazy, but before repeating it I must tell you exactly what happened.

At first it didn't seem so odd that a fly should fly upside down if that made it happy; I had never observed such behavior before, but science teaches us that there is no reason to doubt our senses before every novelty. I thought perhaps the poor creature was deranged or its centers of balance and orientation had been damaged, but I very soon saw the fly was as vital and lively as his two comrades who flew with great orthodoxy right side up. That fly just flew upside down, which among other things enabled it to land nicely on the ceiling; it would approach and land there every so often without the slightest effort. There were, as always, drawbacks. Every time it tried to land on my box of Havanas it had to "buckle the buckle" as English aviation texts translated in Barcelona nicely put it, while its two companions stood like royalty on the *Made in Havana* banner where Romeo was energetically embracing Juliet. When it had had enough of Shakespeare it flew off again on its back and joined its companions in sketching those insensate lines that Pauwels and Bergier persist in calling Brownian. It all was strange, yet it seemed curiously natural, as if it couldn't be any other way; abandoning poor Nancy in the arms of Sykes (what can you do about a crime committed a century ago?), I climbed up on my armchair to try to get a closer look at this behavior in which the supine met the bizarre. When Mrs. Fotheringham came to tell me that dinner was ready (I live in a pension), without opening the door I answered that I'd be there in a couple minutes, and since we were on the subject of time, I also asked if she happened to know how long a fly lives. Mrs. Fotheringham, who knows her boarders, replied without any surprise that it was between ten and fifteen days and that she was not going to let the rabbit pie go cold. As soon as I heard the first of these items of information I decided—I pounce on these decisions like a panther—to investigate and tell the world of science about my small but alarming discovery.

As I explained later to Polanco, I immediately saw the practical difficulties. Whether it flies right side up or upside down, a fly escapes from anywhere with well-known ease; to imprison it in a pitcher or a glass container could alter its behavior or accelerate its death. Of its twelve or fifteen allotted days, how many remained for this tiny animal now placidly floating feet-up a foot from my face? I realized that if I called the Museum of Natural Science they would send out some fellow with a net and my incredible discovery would go fwttttt. If I filmed it (Polanco made films, but with women) I would run a double risk: that the lights would interfere with the flight mechanism of the fly, turning it into a normal one, to the immense annoyance of Polanco, myself, and, indeed, probably even the fly; and that viewers would undoubtedly accuse us of some shameful photographic trick. In less than half an hour (I had to keep in mind that the fly was aging faster than I was) I decided that the only solution was to reduce the dimensions of my room little by little until the fly and I were contained in a minimum of space, an unprecedented scientific condition that would give my observations an unassailable precision (keep a diary, take pictures, etc.) and allow me to prepare my report, once I had called Polanco as a witness not so much to the flight of the fly as to my mental state.

I will not dwell on the description of the labors that followed, the battle against the clock and Mrs. Fotheringham. Once I had solved the problem of coming and going while the fly was away from the door (one of the other two escaped on my first effort, which was lucky; the other I resolutely squashed with an ashtray), I began to gather the necessary materials for reducing the space, not without first assuring Mrs. Fotheringham that it was only a matter of temporary modifications, and passing her porcelain sheep, the portrait of Lady Hamilton, and most of the furni-

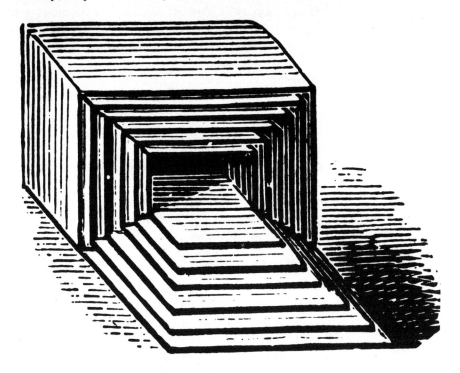

ture out to her through the door, an operation that ran the terrible risk of leaving the door wide open while the fly slept on the ceiling or washed its face on my writing table. During the early stages of these activities I was forced to give more attention to Mrs. Fotheringham than to the fly, since I detected in her a growing inclination to call the police, which would mean that she would no longer be able to hear me through the chink in the doorway. What most alarmed Mrs. Fotheringham was the arrival of the reinforced cardboard because she couldn't imagine what it was for, and I didn't dare tell her the truth since I knew her well enough to be sure that the manner in which flies fly would leave her royally indifferent: I just assured her that I was beginning some architectural experiments based loosely on the ideas of Palladio concerning perspective in elliptical theaters, a concept she greeted with the expression a turtle might assume on similar occasions. I promised that I would pay for any damages, and in a few hours I had installed the cardboard six feet in from the walls and ceiling, thanks to those products of genius, Scotch tape and stick pins. The fly did not appear unhappy or alarmed; it kept on flying feet upwards, and it had already consumed a good portion of the sugar and thimbleful of water I had left solicitously in the most convenient place. I should not forget to mention that Polanco was not at home (this is all very precisely noted in my journal) and that a woman with a Panamanian accent answered the phone to display her total ignorance of the whereabouts of my friend. Solitary and withdrawn as I am, I could only confide in Polanco; hoping he would turn up, I decided to continue reducing the "habitat" of the fly so that the experiment would conclude under optimum conditions. I was lucky that the second batch of reinforced cardboard came in much smaller sizes than the first, as any owner of stacking dolls can appreciate, and Mrs. Fotheringham watched me bring it into the room without taking any measure beyond covering her mouth with one hand and waving a multicolored plume in the air with the other.

I was afraid, as you can appreciate, that the life cycle of the fly might be drawing to a close, and even though I know that subjectivity falsifies experience, it still seemed to me that the fly was spending more of its time resting and washing itself than before, as if flying made it uncomfortable or tired. I gently stimulated it with a few sweeps of my hand in order to assess its reflexes, and the little creature, I swear, flew up like an arrow, with its feet in the air, and, still on its back, surveyed the cubic space that was growing ever smaller, occasionally landing on the cardboard ceiling with a careless perfection that it lacked when it landed on my nose or the sugar. Polanco still had not returned home.

The third day, mortally afraid that the fly would reach the end of its term any moment (how dreadful it was to think that I might suddenly find it on the ground, immobile forever and no different from other flies!), I brought in the third batch of cardboard, which reduced my observation space so much that I could no longer stand up and I had to construct an angled observation platform out of two pillows and a small mattress that Mrs. Fotheringham brought me, crying. At this stage of my work the main difficulty was coming and going; each time it was necessary to open and close three successive layers of cardboard very carefully, being sure not to leave the smallest crack, at last reaching the door to my room, where various residents were beginning to congregate. So when I heard Polanco's voice on the phone I let out a cry that he and his otorhinolaryngologist chastised me severely for later. I began a babble of explanation, which Polanco cut short by offering to come over at once, but since the two of us and the fly could not all fit in such a small space at the same time, I realized that I would have to bring him up to date so he could go in by himself and bear witness that the fly might be crazy but I was not. I arranged to meet him at the cafe on the corner, and there, over a couple of beers, I told him the story.

Polanco lit his pipe and looked at me a while. He seemed impressed and also, I thought, a little pale. I think that I have already said at the beginning that he asked me if I was sure about what I had told him. I must have convinced him, because he kept on smoking and meditating, not seeing that I didn't want to waste a moment (and if it were already dead? if it were already dead?), and I paid for the beers so that he would have to decide once and for all.

When he still didn't decide I became livid and pointed out his moral obligation to assist me in an experiment that would not be taken seriously without a credible witness. He shrugged his shoulders as if suddenly sad.

"It's useless, kid," he finally said. "They might believe you without my corroboration. But me . . ."

"You? Why wouldn't they believe you?"

"It's a sad story, friend," Polanco murmured. "Listen, it's not normal, it's not decent for a fly to go around upside down like that. It's not logical when you think about it."

"But I tell you it does fly that way!" I shouted, startling a number of the customers.

"Sure it does. But it's still flying just like any other fly, it's just the exception that proves the rule, it's just made half a turn, that's all," Polanco said. "No one would believe me, even though it's there plain as day, because it can't be demonstrated. So the best thing to do is for us to go get rid of that cardboard before you get tossed out on your ear. Right?"

On the Short Story
and Its Environs

*Léon L. affirmait qu'il n'y avait qu'une chose de plus épou-
vantable que l'Épouvante: la journée normale, le quoti-
dien, nous-mêmes sans le cadre forgé par l'épouvante.
"Dieu a créé la mort, Il a créé la vie, soit," déclamait L.L.
Mais ne dites pas que c'est Lui qui a également créé la
"journée normale," la "vie de tous les jours." Grande est
mon impiété mais devant cette calomnie, devant ce blas-
phème, elle recule.*

Piotr Rawics, *Le Sang du ciel*

Horacio Quiroga once attempted a "Ten Commandments for the
Perfect Story Teller," whose mere title is a wink at the reader. If
nine of his commandments may easily be dispensed with, the
tenth seems to me perfectly lucid: "Tell the story as if it were only
of interest to the small circle of your characters, of which you may
be one. There is no other way to put life into the story."

This concept of the "small circle" is what gives the dictum its
deepest meaning, because it defines the closed form of the story,
what I have elsewhere called its sphericity; but to this another,
equally significant observation is added: the idea that the narrator
can be one of the characters, which means that the narrative situation itself must be born and die within the sphere, working from
the interior to the exterior, not from outside in as if you were
modeling the sphere out of clay. To put it another way, an awareness of the sphere must somehow precede the act of writing the
story, as if the narrator, surrendering himself to the form he has
chosen, were implicitly inside of it, exerting the force that creates
the spherical form in its perfection.

I am speaking of the modern story begun, one might say, with
Edgar Allan Poe, which proceeds inexorably, like a machine destined to accomplish its mission with the maximum economy of
means: the difference between the story and what the French call

the "nouvelle" and the English call the "long short story" lies precisely in the successful story's insistent race against the clock: one need only recall "The Cask of Amontillado," "Bliss," "The Circular Ruins," and "The Killers." This is not to say that longer stories may not be equally perfect, but I think it is evident that the most characteristic stories of the past hundred years have been created through the relentless elimination of all the elements proper to the novella and the novel: exordiums, circumlocutions, situation development, and other techniques; a long story by Henry James or D. H. Lawrence may be as pleasing as one of the stories I have mentioned, but it is worth noting that while these authors enjoyed a thematic and linguistic freedom that, in a certain sense, made their work easier, what is always astonishing in stories that race against the clock is the overpowering way they employ a minimum of elements to transform certain situations or narrative territories into a story with ramifications as extensive as those of the most developed novella.

What follows is based in part on personal experience and will perhaps show—from outside the sphere—some of the constants

that govern stories of this type. Consider again brother Quiroga's commandment, "Tell the story as if it were only of interest to the small circle of your characters, *of which you may be one.*" To be one of the characters generally means to narrate in the first person, which immediately places us on an interior plane. Many years ago in Buenos Aires, Ana Maria Barrenechea chided me in a friendly way for using the first person excessively, I think with reference to the stories in *Secret Weapons*, although we may have been talking about *The End of the Game*. When I mentioned that there were several stories in the third person, she refused to believe me until I got the book and showed her. We theorized that the third person may have been acting as a displaced first person and that memory tended to homogenize the stories in the book.

Then or a little later, I arrived at another explanation from a different angle; I realized that when I write a story I instinctively try to distance myself by means of a demiurge who will live independently, so the reader will have the impression that what he is reading arises somehow out of himself—with the aid of a *deus ex machina*, to be sure—through the mediation though never the manifest presence of the demiurge. I know that I have always been irritated by stories in which the characters have to wait in the wings while the narrator explains details or developments from one situation to another (an explanation in which the demiurge cannot participate). For me the thing that signals a great story is what we might call its autonomy, the fact that it detaches itself from its author like a soap bubble blown from a clay pipe. Although it seems paradoxical, narration in the first person is the easiest and perhaps the best solution to this problem, since *narration* and *action* are then one and the same. Even when the story is told in the third person, if the telling is a part of the action, then we are in the bubble and not in the pipe. Perhaps that is why, in my third-person stories, I have always tried to maintain a narration *stricto senso*, without those acts of distancing that constitute judgements on what is happening. I think it is vanity to want to put into a story anything but the story itself.

This necessarily raises the question of narrative technique, the special relationship between narrator and narration. For me, this relationship has always been a polarization. While there is the obvious bridge of language that goes from the desire for expression to the expression itself, this bridge also separates me as writer of the story from what I have written, which, at its conclusion, remains forever on the other bank. An admirable line of Pablo

Neruda's, "My creatures are born of a long denial," seems to me the best definition of writing as a kind of exorcism, casting off invading creatures by projecting them into universal existence, keeping them on the other side of the bridge, where the narrator is no longer the one who has blown the bubble out of his clay pipe. It may be exaggerating to say that all completely successful short stories, especially fantastic stories, are products of neurosis, nightmares or hallucinations neutralized through objectification and translated to a medium outside the neurotic terrain. This polarization can be found in any memorable short story, as if the author, wanting to rid himself of his creature as soon and as absolutely as possible, exorcises it the only way he can: by writing it.

This process does not occur without the conditions and atmosphere that accompany exorcism. To try to liberate yourself from obsessive creatures through a mere literary technique might give you a story, but without the essential polarization, the cathartic rejection, the literary result will be precisely that, literary; the story will lack the atmosphere that no stylistic analysis can succeed in explaining, the aura that wells up in the story and pos-

sesses the reader the way it has possessed the author, on the other side of the bridge. An effective story writer can write stories that are valid as literature, but if he ever knows the experience of freeing himself of a story the way you rid yourself of a creature, he will know the difference between possession and literary craft; and, for his part, a good reader will always distinguish those that come from an ominous undefinable territory from those that are the product of a mere *métier*. Perhaps the most important difference—I have already mentioned this—lies in the story's internal tension. Skill alone cannot teach or produce a great short story, which condenses the obsession of the creature; it is a hallucinatory presence manifest from the first sentences to fascinate the reader, to make him lose contact with the dull reality that surrounds him, submerging him in another that is more intense and compelling. From a story like this, he emerges as from an act of love, expended, separate from the outside world, to which he slowly returns with a look of surprise, of slow recognition, often with relief, sometimes with resignation. The person who writes this story has an even more attenuating experience, because his return to a more tolerable condition depends on his ability to transfer the obsession, and the tension of the story is born from the startling elimination of intermediate ideas, preparatory stages, all deliberate literary rhetoric, to set in play an almost inevitable operation that will not tolerate the loss of time: the creature is there, and only a sudden tug can pull it out by the neck or the head. Anyway, that's how I wrote many of my stories, including some relatively long ones, such as "Secret Weapons": through an entire day relentless anguish made me work without interruption until the story ended, and only then, without even reading it over, did I go down to the street and walk by myself, no longer being Pierre, no longer being Michèle.

So it can be argued that a certain type of story is the product of a trancelike condition, abnormal according to the conventions of normality, what the French call a "second state." That Poe created his best stories in this state (paradoxically reserving for poetry a cold rationality, or claiming to) is proven more by the traumatic, contagious, and, for some, diabolical effect of "The Tell-Tale Heart" or "Berenice," than by any argument. Some will say I exaggerate when I say that only in an extraorbital state can a great short story be born; they will observe that I am talking about stories whose very theme contains "abnormality," like the stories of Poe that I have mentioned, and that I am relying too much on my own experience of being forced to write a story in order to avoid something much worse. How can I convey the atmosphere that precedes and pervades the act of writing? If Poe had written on this subject, these pages would not be necessary, but he shut the circle of his hell and kept it to himself or converted it into "The Black Cat" or "Ligeia." Nor do I know other accounts that could help us comprehend the liberating, chain-reaction process of a memorable short story, so I refer to my own experience as a story writer, and I see a relatively happy and unremarkable man, caught up in the same trivialities and trips to the dentist as any inhabitant of a large city, who reads the newspaper and falls in love and goes to the theater, and who suddenly, instantaneously, in the subway, in a cafe, in a dream, in the office while revising a doubtful translation about Tanzanian illiteracy, stops being him-and-his-circumstances and, for no *reason*, without warning, without the warning aura of epileptics, without the contractions that precede severe migraines, without anything that gives him a chance to clench his teeth and take a deep breath, *he is a story*, a shapeless mass without words or faces or beginning or end, but

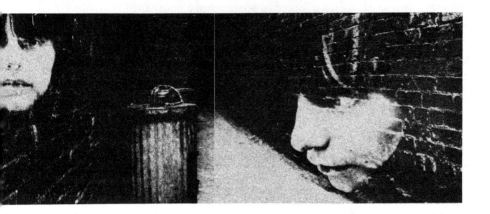

still a story, something that can only be a story, and then, suddenly, Tanzania can go to hell, because he puts a paper in the typewriter and begins to write, even if his bosses and the whole United Nations scream in his ears, even if his wife calls because the soup is getting cold, even if terrible things are happening in the world and one must listen to the radio, even if he has to go to the theater or telephone his friends. I recall a curious quotation from, I think, Roger Fry: a precocious child who was talented at drawing explained his method of composition by saying, "First I think and then I draw a line around my think." In the case of my stories, it is the exact opposite: the verbal line that will draw them is started without any prior "think"; it is like a great coagulation, raw material that is already taking shape in the story, that is perfectly clear even though it might seem that nothing could be more confused; in this it is like the inverted signs of the dream— we have all had dreams of midday clarity that became formless shapes, meaningless masses, when we awoke. Do you dream while you are awake when you write a short story? We already know the limits of dreaming and waking: better ask a Chinese philosopher or a butterfly. But while the analogy is obvious, the relationship is inverted, at least in my case, because I begin with the shapeless mass and write something that only then becomes a coherent and valid story *per se*. My memory, no doubt traumatized by a dizzying experience, retains those moments in detail and allows me to rationalize them here in the context of the possible. There is the mass that is the story (but which story? I know and I don't know, everything is seen by another me, who is not my conscious self, but who is more important at this moment apart from time and reason); there is anguish and anxiety and the miraculous, because both sensations and feelings are contradictory at these times. To write a story in this way is both terrible and marvelous; there is an exultant desperation, a desperate exultation—it's now or never, and the fear that it might be never enrages the moment, sends the typewriter clacking at full throttle, makes me forget the circumstantial, abolishes surroundings. The black mass takes shape as it advances, proceeding, incredibly, with extreme ease, as if the story were already written in invisible ink and only a sweep of the brush were required to bring it forth. To write a story this way involves no effort, absolutely none; everything has already taken place in advance, at a level where "the symphony stirs in the depths," to quote Rimbaud, which is what caused the obsession, the abominable clot that has to be worked out with words. So, since everything is decided in a place that is foreign to my everyday self, not even the ending presents problems, I can write without pausing, making the episodes come and go, because the resolution, like the beginning, is already included in the clot. I remember the morning when "A Yellow Flower" came to me: the amorphous block was the idea of a man who encounters a youth who looks like him and who begins to suspect that we are immortal. I wrote the opening scenes without the slightest hesitation, but I didn't know where things were going, I didn't even think about the resolution of the story. If someone had interrupted me then to say, "At the end the protagonist will poison Luc," I would have been dumbfounded. At the end the protagonist does poison Luc, but this occurred in the same way as everything that preceded it, like a ball of yarn that unravels as we pull on it. The truth is that my stories do not possess the slightest *literary* merit, the slightest effort. If some of them may last, it is because I have been able to receive and transmit what was latent in the depths of my psyche without losing too much, which comes from a certain experience in not falsifying the mysterious, keeping it as true as possible to its source, with its original tremor, its archetypal stammer.

What I have said may have put the reader on the scent: the origins of this type of story and poetry, as we have understood it since Baudelaire, are the same. But if poetry seems to me a sort of second-level magic, an attempt at ontological possession, not a physical possession as in magic properly speaking, the story has no essential intentions, it does not seek or transmit a knowledge or "message." Still the genesis of the story and the poem is the same: they are born of a sudden estrangement, of a *displacement* that alters the "normal" pattern of consciousness; in a time when modes and genres have given way to a noisy critical bankruptcy, there is some point to insisting on this affinity, which many will consider preposterous. My experience tells me that in a sense a short story like the ones I have been describing does not have a *prose structure*. Every time I have undertaken to revise the translation of one of my stories (or tried to translate a story by another, as I did once with Poe), I have been struck by the degree to which the effectiveness and the *meaning* of the story depend on those values that give poetry, like jazz, its specific character: tension, rhythm, internal pulsation, the unexpected within the parameters of the anticipated, that *fatal liberty* that cannot be altered without an irrevocable loss. Stories of this type are affixed like indelible scars on any reader who can appreciate them: they are living creatures, complete organisms, closed circles, and they breathe. *They* breathe, not the narrator, like poems that endure and unlike prose, which transmits the breathing to the reader, communicates it the way you send words through the telephone. And if you ask, "Isn't there communication between the poet (the short story writer) and the reader?", the answer is obvious: the communication operates *from within* the poem, not *by means of* it. It is not the communication of the prose writer from telephone to telephone; the poet and the storyteller direct autonomous creatures, whose conduct is unforeseeable and whose final effects on the reader do not differ essentially from their effects on the author, the first to be surprised by his creation, a reader surprised by himself.

A brief coda on fantastic stories. First observation: the fantastic as nostalgia. All *suspension of belief* operates as a truce from the harsh, implacable siege that determinism wages on man. In this truce, nostalgia introduces a variation on Ortega's observation: there are people who at a certain time cease to be themselves and their circumstances, there is a moment when you want to be both yourself and something unexpected, yourself and the moment when the door, which before and after opens onto the hallway, opens slowly to show us the field where the unicorn sings.

Second observation: the fantastic demands an ordinary passage of time. Its eruption instantly alters the present, but the door to the hallway remains the same in the past and in the future. Even a momentary alteration in the ordinary reveals the fantastic, but the extraordinary must become the rule without displacing the ordinary structures in which it is inserted. To discover Beethoven's profile in a cloud would be disturbing if it did not soon become transformed into a ship or a bird: its fantastic nature would only be confirmed if the profile of Beethoven endured while the other clouds devolved in their eternal random disorder. In bad fantastic literature, supernatural profiles are usually introduced like instant and ephemeral stones within the solid mass of the usual: thus the woman who has earned the thorough hatred of the reader is justly strangled at the last moment by a fantastic hand that comes down the chimney and leaves through the window without the slightest difficulty, even though the author finds it necessary to serve up "explanations" of the sort involving vengeful ancestors or evil spirits. I will add that the worst of this sort of literature elects the opposite procedure, that is, it displaces ordinary time in favor of a sort of "full-time" fantastic, invading almost every aspect of the scene with a vast supernatural cotillion, as in the popular model of the haunted house, where everything assumes unaccustomed manifestations from the moment in the opening sentences when the protagonist rings the bell until the story lurches to a halt beneath a garret skylight. In the two extremes (insufficient installation in ordinary circumstances and almost total rejection of them), the story sins through impermeability; it works with momentarily justified materials among which there is no osmosis, no convincing formulation. The good reader senses that none of these things had to be there, not the strangling hand, nor the gentleman who determines to spend the night in a desolate dwelling on a bet. This type of story, which deadens anthologies of the genre, recalls Edward Lear's recipe for a pie whose glorious name I have forgotten: take a hog, tie it to a stake, and beat it violently, while at the same time preparing a gruel of diverse ingredients, interrupting its cooking only to continue beating the hog. If at the end of three days the glop and the hog have not formed a homogeneous substance, the pie must be considered a failure, the hog released, and the glop consigned to the garbage. Which is precisely what we do with stories in which there is no osmosis, where the fantastic and the ordinary are brought together without forming the pie we want to enjoy trembling.

News about Funes

From time to time, someone comes looking for me and asks: Well then, what about you and incest (or, you and the labyrinth ((or, you and the idea of the double (((or, you and tramways as points of passage ((((or, you and covered galleries, ditto (((((or, you and the influence of Raymond Roussel)))))))))))))))), but this time it was worse, because a certain Julian Garavito from the journal *Europe* has now written: Well then, you and the secret thread that unites your stories; and I was quite astonished, because my stories fall on my head from time to time like coconuts from the coconut palm, and in the end they have been collected in three or four volumes where they seemed to be doing quite well, until Garavito informs me that there is a secret thread tying them together, which troubles me, because I always thought that coconuts were eminently independent fruits that just grow in trees and fall when the fancy strikes them.

Criticism is like Periquita the pianist who does what she can, but up to now the weaving the critics have done with the threads of my work has demonstrated the distance between reality and its interpretation. Garavito has reviewed a series of stories published by Gallimard under the title *Gîtes*, and while at the outset he protests, rightly, the practice of jumbling together stories from different periods and different books, suddenly he finds the thread that connects the coconuts, the thread he calls the constant, which, naturally, fills him with extreme joy, because coherence is a thing that always delights everyone, you figure it out. And there it is—Funes; and I am, as I have said, astonished, because Garavito continues, These French editors are murder, they've jumbled everything up and naturally they have broken the thread, the proof is that in your *Bestiary*, which appeared in 1948, you introduced a Luis Funes, alive, and years later, in "After Dinner," you told the story of his suicide, while now in this mess of a French edition, Funes commits suicide halfway through the volume and reappears in the peak of health in the final story.

It's a dizzying adventure for me to hear someone telling me that I have used the same character in two stories to reveal the constant, because, while this is in no way true, it remains a fact that the name Luis Funes appears in two of my stories, which I have just found out thanks to a French critic who not surprisingly is looking for constants. I call this dizzying because, when I think back to the distant *Bestiary*, I remember "the Funeses," and that one of them was named Luis, but when I wrote the story and through the years, it never occurred to me to put the two together in evoking that person; he was simply Luis, as Nino was simply Nino and Rema was Rema. It was not until Garavito's research that I discovered that Luis was a member of the Funes family, was named Luis Funes, that many years later, in Paris, I used this same name for one of the characters in "After Dinner" and that this Luis Funes was alive in the first story and died in the second, supporting the theory that he was one and the same.

This sort of thing leaves me at once perplexed and full of hope. Maybe it is true, maybe the person who committed suicide in "After Dinner" was the same one who suffered from the wickedness of his brother in *Bestiary*; if not, why among so many possible names did I return to this one after fifteen years? Perhaps Luis Funes did not commit suicide because his friend Rubirosa discovered that he was a spy, but because the memory of a tiger and a brother clawed was stronger than that of the improbable happiness of Rema. It is fine to write all this ironically, but behind it lies something else, the terrible figures woven in darkness by the Spinners. So it is without irony that I thank Juan Garavito, weaver on the side of the light.

Advice for Tourists

> *they eat feces*
> > *in the dark*
> > *on stone floors.*
> *one-legged animals, hopping cows*
> > *limping dogs   blind cats*
>
> *crunching garbage in the market*
> > *broken fingers*
> > > *cabbage*
> > *head on the ground*
> *who has young face.*
> > *open pit eyes*
> *between the bullock carts and people*
> > *head pivot with the footsteps*
> > > > *passing by*
> *dark scrotum spilld on the street*
> > *penis laid by his thigh*
> > > *torso*
> *turns with the sun*
>
> *I came to buy*
> > *a few bananas by the ganges*
> > *while waiting for my wife*

Gary Snyder, "The Market"

The little girl is seated on the flagstones of the plaza, playing with other children who are passing from hand to hand a little bit of cord, a burnt match, adding and subtracting in mysterious bartering. She is naked, she has some gold rings and a jewel that gives a rosy glimmer to the side of her nose; her diminutive sex is like a waxing moon between her dark legs. The boy crouching at her right is also naked, and his pointed buttocks scrape against the flagstones when he moves gleefully over some play of the game. The others are older, between nine and ten, the skeletal outlines of their bodies show through rags that have known many bodies before. The girl is concentrating on the game, she receives and gives the little stick, she says a sentence that the others repeat laughing, the game continues; a streetcar passes with a shaking of old tracks that causes the air and the ground to tremble, but the children do not watch it; the rails are barely two feet from their legs, the streetcar passes between them and other groups of children and adults lying or seated on the flagstones of the plaza. No one pays the slightest attention to the streetcars that pass every two or three minutes with ringing bells and shouts from the passengers trying to push through the crowded platforms. The naked girl looks at the boy squatting at her right, she hands him a scrap of tissue, and says the sentence she has to say, and the boy passes the tissue to the next child. Nearby a decrepit woman without age or sex stirs a mixture in a pot hanging from a little tripod above a fire of trash, puts in her hand to pick out a floury piece of dough and presses it between her hands; she gives it to the old man stretched out beside her on the flagstones, his feet almost grazing the rails, and looks at him without speaking as he revolves the paste in his toothless mouth, trying to mash it before swallowing; then the old woman turns to a girl who is nursing a baby and reaches out a lump of dough to her, before taking the last one for herself; then, with a little stick, she patiently cleans the pot and sets it next to the tripod and heaps embers over the fire to conserve it. The two squatting men who complete the group talk to each other and show each other papers; one points to the front of the railway station, at the end of the large plaza, and the other nods, jetting a splendid and repugnant blob of betel to the ground next to the old woman's foot. Within the circle two naked children run, trip, land on the legs of the old man or in the arms of the men, who hold them, smiling, and say something to them without impatience, warning them to stay within the circle and not to go near the rails. It's thirty-five degrees centigrade in the shade, but in the plaza there is no shade.

It's very interesting, you arrive in Calcutta by plane, for it would not occur to anyone to go by train in this heat and with all the delays, you lodge in a big downtown hotel, the only ones prepared to receive Europeans or wealthy Indians, you watch your luggage pass through the links of an interminable human chain, starting at the door of the taxi and ending at the side of your bed, hands that pass the bags and then reach out under big anxious smiles, a chain of tips that you scrupulously distribute, wanting to be alone and take a bath and drink a glass of something cold;

you arrive in Calcutta by plane and you rest a while in your hotel before going out to discover the city, and at some point you consult *Murray's Guide* and from four or five choices you decide to go to the railway station, Howrah Station, you decide even though you arrived in Calcutta by plane and trains don't interest you at all in this country where there is so much heat and timetables have no meaning.

Nonetheless, you have decided to go see Howrah Station, not only because the guidebook says it has a picturesque quality, but because some friend in Delhi or Bombay has told you that if you want to know India you have to spend some time at Howrah Station, so you put on the lightest possible clothes, you try to make it ten in the morning or seven in the evening, and you hail a cab to the evident surprise of the driver, who can't understand how a European can leave a hotel to go to Howrah Station without any luggage, so you leave some extra money in his hands and in the many other outstretched hands between the door of the taxi and the numbered seat on the train from Benares or Madras. You explain to the driver that you just want to go to Howrah Station to

see what it is like, and the driver smiles and agrees because there is nothing to be gained from trying to understand such an absurdity. Then there is the *city*, the traffic that puts the lie to everything expected or assumed about traffic, the sun blazing down, the sticky perspiration that seeps from your armpits and forehead and thighs although the driver doesn't have a drop of moisture on his face with its fine black beard, a ride that seems never to end even though your watch shows only a few minutes have passed, as if the concentration of humanity in the streets, the traffic of carts, streetcars, and trucks, the markets teeming in vague shadowy recesses out to the anthill walkways and into the very street where everything mixes together amid shouts, protests, and peals of laughter, this all took place in a time different from yours, an interminable, fascinating, and exasperating suspension, until at a certain point you reach the river district, the smell of warehouses and factories, a curve in an avenue, and suddenly, looking like an antediluvian monster beneath a deluge of roofs, signs, used-clothing shops, telegraph wires, behind this maniacal use of every available corner of space, Howrah Bridge looms, with its

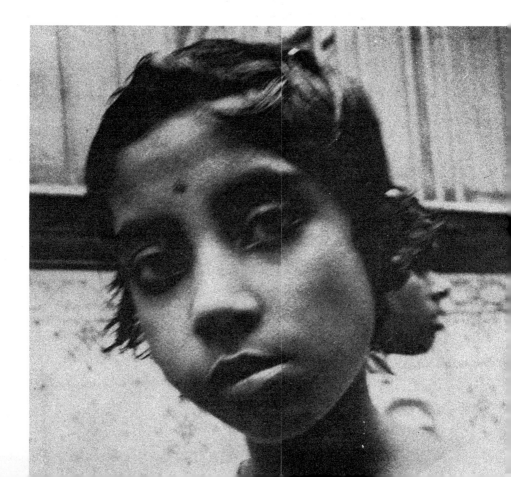

gigantic structure of steel and worn cables the enormous carcass
of a monster that has fallen over the river, and the driver turns to
tell you that the station is on the other side, that you only have to
cross the bridge and you will be at the station, and if the *sah'b*
wants to go to the temples or the botanical garden afterwards, all
day in the excellent taxi low fare, all day in his taxi if the *sah'b*
wishes. The water is underneath already, if it is water, this vis-
cous gray substance from which emerges a cloud of heat and rot
and the smoke of scows; entering the bridge means a full-speed
assault through streetcars and trucks all rushing furiously to be
the first in line when the bridge narrows and you have to slow
down, feeling through the window the eyes of those going on foot:
the multicolored snake between the railing and the road, the men
who run forward at every halt in the traffic to beg alms, beating
on the window you have prudently raised, offering you fruits
and vegetables as if a white-dressed European could buy that sort
of thing in the middle of a bridge, offering their wares in a language where, amid incomprehensible allusions, the words "rupee please, me very poor, please sah'b, baksheesh please, rupee
sah'b" inevitably arise; and the driver stops again without warning, a child's hand appears for a moment against the door, a body
is thrown back violently, behind you hear laughter and perhaps
insults, the bridge advances as if a dinosaur were swallowing a
gelatinous mass in which our taxi, the trucks, and the streetcars
are solid elements floating on the sea of men and women and children who fill the bridge on both sides and cross among the vehi-
cles in an interminable zigzag, until at last the digestion is complete, you are expelled from the anus of the monster onto an
avenue full of all the detritus from the bridge and that is the plaza
of Howrah Station, you have reached the end of your trip, *sah'b*.

The naked girl, any of the innumerable naked girls in the plaza
or the galleries of the station, has moved next to her mother, who
is busy tying and untying a heap of clothes and rags, and she has
taken her little brother, who is lying on the ground crying, into
her arms, laboriously lifting him to her waist with the belt in
which she puts the naked infant's feet, and she runs to beg from a
group getting off a streetcar, but to reach them she has to clear her
way through the endless labyrinth of families clustered on the
ground, the fire of cooking pots in her nose, the fragments of dirty
matting that signal a possession, a territory, heaped up with
dishes, combs, pieces of mirrors, tin cans of nails or wires, sometimes, incongruously, a flower found in the street and put there

because it is beautiful or sacred or simply a flower. You have gotten out of your taxi before reaching the entrance of the station and you have dismissed the driver, who persists in offering to wait, who follows, argues, now you are going to cross the plaza and observe the people, the local customs, of Calcutta, until you reach the station and explore the inside. That white-haired woman with her face hidden, who is sleeping on her back against a lamppost barely two yards from the streetcar rails, seems dead; she can't be, yet she must be sleeping very soundly because flies are swarming over her face and almost seem to enter her half-open eyes. The children who play around her, dropping streams of mangoes and papayas, bits of rotten fruit they intercept with their hands or their bodies, laughing and running, don't seem to bother the old woman, so there is no reason for you to stop, and besides, the mere intention of observing something instantly attracts the notice of those who are walking nearby or who are seated or lying on the cobblestones of the plaza, and then there is no way to avoid the ring of people, the fingers that grasp your pants, children's fingers that barely reach your knees, that cling timidly to your

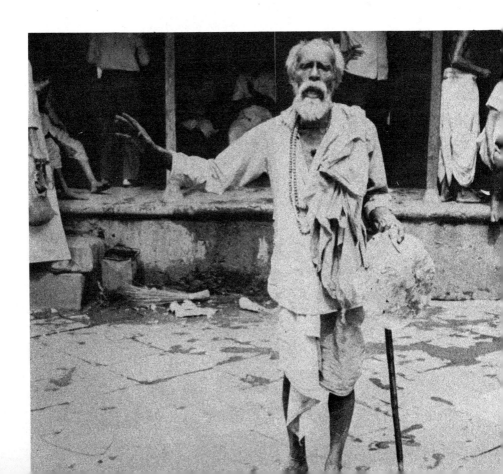

pants as they repeat *baksheesh sah'b, baksheesh sah'b,* while other children rub their stomachs with their hands or extend them in supplication like small empty bowls. You have not lowered your eyes quickly enough from that body stretched out with its mouth open, you haven't kept walking as if you hadn't seen a thing, the only way to keep the others from noticing you so much; to you it seemed strange that a woman could sleep with her eyes half-open while the sun and the flies moved across her face, and you hesitated a moment to make certain she was sleeping; now they have grabbed your pants, a ragged woman has raised her naked baby to you, its mouth covered with sores, a vendor with a basket of trinkets rapidly explains his merchandise's advantages, a boy about ten repeatedly rubs the band of your Contaflex and you remove his hand with a gesture meant to be friendly, look for money in your pockets, give it to the smallest ones so that they will let go of your pants, you succeed in escaping from the ring and you continue across the plaza; perhaps only at that moment you realize that these thousands of families, this multitude walking or lying on the ground, are not in the plaza the same way that you or

someone else might be in a plaza in his country—they live in the plaza, they are the population of the plaza, they live, sleep, eat, get sick, and die in this plaza, beneath this indifferent cloudless sky, in this time without future because there is no hope. You have entered hell with only five rupees, now you suspect that the woman was dead and that the playing children, throwing bits of mango, knew that the woman was dead, and that a truck will come from town to take her away when someone bothers to tell the policeman directing traffic at the entrance to the plaza. *Murray's Guide* was quite right: the scene is picturesque.

The mother nursing the smallest of her five children has begun to cut up the vegetable her husband found between two wagons on the bridge. The naked girl returns with her brother on her arm and sets him on the ground next to his mother; she is tired, she wants to eat and sleep, she has not brought any money, she knows her mother will not say anything, because only rarely does she bring any home, and soon she is distracted by her brothers' games, what is going on in other circles, around other pots and other fires. The family circles partially break when someone enters to trade or beg or run a paid errand, but someone always remains, someone always guards the place on the plaza where the family lives, because if they abandon it for a minute they lose it forever, another circle will split in two, a young couple with their children will break away from their parents to claim this new territory and quickly install there their heap of rags, of scraps. Thus these least privileged ones adapt to living beside the rails where death passes every three minutes, or on the perimeter of the plaza, where the traffic that comes and goes from the bridge passes, at the edge of the road full of trucks and cars. You have tried to calculate the number of people who live seated or stretched out on Howrah Plaza, but it is difficult in this heat that clouds the eyes, and these children who keep arriving from everywhere to beg from you, and then, to think, people *living* . . . It is best to avoid the largest groups, smiling vaguely at some big-bellied child who raises his enormous black eyes in supplication, and at last you reach one of the entrances of Howrah Station, fleeing the sun to lose yourself in the vast somber hall; it is only when your shoe barely misses a woman's hand that you realize that nothing has changed, that the hall continues the world of the plaza, that the floor is occupied by a silent or vociferous throng, more dense than outside, with innumerable men and women carrying luggage or parcels or clothes, circulating among the seated or lying people without your ever knowing which are travelers waiting for trains, and which, in this other, privileged circle of hell, protected from the sun of the plaza, merely watch the trains with a vague, muddy indifference. Perhaps at that moment you recall the brochures of tourist propaganda you were given in the Air India Boeing, not to mention *Murray's Guide*; or maybe the session of parliament at Delhi which you attended by special invitation to hear a speech by Indira Gandhi. It's possible that exactly there, with your foot beside the hand of a woman stretched out on her side, eating some seeds inside a very green leaf, you realize that only madness become action and then system (because revolutions are an unthinkable madness for the Air India

pamphlets, *Murray's Guide*, and Indira Gandhi) can put an end to what is happening at your feet, where a dog has just vomited a black mass, a sort of maldigested toad, next to the head of a child who reaches out and places his hand in the vomit in the time it takes you to turn around and flee to an exit; what is going on around you is nothing, really absolutely nothing that made you turn your head and leave, it is even something that you may manage to forget this very night, as you escape from the heat in the marvelous bathtub in the hotel, but it goes on, it has gone on night and day since Howrah Station opened its doors, and in some other part of the city and the country for years before the English built Howrah Station, and the hell that you are fleeing conveniently, since the driver has waited outside after all, sees you from the distance, and has already opened the door laughing in a friendly way, demonstrating his fidelity and his efficiency, is a hell where the condemned have not sinned nor do they know why they are in the hell, they have been there, renewing their numbers, forever, watching the passage of the few able to overcome the barriers of caste and distance and exploitation and sickness, closing the family circle so that the little ones don't stray too far and don't get smashed by a truck or violated by a drunk, hell is this place where outcries and games and tears continue as if they didn't continue, this is not

something that occurs in time, it is an infinite recurrence, Howrah Station in Calcutta any day of
any month of any year that you have the desire to
go see it, it is there now as you read this, there and
here, this that happens and that you, which is to
say, I, have seen. Something truly picturesque,
unforgettable. It is worth the trouble, believe me.

A Country Called Alechinsky

He doesn't know that we like to roam through his paintings, that we have long loved to adventure through his drawings and engravings, examining each twist and each labyrinth with a secret attention, with an endless palpation of antennae. Perhaps it is time to explain why, for several hours, even at times for an entire night, we renounce our avid anthill activities, the endless lines coming and going with little bits of herbage, crumbs of bread, and dead insects; why we wait anxiously for the shadows to fall over the museums, galleries, and studios (his in Bougival, where the capital of our realm is located), to abandon these tiresome labors and to climb into the enclosures where the games await us, to enter the smooth rectangular palaces of our festivals.

Years ago, in one of those countries that men set up and run, to the great delight of us all, one of us accidentally climbed onto a shoe; the shoe started moving and entered a house: there we discovered our treasure, the walls covered with fantastic cities, se-

cret passages, vegetation and creatures that cannot be found anywhere else. In our most secret
annals is written the story of that first discovery:
the explorer stayed an entire night after finding a
departure point in a small painting where foot-
paths intertwined and contradicted each other
like an endless act of love, a recurring melody
that furled and unfurled the smoke of a cigarette
passing through the fingers of a hand to open into
a head of hair that was full of trains entering the
station of an open mouth in a landscape of slugs
and orange peels. Her story moved us, changed
us, made us into a people hungry for liberty. We
decided to cut back our work hours once and for
all (we had to kill some of our bosses) and to give
our sisters everywhere the keys that would admit
them to our youthful paradise. Emissaries provided with minuscule reproductions of engravings and drawings undertook long journeys to
spread the glad news; little by little determined

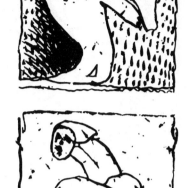

explorers located the museums and mansions containing the can-
vas and paper lands we loved. Now we know that men possess
catalogues of those territories, but our own is an unbound atlas of
pages that at the same time describe and are our chosen world;
and of that we speak here, of vertiginous harbor charts and ink
compasses, of itineraries with crossroads highlighted, of frightening and joyful encounters, of infinite games.

If at the beginning, too used to our sad life in
two dimensions, we remained at the surface,
where the delight of losing and finding and rec-
ognizing ourselves again at the end of shapes and
paths was enough for us, we soon learned to go
beneath appearances, to go behind a green to find
a blue or an acolyte, or a peppery cross or a village
festival; the areas of deep shade, for example, the
india ink lakes that we avoided at first because
they filled us with fainthearted doubts, turned to
caves in which fear of becoming lost gave way to
the pleasure of passing from one penumbra to
another, of entering the magnificent war between the black and the white, and those of us

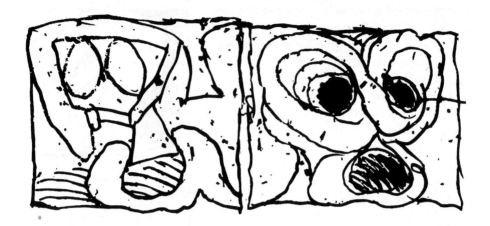

who reached the deepest point discovered the secret: only from underneath, from the inside, could the surfaces be deciphered. We understood that the hand that had drawn the figures and routes to which we allied ourselves was a hand that had likewise reached up from within the paper's deceptive atmosphere; its real time was situated on the other side of the outside space that cast lamplight onto the engravings or filled them with sepia icicles. To enter our nocturnal citadels was no longer a group tour with a guide to comment and destroy; now they were ours, we lived within them, we loved in their apartments and drank the moon's dripping honey from terraces full of multitudes as ardent and frenzied as ourselves, statuettes and monsters and twining animals occupying a common space, which we accept without misgivings as if we were painted ants, free moving inks of the drawing. He doesn't know this, at night he sleeps or goes out with

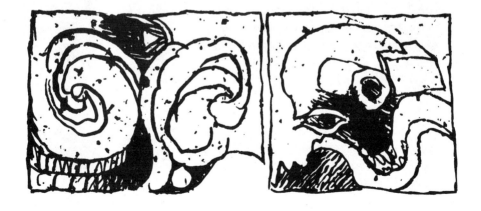

friends or smokes as he reads and listens to music, those meaningless activities that do not concern us. Tomorrow, when he returns to his studio, when the guards begin their rounds in the museums, when the first aficionados enter the art galleries, we will no longer be there, the sun's cycle will have returned us to our anthills. But we will secretly wish to let him know that we will return with the shadows, that we will scale ivy and countless windows and walls to arrive at last at the ramparts of oak or pine beyond which awaits, tense in its fragrant skin, our sovereign night. We think that if sometime, with a light in his hand, insomnia leads him to one of his paintings or drawings, we won't be alarmed by his pajamas, which we imagine are black and white striped, and that he will pause, questioning, amused and ironic, watching us for a long time. Perhaps he will be slow to discover us, because the lines and colors that he has put there move and tremble and come and go just as we do, and in this traffic that explains our love and our confidence we might perhaps pass unnoticed; but we know that nothing can escape his eyes, that he will begin to laugh, that he will think we are scatterbrained because our thoughtless wanderings are altering the rhythm of the drawing or even introducing a scandal into a constellation of signs. What can we say to exonerate ourselves? What can ants do against a man in his pajamas?

Toward a
Speleology
of the Domicile

The rites of passage of our race seem always to alternate between history and clairvoyance, between the sanctioned doors of the past and the uncertain ones of the future. Blessed with an unwaveringly entropic world, the characters in a James Ballard novel, pursuing a dream of primordial truth, descend oneirically to their origins, retracing the path of the species, until in their dreams they attain the fern forests, the vital pollen of the aboriginal sun, the hopeless starting point; then, drunk on the past, these perfect historians of themselves set off in search of the midday sun and awake to a new catastrophe, where an absurd death awaits them. I think this could serve as a metaphor of contemporary man, clairvoyant of history or historian of clairvoyance, bound to the belief that the doors of the self open onto the past or that ivory gates gleam on the horizon.

I have become convinced that these doors are smokescreen images. I want to speak of another entranceway that can just be made out "through a glass, darkly." Bluebeard insists, with a cynical smile, "Never open that door"—but the poor young girl whom some call Anima will not fulfill, with deep complicity, the fate of the legend's heroine. She will not open the door. Her defense

mechanisms will operate so perfectly that she will not even see the door. Although it is within reach of her desire, she will continue to search for the entrance with a book in one hand and a crystal ball in the other. Don't you want the real key, Anima? Judas is seen as the necessary instrument for teleological redemption, with its abominable price of blood and crossed wood—Bluebeard, another version of Judas, seems to say that disobedience can effect redemption here and now, in our godless world. In an archetypal light, any prohibition is clearly an urging: Open the door, open it now. The door is behind your eyelids. It is neither literature nor prophecy.

But you have to be able to see it, and to see it I propose to dream because a dream is a displaced present arrived at by a purely human operation, a saturation of the present, a piece of ambergris afloat within the now, yet apart from it, for dreaming has its own present, and its disquieting forces appear outside Kantian space and time.

In this present, Anima not yet knowing how to control the forces she releases, in this pure existence, dreamer and dream not separated by categories of knowledge, everyone is his own dream, both the dreaming and the thing that is dreamed; in this present the door waits for the hand to reach out to it. We only have to open it ("Never open that door," says Bluebeard), and this is how: we have to learn to wake within the dream, to impose our will on this oneiric reality of which until now we have only passively been creator, actor, and spectator. Whoever wakes up free within his dream will have passed through the door and become at last a *novum organum*, with staggering implications for the individual and the species: returning from oneiric wakefulness to quotidian wakefulness with the same flower between the teeth, establishing a conciliatory bridge between night and day and dismantling the ungainly binary machine that separates Hypnos from Eros. Or, more beautifully, learning to sleep in the heart of the first dream to gain entrance into a second one, and to go on: to manage to wake again within the second dream, and so open another door, and to continue to sleep and wake within a third dream, and to continue to sleep and dream, like stacking Chinese dolls.

"Never open that door," says Bluebeard. What will you do, *animula vagula blandula*?

Silvia

Now you will learn how something might have ended that never even began, that started in the middle and stopped at no precise point, but faded into another fog. First I must mention that many Argentines spend part of their summer in the Luberon valleys, and that we residents of the region often hear their sonorous voices, which seem to suggest wider spaces, and that with the parents come the children, and with them Silvia, trampled flowerbeds, lunches with meat on forks and in cheeks, terrible shouting followed by Italian-style reconciliations, what they call family vacations. These visitors don't bother me much, because I am protected by a well-deserved reputation for unsociability; the screen opens just enough to admit Raul and Nora Mayer, and of course their friends Javier and Magda, which means their children and Silvia too, a barbecue at Raul's two weeks ago, something without a beginning, but above all Silvia, the absence that now fills my solitary home, rubs her golden medusa against my pillow, and makes me write what I am writing with an absurd hope of conjuration, a sweet golem of words. Certainly I must also include Jean Borel, who teaches Latin American literature at a Western university, his wife Liliane, and little Renaud, in whom two years of life have accumulated tumultuously. All these people for a barbecue in the garden of Raul and Nora's house, under a vast linden tree, where, at the hour of childish combat and literary discussion, it is hardly restful. I arrived with bottles of wine and a sun that was setting in the hills. Raul and Nora had invited me because Jean Borel wanted to meet me, but didn't want to approach me alone: Javier and Magda were also staying in the house then, and the garden was a half-Sioux, half-Gallo-Roman battlefield, where plumed warriors fought to the end with soprano voices and handfuls of mud, Graciela and Lolita allied against Alvaro, and in the middle of the uproar, poor Renaud tottering along with his rubber pants full of maternal cotton, wandering from one band to the other, an innocent and execrable traitor watched over only by Silvia. I know that I am mentioning a lot of names, but the order and the genealogies were slow to come to me, too: I remember that I got out of the car with the bottles under my arm, and a few yards ahead I saw the headdress of the Invincible Bison appear among the shrubs, his diffident smirk on encountering a new Paleface; the battle for the fort and the captives unfolded around a small green tent that seemed to be the general headquarters of the Invincible Bison. Ignoring a perhaps decisive offensive, Graciela dropped her messy weapons and cleaned her hands on my neck; then she sat indelibly on my knees and explained that Raul and Nora were above with the other grown-ups and would be down soon, trifling details compared to the rude battle in the garden.

Graciela has always felt an obligation to explain everything to me, based on her notion that I am a little dim. For example, this afternoon the Borels' little boy didn't count for much: "Don't you know that Renaud is only two years old, he still makes poop in his pants, he did just a little while ago, and I started to tell his mother that Renaud was crying, but Silvia lifted him up to the sink, washed his bottom, and changed his clothes, and Liliane didn't find out, because she gets mad, you know, and spanks him, and then Renaud starts to cry again, he's always bothering us and doesn't let us play."

"And the other two, the big ones?"

"They're Javier and Magda's kids, don't you know, silly. Alvaro is the Invincible Bison, he's seven years old, two months older than me, and lots bigger. Lolita is only six, but she still plays with us, she's the Invincible Bison's prisoner. I'm the Queen of the Woods and Lolita is my friend, so I have to save her, but we'll have to finish tomorrow, because now they're calling us for our baths. Alvaro cut his foot and Silvia put on a bandage. Let me down, I have to go."

Nobody was tying her down, but Graciela always needs to affirm her liberty. I got up to greet the Borels, who were coming down from the house with Raul and Nora. Someone, I think Javier, served the first *pastis*; at nightfall the conversation began, the battlefield changed with nature and age, it became a pleasant study of people getting acquainted; the children were bathing, there were no Gauls or Romans in the garden, and Borel wanted to know why I didn't return to my country. Raul and Javier smiled compatriot smiles. The three women occupied themselves at the table; they looked strangely alike, Nora and Magda sharing a Rio Plata accent, Liliane's from the other side of the Pyrenees. They called us to drink the *pastis*, and we discovered that although Liliane was darker than Nora and Magda, there was something they shared, a similar kind of rhythm. We talked of concrete poetry, of the *Invençao* group, and Borel and I discovered a common ground in Eric Dolphy; with the second glass the smiles of Javier and Magda brightened: the other two couples still lived in that time where group discussions revealed disagreements, brought to light the differences that create intimacy. It was almost dark when the children began to reappear, clean and tired, first Javier's, discussing money, Alvaro obstinate and Lolita petulant, then Graciela, holding the hand of Renaud, who already had a dirty face again. They gathered around the little green tent, we discussed Jean-Pierre Faye and Philippe Sollers, with the darkness the fire became visible through the trees, and it colored the tree trunks with shifting golden reflections reaching to the end of the garden; I think at the moment I first saw Silvia I was seated between Borel and Raul at the round table under the linden tree, with Javier, Magda, and Liliane; Nora was in and out with refreshments and plates. It seems strange that I didn't introduce myself to Silvia, but she was very young, and perhaps wanted to remain at the edge of the group; I understood the silence of Raul and Nora: Silvia was obviously at that difficult age, refusing to join the games of the adults, preferring to lord it over the children around their green tent. I could not see much of her, but the fire flared up on one side of the tent, and then I saw her there, stooped over Renaud, washing his face with a handkerchief or a rag; I saw her tanned thighs, thighs slight and defined at the same time, like the style of Francis Ponge of whom Borel was speaking to me; her calves were in the shadow, like her body and face, but her long hair shone from time to time with the wing-beats of the flames, her hair that was also golden. All of Silvia appeared in fiery tones hammered bronze; her short skirt rose to the tops of her thighs, and Francis Ponge has been shamefully ignored by the young French poets, but now, through the efforts of the *Tel Quel* group, he is finally recognized as a master. It was impossible to ask who Silvia was, why she was not among us, and besides, maybe the fire lied, maybe her body was ahead of her age and the Sioux were still her natural territory. Raul was interested in the poetry of Jean Tardieu, and we had to explain to Javier who he was and what he had written; when Nora brought me the third *pastis*, I couldn't ask about Silvia, the discussion was too lively and Borel ate up my words as if they were worth something. I saw a little table go up next to the tent for the children to eat separately; Silvia was no longer there, but the darkness had swallowed up the tent and maybe she was seated farther away or had gone into the trees. Asked for an opinion on the success of Jacques Roubaud's experiments, I could hardly surprise the others by my interest in Silvia, could hardly tell them that the sudden disappearance of Silvia had vaguely disturbed me. When I finished telling Raul what I thought of Roubaud, the fire again fleetingly illuminated Silvia, and I saw her go by the tent, holding the hands of Lolita and Alvaro; behind came Graciela and Renaud, jumping and dancing in a last Sioux appearance; of course Renaud fell on his mouth and his first wail made Liliane and Borel jump up. From the group of children came Graciela's voice: "It's nothing, it's over!" and his parents returned to their discussion with the characteristic lack of concern of everyday conventionality toward the wounds of the Sioux; now I was called on to pass judgement on the aleatory experiences of Xenakis, for Javier showed an interest in them that Borel found excessive. Between Magda and Nora I saw Silvia's silhouette in the distance, again bent over Renaud, playing a little game to console him; the fire defined her legs and profile and I made out a fine, avid nose, lips of classical sculpture (but hadn't Borel just asked me something about a Cycladic statuette for which he thought me responsible, and hadn't Javier's reference to Xenakis turned the conversation onto something more significant?). I felt that if anything ought to be known at this moment it was Silvia, up close, away from the magic of the fire, to return her to the probable mediocrity of a timid girl or to confirm that silhouette too beautiful and alive to remain but a spectre: I should have said so to Nora, with whom I have an old friendship, but Nora was laying the table and putting out paper napkins, not without encouraging Raul to buy Xenakis's latest record immediately. From Silvia's territory, invisible again, came Graciela the little gazelle, the little know-it-all; I offered her old perch with a smile and a boost onto my knees; I took advantage of her excited description of a hairy beetle to remove myself from the conversation without Borel thinking me discourteous. I could at least ask in a low voice if Renaud had hurt himself.

"No, silly, it was nothing. He always falls, he's only two years old, you know. Silvia washed off the bump."

"Who is Silvia, Graciela?"

She looked at me with apparent surprise.

"A friend of ours."

"But is she the daughter of one of the people here?"

"You're crazy," said Graciela reasonably. "Silvia is *our* friend. Right, Momma, Silvia is our friend?"

Nora sighed, placing the last napkin beside my plate.

"Why don't you go back and play with the children and leave Fernando in peace? . . . If you get her started about Silvia, she'll go on forever."

"Why, Nora?"

"Because ever since they invented her we've been hearing about nothing but their Silvia," said Javier.

"We didn't invent her," said Graciela, holding my head in her hands to keep me from the adults. "Ask Lolita and Alvaro, you'll see."

"But who is Silvia?" I repeated.

Nora was already too far away to hear, and Borel was still talking to Javier and Raul. Graciela's eyes were fixed on mine, her mouth sticking out like a trumpet, half in mockery, half in a know-it-all gesture.

"I told you, dummy, she's our friend. She plays with us when she wants to, but not Indians because she doesn't like that. She's too big, you know. And that's why she takes care of Renaud so much, because he's only two and he poops in his pants."

"Did she come with monsieur Borel?" I asked in a low voice. "Or with Javier and Magda?"

"She didn't come with anyone," said Graciela. "Ask Lolita and Alvaro, you'll see. Don't ask Renaud, because he's too little and won't understand. Let me go, I have to go."

Raul, who has a certain radar, broke off a reflection on letters to throw me a sympathetic look.

"Nora warned you, if you keep on her, this Silvia will drive you crazy."

"It was Alvaro," said Magda. "My son is a mythomaniac and he contaminates everyone."

Raul and Magda were still looking at me, and there was a fraction of a second when I could have said, "I don't understand," to force an explanation, or, more straightforward, "But Silvia is there, I just saw her." I don't think, now that I have had so much time to think about it, that Borel's casual question kept me from speaking. Borel had just asked me something about *The Green House*; I began to talk without knowing what I was saying, and then, as a result, I was no longer speaking to Raul and Magda. I saw Liliane coming from the children's table, where they sat on stools and old boxes; the fire spread its illumination like the engravings in Hector Malot or Dickens novels, the branches of the linden momentarily crossed a face or a raised arm, we heard laughter and protests. I talked about Fushia with Borel, I was carried along with the current on the raft of memory where Fushia was so terribly alive. When Nora brought me a plate of food, I murmured to her: "I don't quite understand about the children."

"There you are, you've fallen too," said Nora, with a sympathetic look at the rest. "Good thing they're going to sleep soon, because you're a born victim, Fernando."

"Don't pay any attention," interjected Raul. "You're obviously not used to it, you take the kids too seriously. You have to listen to them the way you listen to rain, old friend, or you will go mad."

Perhaps at that very moment I lost the possibility of entering Silvia's world. I will never know why I accepted the easy explanation that it was a joke, and my friends were just kidding me (not Borel, Borel stuck to his path, which would soon reach Macondo); again I saw Silvia, who had just emerged from the darkness and leaned between Graciela and Alvaro as if to help them cut their meat or take a bite; the shadow of Liliane coming to sit with us intervened, someone offered me wine, and when I looked again, Silvia's profile was as if ablaze from the coals, her hair falling over her shoulder, and then she disappeared, melting into the darkness around her waist. She was so beautiful that the idea of a joke offended me, it was in bad taste. Looking down at my plate, I started to eat, listening with one ear to Borel inviting me to some university colloquiums; if I told him I wouldn't come, it was Silvia's fault, her involuntary complicity in my friends' unwelcome joke. That evening I did not see Silvia again; when Nora took the children their cheese and fruit, it was she and Lolita who tried to keep Renaud awake enough to eat. We began to speak of Onetti and Felisberto, we drank so much wine in their honor that a second wave of bellicose Sioux and Cherokees enveloped the linden tree, and the children were collected to be put to bed, Renaud in the arms of Liliane.

"I had an apple with a worm in it," said Graciela with enormous satisfaction. "Good night, Fernando, you are very bad."

"But why, my love?"

"Because you never came once to see us at our table."

"You're right, I'm sorry. But you had Silvia there, didn't you?"

"Yes, but . . ."

"He's got the bug," said Raul, looking at me with something that might have been pity. "That's going to cost you, I'm afraid the famous Silvia will trap you for good, you'll be sorry, friend."

Graciela moistened my cheek with a kiss that smelled strongly of yogurt and apple. Much later, after a conversation in which sleepiness began to slow our responses, I invited them to dinner at my house. They came last Sunday around seven, in two cars; Alvaro and Lolita brought a kite of sorts, and under pretext of getting it airborne they immediately trampled my chrysanthemums. Noticing that no one was keeping Raul from heading for the grill, I left the women, who were attending to drinks; I invited Borel and Magda into the house, installed them in the living room in front of my Julio Silva painting, and stayed with them a while, pretending to be listening to what they said. Through the large window we saw the kite in the wind, we heard the cries of Lolita and Alvaro. When Graciela appeared with a bouquet of flowers, probably put together at the expense of my best bed, I went into the twilit garden and helped them get the kite up higher. Shadows bathed the hills and the hollows of the valley and advanced into the poplars and cherry trees, but without Silvia; Alvaro hadn't needed Silvia to get his kite up.

"It flies well," I said approvingly, letting it in and out.

"Yes, but be careful, sometimes it dives, and these poplars are very tall," Alvaro warned me.

"It never dives when I fly it," said Lolita, jealous, perhaps, of my presence. "You've let out too much string, you know."

"He knows better than you," said Alvaro in rapid masculine alliance. "Why don't you go play with Graciela, can't you see you're bothering us?"

We remained alone, playing out the string of the kite. I waited until Alvaro accepted me, conceding that I was as capable as he of directing the green and red flight that disappeared farther into the shadows every moment.

"Why didn't you bring Silvia?" I asked, pulling a little on the string.

He gave me a sideways glance of surprise and scorn, and took the string from my hands, subtly demoting me.

"Silvia comes when she wants to," he said, drawing in the string.

"Okay, today she didn't come then."

"What do you know? She comes when she wants to, I told you."

"Ah. And why does your mother say you invented her?"

"Look how it flies," said Alvaro. "Boy, this is a great kite, it's the best one ever."

"Why don't you answer me, Alvaro?"

"Mama thinks I invented her," said Alvaro. "So why don't you think so too?"

Suddenly I noticed Graciela and Lolita by my side. They had overheard the last sentences, they were watching me steadily: Graciela slowly turned a violet posy between her fingers.

"Because I'm not like them," I said. "I saw her, you know."

Lolita and Alvaro exchanged a long look, and Graciela approached and put the flower in my hand. The string of the kite tightened suddenly. Alvaro gave it play, and we were lost in the shadows.

"They don't know because they're stupid," said Graciela. "Show me where your bathroom is and come with me while I pee."

I took her up the outside staircase, I showed her the bath and asked her if she could find her way down. In the doorway of the bathroom, with an expression containing something of recognition, Graciela smiled at me.

"No, you can go, Silvia will take me down."

"Oh good," I said, fighting vaguely against something I didn't understand, absurdity or nightmare or mental disorder.

"Sure, dummy," said Graciela. "Don't you see her there?"

The door of my bedroom was open, the naked legs of Silvia were draped over the red bedspread. Graciela went into the bathroom and I heard her slide the latch. I entered the bedroom, I saw Silvia sleeping in my bed, her hair like a golden medusa on my pillow. I closed the door behind me, I approached I don't know how, there are gaps and slashes here, water that rushes over my face, blinding and deafening me, a sound like fractured profundities, a moment without time, unbearably beautiful. I don't know if Silvia was naked, for me she was like a poplar of bronze and of dream, I think I saw her nude but then I am not sure, I must have imagined beneath her clothes the line of calves and thighs that drew her silhouette on the red bedspread, I followed the soft curve of her buttocks, exposed by the advance of a leg, the shadow of the hidden waist, the small imperious pale breasts. "Silvia," I thought, speechless, "Silvia, Silvia, but how . . ." The voice of Graciela reached me through two closed doors as if she were shouting in my ear: "Silvia, come get me." Silvia opened her eyes, sat up on the side of the bed; she wore the same short skirt as the first night, a tank top, black sandals. She passed by my side without seeing me and opened the door. When she went out, Graciela went running down the stairs, and Liliane, carrying Renaud in her arms, passed her on the way to the bathroom for mercurochrome for his eight-thirty injury. I helped her to calm and to cure, Borel came up, disturbed by the wails of his son, gave me a smile of reproach for my absence, and we went down to the living room to have another drink; everyone was looking at the Graham Sutherland painting, phantasms of that sort, full of theories and enthusiasms that disappeared into the air with the tobacco smoke. Magda and Nora were watching the children to see that they ate a strategic distance apart; Borel gave me his address, insisting that I send him the contribution I promised a Poitiers journal. He told me he was leaving the next day and that they were taking Javier and Magda to show them the region. "Silvia will go with them," I thought darkly, and I looked for a box of candied fruit, a pretext for going to the children's table to linger with them a moment. It wasn't easy to ask them, they ate like wolves, and they snatched away the sweets in the best tradition of the Sioux and the Tehuelches. I don't know why it was Lolita I asked, as she was wiping her face with a napkin.

"How should I know?" said Lolita. "Ask Alvaro."

"Me either," said Alvaro, hesitating between a pear and a fig. "She does what she wants, maybe she'll go."

"But which of you did she come with?"

"None of us," said Graciela, giving me one of her best kicks under the table. "She came, and now, who knows, Alvaro and Lolita are going back to Argentina, and Renaud, he's too little, you don't think she'd stay with him, this afternoon he ate a dead wasp, it was disgusting."

"She does what she wants, the same as us," said Lolita.

I returned to my table, I saw the day end in a cloud of cognac and smoke. Javier and Magda returned to Buenos Aires (Alvaro and Lolita returned to Buenos Aires) and next year the Borels were going to Italy (Renaud would go to Italy next year).

"It's we, the oldest ones, who will stay," said Raul (so Graciela would stay, but Silvia was the four of them, Silvia was only there when all four were together, and I knew they would never be together again).

Raul and Nora are still here, in our Luberon valley. Yesterday I went to visit them and we chatted again under the linden tree; Graciela gave me a doily she had made and they passed along the greetings of Borel, Magda, and Javier. We ate in the garden, Graciela refused to go to bed early, she played Fortunes with me. There came a moment when we were alone, Graciela was searching for the answer to the question about the moon; she wasn't sure, so her pride was hurt.

"And Silvia?" I asked her, tousling her hair.

"Look how dumb you are," said Graciela. "You think she's going to come tonight for only me?"

"Good," said Nora, coming out of the shadows. "It's good she doesn't come for only you, because we've already had enough of those stories."

"It's the moon," said Graciela. "Boy, what a dumb question."

Your Most Profound Skin

Pénétrez le secret doré
Tout n'est qu'un flamme rapide
Que fleurit la rose adorable
Et d'où monte un parfum exquis
                    Apollinaire, "Les Collines"

Every amorous memory retains its madeleines and I want you to know, wherever you are, that mine is a fragrance of blond tobacco that carries me back to the ripeness of that night, to the luminous moment of your most profound skin. Not the tobacco that one inhales, the smoke that papers one's throat, but that vague, equivocal scent that the pipe leaves on one's fingers, which at a certain moment, with some distracted gesture, raises its whip to summon your memory, the shape of your back against a sail of white sheets.

Don't look at me out of your absence with that rather childlike gravity that makes of your face a young Nubian pharaoh's mask. I think we always understood that we would give each other only the pleasures and casual excitements of drink and empty midnight streets. But I retain more of you than that; in my memory you reappear nude, turned over: our more precise planet was that bed where slow, imperious geographies were born of our travels, of welcome or resisted departures, of embassies with baskets of fruit or hidden bowmen; and with each pool, each river, each hill and plain we won new territories, amid the obscure murmurings of allies and enemies. O traveler of yourself, machine of forgetfulness! And now I pass my hand across my face with a distracted gesture and the fragrance of tobacco on my fingers brings you back to tear me away from my accustomed present, to show your antelope form once again on the screen of that bed where we traced the interminable paths of an ephemeral encounter.

With you I learned parallel languages: the one of your body's geometry that filled my mouth and hands with tremulous theorems, the one of your different speech, your insular language that often confused me. With the tobacco scent a precise memory now returns that holds the entirety of a moment that was like a vortex, I remember that you said, "Don't," and I didn't understand because I thought that nothing could trouble you in that tangle of caresses that made of us a skein of black and white coils, in that slow dance where we each pressed against the other to relent to the soft pressure of muscles, of arms, revolving slowly and unraveling to form yet another skein, repeating the passage from top to bottom, rider to colt, archer to gazelle, like hippogriffs face to face, dolphins arrested in mid-leap. Then I knew that your complaint was another word for modesty and shame and that you could not satisfy this new thirst as you had the others; you pushed me away in supplication, with that manner of hiding your eyes, of putting your chin against your throat to keep all but the black haunt of your hair from entering my mouth.

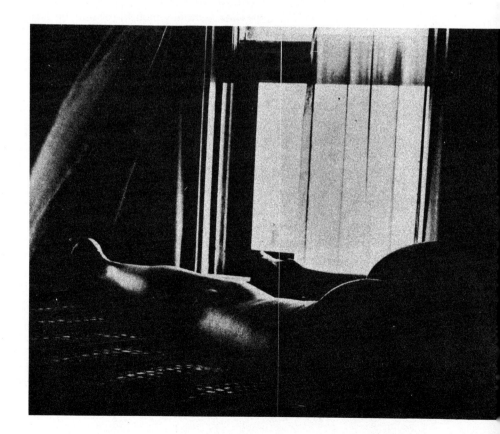

You said, "Please don't," and from where you lay on your back you looked at me with eyes and breasts, with lips that traced a flower of slow petals. I had to open up your arms, to whisper an ultimate desire with my hands that passed over the sweetest hills, feeling you relent little by little and turn on your side to offer the silky wall of your back where a thin shoulder blade was the wing of a fallen angel. I troubled you and from your hesitation would be born the perfume that now returns me to the modesty that preceded another accord, the final one, that carried us to another trembling response. I know that I closed my eyes, that I lapped the salt of your skin, that I descended, turning you back, feeling your midsection like the taper in a pitcher where hands are thrust in ritual offerings; at a certain moment I became lost in the hidden, narrow path that denied my lips their pleasure while everywhere, from your highlands and low countries, your modesty murmured in abandonment of its final resistance.

With the fragrance of the blond tobacco on my fingers rises again the stammer and the tremor of that dark encounter; I know that my mouth sought your trembling mouth, the only lip that still encircled your fear, the ardent pink and bronze contour that admitted my farthest voyage. And as always I didn't feel in that rapture what memory brings back to me now through a vague scent of tobacco, but that musky fragrance, that exquisite shadow, forged a secret path out of its necessary momentary forgetting, an unnameable game of flesh that hid from awareness the movement of the most dense and implacable machines of fire. There was no taste or scent then, your most hidden country appeared as image and contact, and only today my fingers tainted with tobacco bring back to me that moment when I stretched across you to slowly reclaim the keys of passage, to ravish the sweet space where your modesty preserved its final defenses, when with your mouth pressed into the pillow you sobbed in supplication, in deep acquiescence, your hair spread over the pillow. Later you understood and you were no longer ashamed, you ceded to me the city of your most profound skin from many different horizons, after fabulous sieges, negotiations, and battles. In this vague vanilla of tobacco that today taints my fingers opens the night of your first and final hesitation. I close my eyes and breathe in the past the fragrance of your most secret skin, I don't want to open them again to this present where I read and smoke and imagine I'm still alive.

Good Investments

Gomez is a wan and modest man who asks nothing of life but a small place in the sun, a newspaper with its elevating reports, and a boiled ear of corn without too much salt but with plenty of butter. So it should surprise no one that on attaining age and adequate funds this gentleman goes to the country and seeks out a region with pleasant hills and villages to buy a square yard of land where he can "feel at home," as the expression goes.

This business of the square yard might seem strange, and it would be under ordinary circumstances, that is, without Gomez and Literio. Since Gomez is looking for only one square yard of land on which to set his chaise longue and his primus stove—the former for reading his paper and the latter for boiling his corn— he has a lot of trouble because nobody has a single square yard for sale, they have innumerable square yards and selling one in the middle or on the edge of the others would raise problems of property records, community life, and taxes, and besides it's ridiculous, it isn't done, what folly. And just as Gomez is carrying his chaise longue, his primus, and his corn and beginning to get discouraged after having traveled over the better part of the hills and valleys, he discovers that Literio has a space between two lots that measures exactly one square yard, and since the two properties were purchased at different times, the space pos-

sesses a personality all its own even though it may look like just a jumble of plants with a thistle in the north. The notary and Gomez laugh up their sleeves as he signs his name, but two days later Gomez takes his place on his property, where he spends the whole day reading and eating until at dusk he retires to the village hotel where he has rented a decent room because Gomez may be crazy but he's no idiot, and this even Literio and the notary soon realize.

Thus summer in the hills passes agreeably, although occasionally tourists who have heard of the matter show up and peep at Gomez lying back and reading his paper. One night a Venezuelan tourist ventures to ask Gomez why he only bought one square yard of land and what the possible use of it can be beyond being a spot for his chaise, and the Venezuelan tourist and his companions are dumbfounded by his reply: "You seem ignorant of the fact that a property of land extends from the surface down to the center of the earth. Only calculate." Nobody calculates, but they all have a vision of a square shaft going down and down to no one knows where, and somehow this seems more important than the corresponding image of an area of three acres going down and down and down. So when the engineers arrive three weeks later everyone realizes that the Venezuelan hadn't been fooled, that he had divined Gomez's secret, that under his land lies oil. Literio is the first to permit them to ruin his fields of alfalfa and sunflowers with insane drilling that

releases foul gasses into the air; the other landowners also drill night and day, everywhere, and there is even one poor tearful woman who has to move the bed where three generations of honest laborers had slept because the engineers pinpointed an active zone right in the middle of her bedroom. Gomez watches these operations from a distance without concerning himself unduly, although the noise of the machines distracts him from his newspaper reports; naturally no one has brought up the subject of his land and he is not a curious person and only answers when spoken to. That is why he says no when the representative of the Venezuelan oil company admits defeat and comes to ask him to sell his square yard. The representative has orders to buy at any price and begins to quote figures that rise at the rate of five thousand dollars per minute, so that after three hours Gomez folds up his chaise, packs his primus and the corn in his valise, and signs a paper that makes him the wealthiest man in the country if and when they discover oil under his land, which happens exactly a week later in the form of a geyser that drenches Literio's family and all the chickens in the vicinity.

Gomez, much surprised, returns to the city he started from and takes an apartment on the top floor of a skyscraper that has a terrace out in the sun for him to read his paper and boil his corn without Venezuelan pests coming to disturb him or blackened chickens running back and forth, with the indignation that these animals always exhibit when one covers them with crude oil.

The Broken Doll

These pages may interest a certain type of reader of *62* by clarifying some of its intentions or multiplying its uncertainties—different ways, perhaps, of reaching the same destination when one is navigating crosscurrents.

We know that attention acts as a lightning rod.* Merely by concentrating on something one causes endless analogies to collect around it, even to penetrate the boundaries of the subject itself: an experience that we call coincidence, serendipity—the terminology is extensive. My experience has been that in these circular travels what is really significant surrounds a central absence, an absence that, paradoxically, is the text being written or to be written. In the years when I was working on *Hopscotch*, this saturation reached the point that the only legitimate response was to accept without comment the meteor shower that came through the windows of streets, books, conversations, and everyday circumstances and to convert them into the passages, fragments, and required or optional chapters of the *other* that formed around an ill-defined story of searches and missed encounters; that, in large part, accounts for the method and presentation of the story. But already in *Hopscotch* there is a prophetic allusion to Gide's admonition that the writer should not take advantage of such

*Just as distraction does. In "Glass with Rose" (p. 236) I have described an experience that later became the basis for *62*.

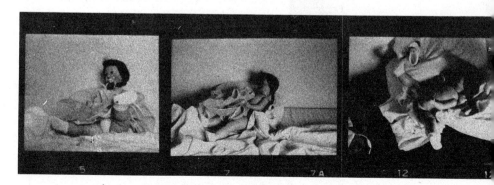

chance encounters; if, years later, 62 explored one of the avenues anticipated there, it had to do so in an original way, encountering and taking on completely different risks. I will not provide a synopsis of the book, which the reader may already know; but he may not have noticed that the text rejects all momentary connections, that it transforms them to other points of view, and that literary quotations and allusions to facts relating to its theme have been eliminated in favor of as linear and direct a narration as possible. The characters rarely allude to external literary elements or to texts that their situation momentarily paraphrases: everything is reduced to a reference to Debussy, a book by Michel Butor, a mention of the countess Erszebet Bathori, vampire. Anyone who knows me would concede that this search for literality was not easy. In my memory, in what happened to me every day as I was writing the novel, in my dreams and encounters, my concentration on that fixed subject was once again translated into a meteor shower of disturbing coincidences, confirmations, and parallels. That is what I wish to speak of here, because, having kept the promise that I made to myself not to incorporate them into the text, I can now have the pleasure of showing them to those who like to tour the writer's kitchen, to share those encounters with other times and places that are what is most real in the reality of his existence.

At the beginning, when the characters' more or less unconscious ritual dance was still taking shape within a text struggling to chart a path into its special territory, my chance readings began to suggest clear directions. Aragon's *La Mise à mort*, for example, that passage that flew off the page like a bat:

> A novel for which there is no key. One does not even know the protagonist, hero or antihero. It is a succession of encounters, of people barely seen and fast forgotten, and

others of no interest who constantly recur. Oh, life is all screwed up. One tries to give it a general significance. One tries. Poor thing.

Aragon was speaking of *La Mise à mort*, but I saw that these words were the perfect epigraph for my novel. I have already said that I had decided to strip the text naked, not only as a counterpoint to *Hopscotch* (and to those readers who always expect "Twenty years later . . ." when they finish *The Three Musketeers*) but also because I foresaw the time when I could write some pages *post facto* where this and other encounters could illuminate the book from other angles, so that the reader would know them before it or after it, in any event under different physical and psychological circumstances. It is worth mentioning, as an aside, that the interactions of life and reading are seldom considered by the novelist, as if only he and his creations were within the space-time continuum, while his reader were an abstract entity that someday would hold an assemblage of 250 pages in the fingers of its left hand and spend some time going through them. I know all too well the extent to which daily interruptions alter, impede, and sometimes create or destroy my work; so why not present these intermissions or ruptures to the reader and give him, before or after the principal game, some supplemental pieces of the model kit? (Even better: in the happy days of serial stories, novelists could take advantage of the reader living days or weeks between the chapters of those fictional lives that occupied a different time frame. Why not take into account the *other story* of those intervals? I searched in Dickens, Balzac, and Dumas for some exploitation of this both dangerous and privileged position, without discovering conclusive signs. Still, Dickens knew that his American readers were anxiously waiting on the waterfront for the ship that would bring them the latest epi-

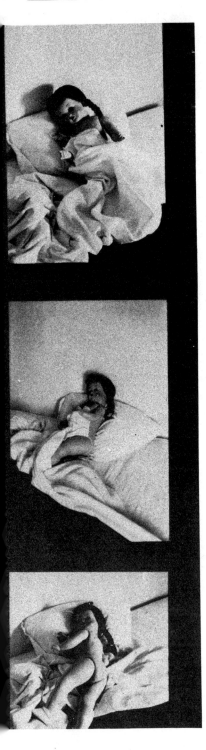

sodes of *The Old Curiosity Shop*, and that well before its tielines reached the dock an anguished question would rise from the wharf to greet those on board: "Has Little Nell died?")

You will see how your memory of a book, its already fading phantom, can take strange twists when the author makes the reader wait for him to give another turn to the screw with candle in hand and blank pages before him: wouldn't that make their relation more intimate, wouldn't it at least better overcome the hostile hiatus between the text and the reader, just as contemporary theater struggles to overcome the hiatus between stage and audience? For such reasons it seemed to me that if the reader of *62* was to be present in the special becoming of the novel (where diachrony, temporal succession, is negated by the very nature of what is recounted, while causality continues to operate with a duration that we may call "affective," in the sense that Julien Benda speaks of affective versus purely intellectual logic—a duration that is actually a form of synchrony giving the story its internal coherence), it would likewise make sense for me to lead him afterwards to some of the inter-, re-, trans-, and pre-ferences that assailed me as I was writing, which I deliberately eliminated. Those lines of Hölderlin, for example, that I was reading in the days when Juan entered the Polidor restaurant and a doll began to complete its disgraceful destiny, those brief lines of mad Hölderlin that my memory infuriatingly repeated:

> But time, nonetheless,
> we interpenetrate:
> Demetrius Poliorcetes,
> Peter the Great.

Scardanelli succeeded in reaching, in living in, the moment in which different times are intertwined and consumed like smoke from different cigarettes in the same ashtray, and Demetrius Poliorcetes coexisted with Peter the Great just as

in those days it often happened that some character of mine who lived in one city would go out to walk with someone who was perhaps in another. And it did not seem extraordinary to me that at that time, reading Vladimir Nabokov's *Pale Fire*, a passage of the poem came into my own time, came from the past of a book already written to describe metaphorically a book that was barely beginning to enter the future:

> But all at once it dawned on me that *this*
> Was the real point, the contrapuntal theme;
> Just this: not text, but texture; not the dream
> But topsy turvical coincidence,
> Not flimsy nonsense, but a web of sense.
> Yes! It sufficed that I in life could find
> Some kind of link-and-bobolink, some kind
> Of correlated pattern in the game,
> Plexed artistry, and something of the same
> Pleasure in it as they who played it found.
> It did not matter who they were. No sound,
> No furtive light come from the involute
> Abode, but there they were, aloof and mute,
> Playing a game of worlds, promoting pawns
> To ivory unicorns and ebon fauns—
>
> . . . .
> . . . Coordinating there
> Events and objects with remote events
> And vanished objects. Making ornaments
> Of accidents and possibilities.

All that appeared like the words of an oracle: "Not text but texture." The awareness that the texture has to generate the text rather than merely conventionally weaving the plot and being at its service. And thus to find "some kind of correlated pattern in the game," the rules of the game that inevitably coordinate "events and objects with remote events and vanished objects." For a long time that had been my rationale for *62*: the exploration of exploring, the experiment of experimentation, all without renouncing the narrative, the organization of another lit-

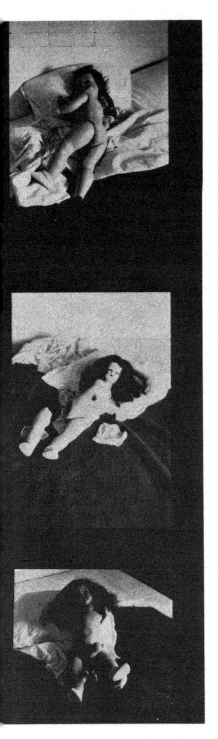

tle world where we could recognize and entertain ourselves and walk along with Feuille Morte and be shipwrecked with Calac and Polanco. But just then, naturally, I had to find in my hands a text of Felisberto that had been unknown to me (these Uruguayans hide their best works), in which I discovered a plan of action that showed me the light in my hour of greatest doubt. "I do not believe that I should only write about what I know," said Felisberto, "but that I should write also of the *other*." Faced with a narration in which a rupture of all logical, and especially psychological, bridges was the first precondition for experience, faced with an often exasperating effort to eliminate all the conventional props of the genre, Felisberto's sentence reached me like a hand extending the first bitter yerba maté of friendship under the wisteria. I realized that he was right, that I had to keep *moving forward*. For who knows "the other"? Neither the novelist nor the reader, with the difference that the novelist who is moving forward is the one who discerns the doors in front of which he and the future reader will linger, testing the latches and feeling the way. His task is to reach across the distance between the known and the other, because in this already lies the beginning of transcendence. The mysterious does not spell itself out in capital letters, as many writers believe, but is always *between*, an interstice. Did I perhaps know what was going to happen after Marrast sent his anonymous letter to the anonymous neurotics? I knew some things, that the bureaucratic and aesthetic order of the Courtauld Institute would be shaken by his senseless, yet—within the mechanics of the story (*a web of sense!*)—necessary and almost inevitable action; but on the other hand I didn't know that Nicole would offer herself to Austin a hundred pages later, and this was part of "the other," that waiting for the moment when "the known" was surpassed.

This sense of virtual porosity, of moving forward only by opening interstitial inroads with no pretense of covering the whole surface of the phenomenological sponge, was marvelously illuminated during those weeks by an Indian text, strophe 61 of the *Vijnana Bhairava*, which I encountered in a French journal: "Whenever one perceives two things, and observes the gap between them, he must enter that gap. If the two things can be eliminated simultaneously, then Reality will blaze in the gap." In the modest little world of the novel I was setting out to write, night after night, many such gaps (which I called interstices and which applied as much to space as to time—distant repercussions would initiate a blazing *gestalt*, converting a previously unrecognizable design into a speech of Helene or an act of Tell or Juan) went on filling up with reality, becoming the reality revealed by the Indian text. And then, while I was still writing in a purely receptive frame of mind, open to any surprise, the book of which I as yet knew little, I chanced (this may be hard to believe: it seems more logical to suppose that I intentionally sought out these correspondences) upon a passage by Merleau-Ponty concerning *signification*: "The number and richness of man's signifiers," said Merleau-Ponty in a discussion of Mauss and Lévi-Strauss, "always surpasses the set of defined objects that could be termed signifieds." And right after that, as if offering me a cigarette: "The symbolic function must always precede its object and does not encounter reality except when it precedes it into the imaginary. . . ."

I would certainly have incorporated this sort of thing into the book immediately when I was writing *Hopscotch*—especially something that happened to me while I was traveling in northern Italy, though it wasn't by certain red houses along the road from Venice to Mantua but on the coast between Cernobbio and Crotto. (Analogously, the strophe of the Indian text was 61, not 62 . . .) Along the route, when I stopped to look at Lake Como in the distance, I found myself in front of a house at the entrance of which was one of the most miserable inscriptions that the petite bourgeois world has given birth to:

> Porta aperta per chi porta
> Chi non porta parta*

---

*A play on the Italian words *porta* (door), *aperta* (open), *portare* (to carry), and *partire* (to leave), which is difficult if not impossible to convey in English; the sense is approximately: "This door will open if you've got gifts—if not, git!" (translator's note)

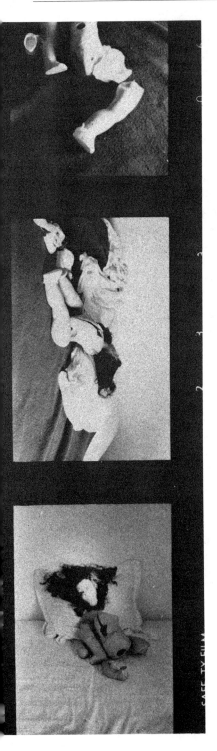

Was there any way that the Scroogish inventor of this base play on words, whom I pictured as a fat, distrustful spider wedged between prosciutto hams and cacciacavallo cheeses, could have imagined that he too would figure in someone else's throw of the dice? I had arrived in front of his house with the tourist's vague spirit of receptivity, in which thoughts and sensations blend into a single being, and this occurred just as Marrast was writing his letter to the anonymous neurotics association so that they would investigate the supposed mystery of the branch of *hermodactylus tuberosis*. With Marrast's eyes I read the ignoble words on the plaque and understood them in another sense; I continued on to Crotto telling myself that the play on words hid a key to the reality that the dictionary tries in vain to lock inside every free word. Only the person who carries something with him will find the door open, and therefore the novelist who points out the door to the *other* (Marrast would point it out explicitly to the anonymous neurotics) would be the first to gain access, because what he carried was the door itself, the opening onto the mystery; the fact of carrying (*portare*) became based on the very notion of the door (*porta*) between Cernobbio and Crotto, between Cortázar and Marrast.

Months later, in Saignon whose hills overlook Apt, the Apta Iulia of Augustus's legions where I once competed at Marco against a Nubian gladiator, I gradually began to enter the night of the King of Hungary Hotel, refusing to settle for a Monk Lewis or Sheridan Le Fanu facility but resolving instead to let Juan live his strange adventure with the peevish skepticism of all well-traveled Argentines. Among the readings that I bought from Paris was an issue of that incredible review called *The Situationist*, about which I can only say that it is written by obsessives, a great merit in a time when literary reviews tend to a depressing sanity. Devoted to nothing less than the topology of labyrinths, the issue contained texts by Gaston Bachelard, among them the following, whose inclusion in my book would have illuminated *al giorno* the King of Hungary and so many other hotels of *62*: "An *analysis situs* of the active instants can ignore the longitude of the intervals, just as the *analysis situs* of the geographic elements can ignore their magnitude. The only thing that matters is their grouping. There is thus a causality of order, a causality of the grouping. The efficacy of that causality becomes more noticeable as one approaches actions that are more composed, more intelligent, more alert. . . ."

Someone had to say it better, to believe it more strongly, to shut it more effectively within the box of literature. And in case that is not enough, this addition that summarizes the deliberate temporal fluctuation of my book: "All duration is essentially polymorphic; the true action of time reclaims the richness of coincidences. . . ."

And now, to reach the end of these parallel routes, I remember the morning when I finished *62*. I had got up at six, having slept badly, to write the final pages and to see the end of the book take place with a by now familiar, recurrent surprise, since in my stories or novels I experience something like a sharp twist of the rudder in the last moments of work, everything organizes itself in a new way, and suddenly I am outside the book, looking at it as if at a rare creature, knowing that I have to write the word END but lacking the strength to do so, orphaned from the book or it from me, both of us forsaken, each now in his own world despite what will later be corrected or changed, two different orbits, handshake in an intersection, best of luck, good-bye. And then, thirsty and ill at ease, I made some maté, I smoked and watched the sun rise over Cazeneuve, I played for a while with Theodor W. Ador-

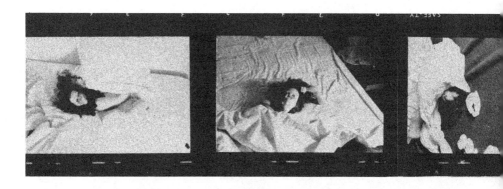

no, who always came at that hour looking for milk and caresses, on the third cigarette I got the urge to read Rimbaud, and between two of Theodor's pats, I opened *Deserts of Love* and my eyes fell upon a fragment that I couldn't believe was, like me, located on the other side of the word END, so well did it continue the visions of those last hours of work:

> I went out into the endless city. O weariness! Immersed in the unhearing night and flight from happiness. It was like a winter night, when snow smothers the world entirely. I cried, "Where is she?" to my friends, but their answers only misled me. I passed before the windows of the place she spends her nights; I ran through a sunken garden. I was turned away. Because of that, I wept without restraint. Finally I descended into a dusty excavation where, seated on the foundation framing, I gave full vent to my tears of that night.

This was Juan searching for Helene near the end, it was Nicole on the waterfront, it was me, sensing a glove falling forever down, being pulled down by the package tied with a yellow cord, something that would be broken for a second time beneath the body of a murdered woman. I could no longer be surprised that a few days later, Aragon, who had begun this alliance of forces surrounding my book, again spoke to me from a poem:

> Laisse-les ouvrir le ventre à leurs jouets saccager les roses
> Je me souviens je me souviens de comment tout ça s'est passé.

The Entrance into
Religion of
Theodor W. Adorno

/ written almost nothing on cats, a very strange thing since cat
and I are like the two little worms of Yin and Yang intertwining
about each other (that is the Tao) and it has not escaped me that
every cat in Spanish (*gato*) is master of the three letters of the
Tao, with the *g* like the little hole that Navajo women leave in their
ponchos so as not to suffocate the soul imprisoned within it; but
Kipling has already demonstrated that the cat "walks by himself": and there is no Tao or magic phrase that can keep him from
his hours and haunts / W. Adorno has walked a good deal through
the Saignon pages, I must explain that his Yin and my Yang (or
the reverse, according to the moon and herbs) were joined in
friendship and intertwined without a contract, without that business of somebody gives you a kitten and you give it a cup of milk
so that the animal develops conditioned reflexes, stakes out his
territory, and sleeps on your knees and hunts your mice, the sad
pact old people make with their cats, that cats make with old people. Nothing of that, my wife and I saw Theodor arrive on the
path that descends to our house from Luberon: he was a base,
dirty cat, black beneath the dusty ash that failed to cover his
wounds, because Theodor, along with ten other Saignon cats,
lived on the compost heap like scavenging bag people, and each
herring skeleton was Austerlitz, the Catalonian fields, or Cancha
Rayada, bits of torn ears, bloody tails, the life of a wild cat. But
this animal was more intelligent, as we quickly saw when he
started mewing at us from the entrance, not letting us approach
him but indicating that if we were to place milk in an acceptable
no cat's land he would condescend to drink it. We complied and
he saw that we need not be scorned; we observed the neutral zone

by mutual, tacit accord, without recourse to the Red Cross and the United Nations, a door remained respectfully open as a concession to dignity, and a little later the black patch began to sketch its wary spiral across the red tiles of the living room, sought a rug by the fireplace, and reading a book of Paco Urondo I heard the first sign of our alliance come from there, a bold purring, the release of a stretched-out tail, and sleep among friends. Two days later he allowed me to brush him, in another week I cured his wounds with sulfur and oil; all that summer he came mornings and nights, never consented to sleep in the house, are you kidding, and we didn't insist because we had to return to Paris soon and couldn't take him with us, gypsies and international translators don't have cats, a cat is a fixed territory, an agreeable limitation; a cat is not traveling, its orbit is slow and small, it goes from a bush to a chair, from an entrance hall to a place for meditations; its designs are deliberate, like those of Magritte, cat of painting, never Jackson Pollock or Appell / day that we left, inevitable guilty feeling: and if he had been weakened, if all that milk and spaghetti and petting had left him at a disadvantage for the trials by fire, the machos with ripped ears and the manners of ravaging troops? He watched us go, sitting on a little stone, clean and shining, comprehending, accepting. That winter I thought of him often, we spoke of him with elegiac voices. Summer came, Saignon came, when the first time we went to throw out the garbage we were again astonished to see eight cats leap away at once, tabbies and blacks and whites, but not Theodor, his white bib unmistakable amid such commotion. Fears confirmed, natural selection, law of the strongest, poor little animal. Five or six days later, eating in the kitchen, we saw him seated on the other side of the window glass, lunar Mizoguchi phantasm. His mouth sketched a miaow that the window made silent cinema; my eyes moistened like an idiot's, I opened the window and prudently offered my hand, knowing that eight months of absence erode and destroy a relationship. Dirty and sick, he let me take him in my arms, although once on the ground he appeared shy and distant and claimed his dinner as a natural right; he went away almost at once with that habit of his of approaching the door and miaowing as if his heart were broken. The next morning he was there playing, happy and at ease, right away the brush and the sulfur. The next year was the same except that he waited almost a month to return, we castigated ourselves, suspecting he had died, grieving, but he came, thinner and sicker than ever, and that was the third and final year of the pagan and happy life of Theodor W. Adorno, when I photographed him and wrote about him and returned to cure him of what was probably a hairball attack, complicated by Theodor's being in love, which made him completely stupid: he walked past the house head up and whining, in the afternoon he crossed the garden as if in a trance, floating over the clover, and once when I followed him discreetly I saw him go down a path that led to one of the farms in the valley and get lost in a shortcut, yowling and crying, Theodor Werther, demolished by love for some cat of scabious access. What would fate hold in store for this idyll with the washerwoman of Vaucluse? It would be Juan de Mañara's fate, not Werther's: this year I found it out, after two months of Saignon with the irrefutable absence of Theodor. Dead, this time indubitably dead, his throat opened by one of the toms of the dump, poor Theodor so weak and in love, that sort of thing? / eleven-thirty is the best time to buy bread and on the way mail letters and dump the garbage; I climbed the path thinking of nothing, as almost always in moments of revelation (to study once more how all profound distraction opens certain doors and how you have to allow yourself to be distracted when you are unable to concentrate) / express mail, and this one air mail, *allez, au revoir monsieur Serre*, a round and hot loaf of

bread, a chat with M. Blanc, exchange of meteorologic thoughts with Mme. Amourdedieu, suddenly the little patch of shadow under the yellow excess of midday, the door of Mlle. Sophie, the patch of shadow curled up in front of the door, it can't be, how can it be, the devil, in the daylight all cats are black and how could the great pagan be taking the sun in front of the door of Mlle. Sophie, tiny Christian lady of Saignon, with glasses and bonnet and a mouth lost between a nose that falls and a chin that rises. Theodor, Theodor! I pass alongside and he doesn't look at me, I say softly: *Théodore, Théodore, chat*, and he doesn't look at me, Juan de Mañara has entered into religion, I see the platter of milk and the ribs fragile as Mlle. Sophie's own, the paltry rations of a church mouser smelling of candles and cheap ham, Theodor converted, baptized, ignoring me, prepared for eternal life, convinced that he has a soul, perhaps at night *sleeping in the house*, the ultimate humiliation, the final penance, mea culpa, he who never tolerated a closed door and now the pointy knees of Mlle. Sophie, the bordered tablecloths, the speeches and purrs at the same time, Christian life in a Provençal village. And the Tao, and the loves, and that way of playing with paper balls that we made from the Sunday supplements to *La Nacion*? / returned to see you two or three times and you never recognized me and that's fine because I will not reclaim you either, what right do I have, you the freest of pagan cats and most imprisoned of Catholic cats, stretched out before the door of your sacristan like a watchdog. O Theodor, how fine it was to see you coming down the path tail in the air, moaning for your tabby among the lavender, how sweet it was to meet you again each year, the days you followed your caprices, the moonlit nights you chose to come haughtily through the window and spend some hours with us before returning to a freedom you, like so many of us, have exchanged for cat's delight, the promise of heaven.

Make a Little Star

Make a little star right at the top of the page and the field of operation will appear clearly. The hand that holds the knife descends on virgin flesh. As it penetrates, the surgeon coldly listens to the deep respiration of bound and anesthetized time. But who dies and who listens? You fall into another sleep and dream of waking to begin to write. As usual, the true chains are elsewhere. It was useless having choreographed the dance so well, for suddenly everything falls away and the dancer becomes the dance, something rises from the depths to subsume the mime and everything on the surface. It was all so calculated, so precisely prescribed: the appropriate lighting, potent pentothal, the little star you put at the top of the page. Nothing was overlooked for the pure white skin's rite of passage to hesitation, the blush of shame, ephemeral refuges. The priest was there to direct the rites. Even now he bends over the victim, madly multiplying the parallel incisions. But who really does the deed? Will no one tell him that he too is bound in the wrappings of the shadowy mummy, bound by the impure blood of those who cannot distill powers through these incisions, these words written in the blinding illusion of freedom?

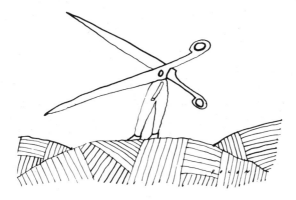

No, No, and No

Mr. Silicose is completely mad if he thinks that I am going to give him an ant. At the moment he is only asking for one, hoping to persuade me by his moderation, but at the beginning (the afternoon of 22 November) he asked for a lot more, he wanted whole anthills, legions of ants, practically all the ants. He's crazy. Not only am I not going to give him the ant but I intend to walk past his house with it on me, just to make him furious. I'll do it like this: first I'll put on my yellow tie and then, having picked out the liveliest and shapeliest of my ants, I will let it crawl over my tie. So it will be a double promenade, me walking in front of Mr. Silicose's house and the ant walking on my tie. Did I say a double promenade? It will be an open spiraling infinity of promenades, because if the ant is walking on my tie, my tie is moving with me, the earth is carrying me along on its ellipse, which is moving through the galaxy, which is wandering around the star Beta in the Centaur, and the very moment that Mr. Silicose, thinking himself immobile, leans over his balcony to see my perfectly formed ant with all its feet and antennae on my yellow tie, he will comprehend, poor man, my flamboyant gesture. He will start to slobber something like macramé from his mouth and nose, and his wife and daughters will try to revive him with smelling salts, and lay him across the sofa in the living room. That living room, I know it only too well, having spent so many evenings drinking iced tea there with that family avid of insects.

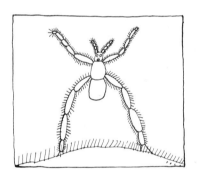

Futile Protection

I am well aware that I am pathologically timid, that just being in the world is steel and flint for me. Even water, usually an ally, sometimes turns dry and hostile between my lips that wish for almonds and lace; in the ambiguous light of dusk, when I dare to walk through the city, soft cloudlike shapes tear vicious cuts in my skin and cause me to run off screaming and conceal myself in doorways. They tell me I should take the metro to be safer, or buy a hat with a broad brim. It's no use speaking to me in the tone one uses with children, I still look warily into the distance where a swallow might be waiting to sharpen its scissors in my neck. The city fathers have even approved funds for my protection, people are concerned about me. I thank you, ladies and gentlemen, I wish I could thank you tenderly and fondly—but you're always there and for me that is the cliff-edge, the shadowy millstone, an unbearable excess of kindness cloaked in coral talons. I find it more and more shameful to complicate the lives of others, but no desert island remains, no infamous thicket, not even a tiny pen to fence me in, from which I could look at you in the light of friendship. Is it my fault, prickly world, that I am a unicorn?

Cycling in Grignan

I insist on rejecting causality, that facade erected by an ontological *establishment* that stubbornly shuts the doors on the most exalting human adventures—I mean, if I drank the glass of wine in the Grignan cafe *after* reading the book by Georges Bataille, that still would not make his girl on the bicycle *before*, casting on her the aura we too readily assign to such special moments; memory would have fashioned a causal chain to connect the book and that occasion, a chain forged by our being conditioned for peace of mind and a quick forgetting. But that's not how it was. First let me mention that Grignan assumes the honor of keeping the memory of Mme. de Sevigné, and the little cafe with its outdoor tables lies in the shadow of a monument where, marble pen in hand, she continues to write her daughter chronicles of a time we can never attain.

Leaving the car under a plane tree, I stopped there for a rest after all the turns on the winding roads through the hills; I like this sort of quiet town at midday, where they serve wine in thick glasses that the hand holds as if returning to something vaguely familiar, an almost alchemical material that no longer exists in the cities.

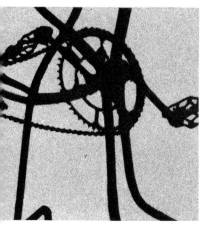

The little plaza was sleeping, occasionally a car or wagon caught your eye. Three friends were joking and laughing near the tables, two on foot, the other astride a bicycle tilted a little on its side, perhaps a model too big for her, one foot resting on the ground, the other playing absentmindedly with the pedals.

They were adolescents, the young ladies of Grignan, going through the period of first dances and last games. The cyclist, the prettiest, had long hair tied in a ponytail that swung from side to side with each laugh, each glance at the tables of the cafe. The others lacked her foal grace, their personalities were already tried and set, they were little bourgeois whose entire future could be read in their bearing; but they were young, and their laughter mingled and rose in the midday air in the conversation of girls that cares more for pleasure than for sense. It took me a while to realize why the cyclist interested me particularly. She was in profile, at times almost with her back to me, and when she spoke she rose and fell lightly on the bicycle seat. Suddenly I saw. There were other customers in the cafe, anyone could see, the two friends, the girl herself, what I had seen. Suddenly it had struck me (as it had her, in a different sense). I no longer saw anything but

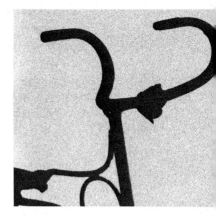

the seat of the bicycle, its vaguely heart-shaped form, black leather terminating in a thick, rounded point, her skirt, a thin yellow fabric clinging to her small firm buttocks, her thighs pressed against the sides of the seat, only releasing when her body jumped forward and touched the metal bar; with each movement the end of the seat pressed for a moment between her legs, moved back, pressed again. Her buttocks moved with the rhythm of their joking and laughing, but it was as if in seeking the contact of the seat they were stimulated, made to advance again in an endless come-and-go and this took place under the sun in the middle of the plaza, with everyone looking without seeing, without understanding. But that is how it was, between the point of the seat and the warm intimacy of that adolescent rump there was no more than the net of a slip and the thin yellow fabric of the skirt. Those two minimal barriers were sufficient to keep Grignan from seeing what would have provoked most vehement reactions,

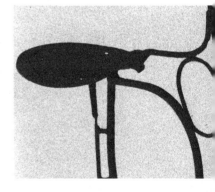

the girl kept pressing the seat and rhythmically releasing, time and again the thick black point inserted into the two halves of the yellow peach, cleaving it as far as the elasticity of the cloth would allow, departing again, recommencing; the joking and laughing continued like the letter that Mme. de Sevigné kept writing in her statue, the slow *per angostam viam* copulation was performed in cadence, interminably, and with each advance or retreat the ponytail swung to the side, whipping a shadow and her shoulders; the pleasure was there even though it was not acknowledged, even though the girl was not aware of the pleasure that turned into laughs, light remarks, the conversation of friends; but something within her knew, hers was the sharpest laughter, her gestures the most exaggerated, as if drawn from outside herself, surrendering to a force that she herself provoked and received, innocent Hermaphrodite seeking the conciliatory fusion, transforming the first sap into shivering foliage. I left, of course, returned to Paris, and four days later someone gave me Georges Bataille's *Histoire de l'oeil*, in which I read about Simone nude on the bicycle, and then I saw the savage beauty of what I tried to describe at the opening of this perhaps too circular text.*

*The French edition omitted this quotation from *Histoire de l'oeil*, which served as epigraph for the Spanish text:
Elle se branlai sur la selle avec une brusquerie de plus en plus forte. Elle n'avait donc pas plus que moi épuisé l'orage évoqué par sa nudité. (translator's note)

The Journey

It could be La Rioja, a province called La Rioja, in any case it is late in the afternoon, almost nightfall; but it began earlier in a country courtyard where a man had told him that the trip was complicated but then you could rest, it began with a recommendation to spend two peaceful weeks in Mercedes. His wife goes with him in the car to the town where he has to buy his tickets: the man had also suggested he get his tickets at the station there to be sure the schedules hadn't changed. In the country, with the life they were leading, they could easily believe that the schedules, like many other things in town, might have changed, as they often do. It would be worth driving to town, even though it would be cutting it close to catch the first train at Chaves.

It's been five hours since they arrived at the station and left their car in the dusty square among the sulkies and carts full of bundles or cans; they hadn't spoken much in the car, although the man had asked about some shirts and the woman had said the bags were packed and they just had to put some books and papers in the briefcase.

"Juárez knew the schedules," says the man. "He told me how to get to Mercedes, he said it was better to get the tickets here and verify the train connections."

"Yes, you told me," his wife replies.

"From the station to Chaves has to be at least a sixty-mile drive. It seems the train to Peulco goes through Chaves a little after nine."

"You'll leave the car with the stationmaster," his wife says, half questioning, half stating.

"Yes. The Chaves train arrives in Peulco after midnight, but it seems there are always rooms with baths in the hotel. The bad thing is it doesn't give me much time to rest, because the next train leaves at five in the morning. I'll have to check. Then there's an easy stretch into Mercedes."

"It's still far, yes."

There aren't many people at the station, only a few local people buying cigarettes at the kiosk or waiting on the platform. The ticket room is at the end of the platform, almost on the gravel of the side track. It is a room with a dirty counter, walls covered with notices and maps, and at the rear two desks and a strongbox. A man in shirt sleeves handles the counter, a girl operates a telegraph set at one of the desks. It is now almost dark but the lights have not been turned on, they use the maroon light that dimly enters through the rear window for as long as they can.

"I have to go back to the house as soon as I get the tickets," says the man. "I have to ship my luggage, and I need to get some money."

"Get the tickets and let's go," says the woman, who has stayed a little behind.

"Yes. Wait a moment while I think. So, I'll go to Peulco first. No, I mean we have to buy a ticket to that place Juárez mentioned, I don't remember exactly."

"You don't remember," says the woman, with that intonation that makes a question not a question at all.

"I'm always like that with names," he says with an ironic smile. "They're gone as soon as you say them. And then another ticket from Peulco to Mercedes."

"But why two tickets?" says the woman.

"Juárez told me that there are two different companies, so you have to get two tickets, but all the stations sell them both, and it's all the same. One of those English things."

"There are no more English," says the woman.

A dark-skinned boy has entered the room and is checking something on the wall. The woman goes up to the counter and rests an elbow on it. She is blonde, with a tired, beautiful face that disappears in a frame of golden hair that seems somehow to illuminate the planes of her face. The ticket agent looks at her for a moment, but she says nothing, as if waiting for her husband to come forward to buy the tickets. Nobody greets anyone in the room, it is so dark it seems unnecessary.

"You have to look on this map," says the man, going to the wall at the left. "Look, it must be here. We are here . . ."

His wife approaches and watches his finger hesitating over the vertical map, looking for a place to set itself.

"This is the province," says the man, "and we are here. Wait, here. No, it must be farther south. I have to go this way, that's the direction, see. And now we are here, I think."

He takes a step back and looks at the entire map, looks at it for a long time.

"This is the province, right?"

"It seems to be," says the woman. "And you say that we're here."

"Here, sure. This must be the road. Sixty miles from this station, as Juárez said, the train must leave from there. I don't see any other possibility."

"Good, so buy the tickets," says the woman.

The man looks at the map for a moment longer and goes over to the ticket agent. His wife follows him, again places her elbow on the counter, as if prepared for a long wait. The boy stops talking with the ticket agent and goes to consult the schedules on the wall. A blue light is lit on the telegraph operator's desk. The man has taken out his billfold and is looking for money; he chooses some bills.

"I have to go from . . ."

He turns to his wife, who is looking at a drawing on the counter, something like a forearm, badly drawn in red pen.

"What was the town I'm going to? I've forgotten the name. Not the second one, the first, I mean. I'm taking the car to the first one."

The woman raises her eyes and looks in the direction of the map. The man makes an impatient gesture, because the map is too far away to be helpful. The ticket agent leans on the counter and waits without speaking. He wears green glasses and a mass of copper-colored hair sticks out of the open neck of his shirt.

"You said Allende, I think," his wife says.

"No, not Allende."

"I wasn't there when Juárez explained the trip to you."

"Juárez explained the schedules and connections to me, but I repeated the names to you in the car."

"There's no station called Allende," says the ticket agent.

"Of course not," says the man. "Where I'm going is . . ."

The woman is again looking at the drawing of the red forearm, which is not a forearm, she now feels sure.

"Look, I want a first-class ticket to . . . I know I have to go by car, it's north of the station. So you don't remember?"

"Take your time," says the ticket agent. "Think calmly."

"I don't have that much time," says the man. "I still have to go by car to . . . I just need a ticket from there to the other station where I make the connection to Allende. Now you say it's not Allende. Why don't you remember?"

He goes closer to his wife and asks her the question as if in disbelief. For a moment he seems on the verge of going back and studying the map again, but he decides not to and pauses, leaning slightly toward his wife, who runs a finger back and forth across the counter.

"Take your time," repeats the ticket agent.

"So . . ." says the man. "So, you . . ."

"It was something like Moragua," says his wife almost as a question.

The man looks at the map, but he sees that the ticket agent is shaking his head.

"That's not it," says the man. "It's not possible that we can't remember, when we have just driven . . ."

"It will come," says the ticket agent. "The best thing would be to divert your attention by talking about something else, and then the name will land like a bird, just today I said so to a man who was going to Ramallo."

"To Ramallo," repeats the man. "No, it wasn't Ramallo. But maybe if I look at a list of stations . . ."

"It's over there," says the ticket agent, pointing to a schedule tacked on the wall. "But as for that, there are something like three hundred. A lot of them are just stops and loading stations, but they all have names, you see."

The man goes to the schedule and puts his finger at the top of the first column. The ticket agent waits, he takes a cigarette from behind his ear and licks the tip before lighting it, looking at the woman who is still leaning on the counter. In the darkness he has the impression that the woman is smiling, but it's hard to make out.

"Give us a little light, Juana," says the ticket agent, and the telegraph operator reaches an arm over to the switch on the wall and a light on the yellow ceiling comes on. The man has reached the middle of the second column, his finger stops, goes back up, goes down again, and moves on. Now it is obvious that the woman is smiling openly, the ticket agent has seen it in the light from the lamp and he is sure, he also smiles without knowing why, until the man suddenly turns around and returns to the counter. The dark-skinned boy has sat down on a bench near the door, so there is another person there, another pair of eyes turning from one face to another.

"I'm going to be late," says the man. "You at least should remember, but I can't remember, you know how I am with names."

"Juárez explained it all to you," says the woman.

"Never mind Juárez, I'm asking you."

"You had to take two trains," says the woman. "First you drive to one station, I remember you told me you would leave the car in care of the stationmaster."

"That's no help."

"All the stations have stationmasters," says the ticket agent.

The man looks at him, but may not have heard. He is waiting for his wife to remember, suddenly it seems that everything depends on her, on her remembering. There isn't much time left now, he has to return to the country house, load his luggage, and leave for the north. Suddenly his fatigue is like this name that he can't remember, an emptiness that weighs more all the time. He has not seen his wife smile, only the ticket agent has seen her. Now he waits for her to remember, he tries to help her with his own immobility, he rests his hands on the counter, very close to his wife's finger, which goes on playing with the drawing of the red forearm, slowly tracing it although she knows it is not a forearm.

"You're right," he says, looking at the ticket agent. "When you think too hard you forget things. But you, at least . . ."

The woman pursed her lips as if drinking something.

"I might be able to remember," she said. "In the car, we talked about going first to . . . It wasn't Allende, right? Then it must have been something like Allende. Look again at the *a*'s and the *h*'s. If you like, I'll look myself."

"No, that wasn't it. Juárez explained the best connection to me . . . Because there's another way to go, but then you have to change trains three times."

"That's too much," says the ticket agent. "Two changes is already enough, with the whole country in the coach, not to mention the heat."

The man makes a gesture of impatience and turns his back to the ticket agent, between him and his wife. Out of the corner of his eye he sees the boy watching them from the bench, and he turns a little more, so as not to see either the ticket agent or the boy, to be completely alone with the woman, who has removed her hand from the drawing and is scrutinizing a painted nail.

"I don't remember," says the man in a very low voice. "I don't remember at all, you know. But you can. Think for a moment. You'll see, you'll remember, I'm sure of it."

The woman rounds her lips again. She blinks two, three times. The man's hand encloses her wrist and squeezes. She looks at him, without blinking now.

"Las Lomas," she says. "Maybe it was Las Lomas."

"No," says the man, "it's not possible that you don't remember."

"Ramallo, then. No, I said that before. If it's not Allende, it must be Las Lomas. If you want, I'll show you on the map."

His hand releases her wrist, and the woman rubs the mark it left and blows on it softly. The man has lowered his head and is breathing with difficulty.

"There's no Las Lomas either," says the ticket agent.

The woman looks at him over the man's head, which is bent close to the counter. Offhandedly, as if testing her, he smiles a little.

"Peulco," says the man suddenly. "Now I remember, it was Peulco, right?"

"Maybe so," says the woman. "Maybe it is Peulco, but it doesn't say much to me."

"If you're going by car to Peulco, it'll take a while," says the ticket agent.

"You don't think it was Peulco?" insists the man.

"I don't know," the woman says. "You remembered a little while ago, I didn't pay much attention. Maybe it was Peulco."

"Juárez said Peulco, I'm sure. It's about sixty miles from station to station."

"It's a lot more than that," says the ticket agent. "It's a bad idea to go by car to Peulco. And when you get there, then what?"

"What do you mean, 'then what?'"

"I mean Peulco is nothing but a junction. Three houses and the station. People go there to change trains. Of course, if you have some business there, that's different."

"It can't be that far," says the woman. "Juárez told you sixty miles, so it can't be Peulco."

The man is slow to answer, he presses one hand against an ear, as if listening to something inside his head. The ticket agent does not take his eyes from the woman, and he waits. He is not sure whether she smiled when she spoke.

"Yes, it must be Peulco," says the man. "If it's so far, it must be the second station. I have to get a ticket to Peulco and wait for another train. You said it was a junction and that there's a hotel. So it is Peulco."

"But it's not sixty miles," says the ticket agent.

"Of course not," says the woman, straightening up and raising her voice a little. "Peulco is the second station. What my husband doesn't remember is the first one, which is sixty miles. That's what Juárez told you, I think."

"Ah," says the ticket agent. "Well, then first you go to Chaves to catch the train to Peulco."

"Chaves," says the man. "It could be Chaves, sure."

"And then from Chaves to Peulco," says the woman, almost as a question.

"It's the only way to go from this area," says the ticket agent.

"You see," says the woman, "if you're sure that the second station is Peulco . . ."

"You don't remember?" says the man. "It sounds right to me now, but when you said Las Lomas I thought that could be it."

"I didn't say Las Lomas, I said Allende."

"It's not Allende," says the man. "Didn't you say Las Lomas?"

"Maybe so, I thought you said something about Las Lomas in the car."

"There's no Las Lomas station," says the ticket agent.

"Then I must have said Allende, but I'm not sure. It's Chaves and Peulco, as you say. Get a ticket from Chaves to Peulco, then."

"Certainly," says the ticket agent, opening a drawer. "But from Peulco . . . because as I said, it's only a junction."

The man has been riffling through his billfold, but these last words stop his hand in the air. The ticket agent leans against the drawer and continues to wait.

"From Peulco I want a ticket to Moragua," says the man, in a voice that seems to hang back, like his hand suspended in the air with his money.

"There's no station called Moragua," says the ticket agent.

"It was something like that," says the man. "Don't you remember?"

"Yes, it was something like Moragua," his wife agrees.

"There are quite a few stations that start with *m*," says the ticket agent. "I mean, from Peulco. You know about how long the trip takes?"

"All day," says the man. "About six hours, or maybe less."

The ticket agent looks at a map covered with glass at the end of the counter.

"It could be Malumba, or maybe Mercedes," he says. "At that distance I don't see any but those two, maybe Amorimba. Amorimba has two *m*'s, maybe that's it."

"No," says the man. "It isn't any of those."

"Amorimba is a little town, but Mercedes and Malumba are cities. I don't see anything else with an *m* in that area. It must be one of those, if you take the train from Peulco."

The man looks at the woman, slowly crumpling the bills in his still outstretched hand, and the woman purses her lips and shrugs.

"I don't know, dear," she says. "Maybe it was Malumba, don't you think?"

"Malumba," repeats the man. "So you think it's Malumba."

"It's not what I think. The gentleman told you that from Peulco it's either that or Mercedes. Maybe it's Mercedes, but . . ."

"Going from Peulco it has to be Malumba or Mercedes," says the ticket agent.

"You see," says the woman.

"It's Mercedes," says the man. "Malumba doesn't sound familiar, while Mercedes . . . I'm going to the Hotel Mundial, maybe you can tell me if that's in Mercedes."

"Yes, it is," says the boy sitting on the bench. "The Mundial is two blocks from the station."

The woman looks at him, and the ticket agent hesitates before putting his hand on the drawer where the tickets are kept. The man is bent over the counter as if that will help him get his money on it faster; he turns his head and looks at the boy.

"Thanks," he says. "Thanks a lot."

"It's part of a chain," says the ticket agent. "Excuse me, but there is also a Mundial in Malumba, for that matter, and probably even Amorimba, although I'm not sure about that one."

"Then . . ." says the man.

"Try Mercedes anyway, if it's not Mercedes you can always take another train to Malumba."

"Mercedes sounds more like it to me," says the man. "I don't know why, but it sounds better. And you?"

"Me too, especially at first."

"Why 'at first'?"

"When the boy told you about the hotel. But there's another Hotel Mundial in Malumba . . ."

"It's Mercedes," says the man. "I'm sure it's Mercedes."

"Get the tickets then," says the woman as if she had stopped listening.

"From Chaves to Peulco, and from Peulco to Mercedes," says the ticket agent.

The woman's hair hides her profile; she is again looking at the red drawing on the counter, and the ticket agent can't see her mouth. Her hand with painted nails gingerly rubs her wrist.

"Yes," says the man after a brief pause. "From Chaves to Peulco and from there to Mercedes."

"You're going to have to hurry," says the ticket agent, choosing a blue box and another, green one. "It's more than seventy miles to Chaves and the train goes through at nine-o-five."

The man puts his money on the counter and the ticket agent starts to give him change, watching the woman slowly rubbing her wrist. He can't tell if she is smiling and it doesn't much matter, but he would still like to know if she is smiling behind the golden hair that covers her mouth.

"Yesterday it rained hard around Chaves," says the boy. "Better hurry, mister, the roads will be muddy."

The man puts his change away and puts the tickets in the pocket of his vest. The woman brushes her hair back with two fingers and looks at the ticket agent. She has her lips together as if to sip something. The ticket agent smiles at her.

"Let's go," says the man. "I barely have time."

"If you leave right away you'll be okay," says the boy. "Be sure to put on chains, it'll be sloppy on the way to Chaves."

The man agrees, and waves a hand vaguely in the direction of the ticket agent. When he has already gone, the woman begins to walk to the door, which has just shut.

"It'd be too bad if after all that he was wrong, wouldn't it?" says the ticket agent, as if to the boy.

Almost at the door, the woman turns her head and looks at him, but the light barely reaches her, and it's hard to tell if she is still smiling, if it is she who has caused the door to slam, or the wind, which almost always comes up at nightfall.

Lunch

When I get up in the morning, the first thing I do is to run into my mother's room and tell her hello and kiss her affectionately on both cheeks.

"Good morning, Brother," I say to her.

"Good morning, Doctor," she answers, fixing her hair.

It is probably worth mentioning at this juncture that I am seven and a half years old and that I sing sol-fa with my aunt Bertha.

"Good morning, Niece," I say as I enter the room where my father worries over his rheumatism.

"Good morning, dear," says Father.

I add for your further information that I am a little boy, red-headed and extremely casual.

After these ablutions, the family assembles around bread and butter and *Figaro*, and I am the first to wish a good day to my older brother, who is buttering his slice of baguette.

"Good morning, Mother," I say to him.

"Good morning, Medor," he replies. "Down boy!" he adds emphatically.

Thus the entire family gathers together to consume the *cafés au lait* prepared by my grandfather with his customary care. Naturally I do not neglect to convey my appreciation.

"Thank you, Germaine," I tell him.

"Not at all, dear sister," answers Grampa.

These tender effusions are always interrupted by the untimely arrival of the mailman with the telegram from Uncle Gustave, who is a farmer in Tananarive, and my older brother assumes responsibility for reading its woeful tidings:

SUGARCANE WIPED OUT TYPHOON MONICA STOP
WHAT WILL BECOME OF ME STOP SHIT STOP

It is unsigned but in my family we all know each other.

"I knew it," says Mama, beginning to cry.

"What a jerk," says the doctor.

"Children, be still," says my older brother.

"We may be children but Uncle Tatave is still a turkey," says my sister.

"Down, Medor," says Mother.

"If I may say a word," says Germaine.

"Of course, Grandfather," my sister says.

"Are you going to quiet down or not?" shouts my older brother.

"Is that any way to speak to your mother?" says my niece.

"I'm sorry, Mother," Mother says.

"Hypocrite," I say to her.

"Really, Doctor, please," says my brother.

"My opinion," says Germaine, "is that the coffee is going to get cold parce que the telegram."

"He's right," says Medor.

"Thank you, Grandfather," adds my niece.

"Not at all, Victor," says Germaine.

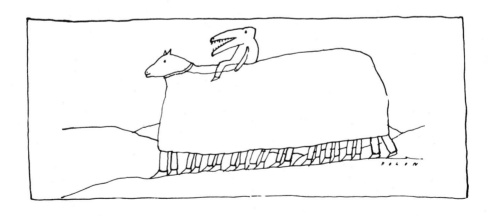

Short Feature

Auto tourist, vacationing in the mountains of central France, grows bored away from the city and its nightlife. Young girl by road makes ritual car-stopping gesture, asks timidly whether Beaune or Tournus. A road, a few words exchanged, a fine profile, occasionally full face, laconic answers to questions from the tourist who now looks at bare knees against red seat. At a turn the car goes off the road and is hidden by thick woods. Out of the corner of his eye he sees her cross and recross her hands on her miniskirt while terror little by little. Under the trees a shelter of plants where one could, getting out of the car, the other door, brutally seize her shoulders. The young girl looks as if she didn't, lets herself be led out of the car knowing that in the solitude of the woods. When hand on skin to lead her under the trees, revolver out of the bag and on the temple. Afterwards the billfold, verify that it is indeed a fat wad, on the way back she makes off with the car which she abandons a few miles farther on not leaving a single fingerprint because in this business you have to think of everything.

The Lip-Biter's Discourse

I have an odd lip-biter. As soon as the chimes of Saint-Roch die out, my lip-biter stands up on its feet and directs its daily discourse to me. Ensconced in my wicker chair, I have tried for years to pretend not to hear, for the topics of this creature almost never interest me—but so far my lip-biter has always been more clever than I. Thus, as soon as he begins his speech, delivered in a mostly onomatopoeic manner that I nonetheless understand without too much trouble, I am forced to be, as the saying goes, all ears, and to make a show of wholehearted appreciation and approval.

If that were the end of it, I could resubmerge myself in Saint-Simon's *Mémoires* after twenty minutes, but my lip-biter is still far from satisfied. As soon as his speech is over, he insists that I recap it for him in a few sentences. This is the most painful moment of the evening, for I often lose the thread of his thoughts. To give but one example, if his speech tonight was based on the sound *a*, on which he is capable of fashioning interminable mod-

ulations, harmonic changes, and transformations toward *e* or *o* (in other words, the whole scale of *aae, aee, aoa, aoo, aeoa, aeeoo*, etc.), my failure to follow the logical connection between two points of his argument will cause the whole structure to come tumbling down. Then the fury of my lip-biter knows no bounds, and I suffer the consequences. First there is the matter of the ashtray. If he is annoyed, for the reasons I have just mentioned (although the variations are infinite), there's no point in asking him to bring me my ashtray so that I can smoke my nine-thirty cigar, since he will behave unpredictably, either dropping it into a basket of papers or hiding himself under the game table and watching me from there, his mouth between his feet, looking vaguely sphinxlike. As for me, my inability to summarize his speech almost always puts me in a state about which I can only say that it leaves me a bilious whirlpool of conflicting emotions. Such

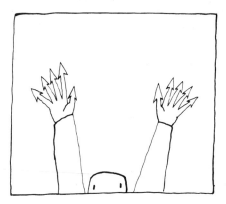 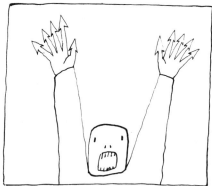

a situation can't help but create tensions that time, that abominable watch-winder, multiplies like funhouse mirrors. It seems almost natural, although that word seems a little out of place here, that we end up throwing the most elaborate insults into the fray, and that my lip-biter, indifferent to the grave consequences of his behavior on the household economy, rips my cambric handkerchief out of my hands to dry the tears that in his excitement gush as freely from his nose as from his blazing eyes. That's when I gauge the hold that I have on my lip-biter, because the creature never dares to carry the affair beyond the business of the ashtray or the handkerchief, even though, in view of my forced immobility, he could easily force me to submit to treatment that would be inconvenient to say the least. I have to remind myself that a lip-biter's soul does not extend beyond its little finger, which leads one to a bit of compassion and forgiveness, if only out of a desire for peace and quiet. Because then there is silence in the house; with or without my summary, the speech is over, the ashtray has been brought or denied, the handkerchief torn or not from my hand. There's nothing left to do but stare fixedly at each other, each in his own place, as the great vault of night descends upon us. Our breakfast won't be brought until quarter after seven in the morning. We still have plenty of time.

Glass with Rose

The state that we describe with the word *distraction* is perhaps only another form of attention, its symmetrical and more profound manifestation located in another region of the psyche: an attention directed *from* or *through* or even *toward* that more profound region. It is not unusual for the subjects of such distraction (in what we call stargazing) to instantly create a dazzling homogeneity from the successive appearance of heterogeneous phenomena. In my habitual stargazing condition a series of phenomena initiated by the noise of a door closing, which precedes or

superimposes on one of my wife's smiles, and recalls a passageway in Antibes and the image of a rose in a vase, composes a pattern that is separate from all these elements and completely unaffected by their associative or causal ties, which proposes—in this unrepeatable instantaneous flash already disappearing into the past—the covision of another reality in which what is for me the sound of a door, a smile, or a rose constitutes something completely different in essence, in significance. One might say that the *poetic image* is also a re-presentation of elements of ordinary reality, articulated in such a way that its system of relations favors this covision of another reality. The difference lies in the fact that the poet is a voluntary or involuntary but always intentional transporter of these elements (intuiting a new articulation, recording its image), while for a stargazer the covision occurs passively, irresistibly: the door shuts, someone smiles, and he *experiences* an instantaneous estrangement. Personally, I am inclined to both forms, to the more or less intentional and to the totally passive, but it is the latter that carries me away from myself most forcefully and gives me a perspective on reality in which I am sadly unable either to remain or to move forward. In the example I mentioned, the elements of the series—*door shutting—smile—Antibes—rose*—no longer have their usual meanings, without my knowing *what* they have become. The transformation is like the phenomenon of *déjà vu*: as soon as the series begins the first elements become *door-smile*, and what follows becomes *Antibes-rose*—it becomes part of the complete figure and ceases to function as *Antibes* and as *rose*; likewise, the liberating elements (*door-smile*) are also integrated into the total pattern. One faces a startling crystallization, and if we sense it develop temporally—(1) *door* (2) *smile*—we can be sure that this is only because of psychological conditioning or the mediation of

the space-time continuum. In reality *everything occurs in a (is) simultaneity*: *door, smile*, and the rest of the elements that make up the pattern appear as facets or links, like a lightning bolt that transforms the glass outside of time. It is impossible to retain this vision, since we don't know how to dis-place ourselves. There remains only an anxiety, a trembling, a vague longing. Something was there, perhaps quite near. And now there is nothing but a rose inside a glass, on this side where *a rose is a rose is a rose*, and no more.

Ecumenics Sine Die

Les bourgeois c'est comme les cochons
Plus ça devient vieux, plus ça devient con
Jacques Brel song

"No sir," said Polanco indignantly, "I will never understand them insulting the bourgeois like that. If you think about it, they're the true citizens of the world. Why not? A Venezuelan, a Spanish, a French, and a Saudi Arabian bourgeois are much more united than a Chinese, a Peruvian, and a Russian Communist—who can be as Communist as you like but will always be separated by virulent nationalism. The bourgeois on the other hand share a single country, which is the bourgeoisie, and there they all lay the furniture out the same way: money here, religion there, sexual morality over there, and over there the striped shirt. All they're missing is Latin to bring back the longed-for catholicism of the Middle Ages; and these days, with translating machines, McLuhan, and English in twenty quick-and-easy lessons, believe me kid, they won't have much trouble."

It Is Regrettable That

Our living room is fairly large, but to think that in it Robert

We don't have too much furniture, which leaves a lot of room to receive parents and friends when they come to

Me in the chair by the lamp and my wife almost always on the stool where she can

There is only one table, narrow and long, that we use for

You can move around freely, look at the shelves in the library, and sit on the banquette built into

I think that is just where Robert was going to sit when, in the middle of the living room

It must have been ten in the evening, maybe ten-ten, the Mouniers agree, while my wife

Let's say ten-o-five, not to

Actually, we had just served coffee and Robert said something to Mme. Cinabre that

I think I remember that he had taken a cigarette and on the way to the banquette had

Anyway, he had put the cigarette in his lips when he stopped and

We heard the commotion and my wife looked up from her knitting and looked at Robert as if she couldn't

As for the Mouniers, they were sitting on the floor near the fireplace when

As for me, I had in my hand the cup of

A quiet agitation and Robert foundering, looking down at his feet as if it were so

My wife had always said that there in the living room it would be possible to

Not Paul, Paul was sure he would never

As far as I'm concerned, I would never want to be involved but I have to say just the same that Robert could

But I have to admit that on the spur of the moment it's quite understandable how a man

The cigarette in his mouth must have seemed strange to him because he took it out and held it between two fingers while

Mme. Cinabre, as you can imagine, could think of nothing but to make vague signs with

The Mouniers, who were on the floor, could see better and they exchanged glances as if

It must have been the left foot because Robert fell back, leaning against

"We must," said my wife after

"Wait just the same until," I replied, I who on principle

Sometimes it seemed so awful, and then, finally

"Who knows the depths of that area where," whispered Paul as if we didn't

The word *fathom* has always fascinated me, ever since

"Toss aside your cigarette when," the Mouniers suggested, demonstrating

And also *beacons, breakwaters, gales, foresail,* and

Probably fearing a fire that would only

It was not even ten-thirty and Robert could still expect

But who would have thought to go to him with

Especially considering that he already

"An agitation as if," said Paul, who was the one of us least

From where they were the Mouniers could see the rise of the

I think that he cried out once or twice but in such cases it is difficult to

"We have to throw him a," I said without too much

At least try with this

So plain in appearance, but a living room where

"It doesn't matter what," said Mme. Cinabre with a certain

She said that literally, as if we

Besides, the Mouniers were already sure that both feet

"I strongly doubt that they will function without," said Paul, who was the one of us most

I decided he was speaking of the pumps, because in fact the

At the last moment he threw away the cigarette, apparently in order

We could make it out as a little white staff that pitched and

In such cases you think of gulls, never of kingfishers, which would be

"If he had time to report his latitude to," said Paul, as if

The expression "wireless telegraphy" came into my mind, which in our time has fallen into

My wife had the impression that the knees of

But then again, what good is it to spread fear when it had not yet

We could telephone, but then we would have to explain that

The Mouniers seemed to want to help him by handing him the end of a

Yet they were undecided, which is natural, considering

We felt in sympathy with the Mouniers, but not when they wanted to take the

"It's almost to the," said Paul, with his air of

My wife stuck her knitting needles in the skein and looked at me, waiting perhaps for me to

It wasn't as easy as that, first you had to recognize that

We all tried not to disturb Robert, although

Moreover it was not a matter that the maid

It is well known that once admitted outsiders will

Paul ran to be sure that the doors and window would not let anyone

What was discouraging was that his cries were growing more and more

"These are surely albatrosses like," said Mme. Cinabre with that nostalgic tone she always

One of the Mouniers began to make swimming motions, not realizing that

The other, more aware of

I was moved by their courage, because in a house of well-educated people

"We have to ask if it wouldn't be better once and for all," said my wife, making a gesture that we

She expressed everyone's opinion that

I must admit that you had to feel a certain relief

Not for us apparently but for him, because finally the poor

The word is borborygmus and even

It's not a nice word but honesty obliges me to

"One might say a medusa who begins to," said Mme. Cinabre at last, whose images

Yes, a little, because the hair

As if innumerable minuscule fingers opened and closed upon the

My wife went out, carefully carrying the cup of undrunk coffee, and it seemed to us that

That sort of gesture merits a silent acknowledgment, because isn't it

After all, in a house like ours where

No one could say that we didn't do our best to

Marcel Duchamp; Or, Further Encounters Outside of Time

The games of time (which Alejo Carpentier calls the wars of time—wars of the flowers, games of Russian roulette) are games of billiards where caroms on a single surface reduce before and after to mere historical conveniences. This afternoon I had a game with Marcel Duchamp, another game among many. So it is not surprising that between the windows of this "this afternoon," which goes back two months, and *this* afternoon, as I correct and rewrite an awkward, stumbling text, occurred the ultimate rupture of Duchamp and time: here in Paris, three days ago, Duchamp died, dead as the *Great Glass* in Philadelphia, his cold final jest, snow settling slowly in the heart of a paperweight while the vulgar sun of habit and time goes on shining outside. Faithful to the lesson of the *Great Glass*, I will limit myself to the present of two months ago, I will speak of Duchamp as if I had not learned of this trivial accident, of what Mallarmé called *un peu profond ruisseau calomnie la mort*. Stricken by an embolism as he brushed his teeth before bed, Duchamp is now his final readymade, with the silent irony of being once more in the middle of the show, spared conventional greetings, a proud and distant cat who knows how to dream up, when he is bored, a perfect ball to play with.

The *petite histoire* of what happened to me today in Saignon began two years ago, became clear this afternoon at quarter after three, and rebounded backwards in time to strike another ball that I imagine in the year 1958 or 1959. Some readers will recall that earlier I wrote of a "bachelor machine" invented by Juan Esteban Fassio, and that there I alluded to Marcel Duchamp's visit to Buenos Aires in 1918, a journey so vague and imprecise that its reality cannot be doubted in the field of uncertainties in which he and I travel. There I described a series of unforeseen convergences, including Fassio and the author of *Hopscotch* working separately, unaware of a bridge that would finally link them, thanks to the transparent machinations of the *marchand du sel*. And today . . .

I hate ellipsis points, but what developed this afternoon is like a sort of metaphysical yawn, a break in the continuum, and total apprehension of those arrythmias depends on a not always easy openness to the mysterious. In New Delhi some months ago, Octavio Paz gave me an admirable essay on Duchamp to read, and there I found another mention of his elusive sojourn in Buenos Aires. Duchamp had told Octavio that he had spent a few months in our capital, doing nothing but playing chess at night and sleeping by day; he added that his arrival coincided with a coup d'état and other political perturbations "which complicated circula-

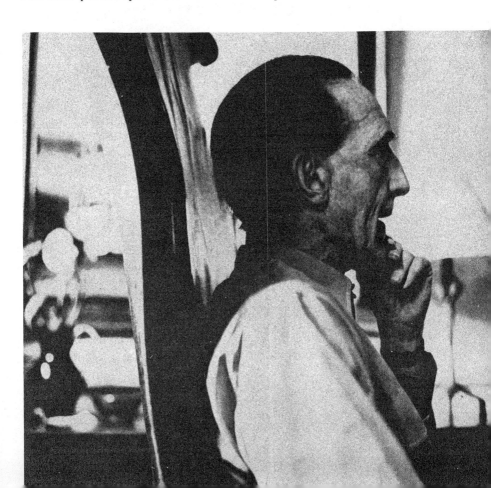

tion." As far as I know, 1918 was one of the few years in which there was not a coup d'état in my country, but the specialists can clarify that aspect of the matter, which is of no importance here; incidentally, to Duchamp's assertion that he did not meet a single "artist, poet, or thinking individual" in Buenos Aires, Paz rightly replied, "How unfortunate: I can't think of any temperament that would have been closer to yours than Macedonio Fernandez's." And truly this was unfortunate, but in Paris too, in the Café de la Régence, Duchamp saw Raymond Roussel from a distance and "neglected to introduce himself." Why not add that in 1942 I saw Vicente Huidobro at a distance on a Chilean beach and didn't want to bother him by introducing myself? There are so many better ways to get acquainted, a fact overlooked by frenetic arrangers of meetings; you don't call up eagles on the phone.

Now (which is to say, after the ellipsis points), this afternoon at three-fifteen, the mediocre little book by Pierre Cabanne, *Entretiens avec Marcel Duchamp*, presents me with the following:

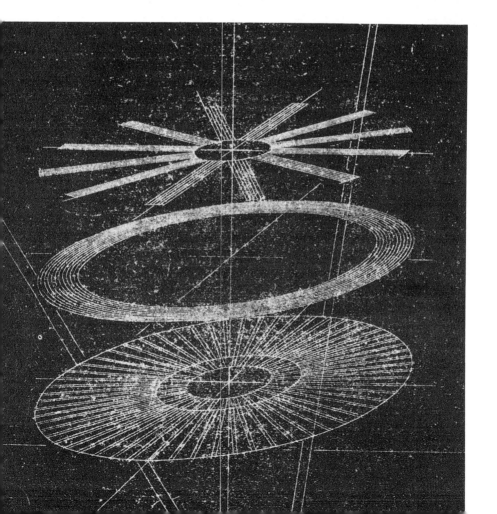

DUCHAMP: . . . in June/July of 1918 I left (the United States) for a neutral country called Argentina.

CABANNE: Carrying what you called "travel sculptures . . ."

DUCHAMP: Yes, travel sculpture . . . and in addition a number of rubber objects.

CABANNE: These were, in fact, little pieces of rubber of various sizes and colors, that you fastened to the ceiling . . .

DUCHAMP: And that filled the whole room, of course. They were mostly little bits of rubber bathing caps, which I cut up and glued in place, and which had no particular shape. At the bottom of each piece there was a thin rope and these were tied to the four corners of the room, so that when you entered the room you couldn't move around because these ropes blocked your way.

Much later, in '58 or '59, a ball in this billiards game that had been tapped by Duchamp's cuestick reached a book of mine, in which a certain Oliveira filled a room in Buenos Aires with rope so that no one could move through it. Who knows whether that room resembled the one where Marcel Duchamp hung his rope forty years earlier; a hotel can be converted to a madhouse in time, and vice versa, we've seen it happen. Without mentioning that if Marcel Duchamp had been offered a job in a circus or an asylum in 1918, he was capable of accepting. In what consists *my freedom?* Oliveira thought himself free that night, yet he did nothing but repeat the actions of Marcel on another night in Buenos Aires; between the two, unknowingly the bridge, I close the circuit. And that is enough for me, I won't complain. Better to be silent now, as they are.

Don't Let Them

It's obvious that they will try to buy out any poet or story writer with Socialist ideals whose writing has an influence in his time; it is no less obvious that only the writer himself can make sure that this doesn't happen.

But what is harder and more painful is to resist the pressure from your readers and those who share your views (the two are not always the same) to make you submit to every sort of sentimental and political extortion and let politeness lead you into the most public and spectacular forms of "compromise." There will come a day when they will ask you not for books but for lectures, debates, conferences, signatures, open letters, polemics, political commitments.

The poet or story writer's most arduous struggle is maintaining the delicate equilibrium that will allow him to continue to create work with air under its wings without becoming a holy monster, a worthy freak exhibited in history's daily carnival, so that his compromise can be worked out in the appropriate domain, where his foliage can put forth new growth.

Bitter but necessary moral: Don't let them buy you out, friend, but don't sell yourself either.

To Dress a Shadow

The hardest thing is to surround it, to fix its limit where it fades into the penumbra along its edge. To choose it from among the others, to separate it from the light that all shadows secretly, dangerously, breathe. To begin to dress it casually, not moving too much, not frightening or dissolving it: this is the initial operation where nothingness lies in every move. The inner garments, the transparent corset, the stockings that compose a silky ascent up the thighs. To all these it will consent in momentary ignorance, as if imagining it is playing with another shadow , but suddenly it will become troubled, when the skirt girds its waist and it feels the fingers that button the blouse between its breasts, brushing the neck that rises to disappear in dark flowing water. It will repulse the gesture that seeks to crown it with a long blonde wig (that trembling halo around a nonexistent face!) and you must work quickly to draw its mouth with cigarette embers, slip on the rings and bracelets that will define its hands, as it indecisively resists, its newborn lips murmuring the immemorial lament of one awakening to the world. It will need eyes, which must be made from tears, the shadow completing itself to better resist and negate itself. Hopeless excitement when the same impulse that dressed it, the same  thirst that saw it take shape from confused space, to envelop it in a thicket of caresses, begins to undress it, to discover for the first time the shape it vainly strives to conceal with hands and supplications, slowly yielding, to fall with a flash of rings that fills the night with glittering fireflies.

Saint-Tropez Night

for Joyce Mansour on his yacht,
privileged observation point

At ten at night the wharf and the city, the wharf and the decks of
the yachts with stairs going down to the wharf and to the city, its
people, those who roam the wharves in summer and those who
cruise in the yachts docked along the wharf and those who live in
the city, an oozing magma beneath the lights of the cafes and
shops on the streets of the port, the street lamps and the lanterns
of the yachts, a single mass flowing and oozing from the streets to
the wharf, from the yachts to the street, the magma of adolescents
oozing and flowing in the world of adults oozing and flowing in
the world of the elderly, a derisive skeleton of transit because the
body is plastic and flowing, Saint-Tropez at night oozes and flows
like seminal fluid, an interminably slow ejaculation that flows and
oozes from the wharves to the yachts, from the streets to the
wharf, the miniskirts and bleached hair and pants tailored to crev-
ices and protuberances, a circulation without defined laws, wharf
above or street below, golden chains with crosses between breasts
open like magnolias, splendid queens with colored headbands
and arms fastened to their hips, hands forward, Egyptian-style,
couples intertwined on the decks of the yachts, on the wharf, in
the street, the encounters and departures of transistors, carried
with oscillating indifference, from which music and the voices of
the announcers mix to make new noises, ephemeral mixtures like
the color combinations of blouses and hair, sometimes a contact
of hands and lips which is invented and prolonged when a couple
interrupts the current to be lost in their dream or their illusion of
the moment, immobile in whatever part of the city, the wharf, the
deck of a yacht, kissing in abolition of time that seems always to
speed along the seminal fluid that advances and undulates from
the yachts to the street, from the wharf to the yachts below the
floodlights and noise of the city: any point of observation on the
decks, on the wharf, or in the street is the same point of observa-

tion, a point from which will be seen the identical oozing of the
world of adolescents dominating the world of adults, the ambiguous couples and the even more ambiguous loners, the privileged
come-and-go of sensation, the passage of golden prisoners, the
file of those condemned to an endlessly costly and precarious idle-
ness, to a search that stretches from the wharves to the streets,
from the yachts to the wharf, a total incommunication that mixes
and confuses semi-nude young women, homosexuals bound to
their own beauty like languishing Narcissuses, who have spent
the entire day choosing a bracelet that is now displayed with a
disdainful smile that becomes the signal for the Norwegian sailor
or the elderly Yankee to propose the first cocktails, a sliding of
thighs and rumps, bare feet and tanned shoulders, from the
yachts to the street, from a cafe to a restaurant, interminably the
same diversity of skins and languages and laughs and music, with
no other end than an end to the night less dull than the one before,
or perhaps perfecting an experience of satiety, a cry from dead-
ened lips or liberating drugs, the hidden anxiety that moves that
serpent without head or tail tied to his own recurrence: except the
immobile motorcycle, planted like a bull in the middle of the
wharf, almost touching the stairs of one of the yachts where they
dance and drink and observe the chromed motorcycle that has
been there since the beginning of the night because its owner
must have gone aboard one of the yachts or into one of the houses
with windows opening onto the wharf, a Harley-Davidson removed from the series, a metal-plated minotaur that seems to
weigh heavily on the ground with a weight that goes beyond its
wheels and double support, a machine designed to conquer space
and the wind, a fuel tank of aluminum ending in a double exhaust,
accelerated by means of a lever beneath and attached to the flanks,
a red leather seat like an enormous horizontal heart where the
eyes fixed on the motorcycle probably imagine the buttocks of a
young English millionaire going a hundred-twenty miles an hour
through the hills at dawn, nude after an orgy and carrying on the
rear seat a mulatto with her hair trailing in the wind and her
breasts pressed against his shoulder blades as he revs the motor,
full of the delirium of highway and horizon, whatever the fantasy
of those who stop to look at the petrified machine, as self-con-
tained as anger ready to redden and strike out against the multitude that flows and oozes from the wharf to the streets, from the
yachts to the wharf, pausing singly, in couples, or in unruly
crowds that surround the Harley-Davidson abandoned by its

owner at the foot of the steps of a yacht where he may not be
among those who are drinking champagne on the deck and dancing semi-nude beneath shadows of masts and furtively descending into the cabins, and now some young woman touches the bow-
els of the motorcycle with the tip of her finger, runs a hand across
the handlebars, makes a gesture of mounting the red seat and then
does mount, gets settled among annoyed or insolent laughter,
feigns moving forward to accelerate the immobile machine that
holds her disdainfully, obliges her to dismount, to yield her place
to a drunken fisherman who jumps on the machine, grasps the
handlebars and imitates the roar of the motor, and is about to fall
off when a companion takes him from the seat with crude jokes,
and there are those who pretend indifference or knowledge of the
machine, men admiring the double exhaust, the size of the motor
encrusted in the genital guts of the metal bull, women darkly
excited by a machine that could carry them to the pleasure of
luxury hotels, to Fellini or Pieyre de Mandiargues festivals, like a
forerunner of the apartment with air conditioning and colored
fish, leopard wraps and generous checks, real life without type-
writers or storefronts in the morning, and sometimes not so much
this American dream but adventure that justifies the summer va-
cation, an invitation, a gesture, speeding through dunes into the
night, the taciturn Swede or occasional Italian who cuts the engine with a disdainful push to spread her mouth open or mouth
closed on the sand and possess her with neither pleasure nor cruelty, coldly, like the immobile machine that attends the ravishing,
the chromed bull that a blonde woman with heaving breasts caresses becoming momentarily Pasiphaë while her friend forgets
her, lost in an inspection of cylinders, odometer, and retracting
mirrors: the Omphalos, the center of the Saint-Tropez night, the
place of passage, the border where pause the trembling multitudes of the chosen, the privileged ones of the Western world, the
flower of European culture, the most precious lords of the consumer society, the hope of Christianity and liberalism and free
enterprise, the adolescents with wet mouths and uncertain geni-
tals, the men and women who crown the races and nationalities in
the streets and the wharf and the yachts, mixing and flowing in
a silent, rancorous collective orgasm that curls the mouths and
burns the bellies and the buttocks: the motorcycle coveted, caressed, violated, masturbated with eyes, hands, hair, shoulders,
buttocks of those who contemplate it, circling around it, joking,
pretending to dislike it or to know it intimately, pretending to

ignore it while they adore it, prostrating themselves before it, beneath it, submitting to its dominion, the macho motorcycle goat of the Saint-Tropez sabbath demanding the most lewd kiss from the platinum witches, the queens moist with love, luxurious epilog of a time that smells like an orchid, phosphorescent and slavering, lovely with fatuous fires, oozing in its vomit of luxury, poorly digested caviar, Joyce Mansour, that can be seen quite well, from the deck of your yacht that really can be seen quite well.

Regarding the Eradication of Crocodiles from Auvergne

The problem of the eradication of crocodiles from Auvergne has long troubled the governors and administrators of that region, who have stumbled over all sorts of obstacles in carrying out their task and have often been on the verge of abandoning it with plausible, but clearly fallacious, pretexts.

The pretexts are plausible because, in the first place, no one has ever admitted seeing a crocodile in Auvergne, so that from the start any attempt to exterminate them is surrounded with difficulties. The most sophisticated investigations, based on the latest findings of the Butantan Institute and the FAO, like similar investigations in which one never addresses the central proposition directly, instead accumulating tangential data that can, using a structuralist methodology, expose the object sought, have always resulted in complete failure. Both the police forces and the psychologists who have conducted these investigations believe that the negative responses and bewilderment of the interrogated subjects prove unequivocally the existence of vast numbers of crocodiles in Auvergne and that, given the mentality of the inhabitants of that region, there must be a tacit, ancestral understanding among them that causes them to react with wide-eyed astonishment when they are interviewed in their farms and fields and asked if they have ever seen a crocodile in the immediate vicinity, or if a

crocodile has ever eaten their eggs or their children, that is, their means of existence and continuance.

There can no longer be any doubt that nearly all the inhabitants have seen crocodiles, but the belief that the first to speak out will suffer grave injury to person and property makes them bide their time in the hope that someone else, driven beyond his endurance by the devastation these pernicious animals have wrought on his fields and stables, will decide to lodge a complaint with the authorities. According to the calculations of the OMS, four or five centuries have already elapsed in that expectation, and obviously the crocodiles have taken advantage of this to multiply and proliferate freely throughout Auvergne.

In recent years the authorities have managed to convince a few of the more educated and intelligent countrymen that they will not be harmed if they reveal the existence of the crocodiles, whereas their eradication will instead greatly improve the quality of life in this French province. To this end, social workers and psychologists specially sent from the urban centers have offered the strongest assurances that announcing the existence of the crocodiles will not bring one any harm—certainly no one will be asked to leave his lands to repeat his testimony in Clermond Ferrand or any other city, his property will not be invaded by police, and his wells will not be poisoned. All that is needed, in fact, to launch a full-scale attack on these dangerous beasts is for one inhabitant to say the word, and the authorities will set in action a plan that has been in the works for years for the greater public good.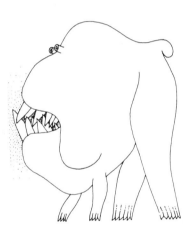

Nothing has come of these promises. As yet no one has admitted seeing a crocodile in Auvergne, even though our investigators possess scientific evidence showing that even very young children are perfectly aware of their existence and talk about it among themselves when they are playing or drawing, so the crocodiles continue to enjoy the malignant impunity afforded them by their spurious nonexistence. Needless to say, these circumstances make their eradication more than problematical, and the danger of swimming in the streams or walking through the fields grows greater every year. The frequent disappearance of minors, which the police are forced for statistical purposes to attribute to speleological mishaps or white slav-

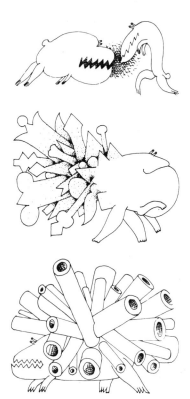

ery, is undoubtedly the work of the crocodiles. Often neighboring farmers argue and even kill each other over vanished cows and sheep for which they hold each other responsible. From the obstinate silence that follows these bloody disputes, the psychologists have drawn the conclusion that the true culprits were crocodiles, and that the personal accusations came from the desire to feign an ignorance that in the end benefits no one. How else can we explain the fact that no one has ever found the skeleton of a crocodile that has died of age or illness? The region's trout fishermen could surely answer that question, but they too hold their tongues; yet it is not difficult to guess the reason for the fires frequently lit at night under the pretext of making woodash, where under thick layers of branches and trunks lie remains that would finally prove the existence of these dangerous animals.

In the hope of surprising a slip-up, an involuntary admission, or some other lucky break that will at last furnish the official proof that is required, the authorities long ago made the necessary arrangements for the eradication of the vast numbers of crocodiles that infest Auvergne. Thanks to the enlightened cooperation of UNESCO, the best African, Indian, and Thai specialists have explained methods and provided instruction that will permit the eradication of the plague within a few months. In every district headquarters there is an official who controls strategically situated stockpiles of arms and the most lethal poisons and has the power to execute a bold offensive against the crocodiles. Each week practice exercises are carried out in the police schools for the battle against the crocodiles and, with the coming of autumn, the season when these reptiles lay their eggs and show a greater tendency to lie in the sun and become lethargic, these forces will initiate extensive maneuvers in the rural areas, including dragging the rivers, exploring the numerous caves and pits, and systematically searching the fields and barns where the females can hide to raise their young. All of this, however, has so far assumed the guise of an ordinary campaign against annoying insects, predatory birds, and illicit hunting, because the authorities, understandably, shrink from exposing themselves to ridicule for persecuting animals whose existence is not borne out by any concrete evidence. Nonetheless, inhabitants are surely aware of the real purpose of these operations and contribute cheerfully to their execution, which will result in the obvious benefits already mentioned, since the psychologists who accompany the police on their forays have noted that any casual mention of crocodiles, made casually or to entice an unofficial statement, are greeted with signs of astonishment and hilarity, which, even if they don't fool anyone, compromise the smooth development of the operations, which demand absolute cooperation between the inhabitants and the armed forces.

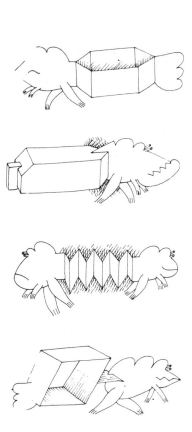

In summary, though this assertion may appear a bit abstract, Auvergne may be considered effectively protected against crocodiles, whose depredations will be terminated with unusual efficiency. From a strictly theoretical and logical point of view, we can even affirm that crocodiles do not exist in Auvergne, since everything is prepared for their extinction. Unfortunately, as long as circumstances do not permit these operations to be undertaken, Auvergne will remain infested with crocodiles, which constitute a permanent threat to the economy and well-being of that lovely region of France.

All Spheres
Are Cubes

The first problem is always my aunt. When I tell her that all spheres are cubes, she turns the color of spinach. She freezes in the doorway, leaning on her broom, and looks at me with an expression in her eyes that suggests a temptation to spit on me. Then she goes and sweeps the patio without singing the boleros that are the joy of our home in the morning.

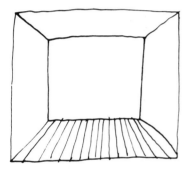

The second difficulty is the sphere itself. Unfortunately, as soon as I plunk it down on an inclined plane, where any cube should be happy, it pulls up all its little feet and heads for the ground like a bolt of lightning, rolling, for good measure, under the dresser where by a strange coincidence fuzzballs gather in large numbers. Getting it out from under there is a nasty business, I have to roll up my sleeves and since I am allergic to dust I begin to sneeze so hard that great clouds of it come out with the cube and immediately set off a severe asthma attack, I'm unable to go to the office, Mr. Rosenthal threatens to withhold a day of my pay, my father starts to look the way he did when he slept under the skies on his desert expedition, and my aunt always ends up retrieving the sphere and putting it where the family thinks it ought to be, in other words, on the bookcase in the living room between the works of Dr. Cronin and the stuffed bird that belonged to my brother who died in infancy.

My father has asked me twice why I persist in such nonsense, but I have not dignified this with an answer because his passivity discourages me. Can it be that everyone is willing to let this miserable ball impose its will on them? Again I struggle with the sphere that is, I know, a cube; I set it on an inclined plane, my

aunt turns to spinach, the dustballs, vicious cycle. Then I wait for my asthmatic attack to end, and I place the sphere back on the inclined plane, because that is where it should go, and not in the living room next to the little bird.

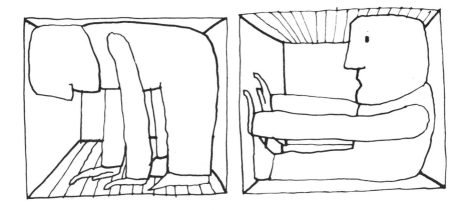

Strange Choices

He is not sure.

He is not at all sure.

They have offered him a banana, a treatise by Gabriel Marcel, three pairs of nylon socks, a coffee maker still under warranty, a flexible blonde, early retirement, but he still isn't sure.

His reticence causes insomnia in several functionaries, a priest, and the local cops.

Since he isn't sure they have begun to ask whether they may not have to expel him from the country.

They have delicately insinuated as much.

He has replied, "In that case I'll take the banana."

Naturally, they were suspicious.

It would have been more reassuring if he had chosen the coffee maker, or at least the blonde.

It just seems strange that he would choose the banana.

The whole matter will have to be reviewed from the beginning.

Salvador Dalí:
Sin Valor Adalid

Haces bien en poner banderines de aviso
Federico Garcia Lorca, *Oda a Salvador Dalí*

Everyone has his compasses and barometers; personally, I have always found that Dalí serves admirably for judging the orientation of those who judge him. When I want to know quickly about someone who is introduced to me without better references, I arrange to fit Dalí into some opening in the conversation. If they say (I summarize an opinion that might take ten minutes), "He is a magnificent son of a bitch," I feel that contact has been made and that things will go well. If on the other hand the response is along the lines of "Except for his painting, he is a morally depraved being," I terminate the conversation and beat a hasty retreat because I have obviously come across a *good* man and few things in life bother me more than that. The two opinions seem alike, since they both involve (and sometimes belabor) a moral judgement, but you have to be there, to hear the tone and implications of the two opinions to understand how they differ. That Dalí is a son of a bitch is a euphemism that falls upon the head (another euphemism) of a poor Spanish lady, when it is really he who deserves a brickbat smack in the

moustache-antennae. No one has resisted such brickbats less than Salvador Dalí, accepting, even welcoming them; his infamy is like Aretino's, Curzio Malaparte's, Louis-Ferdinand Céline's, Maurice Sachs's, Jean Genet's, William Burroughs's. Some comments about Sachs I wrote in 1950 and rediscovered today among some old pages perfectly clarify this viewpoint: "N. and his wife were scandalized by the ignoble figure of Sachs, as he appears in

The Sabbath. I attempted not a defense (what is there to defend there?) but a check against that overflowing of loathing behind which one perceives the salving of consciences. Certainly Sachs is a perfect *salaud*, but my friends should not forget that *he is the first to admit it.* We are surrounded by lives of bad faith beginning with our own, and we seldom acknowledge it beyond saying "I, a poor fisherman, etc.," or "Among my many faults, etc." Sachs never lapses into this sort of periphrasis, which disguises an underlying message: "Sure, everyone has his faults, but after all . . ." He is honest enough to know that he is not honest; beginning a possible biography, he sends his calling card: *Maurice Sachs, swine.* What does your card say, N.? What does mine say?

"The error of N. may lie in his failure to make the critical distinction between what is told in *The Sabbath* and the act of telling it. It's the same with Céline or Genet. Much of what he relates is atrocious, but *his* telling it gives it a significance beyond the 'fictional.' If N. is right about Sachs's moral exhibitionism, the way we *vicariously* enjoy pathological states (most often through popular psychoanalytic or criminological studies, which are brothels for bystanders) should make us recognize the value *sui generis* of someone who assumes such states and narrates them without the refuge of the third person, without the mediation of a couch and the symbolism of dreams and families. Let's be honest at least in this admission: every 'horrible' book—*The Sabbath, Journey to the End of the Night, Miracle of the Rose*—calls into question

the entire literature built on Judeo-Christian morality, defies it and demands truths more applicable to values that are perpetually in crisis. Before these harsh, unavoidable, and insistent cesspools, those who continue to seek in literature an aesthetic version of the eternal battle between Ormuz and Ariman, confident that the battle will favor Ormuz, are outraged by the seemingly incomprehensible phenomenon of Ariman sometimes being able to speak directly rather than being limited to counterblows and games of negation. This simply isn't done, a swine has no right to be a great writer; he cannot be allowed to dwell with us in the city of letters."

Dalí, it goes without saying, is as much Ariman as Leonardo da Vinci or any of those artists and thinkers whom he claims to incarnate, and thus to place behind him. To send him to the devil is to render him homage that will immediately win us a telegram from him. The historical and social function of Dalí is fundamentally Socratic, but like a negative Socrates, disinterested in *progress* on any level. He is the *monster*, which is to say, that apparent exception that all of a sudden lays bare the monstrosity, until then dissimulated, of normal persons. If Dalí is guilty of ignoble actions (I have no personal knowledge of any, and those I've heard of do not seem so shocking), none of them can possibly attain an infamy universal enough to justify the choir of virtuous protests and condemnations that always greet them. There is a horror of Dalí much like the sadistic hypocrisy that feigns horror before the execution. Dalí calmly mounts the stairs, passes the rope around the neck of André Breton or Pablo Picasso, and hangs them without the slightest remorse. But the horrified crowds who attend the executions contain many who have hanged Breton and Picasso privately for years, who have quartered them and burned them on slow fires over countless cups of coffee, in gatherings in Valencia or Paris or Buenos Aires, but who steal away when asked to sign for their opinions. Dalí is a new Socrates for his ability to reveal individual and collective failings, and he is Christ for his assumption of the sins of the world; to the positive images of the sophists and messiahs he opposes a mere maieutic concern; once stupidity, vanity, received ideas, artistic tradition, spiritual progress as the bourgeois understands it have been laid bare and sufficiently ridiculed by his own actions and especially by the reactions that his actions occasion and desire, he loses interest in the affair. The beautiful, the good, and the true matter little to him and even less washing away the sins of the world. He is not the friend of Alcibiades nor the lamb of God; he is an old Catalan *compadre*, with more tricks than a circus horse, he is a witness to the century, a stupendous son of a bitch. When Federico eulogized him for flying the flags of warning, he was right. His scissors have sheared a multitude of Samsons overly sure of their moral strength. Someday, perhaps, humanity will write its history without people like Dalí; for the moment it can only deny him, the way lepers cover the mirrors in their houses. Beside the famous, just, and Latin anagram *Avida dollars*, I would like to set another that is more pleasant, symbolic, and French, with which I take my leave: *Dors, Dalila, va.*

Intolerance

I have never been able to abide yawning, especially out of the mouth of a policeman. It's more than I can bear. If I see one yawning on a streetcorner I walk over and give him one of those back-and-forth slaps that are like a pigeon's wings flapping. That has already cost me three broken ribs and a total of fifteen months in jail, not to mention bruises and scrapes. But there is nothing I can do and the only way these misfortunes can be avoided is by encountering policemen who like their work and devote themselves passionately to the problems of traffic circulation. It's even worse with priests: if I catch one yawning, my indignation knows no bounds. As soon as I can, I go to mass and scrutinize the officiant from the front rows. If I surprise him in a yawn at the moment of elevation, as has happened to me twice now, something stronger than me drives me to the altar and you don't want to know the rest. There are voluminous dossiers about me in the pontifical courts, I know, and in certain churches I am anathema and get the heave the minute I enter the nave. Personally, I love to yawn, it's hygienic and my eyes fill with tears that flush out many impurities. But the idea of yawning would never occur to me as I wait, with my stenographer's notebook in hand, for Mr. Rosenthal to dictate one of his letters in which he rejects some proposal with a great waste of words. Sometimes I get the impression that Mr. Rosenthal is disturbed by my failure to yawn, because my concentration on my work has obliged him to raise my salary. I am almost sure that if a yawn were sometime to escape me Mr. Rosenthal would silently thank me; it is clear that he finds so much professional interest unsettling. But I carefully disguise the yawns that accumulate in my throat and palate over four and a half hours; therefore, if I see a policeman yawn when I leave, I can't contain myself and rush over to give him a few slaps. It's strange, but it doesn't give me any satisfaction, it's a little as if in

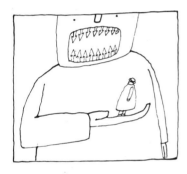

that moment I were both Mr. Rosenthal and the cop, I mean, as if Mr. Rosenthal were slapping me in the middle of the street. I almost prefer the kicks and jail, or excommunication if it's a priest, because those are things that conçern only me, not one of these episodes where nobody is sure who is who.

Stairs Again

Somewhere among the works of someone I would rather forget it is said that there are stairs for climbing and others for going down; what is not mentioned is that there can also be stairs for going backwards.

Users of these practical devices readily understand that all stairs go backwards if you climb them backwards, but *what remains to be seen* is the result of such an unusual activity. Try it on an exterior stairway; once you get past the impression of inconvenience (and vertigo), with each step you will discover a new horizon, which emerges from the preceding one but at the same time corrects, criticizes, and expands it. Now recall how a moment ago, when you climbed the usual way, the world, behind you, was abolished by that same stairway, by its hypnotic succession of steps; whereas you only have to climb up backwards for the horizon, at first blocked by the wall of your garden, to leap out to the Peñaloza fields, then embrace the Turkish mill, burst through the cypresses of the cemetery, and with a little luck at last attain the true horizon, that of the schoolteacher's definition. And the sky? And the clouds? Count them when you are at the very top, drink the sky that falls upon your face through its immense funnel. Maybe then, when you make a half turn and enter

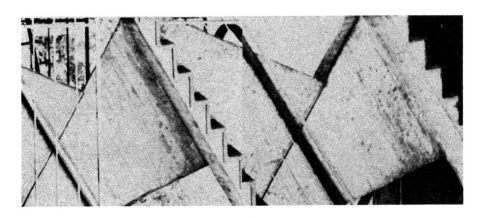

the rooms on the top floor of your house, your everyday domestic life, you will realize that there too you should look at things the same way, that a mouth, a love, a novel, should all be climbed backwards. But be careful: it is easy to totter and fall, some things can only be seen by climbing backwards while others resist, fearing this way of climbing that lays them bare; insisting on their viewpoints behind their masks, they revenge themselves cruelly on those who climb backwards the better to see the rest, the Peñaloza fields or the cypresses of the cemetery. Beware of that chair, beware that woman.

How the Jaguars Sap Our Strength

We have to recognize that we are much weakened by the jaguars. In our house on the rue Blomet there are jaguars in every corner. You might not have noticed, since they are not often spotted, but ultimately that is how they infiltrate us. Believe me, in the morning we'll find they have even gotten into the butter; look at Hortense, my wife, who butters her toast so sadly, and perhaps you will be able to see the minuscule red thread that converts the stick of butter into something that wavers between a fantastic marzipan and a polyvalent toothpaste. The jaguar has been through there, scratching Hortense's fingers along the way, and that is why Hortense is so sad as she butters her toast. And that's not even mentioning the jaguars in the shower, that former caress now capable of flaying us with its wet slap. One time I was nearly scalped, but now I have the solution: I no longer wash myself—and the die is cast.

There are the large ones, of course, the terrible ones that come out in the night, but if we think about it we have to admit that the small ones (so cute, little bugs!) are the most annoying. There is the jaguar of the lampstand, the one of the chiming clock, the one who hides in a sock, the one who does his figuring with us, 44, 35, 2271, and carry 3, who stubbornly subtracts us, divides us, reduces us to a vague step in even vaguer statistical calculations. Among the small ones (there are some like pencil erasers or matchbooks) the most notable is the one who hates commas, so that as soon as you write one your sleeve wipes it off the page; I am taking advantage of his not having appeared today to put commas all over the place. Hortense, who keeps a sense of perspective, says that the worst of the jaguars is the one in the vacuum cleaner, because his tendency to vomit has always horrified us. Oh, you would think you were in a madhouse if it weren't for the others, the real ones, because in the final analysis you can't take the tiny ones too seriously. But you don't see the big ones very often, almost never, they are cloistered like nuns. There is mostly the smell (in bed at night, on the stairs in the morning) and the infrared friction on her marvelous skin that wakens my poor Hortense from her dreams. They seldom roar but they are there, silently growling around the bed, under the table, or in the cupboards. We live terribly weakened by these large jaguars and can hardly get up the strength for our activities, work, hygiene, or even love. If they jumped out at this very moment, what a maelstrom of claws and tongues there would be! A strict but passive vigilance grants us a reprieve, guarantees that although they circle around us weaving their fiendish plots, at least they will not spring at us from the front. What reassures us is the notion that everything is in a sense a jaguar, that the bed itself, that ultimate fortress of the Christian couple, is a jaguar, and the house too, oh yes! the house itself could be a jaguar, even if sophisticated minds hesitate to accept that hypothesis. Thus the very magnitude of our suspicions ends up calming us a little, for we feel that we are caught in a conveyor belt that runs from the smallest one in the tea canister to the most enormous, whose size surpasses our poor understanding. I know that Hortense refuses to accept such thoughts of knobby velvet push-rods, choosing to limit herself to the visible confines of the bedroom and stairs, but I insist on expanding her comprehension of these matters; sometimes I have managed to surprise in her eyes a look of melancholy lucidity, and I tell myself that she too could climb mentally from jaguar to jaguar to reach the one that includes all the others. Because to tell the truth, not only the house but also the city is a jaguar, the city and around it the country, that proud nation whose essential nature is revealed when you think of its eternal antagonism toward the Russian bear, the Prussian eagle, the English bull, and high French culture. And that is how the jaguars sap our strength, so Hortense and I now prefer to live in the country, as far away as possible, even at the edge of those swamps where chunks of rotting cork float, where owls go only when the weather permits.

The Canary
Murder Case II

It's terrible, my aunt invited me to her birthday party, I bought
her a canary as a present, I arrived and no one was there, my
datebook was wrong, on my return the canary sang like crazy on
the subway, waves of passengers were getting on, I bought a ticket
for the creature so they would respect it, as I got off I hit a woman
in the head with the cage and she snarled at me, I reached home
bathed in birdseed, my wife had run off with a notary, I stiffened
and fell down in the hall and crushed the canary, the neighbors
called for an ambulance and took it off on a stretcher, and I stayed
all night sprawled out in the hall, eating birdseed and listening to
the telephone in my room, it must have been my aunt calling and
calling so I wouldn't forget her birthday, she always counts on my
present, poor aunt.

On Graphology
as an Applied Science

It happened that a gentleman had an idea: if all handwriting preserves within its fly tracings the character and therefore the destiny of a person, like the grooves on a disc when you know how to be a stylus, then you would only have to write exactly like Napoleon to set in action the inverse process and produce, not a Dvořák quartet brought to you by a spiral and a little motor, but Bonaparte, who at this very moment, having completed five months of handwriting study, leaves his house on the rue de la Convention and doesn't go a block before he is seen by four streetsweepers going about their tasks, and the legendary magnetism of the Eagle of Austerlitz overwhelms not only the streetsweepers but also a woman selling eggs in a doorway, instantly transforming them into soldiers, not to mention a number of priests, three masons, and the salespeople at the nearest hardware shop, all of whom rush to line up behind the Emperor, so that a small but select and, most of all, fervent troop advances along the rue Vaugirard as several dumbfounded neighbors contemplate this spectacle from their windows and discuss it, shocked and horrified, until the moment the Emperor raises his eyes and lifts his arms, and then the first bits of paper about the great triumph rain down all around him, since we are, after all, well into the second half of the twentieth century and the outward signs of idolatry and celebration have changed considerably, thanks to the widespread democratic customs of the Americans.

Naturally, the advance of the Napoleonic column, now approaching the heights of the rue de Rennes, causes alarm in the prefecture, and two paddy wagons, together with the inevitable Red Cross observer, set out to intercept the troops, which have grown considerably along the way, thanks to several vociferous harangues delivered in an impeccable Corsican accent every five blocks, and they appear ready to cross the Seine and invade the Left Bank, where the banking and commercial institutions, warned by radio and helicopter, organize a first line of defense and direct urgent telegrams to the United Nations, the Pope, and the International Monetary Fund, all with response prepaid. All it takes is an order from the Emperor and in minutes a spirited batallion of cadets made up of the kids from the lycée on Boulevard Pasteur overpower the mild resistance of fifty policemen halfheartedly summoned by a prefect who couldn't take a student prank seriously. When a Molotov cocktail made by a plumber from the rue des Canettes—immediately promoted to brigadier—torches a fire engine and several of its occupants, including two ladies who were admiring the length of its hoses, the authorities realize that the situation has got out of control, particularly in view of the sizable segment of the population rushing to place itself at the command of the Emperor, who appears at the end of the line dressed in a wide-lapeled uniform and bicorne brought to him en route by an old-clothes man who lost his paralysis and became a colonel. The attack on the bridges of the Seine, a claw or pincer operation, proves successful, since the mostly academic defense of the city police is destroyed by machine-gun fire from a corps of parachutists who join Napoleon with their arms and chutes in mid-fall, just as it appears they will reduce the rebellion to mincemeat and derision. Over the Solferino Bridge, over the Royal, over the Carroussel the Emperor's hordes advance, the Louvre falls, along with several armored cars and land rockets of German design waiting uneasily beside it, the Tuilleries fall and the children playing with boats in the fountain rush to the hero with bouquets of flowers and their liberated mothers, night falls on the victorious army as it erects tents and starts bonfires to feast beneath the chestnut trees; everyone already knows that next morning the Emperor will launch a march down the broad boulevards where the remaining enemy forces and their reserves of gold are entrenched for a last, desperate stand. The Pope's message arrives around midnight: "Dominus vobiscum, the most primitive peoples make holes here and there for burying their dead, and in place of the fracas of cannonfire a bipartite conference will substitute the . . ." (the text goes on at length). Tired and proud, Napoleon relents; he doesn't know that in London a man is beginning a race against time that will lead to the Emperor's downfall, seated before yellowing pages hastily obtained from venerable collections, surrounded by grim-faced functionaries, dietitians who inject his muscles with rich proteins to ward off sleep. Forty-eight hours later, overruling the dilatory maneuvers of his Chancellor and Security Council, the Emperor gives the order to renew the offensive; he doesn't know that an airplane has just landed at Le Bourget, bringing a man who descends stiffly and laconically, projecting a terrible strength, gives an almost cursory salute, and assumes command of the troops that have been awaiting his arrival. At Porte Saint-Denis the imperial army will meet the regiments of the Iron Duke: a certain Grouchy will fail to arrive on time, a certain Cambronne will say what has to be said on such occasions, the Imperial Eagle will see the sun rise from the roof of the Lafayette Galleries. Right now the proprietor of that noble establishment is asking himself whether its name shouldn't be changed to Waterloo; all that holds him back is a long-standing respect, a few monuments scattered around Paris, that sort of thing. One suspects that he will be persuaded.

Some Facts
for Understanding
the Perkians

They too have invented the wheel and their sturdy chariots roll and resound over the entire land of Perk. Their wheel, however, differs from ours in that its circumference is not at all perfect: at a certain point they have left a bump, a slight protuberance that departs from the circular line and returns to it almost imperceptibly, and in fact it would remain imperceptible if the wheel remained immobile, but the chariots roll and resound over the entire territory of Perk and you have just seated yourself on a nice soft cushion, the cart starts off, travels noisily but smoothly for four or five feet and suddenly you take your first bounce into the air and return to your seat, leap again, seat yourself again, and you will be in luck if the charioteer has thought to adjust the wheels so that the four bumps hit the ground at the same time because then the bouncing will be almost pleasant, like a horse's trot you might say, rising up without violence every ten seconds, but there are also disorderly charioteers in Perk and if the bumps come around at random, it turns out that you just come down from the first one and land on the cushion when the second bump hits the ground and the chariot jumps up into the air again and that's tough, that's a shock, you might lose your balance if, almost simultaneously, another bump hits the ground, or doesn't when you expect it to, there is an oscillation and a dissonance between the cushion, the chariot, and you. It's no use putting your foot down and saying, "In our countries," etc. They will give you a pained look and express regret that "In our countries. . . ." You will have to get back in the vehicle, you can't understand that civilization if you refuse to travel bound by bound, on the cushion and off of the cushion, concordant or successive bumps, one then

three, two by two, three then one or all four followed by a perfectly calm, comfortable ride, which lasts just long enough for
you to begin to settle into your cushion and steal a glance at the
roadway and then woof! a bound, two bounds, cushion, leap,
descent, you go down, cushion comes up, and you meet halfway
(in the worst place), you rebound, then are tossed violently upwards, and the cushion goes down again, deafening silence for
two or three seconds, then back down on the cushion fwoop! and
then nothing more, a little calm bit of road and then woop! another bound.

This then explains why the Perkians have such a convulsive
worldview. In place of a single tree, which we would call *a tree*,
for example, they tend to see at least three, the *cushion-tree*, the
bounding-tree, and the *descending-tree*, and in fact they are
right to have these three views and to distinguish them from each
other, for the cushion-tree is composed of a trunk and foliage
as are our own, the bounding-tree is mostly canopy, and the descending-tree is mainly trunk—but to these three trees are added
many others if it happens that the charioteer has not bothered

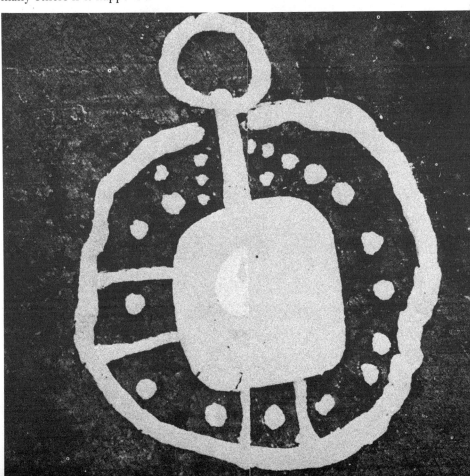

to synchronize the bumps (see above). Then in that total ar-rhythm of rises and falls there can be not only *tttrrreeeeee* but also *tttrrrttteeetttrrrttteee*, as well as countless other variations. There is of course no need to explain that this typographic repre-sentation is only a metaphor to suggest the effect of the convul-sion of images on Perkian semantics, logic, and, ultimately, entire history and culture, of which we will some day speak if the bumps woop per plop mit.

Siestas

One day, in a time without horizon, she remembered how Aunt Adela would listen to the record with the voices and choruses in the afternoon, and her own sadness when the voices would begin—a woman, a man, and then many voices singing something that she couldn't understand, and the green jacket with explanations for adults, *Te lucis ante terminum, Nunc dimittis*; Aunt Lorenza said it was Latin and it was about God and things like that, so Wanda got tired of not understanding, of being sad like when Teresita put on the Billie Holiday record at her house and they listened to it, smoking, because Teresita's mother was at work and her father had also gone out on business or else was napping through siesta, so they could smoke as much as they wanted, but listening to Billie Holiday was a beautiful sadness that made you want to lie down and cry with happiness, it was so good in Teresita's room with the window shut, with the smoke, listening to Billie Holiday. In Wanda's house they weren't allowed to sing those songs because Billie Holiday was black and she had died from taking drugs, Aunt Maria made her spend an extra hour at the piano practicing arpeggios, Aunt Ernestina began her speech about the youth of today, *Te lucis ante terminum* reverberated in the room where Aunt Adela sewed by the light of a crystal globe full of colored water, which concentrated (it was lovely) all the light of the lamp. It was better at night when Wanda slept in the same bed as Aunt Lorenza for then there was no Latin, nor discourses on tobacco and degenerates in the street, Aunt Lorenza put out the light after prayers and they talked for a while about things, usually about the dog Grock, and when Wanda went to sleep she was reconciled, protected from the sadness of the house by the warmth of Aunt Lorenza, who panted softly, a little like Grock, warm and curled up slightly and breathing contentedly like Grock on the rug in the dining room.

"Aunt Lorenza, don't let me dream about the man with the artificial hand any more," Wanda had pleaded the night of her nightmare. "Please, Aunt Lorenza, please."

Afterwards she talked about this with Teresita, and Teresita had laughed, but it was not a laughing matter, and Aunt Lorenza hadn't laughed either, drying Wanda's tears, giving her a glass of water, and calming her little by little, helping her get rid of the images, a mixture of memories of last summer and her nightmare, the man who looked so much like those in Teresita's father's art book, or the dead-end passageway at dusk, where the man dressed in black had trapped her, had approached her slowly, then stopped and looked at her with the moon full on his face, the glasses with the metal rims, the shadow of his bowler hat obscuring his face, and then the movement of the right arm reaching out to her, the mouth with its thin lips, the scream or the flight that had saved her at the end, the glass of water and the caresses of Aunt Lorenza before a slow frightened return to a sleep that lasted into the afternoon, Aunt Ernestina's laxative, fresh soap and advice, the house again and *Nunc dimittis*, but in the end permission to go play with Teresita, even though that girl did not inspire confidence, with the education her mother was giving her, she was capable of teaching her things, but in the end it's better than seeing her with this fallen face, and a bit of distraction can't do her harm, it used to be that children embroidered or practiced scales during siesta, but the youth of today.

"They're worse than fools, they're idiots," Teresita had said, offering a cigarette stolen from her father. "What aunts you have taking care of you, girl. And they gave you a laxative? Did you go or not? Hey, look what Chola gave me, all the autumn styles, but first look at these pictures of Ringo and tell me if he's not adorable, look at this one with his shirt open. Look at his hair, see."

Later she wanted to hear more about the nightmare, but Wanda couldn't stand to talk about it then when a vision of her flight suddenly returned to her, the mad rush through the alley, and it wasn't the nightmare but it must have been the end of the nightmare that she had forgotten when she woke up screaming. At least before, at the end of last summer, she could have talked about it with Teresita, but she never spoke out because she was afraid that Teresita would gossip with Aunt Ernestina, at that time Teresita was still allowed at her house and her aunts wormed things out of her with treats and candy, until they had a falling out with her mother and wouldn't let her over anymore, although they still let Wanda go to her house sometimes when they had afternoon visitors and wanted to be left in peace. Now she could have told Teresita everything but there wasn't any point because it was exactly the same, just like the art book, and nothing actually happened, like those streets in the art book that disappeared into the distance, the same as in the nightmare.

"Teresita, open the window a crack, it's stifling all shut up like this."

"Don't be stupid, then my mom would know we've been smoking. La Rosada has a nose like a bloodhound, it's like walking on eggs around here."

"So? They won't beat you."

"Sure, you'll go back to your place and what do you care. What a baby you are."

But Wanda wasn't a baby, even if Teresita said so sometimes, though not so often anymore since the hot afternoon when they talked about things and Teresita showed her; afterwards everything was different even though Teresita still called her a baby sometimes when she was irritated.

"I'm not a baby," said Wanda, blowing smoke out her nose.

"Okay, okay, don't get on your high horse. You're right, I was just a little upset. The best thing would be to take our clothes off and have some wine with ice in it. I'll tell you something, that nightmare was caused by Papa's picture book, I know the man didn't have an artificial hand in it, but I mean who can figure dreams? Look at me, how I'm filling out."

It didn't show under her blouse, but it was different when she took it off. She became a woman, her face changed. Wanda was embarrassed to undress and show that her chest was almost flat. One of Teresita's shoes went flying toward the bed, the other disappeared under the sofa. It was true, he was just like the men in Teresita's father's art book, men dressed entirely in black who were in almost every picture. Teresita had shown her the book one afternoon during siesta, right after her papa left and the house was as empty and silent as the rooms in the houses in the book. Shoving each other and laughing nervously, they climbed up to the top floor, where Teresita's parents sometimes called them for tea in the library, like proper young ladies, and on those days there was no chance to smoke and drink wine in Teresita's bedroom because La Rosada would sniff them out at once, so they took advantage of the house being all theirs and climbed shouting and pushing like now Teresita was pushing Wanda so that she fell on the blue couch, and she pulled down her slip almost in the same motion so that she was naked in front of Wanda and the two of them looked at each other with slightly breathless smiles until Teresita started to laugh and said was she nuts, didn't she know hair like Ringo's curls grew there. "But I have hair there too," said Wanda. "It started last summer." The same as in the art book where all the women had lots; in almost every picture they came and went or were sitting or lying down in fields or train stations ("They're crazy," was Teresita's opinion) and looked at each other just as they were now and the moon was always full even if it wasn't always in the picture, and everything took place under those full moons, the women walked naked through streets and train stations, passing by as if they didn't see a thing and were terribly alone, and sometimes the men in black suits or gray overcoats watched them come and go or studied precious stones under a glass without taking off their hats.

"You're right," said Wanda. "He looked a lot like the men in the book, and he wore a bowler hat and eyeglasses, he was like them except he had an artificial hand, and that time . . ."

"Enough about the artificial hand," said Teresita. "Are you going to keep on about it all afternoon? You're the one who complained about it being too hot and now I'm the one who's got undressed."

"I have to go to the bathroom."

"The laxative! No, really, your aunts are too much. Hurry up and go, and bring back some more ice with you. Look how Ringo's watching me, the little angel. You like this little belly, sweetheart? Look, rub like this, this way, Chola will kill me when she gets her photo back all wrinkled."

Wanda waited as long as she could in the bathroom to avoid going back again. She was miserable and she resented the laxative, just as later she resented Teresita looking at her on the blue couch as if she were a baby, making fun of her like that other time when she showed her and Wanda hadn't been able to help turning red as a beet, that afternoon when everything was different, first Aunt Adela giving her permission to stay later than usual at Teresita's, after all, it's right next door and I have to wait for the director and the secretary of Maria's school, there's no room in this little house, it would be better for you to go play with your friend, but be careful on the way back, come straight home, none of your gallivanting through the streets with Teresita, I know how she likes to do that, I know her, and afterwards they smoked some cigarettes that Teresita's father had left in his desk drawer, with gold filters and a strange smell, and then Teresita showed her, it was hard to remember exactly how it happened, they had been talking about the art book, or maybe the book business was at the beginning of summer, that afternoon they had on more clothes, Wanda had on her yellow pullover, so it mustn't have been summer anymore, they no longer knew what to say, they looked at each other and laughed, almost without a word they went out into the street and started walking to the station, avoiding the corner where Wanda's house was because Aunt Ernestina kept her eyes open even when she had the director and the secretary over. On the station platform they spent some time pretending to wait for a train, watching the engines that shook the platform and filled the sky with black smoke. Then, or maybe when they had to split up on the way home, Teresita had said, in an offhanded way, you've got to be careful with it, don't rub it off, and Wanda, who had been trying to forget, blushed, and Teresita laughed and said that nobody could know a thing about that afternoon but her aunts were like La Rosada, and if they weren't careful they'd slip up and be found out. Again she laughed but it was true and of course it was Aunt Ernestina who surprised her at the end of siesta when Wanda had been sure no one would come into her room, everyone was napping, and you could hear the sound of Grock's chain on the patio and the buzzing of wasps maddened by the sun and heat, she hardly had time to pull the sheet up to her neck and pretend to be asleep but it was already too late because Aunt Ernestina was at the foot of the bed, without a word she pulled off the sheet and looked at the pajama bottoms around her calves. At Teresita's they locked doors and La Rosada locked her things up with a key but Aunt Maria and Aunt Ernestina worried about fires and talked about children dying in flames, but now Aunt Ernestina and Aunt Adela were not talking about that, first they came over to her without saying a word and Wanda tried to pretend she didn't understand, until Aunt Adela seized her hand and twisted it hard and Aunt Ernestina gave her the first slap and then another and another, and Wanda tried to defend herself by crying, her face pressed into the pillow, crying that she hadn't done anything wrong, that they were hurting her, she had only, but then Aunt Adela took her sandal and spanked her hard holding down her legs, and degeneracy and surely Teresita and youth today and ungrateful children and when she had been sick and the piano lessons and confinement but mostly about degeneracy and sickness until Aunt Lorenza woke up disturbed by the yelling and crying and suddenly it was very quiet, only Aunt Lorenza stayed and looked at her sadly, not calming or comforting her though it was always Aunt Lorenza who gave her a glass of water like now and protected her from the man dressed in black, repeating in her ear that she would sleep well, the nightmare wouldn't come back.

"You ate too much stew, I saw you. Stew is too heavy in the evening, like oranges. Now it's over, go to sleep, I'm here, you won't dream anymore."

"Why are you waiting to get undressed? You have to go to the bathroom again? You're going to turn inside out like a glove. Your aunts are really crazy."

"It's not so hot we have to get undressed," Wanda had said that afternoon, when she took off her dress.

"You're the one who started in about the heat. Bring me the ice and you carry the glasses, there's still some sweet wine but yesterday La Rosada saw the bottle and made a face. Tell me about it! She didn't say anything but she made a face and she saw that I knew she knew. Good thing Papa doesn't think about anything but business, with me stealing his cigarettes all the time. You're right you have some hair but not much, you still look like a kid. I'll show you something in the library if you don't tell."

Teresita had discovered the book by accident, the bookcase locked shut, your father keeps science books there that aren't for people your age, what idiots, they left it open and she found dictionaries and a book with the spine hidden, as if to keep it from being noticed, and there was one with anatomical plates too, but not like the ones at school, these showed everything, but when she pulled out the art book she lost all interest in the anatomical plates because the art book was like a picture story, except it was very strange, unfortunately the captions were in French and she could only make out a few words, *La sérénité est sur le point de basculer, sérenité* must mean serenity but *basculer*, who knows, it was a strange word, *bas* meant stocking, like in La Rosada's Bas Dior, but *culer, culer* stockings didn't mean anything, and the women in the pictures were always naked or in skirts or robes but they never had stockings, maybe *culer* was something else. Wanda thought so too when she showed her the book and they laughed like crazy, it was fun being with Wanda during siesta when they had the house to themselves.

"It's not so hot that we have to take off our clothes," said Wanda. "Why do you always exaggerate? I said it was hot, sure, but I didn't say that."

"So you don't want to be like the women in the pictures," teased Teresita, stretching out on the couch. "Look at me close and see if I'm not just the same as that one where everything is like glass and there's a tiny man walking through a street in the background. Take your slip off, idiot, you're spoiling the effect."

"I don't remember that picture," said Wanda, fingering the elastic straps of her slip indecisively. "Oh, wait, now I remember, there was a ceiling lamp and a blue window frame with a full moon outside. Everything was blue, right?"

That's why they spent so much time on that one picture the afternoon of the art book, even though there were others that were more exciting and even stranger, like the one of Orpheus, who the dictionary said was the father of music and descended to the underworld, but there was no underworld in the picture, only a street with some red brick houses, a little like at the beginning of the nightmare although afterwards it was all different and it was the alleyway again with the man with the artificial hand, and Orpheus was walking naked through the streets with the red brick houses, Teresita had pointed him out right away, but at first Wanda had thought he was another of the naked women, until Teresita began to laugh and placed her finger right there and Wanda saw that he was a very young man and she looked and thought for a long time about Orpheus, wondering who the woman seen from behind in the garden could be and why she was seen from behind, with the lightning-shaped clasp of her skirt half-open, as if that were a way to go about in the garden.

It's a decoration, not a lightning clasp, Wanda discovered. You think it is but when you look close you see it's a kind of hem that looks like lightning. But why does Orpheus walk down the street naked and why does the woman seen from behind wait in the garden on the other side of the wall, it's very strange. Orpheus

looks like a woman with his light hair and those hips. Except for that of course.

"Let's find another one where we can see closer," said Teresita. "Did you ever see a man?"

"No, what do you think?" said Wanda. "I know what they are but how could I see? Like babies' only bigger, right? Like Grock, but he's a dog, it's not the same."

"Chola says when they get excited they get three times as big and that's the time of fecundation."

"Having babies, you mean. Is that fecundation or what?"

"You're such a silly child. Look at this one, it almost looks like the same street but this time there are two naked women. Why does this poor guy paint so many women? Look how they each walk in their own path and they walk by and don't even seem to see each other. They're totally crazy, naked in the middle of the street, and no policeman objects, it couldn't happen anywhere. Look at this other one, there's a man but he's dressed, inside a house, all you can see is his face and one hand. And that woman dressed in branches and leaves, they're crazy I tell you."

"You won't dream anymore," Aunt Lorenza promised her, caressing her. "Sleep well, you'll see, you won't dream anymore."

"It's true, you have some hair but not much," Teresita had said. "It's funny, you still look like a child. Light me a cigarette. Come here."

"No, no," Wanda had said, trying to get away. "What are you doing? I don't want to. Leave me alone."

"What a silly child. Look, you'll see, I'll show you. I won't do anything to you, just be quiet and you'll see."

That night they sent her to bed without a kiss, dinner had been like in the pictures where everything was silent, only Aunt Lorenza looked at her from time to time and served her dinner, in the afternoon she had heard Aunt Adela's record in the distance and the voices reached her like accusations, *Te lucis ante terminus*, she had already decided to kill herself and it made her cry hard to think of Aunt Lorenza finding her dead and them all being sorry then, she would kill herself by hanging herself from the roof in the garden or slitting her wrists with Aunt Ernestina's razor, but not yet because first she had to write a farewell letter to Teresita telling her that she forgave her, and another one to the geography teacher who had given her the nicely bound atlas, and it was a good thing that Aunt Ernestina and Aunt Adela hadn't found out that she and Teresita had gone to the station to watch the trains go by and that they'd drunk wine and smoked cigarettes that afternoon, and she was especially glad that they didn't know about the time she was coming back from Teresita's house at nightfall and instead of coming straight back like they had said she had gone roundabout and the man dressed in black had come up to her and asked the time like in the nightmare, or maybe that was all it was, a nightmare, O dear God, right at the entrance of the passage that ended with the wall covered with vines, and not even then had she realized (but maybe it was just the nightmare) that the man was hiding his hand in the pocket of his black jacket, until he started to take it out very slowly as he asked her the time and it was a hand that seemed to be made of rose-colored wax, with hard fingers all stuck together, and they stuck to the lining of his pocket and he had to tug them out with little pulls, and then Wanda had run away from the entrance of the alleyway, but she had already forgotten that, forgotten having run away and escaped from the man who wanted to trap her at the end of the alley, there was a kind of gap because the terror of his artificial hand and his mouth with its thin lips fixed that moment forever and there was no before or after, and the worst thing was that she couldn't tell Aunt Lorenza that it wasn't just a dream because she wasn't sure and she was so afraid that someone would find out, everything got all mixed together, Teresita, the only sure thing was that Aunt Lorenza was there next to her in the bed with her arms around her promising her a peaceful night's sleep, stroking her hair and promising her.

"You like that?" said Teresita. "You can do it like this too, see?"

"No, no, please," said Wanda.

"Sure, it's even better, twice as good, and Chola does it that way and me too, see how you like it, don't pretend, if you want to, lie down here and do it yourself, now that you know."

"Sleep well, sweetheart," her Aunt Lorenza had said. "You'll see, you won't dream anymore."

But it was Teresita who lay back with her eyes half shut, as if she had suddenly become very tired after showing Wanda, and she looked just like the blonde woman on the blue couch only younger, without so much hair, and Wanda thought of the other woman in the picture who was watching a candle burning even though in the glass room there was a lamp on the ceiling, and there were street lamps outside, and a man in the background who seemed to be coming to the house, to enter the house like in most of the pictures, but none was as strange as the one called *Demoiselles de Tongre*, because *demoiselles* in French meant girls and while Wanda looked at Teresita who was breathing hard as if she were very tired and it was the same as the picture of the demoiselles of Tongre, which must be a place because it started with a capital letter, embracing each other, wrapped in blue and red robes but naked underneath, and one had her breasts exposed and caressed another one and they both wore black berets and had long blonde hair, she caressed her by stroking her back with her fingers as Teresita had done, and the bald man in the gray coat was like Dr. Fontana when Aunt Ernestina took her to see him and the doctor, after talking privately with Aunt Ernestina, had told her to undress, she was thirteen then and beginning to develop, that's why Aunt Ernestina took her or maybe not just for that because Dr. Fontana began to laugh and Wanda heard him tell Aunt Ernestina not to exaggerate and these things aren't as serious as all that and then afterwards he listened to her lungs and looked into her eyes and he had a coat that was like the one in the picture only white, and he told her to lie down on the examining table and he felt her down there and Aunt Ernestina was there but she had gone and looked out the window even though you couldn't see down to the street because the windows were frosted glass until the doctor called her and told her not to be concerned and Wanda watched while the doctor wrote her a prescription for a tonic and some cough medicine and the night of the nightmare was a little like that because the man dressed in black had been friendly at first and smiled like Dr. Fontana and he just wanted to know the time but then came the alley like that afternoon when she took the roundabout route and now the only solution was to kill herself with the razor or by hanging from the roof, as soon as she had written the teacher and Teresita.

"What an idiot," Teresita had said. "First you leave the window open, like a moron, and then afterwards you can't even lie about it. I told you, if your aunts let this get back to La Rosada, since for sure I'm the one they'll blame, I'll be sent away to a boarding school, Papa already warned me."

That was the worst, not being able to tell Aunt Lorenza why

she had left the house the afternoon of Aunt Ernestina and Aunt Adela, why she had gone walking through first one street then another, not knowing what to do, feeling she had to kill herself right away, throw herself under a train, and looking all around because maybe the man would be there again and when she was in a secluded place he would come up and ask her the time, maybe the women in the pictures walked naked through the streets because they too had left their houses and were afraid of those men in their gray coats or black suits like the man in the alleyway, but in the pictures there were many women and now she was walking alone through the streets, but at least she wasn't naked like they were and no one came to embrace her wearing a red robe or to tell her to lie down like Teresita and Dr. Fontana had.

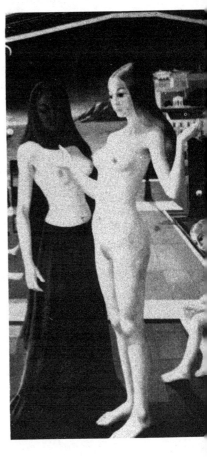

"Billie Holiday was black and she died from taking too many drugs," said Teresita. "She had hallucinations and things like that."

"What are hallucinations?"

"I don't know, something terrible, you scream and writhe. You know, you're right, it's a real heat wave. We should take off our clothes."

"It's not so hot that we have to get undressed," Wanda had said.

"You ate too much stew," said Aunt Lorenza. "Stew's too heavy in the evening, like oranges."

"You can do it this way too," Teresita had said.

Who knows why the picture they remembered the best was the one of that narrow street with trees on one side and a door in the foreground on the other, and right in the middle of the street was a little table with a lamp that was lit even though it was the middle of the day. "Enough about the artificial hand," Teresita had said. "Are you going to go on about it all day? First you complain about the heat and then I'm the one who gets undressed." In the picture she walked on, trailing a dark robe along the ground, in the doorway in the foreground Teresita was looking at the table with the lamp without realizing that the man dresed in black was waiting in the background for Wanda, who was motionless on the side of the street, we aren't us, it's like in the nightmare, you think that's what it is but it isn't, and Aunt Lorenza wouldn't let me have the nightmare

anymore. If she could have asked Aunt Lorenza to protect her
from the streets, to keep her from throwing herself under the
train, not to let the man dressed in black appear, the man who
waited in the distance in the picture, now that she was going out
of her way ("Come straight back and none of that wandering
through the streets," Aunt Adela had said) and the man dressed
in black came up to her to ask the time and slowly trapped her in
the dead-end passageway, pressing her back and back against the
wall covered with vines, she was unable to scream or plead or
defend herself, just like in the nightmare but in the nightmare
there was the gap at the end because Aunt Lorenza was there
soothing her and the taste of fresh water and caresses erased
everything and the afternoon of the alleyway had a gap too at the
end when Wanda had escaped running all the way home without
looking back and bolting the door behind her and calling for
Grock to guard the door because she couldn't tell Aunt Adela the
truth. Now everything was the same as before but she could not
escape or wake up, there was no gap in the passageway now, the
man in black trapped her against the wall and Aunt Lorenza
wasn't there to comfort her, she was alone in that night with the
man dressed in black who had asked the time, who pressed closer
to the wall and started to take his hand out of his pocket, ever
closer to Wanda pressed against the vines, and the man dressed in
black didn't ask the time, the wax hand searched her for something, lifted her skirt, and the man's voice was in her ear, be still,
don't cry, we'll do what Teresita showed you.

Photo and Illustration Credits:

About the Author

JULIO CORTÁZAR was born in Brussels of Argentine parents in 1914. After World War I his family returned to Argentina, where he received a literature degree from the teachers college in Buenos Aires in 1935. From 1935 to 1945 he taught in secondary schools in several Argentine towns. From 1945 to 1951 he worked as a literary translator for Argentine publishing houses, translating the complete prose works of Edgar Allan Poe, as well as works by André Gide, Walter de la Mare, G. K. Chesterton, Daniel Defoe, and Jean Giono. He refused a chair at the University of Buenos Aires because of his opposition to the Perón regime. In 1951 he moved to France, where he lived until his death in 1984, dividing his time between Paris and the Provençal town of Saignon. He accepted President Mitterand's offer of French citizenship in 1981, while insisting that he had not relinquished his Argentine citizenship. Active in Latin American politics, he visited Cuba in 1961 and Nicaragua in 1983; he donated his Prix Médicis prize money for *Libro de Manuel* (1973, translated by Gregory Rabassa as *A Manual for Manuel*, 1978) to the United Chilean Front. During most of his years in France he worked for four months as a translator from French and English into Spanish for UNESCO and devoted the rest of the year to his writing and other loves such as the jazz trumpet. He published poems and plays in the thirties and forties but achieved his first major success with a book of stories, *Bestiario*, in 1951 (selections appear in *The End of the Game and Other Stories*, translated by Paul Blackburn, 1967). His novel *Rayuela* (1963; translated by Gregory Rabassa as *Hopscotch*, 1966) was widely praised and won Cortázar an enthusiastic international following. AROUND THE DAY IN EIGHTY WORLDS is his eleventh major work to be translated into English.

Design by David Bullen
Typeset in Mergenthaler Imprint
with Bulmer display
by Wilsted & Taylor
Printed by Haddon Craftsmen
on acid-free paper